Ghostkin

By
Ellen Mellor

DOUBLE DRAGON PUBLISHING

Double Dragon Press

An Imprint of
Double Dragon Publishing
PO Box 54016
1-5762 Highway 7 East
Markham, Ontario L3P 7Y4 Canada
http://www.double-dragon-ebooks.com
http://www.double-dragon-publishing.com

ISBN-13: 9781724017543

A DDP First Edition September 17th, 2018
Book Layout and
Cover Art by Deron Douglas

For
Candy and Max

Chapter One

It wasn't a dark and stormy night. It was, in fact, cloudless and clear. The moon was nearly full and shone brightly down onto the streets below. On the whole, this was a good thing, because not even ghosts liked it when it rained.

There were actually quite a few ghosts lingering along the main shopping street, most of them near where their mortal lives had ended, like Kerry, who had been twelve years old when she had been run over in front of her best friend. She now haunted the pelican crossing that she should have actually used. One or two remained in a location to which they had an emotional attachment. Mr Gupta, for example, despite dying in his mistress's bed in Walker, haunted the now empty shop that had once been the greengrocers, where he had spent almost all of his waking hours. Ironically, it was his death and subsequent haunting that had ensured the closure of his shop soon after his son had taken over its running. A ghost whose presence makes everything around him several degrees colder than everywhere else maybe really useful for keeping the vegetables fresh but it doesn't do a lot for customer relations. No matter how used people had become to the idea of ghosts, most of them still liked to keep away from them.

There was one ghost, however, who wasn't sticking to a single spot. If it had been possible to see it - which would only happen if it was being watched by another ghost or by a sensitive - it would have been seen to be moving quickly and with apparent purpose up the street. It looked to be heading for the bank. Even with the eyes of someone capable of viewing it, the description wouldn't have been any use if it came to identifying the person whose ghost this was. It was a human figure, probably female and around six feet in height but, other than that, it had no other features. Its face and head were white - actually white rather than Caucasian - and utterly featureless. No eyes, no nose, no mouth. Nothing. It looked like a cloud that someone had managed to sculpt into a figure rather than a real person.

The bank's heavy wooden doors didn't slow it down for a moment as it passed straight through them but, once inside, it paused as if looking around.

Standing in front of the cashier's desks was another ghost. This one was a bit pathetic. Old Mister Hogarth had been there for a few years now after a sudden massive stroke hit him while he stood in line waiting to deposit the bags of copper and silver the kids had spent in his arcade. After all this time, he had faded away almost to nothing so that now all that was left was a slight misty blur in the air. Even his ghostly cooling effect had been counteracted by the bank's highly efficient air conditioning system. He would soon go wherever it was that ghosts went after their psychic energy had finally been used up.

But, that pathetic little remnant was all that the strangely decisive ghost needed. A pale glow lit it up from the inside and, after a few seconds, a shiny wisp of cloud-like energy broke off from its torso and floated across to the spiritual remains of Old Mister Hogarth. Touching him, it grew, engulfing and penetrating him. The mist that had been all that remained of him grew thicker and started to expand as if filling a human shaped balloon. The ground around him turned white with frost as the temperature dropped drastically. After ten or fifteen seconds, he looked almost as solid as he had done when he was alive. Although he looked a little different to how he must have appeared in life. Old Mister Hogarth had apparently been a fan of Dickens while he had been alive and appeared to have, perhaps unconsciously, identified a little too strongly with one of his characters. He was wrapped in chains and attached to the end of each one was a one-armed bandit, a lock-box or a bag of cash.

With a screech of joy that would have been audible, had there been anyone other than the other ghost there to hear it, Old Mister Hogarth launched himself into the air, spewing a stream of glowing ectoplasm. He flew around the walls, getting faster and faster, spraying more and more ectoplasm. As it hit electrical devices that had been left on, they sparked and spat - computers, TV screens and, most importantly to the ghost who had retreated to the porch of the building, the security cameras and psychic foils that the bank had installed to prevent exactly what it now intended to do.

After a few minutes, Old Mister Hogarth was spent, both his glow and shape dying away. He returned to the misty blur that had been his after-life before the other ghost had interfered and beyond. He kept fading until, with a last gentle sigh that could have just been the now badly malfunctioning air-conditioning, he disappeared.

The other ghost knew that it now had no time to lose. The destruction of the psychic foils would have set off some kind of alarm and the police would be on their way. Still, there wasn't a whole hell of a lot they could do, but it would still rather not be around when they arrived.

It dropped through the floor to the basement below. The thick steel door of the walk-in safe posed as little inconvenience to it as the entrance. Inside the vault was as dark as pitch but again, that didn't matter to the ghost who could see as well, if not better, in there as it could in the full light of day.

It looked around at the cash that lay in neat piles on shelves around the walls and then picked it up, seemingly pushing it into its body where it disappeared from view.

It didn't take long for all the cash to have disappeared. Taking one last look around, the ghost floated through the wall and away.

#

The next morning was overcast, dark clouds threatening rain later on in the day. Rachel lay in her double bed, stretched from one corner to the other, looking out of the window and just about deciding not to bother getting up. She could hear her mother bustling about downstairs, while arguing with her father, as usual. Fumbling for the remote control, She flicked on the telly, just as the news was starting. It was full of the usual stuff – war, terrorism, credit crunch, politics and negotiations with faerie. As always, the local news followed immediately after. The Penshaw Wyrm had taken another three people over night. *Really*, Rachel thought, *someone needed to do something about that bloody dragon.*

Both her musings and her peaceful morning were interrupted by the sound of the doorbell. Her mother screamed at her father to keep quiet as she went along the front hall.

Rachel heard someone say "Good morning, Mrs Cantrell."

Recognising the voice, she jumped out of bed and started to drag on leggings and a t-shirt.

"Good morning, inspector," her mother replied.

"Is your Rachel in?"

"She's still in bed, would you like to have a word with her?"

"If you don't mind. Did she have a late one last night?"

"Oh no. She went quite early, just after *Have I Got News For You.*"

"She's not poorly, I hope."

"No. She said she had a book she wanted to finish reading."

By this time, Rachel was coming down the stairs.

"Good morning, Inspector Charlton," she said. "What brings you out so early?"

"It's not that early, Rachel. It's half past ten."

"Well, I was awake late, finishing my book."

"Must be nice being able to lie in on a weekday."

"Well, you know how it is. There's just no work around at the moment."

"Would you like to come into the lounge, officer?" Rachel's mother asked. "I'll make you a nice cup of tea."

"That would be lovely. Thank you, Mrs Cantrell."

"Ignore, Mark," she told him, but looking directly and searingly at the ghost of her husband. "He's in a right mood this morning. Practically 'geisting."

#

Rachel followed Inspector Charlton into the lounge. It was actually two rooms knocked into one, stretching from the front of the house, the part her mother called the lounge, through an arch into the 'dining room' and then through a pair of French doors into the back yard. The walls were decorated with bright flowered wallpaper. Neither Rachel nor her mother actually liked it, but her father refused to let them change it, saying that 'Ma' – that is Rachel's grandmother – had chosen it and he would let them change it over his dead body. Pointing out the obvious didn't help. He sat in his favourite armchair glowering at the policeman as he came in.

"Good morning, Mr Cantrell," the Inspector said.

"Aye. Whatever," Rachel's father replied, before turning his attention towards Rachel. "You been on the nick or summat?"

"That's what I would like to know as well," Inspector Charlton said, as he sat in the other armchair.

"What do you mean, Inspector?" Rachel asked, her face a picture of innocence.

"Last night, at about half past two, the Lloyds on Chillingham Road was robbed."

"What's that got to do with me?" Rachel asked. "I finished reading my book at about one thirty and then went straight to sleep. I dunno."

"Well, there was ectoplasmic residue, no signed of forced entry and their resident ghost had been forced into a 'geist frenzy so I'm thinking that it's looking like a ghostkin did the job..." the Inspector trailed off, looking expectantly at Rachel.

"And I'm ghostkin and I was renned when I was sixteen and the bank job was just down the road, so it must have been me, right?"

"Well, that's certainly one possibility. Unless you have any other ideas?"

"You mean, if I want to get off the hook, I have to grass up someone else? Bugger off, Inspector and don't come back unless you actually have some evidence, eh?"

At the moment, Rachel's mother came into the room, carrying a tray.

"Sorry, mom," Rachel said. "The Inspector isn't staying."

"That's a pity," she said. "It's always nice to have a member of the constabulary visit. It makes you feel safe."

"If only everyone felt that way, Mrs Cantrell," the Inspector said. "There are some real crooks around who don't give a damn who they hurt."

"Oh, I know, officer, I know. I'm just glad that my Rachel has put all that behind her. Was she helpful?"

"Oh, she gave me a suggestion or two."

"That's good. Well, you know we're always happy to help, so please pop around whenever you want."

"Thanks, Mrs Cantrell, I might well come back soon." The Inspector looked at Rachel as she said this.

As the front door closed, Rachel's father stared at his daughter.

"What you been doin', girl?" she shouted. "I didn't fight and die in the war so you could swear at me and go nicking stuff."

"Now, Mark. I've told you before," Rachel's mother said. "That's absolutely no way to speak to your daughter. Rachel is a good girl."

"A good girl, my arse," Mark replied. "You let that girl get away with too much, Mary. You let her laze around in bed until yon time and then wait on her hand and foot. It wasn't like that in my day..."

"Well, it's not your day anymore," Mary replied, sharply. "Rachel may have done wrong in the past, but that's been and gone. And it was only because of your brother's son that she ever went the wrong way."

"Yeah, sod off, dad," Rachel replied.

As soon as she said it, Rachel realised that she'd made a mistake. She should have known better by now. When her mother was in full flow, even if she was defending her, she could shift her target in a moment.

"And, as for you young lady," she said, swinging around. "There is something in what your father says. You stay in bed far too long. You need to think about doing something. You've not done anything for months. At the least, I think I you can help around here a bit – pick up after yourself a bit. Maybe make tea once in a while."

"Yes, mum. Sorry mum."

Her father glared at her before slowly fading away, his luminous, translucent flesh melting away revealing his muscles, internal organs and finally skeleton before disappearing entirely, leaving a faint smell of rotten meat and a cold breeze. Her mother just sat down in her chair, picked up the cup of tea that she had made for Inspector Cantrell and the magazine she had been reading and settled back in complete comfort.

#

Wandering down Chillingham Road, on her way to the paper shop, Rachel passed the bank. Police tape blocked off the entrance and a police officer stood on guard in front of it. As Rachel passed the door Inspector Charlton stepped out of it.

Rachel gave him a wide, toothy grin. It was not returned. Instead, the Inspector stared at her as if she were a piece of crap that he had stepped in. Rachel could tell exactly what he was thinking. The Inspector may be certain that she had done the bank job, but there was no way that he could prove it. And, as far as Rachel was concerned, that was all that was important. She didn't feel the need to be friends with the police.

Passing by the bank, Rachel saw a little girl sitting on one of the benches that dotted the street. Ruby wasn't the sort of girl, even at eleven years old, who would allow herself to be seen crying in public. So, to see her sitting there, not bawling but weeping, utterly bereft, Rachel knew that something was wrong. She went and sat down next to her.

"Hey Ruby," she said to the dark haired girl.

Ruby turned red-rimmed eyes up to her, sniffed hard and dragged the back of her hand across her nose.

"It's Uncle Phil. He's died," she told her, through hiccups of anguish.

"Aw, pet," Rachel said. "That's really shit. I'm sorry."

It may have been really shit for the little girl, but it didn't surprise Rachel at all. Phil Marshall was not a healthy man. It was a regular topic of conversation about what it was that would kill him – the booze that he drank as if he was dying of thirst, the Greggs pasties that he invariably shovelled into his maw when he didn't have a pint in his hand, or working for Fred Mott. Although Rachel wanted to know which one it was – she had money on the pasties – she knew this wasn't the time and Ruby wasn't the person to ask. Phil wasn't actually Ruby's uncle, he was just the latest in a line of men that shared her mother's bed. Although, to be fair, they had been together for a couple of years now. So, maybe it had actually been love. Which made the whole thing even shittier.

"Mam sent us out to get some ciggies," she told her. "I think it's because the man was coming to take him away. She wanted us out of the house, y'know?"

"Yeah, well, it's not something a girl your age should see," Rachel told her.

"I've seen dead people before. I mean, I know your dad." Speaking to Rachel was helping her to pull herself together. Her tears dried up and she even managed a cheeky smirk as she argued.

"A ghost is a bit different to a corpse, though."

"And I've seen them in my dreams as well. And I bet they're nastier than Uncle Phil. At least he isn't going to be moving around."

Rachel knew that she wasn't lying. Her abilities would have meant that her dreams would be wide-screen, Technicolor horror movies, broadcast directly from hell. Ruby was a natural witch. Lots of power, but no control. She was going to be a real poltergeist magnet in a couple of years. Unfortunately, her mother didn't seem to care and hadn't bothered getting her any training.

"That's still different to seeing a relative like that. You been out long?" Rachel asked.

"'Bout half an hour."

"It's probably safe to go back now. Your mom'll want you around."

"Will you get the ciggies for us? The cow in the shop wouldn't sell them to me."

"Well, with the police around, she probably needs to be careful. Come on. Then I'll walk you home."

#

Getting in to the paper shop was delayed by a bunch of orange jump-suited zombins who were slowly picking up litter. Zombins – Court-Sanctioned Zombifications or CSZ as they were correctly known – were convicted criminals who had been executed and their mortal remains re-animated to serve the community for a fixed period before they were finally interred. They were useful but very slow. And of limited intellect. So they were normally led by a live person. In this case, it was a renfield, another criminal whose punishment was to have his will dominated and set to work. He wasn't stupid, well apart from the stupidity it takes to get caught, but the renning – when not done by a vampire, who tended not to be too interested in working for the judiciary – had a tendency to dull the wits somewhat. Rachel could certainly vouch for that.

But there was no point grumbling, even though Rachel and Ruby were forced to stand and wait for five minutes while one of the zombins carefully knelt and scraped up a piece of chewing gum that was ground into the pavement right in front of the door to the shop. If it hadn't been a renfield in charge, she could have said something and got the zombin to move, but they tended not to notice anything other than the job unless it was an emergency. And getting the *Guardian* did not count as an emergency. Still, it meant some time for her to sit and think. Phil Marshall was a fairly major player. With his death, that meant there would be some sort of opening in Fred Mott's organisation. She, Rachel, was loathe to even consider going to work for Mott again, not after the complete screw up that had cost her five years as a renfield and her cousin's life, but she needed to do something. This sitting around all day on her arse was getting dull. There was no way she was going to get a legitimate job, some nine-to-five gig where she had to answer to some jumped-up twat with a Napoleon complex. And, for all that Mott was a first grade shit, with a Napoleon complex, he was also probably the most decent gangster in the whole of the North East, knew what he was doing and recognised talent when it presented itself. Not that describing him as 'the most decent gangster in the North East' was saying much. But, at least Fred was human. Unlike say Bailey or Oberon. Now there was a creature that had really had a fall. Before The Doors re-opened he had been king of Lyonesse. Now he was reduced to selling Dust to junkies. And you didn't get much lower than that.

Finally, the zombin dragged itself up off its knees and shuffled off to another mashed down piece of gum a little further down the road. The shop emptied and then the queue that had built up waiting to get in filed in. There was some of the usual muttering from the usual old geezers who wanted their copy of the *Mail* or the *Express*. But then, if there wasn't something for them to whinge about they'd probably keel over. And then they'd probably come back and haunt the bingo hall. Why was it always the miserable bastards who came back, though? With the notable exception, of course, of John Lennon, but John had admitted that he only came back because he wanted to get one over on Paul. Although how you could tell if he had actually succeeded was a bit of a mystery. After all, McCartney had been a zombie since 1966 and, while his playing hadn't been affected much, he didn't really do much else. He still had a sense of humour though – how many other zombies would dare perform a song called *'Live and Let Die'*?

#

As they walked towards her house, Ruby looked up at Rachel.

"Rachel?" she asked.

"Yes, Ruby."

"You know about dead people, don't you? I mean, because of your dad and because you're a ghostkin."

Rachel nodded.

"Yeah, I guess I know a bit about them."

"Well, I mean... do you know... is Uncle Phil going to heaven?"

Rachel's first thought was *'not a chance'*.

"Of course he is. He loved you and did nice things for you, didn't he?"

"Yeah, he did."

"Well, that's what you've got to do, if you're going to go to heaven."

"Promise?"

"Promise."

That wasn't the biggest lie that Rachel had ever told but it was certainly up there.

"Hang on," she said, her guilt poking at her. "I'm just going to nip in here."

She went into to the florist's shop and returned a couple of minutes later with two bunches of flowers.

Passing one to Ruby, she said, "give that to your mom, give her my best wishes."

"I will. Thanks, Rachel. Whose that one for?"

"My mom. I've not bought her any flowers for ages."

"Really? You buy flowers for your mom?"

"What's wrong with that?" Rachel said, a bit defensively. "She's my mom. I owe her everything."

"I thought you were only meant to buy flowers for people that you fancy or if they're in hospital or something. Not that Uncle Phil ever bought any for mom. Or any of mom's other boyfriends for that matter..."

#

Coming up to the front gate, Rachel handed over the packet of Silk Cut that she had been carrying.

"Make sure your mom gets them. Don't smoke any yourself," she told the young girl. "And tell her that I'm really sorry for her loss. If there's anything I can do to help, tell her to let me know."

"I will. See you Rachel."

"See you, Ruby."

The girl stood on the step for a moment, stealing herself before pushing the door open and slipping inside.

Rachel stared up at the windows of the upstairs flat where the girl and her mother lived for a moment, before turning on her heel and making her way back up the street.

Before she got far she was stopped by a woman calling her name. She turned, expecting Ruby's mother to be there and quickly running words of consolation through her head. She stopped short and the words died on her lips as she saw a woman wearing the dog collar and black shirt that marked her out as a member of the clergy.

"Shit," Rachel muttered to herself as she started to make her way back towards her.

The woman stood and waited for Rachel to approach, a dark, thunderous look on her face. As Rachel got closer, she shook her long, red hair out of her face – a nervous twitch that Rachel recognised from long experience.

The Reverend Susan Donahue was the first woman that her mother had ever actually thought capable of conducting a service properly which was more than likely because she had taken Susan to church with her long before she became Reverend Donahue. Susan had actually been Rachel's first girlfriend, when they had both been about nine. She was the first girl that Rachel had ever kissed who hadn't been a member of her own family. Obviously, it had all been very innocent. The closest they had ever actually managed to get to a date – other than going to church together, which Susan had loved and Rachel had hated – was having Rachel's mother take them to the cinema to see the Disney version of Beauty and The Beast while she sat a couple of rows back from them. Considering how strongly Christian she had been back then, it hadn't surprised Rachel when she had gone to Oxford University to study Theology and then gone on to become ordained. What had been surprising was that she decided to come back to Heaton to take over the running of Saint Gabriel's church. But she had and Rachel's mother had been over the moon.

Unfortunately, a little incident that had occurred when they were fourteen, meant that neither Rachel nor Susan had been able to be friends. They managed to remain coldly civil to one another when Rachel's mother was around but at any other time words tended to be short and bitter and poisonous.

"Rev," Rachel said, wanting to get this over with as quickly as possible.

"Get in the car," Reverend Donahue said. "I'll give you a lift home. I need to drop in and see your mother."

"No, thanks, I'm okay," she replied. "I've got a couple of things I need to get done. I'll just see you around, okay?"

"No. It is *not* okay," she hissed. "Get in the car. Or would you rather I said what I have to say out here in the street?"

With a deep sigh, Rachel turned and trudged towards her car, a sleek black Saab that stood out a mile on this street that tended to be filled with somewhat cheaper makes and models. She was annoyed that she'd missed it as she was walking Ruby back home. If she had, she'd have run a fucking mile and maybe avoided this.

The door lock clicked open and Rachel slid into the passenger seat. Despite her feelings for the Reverend, she couldn't help but watch as she slid into the driver seat. She wasn't tall and she wasn't slim and she didn't have a perfect complexion, but Rachel couldn't help but feel a warmth towards her, despite everything that had happened between them. She guessed that you just never quite managed to get over your first girlfriend. And, to be honest, she'd never really been that interested in leggy, skinny blondes. Maybe Susan had imprinted herself on Rachel all those years ago.

Having said that, the warmth she felt was pretty much always dissipated by actually having to speak to her. She had become the most self-righteous, obnoxious and annoying woman she had ever had the misfortune to meet. It was made worse by her mother's insistence that they were perfect for each other. She couldn't persuade her otherwise, no matter what she said. Not even bringing up the fact that Susan wasn't a lesbian and she was married – to a man who seemed to be an utter twat, as far as Rachel was concerned – could dissuade her. She just smiled and said that 'love would find a way' or some other diabetes-inducing, Radio Two Sunday Love Song crap.

Susan pulled out into the street and headed down the street, away from Rachel's house. This was an interesting tactic, Rachel thought, she'd never been kidnapped by clergy before.

After a couple of minutes, she thought she should probably say something.

"I live in that direction," she said, pointing over her shoulder.

"I know," Susan said, indicating right to turn on to the Coast Road towards the sea.

"So, where are we going?"

"What I have to say to you, is not something I can say to you at home. And I'm not taking you either to my home or the church. So, we're going somewhere we can talk privately."

"You want to hear my confession?"

"Trust me. That's the last thing I want to hear. I already know you as well as I want to."

"And what is that supposed to mean?"

Susan ignored her and kept on driving.

#

After about quarter of an hour, Susan slid the car into a parking space that looked out over the sea towards the lighthouse on Saint Mary's Island. The tide was in and the causeway covered, otherwise Rachel was certain she would have driven straight across to it. As it was, apart from the snack van, which looked about as appetising as those things always did, the car park was entirely empty. Down on the narrow strip of beach in front of them a couple of people were walking their dogs, but they were far enough away that they wouldn't be able to hear anything either one could say, even at the tops of their voices. Well, probably, anyway. And frankly, she wasn't that bothered. She wasn't the one who had decided to drive all the way out here due to some odd desire for privacy. She didn't care. Whether the Reverend wanted to be seen with her or not was entirely her concern. And Rachel liked coming out here. It cleared her head.

She turned to look at Susan, who was sitting in the driver's seat, hands still clamped to the steering wheel, staring out fixedly.

"So. Why did you bring me all the way out here? I'm not sure that God would be happy if you killed me…" Rachel said, laughing half-heartedly as she said it.

Susan flung her head around to stare at Rachel and she realised with shock that her eyes were brimming with tears.

"Maybe that would be for the best. If someone did end your life…" she hissed.

"Now hold on just one fucking minute. Where the hell do you get off saying something like that?"

"What exactly were you doing with Ruby?"

Rachel started to reply, started to shout at her, when her words penetrated and she stuttered to a stop and she found that she could only speak a single, strangled, startled word.

"What?"

"You heard me," she replied. "What were you doing with Ruby?"

"I… What do you mean? Are you suggesting that I…? You are fucking kidding me. You really think that I would do something like that? She's what? Eleven? Twelve?"

Rachel hammered at the car door, the angry red haze slamming down hard and fast, blinding her to everything except the need to get out of the car, to get away, before she really did do something she would regret. After a few seconds of flailing she found the door latch, pulled it and was a jerked to a halt as she discovered that she still had the seat belt clipped into place. Punching at the release, she managed to loose it and pull it free. Clambering out of the car, she stumbled and fell to her knees. Quickly pulling herself up, she started to stalk away, only to discover that she was heading towards the sea. To turn around and go the other way would mean passing back in front of the car, so instead, when she got to the edge of the car park, she stopped and stood there, ramrod straight, staring out at the lighthouse.

A light touch on her shoulder made her jump and she span around quickly. Susan squeaked in a way that under pretty much any other circumstances would have made Rachel laugh out loud, but her anger combined with the way the other woman cowered back fearfully, as if she was fully expecting Rachel to smash her fist into her face, was like the sea had thrown up an ice cold wave over her. Her anger turned from a red hot incoherence into a small hard ball of ice in her chest.

"I know that you don't like me," she said quietly. "And I know it's because of what I did that one time. But do you really think I'm capable of that?"

"I'm… I'm sorry," Susan said. "I don't know what came over me. I'd just been talking to Ellie, consoling her, and she told me that she was glad. That she had seen the way that Phil had been looking at Ruby. And Ruby came in as I was going out and said that you had bought flowers for her, I guess I kind of lost it."

"I bought the flowers for Ellie. They were for Ruby's mother not for Ruby. I'm a fucking idiot. I should know better than to get mixed up in anyone else's family fucking dramas."

"I'm really sorry, Rachel" Susan repeated. "It was wrong of me to jump to conclusions like that."

"Too fucking right you were wrong," she spat. "I'm not one of your fucking priest kiddy-fiddlers, you know? I bet if it was one of them walking Ruby down the road and buying flowers, you wouldn't have said a fucking thing."

Embarrassed and upset by her own over-reaction, Susan covered it by flaring up herself.

"That's ridiculous," she said. "How dare you accuse me of something like that."

"It's no worse than what you've just accused me of," Rachel replied.

"You've got form though. Haven't you? Remember, I was her age when you violated me."

"Two… no three things about that… First – you were at least two years older…"

"And that makes it all right?" Susan interrupted.

"You were two years older," she repeated, ignoring her. "Secondly, I was the same age and thirdly, I have apologised over and over and over again. Isn't that meant to be one of your fucking laws? 'Forgive them who trespass against us' or some such shit."

"Some things are harder to forgive than others."

"Tell me about it. It's going to take a hell of a long time for me to forgive you for this."

"Do you think I care for your forgiveness?" she asked. "Okay, so you wouldn't do that to Ruby…"

"I wouldn't do that to any kid. And if I'd known that Phil Marshall was even thinking about that, I'd have fucking killed him."

"Whatever," Susan continued. "So you wouldn't do that to any kid. Good. Great! I'm glad. You're a hero. Congratulations, you have reached the minimum level for being a decent human being. Now, what about everything else you do? Your soul is not exactly spotless, is it?"

"I was a thief! And I did my time for it. Like I told Charlton, if you think I've done anything since then, fucking prove it."

"I'm not the police though. And I know you," Susan replied.

"No, you're not the police. You're an Anglican priest. You're meant to be better than that. You're meant to forgive people and look for the best in them."

"Some people make it really hard to see."

"Well, fuck you, your self-righteous, stuck up, fucking Reverend

Mother-ness," Rachel said, practically spitting in her face.

Susan span around and stormed back to her car. Getting in, she slammed the door, gunned the engine and, wheels spinning, slewed the car around and shot back up the road out of the car park.

"Fuck," Rachel said, watching as the car's brake lights came on for a moment as it turned on to the main road and accelerated away. Shoulders drooping and chin in her chest, she started to follow it up the road.

#

Lying back on her bed, Rachel slipped free of her body. Silently, invisibly, she sped through the air passing over the heads of passersby, slipping through buses and cars and houses. She loved doing this, being able to see people and peek into their private lives without them suspecting. She'd done it so much when she was younger that her own corporeal body became almost uncomfortable to her. And she'd discovered so many secrets – the habits of her neighbours, her teachers, her friends and enemies. And, to top it off, she almost never had to pay to see a film.

Eventually, she got to a small garage on the far side of Byker, down by the river. It was locked with industrial strength padlocks and heavy steel bars were welded into place on the inside of the door and across all the windows. Basically, if you weren't a ghost, you weren't coming in, unless you were prepared to knock a wall down. And, there was no reason for anyone to suspect there should be anything worth breaking in for. She had bought it under a false identity, paid for it with cash and, once she had it set up as she wanted it, never went there in person, so there should not have been anything to connect it to her.

Inside, several heavy safes were set around the walls. A trestle table stood in the middle of the garage, on top of which lay a heap of black plastic bin bags, bulging and heavy. Rachel materialised and willed herself to turn solid. It wasn't perfect, it felt as if she was handling things through a dozen layers of heavy felt, but it was enough to do what she needed to do.

Tearing one of the bags open loosed a cascade of brown, purple and red pieces of paper. Picking up the banknotes she carefully sorted them into piles. The next few hours were spent sorting and counting, before she finally had them in order and knew how much she had taken the night before. She just hoped that she was going to be able to get it all into the safes. Two hundred and fifty thousand pounds was a lot of money and they were already getting a bit full. She was going to have to get something arranged to get a big chunk of it laundered and shoved into one of her accounts on Jersey. Which was just one more reason she needed to get back in with Fred Mott. He had always had one of the most efficient money laundering operations going. And he would certainly not be averse to taking a slice of the proceeds to make the rest of it nice and clean.

#

The next week or so passed quietly. Rachel made a few phone calls to try and get in touch with people she had known back when she had been part of Mott's organisation, but it seemed that they'd either gone to jail, been renned, zombinned or just disappeared. Which happened fairly regularly when you were a human in a business that attracted the nastier strain of non-humans. After all, it wasn't called the underworld for nothing. And this was one of the reasons that Rachel knew that Mott would take her. Being a ghostkin meant that she had supernatural powers and abilities, but she was still basically human. She didn't drink blood or have uncontrollable urges – well, other than when she saw a cute girl – and she came from this plane of reality. Okay, she was conceived when her father was already dead and the old git was still hanging around, but at least the DNA was still basically the same and she still had human concerns and fallibilities – like cute girls. If she could get in touch with Mott, she knew that she'd be in there.

There was nothing for it. She was going to have to go and see the old bastard in person. Without an invitation. Hopefully, she'd catch him in a good mood.

#

Fred Mott's house was something special. It was a really nice house, five stories tall, hidden away behind the motorcycle shops and non-stop traffic of Westgate Road, it looked out over a little green paradise, trees and grass and flowers. It was idyllic. You would never guess that it was so close to the centre of town, nor that it was home to one of the nastiest men in the city.

Rachel went up to the door and hammered the knocker. It echoed inside the house, a deep booming that sent a shiver down her spine. A crackle of static was followed by a voice.

"Hello, can I help you?" The voice was a pleasant, professional sounding woman, although it was made hollow and tinny by the low quality speaker that was set to the side of the door.

"Hi," Rachel said after spending a moment or two working out which of the many buttons to press. Why a door needed so many buttons, she didn't know, but she figured it was one of those things that came with money. Rachel hoped she'd get to find out for herself someday soon. "My name's Rachel Cantrell. I'd like to speak to Mr Mott if he's available."

"I'll see if he's available. Give me one moment."

The woman's voice was replaced by the silence of an open line before a loud click followed by the gruff voice of Fred Mott.

"Rachel Cantrell? Fuck me, I haven't spoken to you in a long time. What brings you here?"

"I'm looking for a job."

"Really? Come on up, I'm on the second floor at the front. I'm sure you remember where it is."

The door slowly opened. On the other side was a grey-skinned, dead-eyed dead man. No amount of fine clothing and aftershave could hide the basic vague putridity of a zombin that was getting close to the end of its afterlife.

It grunted at her and gestured, carefully, as if it knew that too much movement might endanger its physical existence. Rachel knew, however, that no matter how close to falling apart it may be, the zombin would still be able to tear her apart. It wasn't that it was much stronger than she was, it was, instead, a case of not worrying about the damage it did to itself. If it was ordered to kill her then it would suffer ripped muscles, broken bones and vicious wounds, any one of which would disable a live person, to do its duty.

#

Rachel entered and followed the Zombin passing a woman, presumably the one to whom Rachel had spoken on the intercom sitting in a small office with a glass partition looking out into the hallway. She glanced up at her as Rachel passed , giving her a tight smile, looking as pleasant and professional as her voice had sounded.

On the walls going up the stairs were photographs of girls clad in not very much at all. They weren't artistic, they weren't subtle, they weren't even sexy. They were the sort of thing you'd get in a tabloid newspaper. All in similar poses – pouty lips and pert breasts, wearing little wispy panties. Unsurprisingly, the zombin ignored them.

The front room of the second floor was spacious and well-lit. A huge, oak desk stood in the curve of a bay window that overlooked the garden. Fred Mott sat in a well-padded leather office chair, papers strewn across the desk. He was turned away from the door as it opened, looking out of the window, talking on a mobile 'phone. All that Rachel could see of him was a hand resting on the arm of the chair - a big hand, gold sovereign rings on three of his fingers, a fat, smoking cigar held between two of them. This was a hugely confident man who knew he had nothing to fear. There would be more than just the one decrepit zombin in the house and Rachel assumed that the glass was probably bullet-proof.

"I don't care about that," he was saying. "There's a shipment coming in on Thursday and I want it covered."

He paused while listening to the reply.

"Then get more. You know where they hang out, go and get some... That's your job. If I wanted to do it myself then I wouldn't be paying you, would I?... Just fucking do it, or you'll be joining them on the next shipment."

He stabbed the button to disconnect the line, swung his chair around and slammed the 'phone down on the table.

"Bloody magicians," he said to Rachel. "They can't bloody think for themselves."

He stood and came round to the front of the desk, hand outstretched, giving Rachel a chance to see him. He had changed in the last few years. His muscle had turned to fat and his hair had thinned to a dirty grey gauze over his pate. Lines had deepened around his eyes and across his forehead. But, those eyes still held their sharpness and his chin was still strong. Despite appearances – the soft porn pictures, the almost ludicrously stereotyped gangster image that he put forward and the age, Rachel knew that Fred Mott was not a man to fuck with. He was sharp and he was vicious. If he caught you bullshitting her, he would string you up by your intestines. Literally. Probably as a component for some spell or other.

"Rachel, it's so good to see you. You haven't been to see me since you were released. I just want to tell you how sorry I am for what happened to your cousin."

Rachel shook Fred's hand and sat in the seat towards which she was pointed. Fred returned to his own chair, just as the woman from the office brought in a tray filled with tea things, setting it on the desk..

"Thank you, Clara," Fred said. "Please hold my calls."

She nodded assent and quickly left the room.

"You've changed a bit since last we spoke," he said, turning his attention to Rachel. "You're looking good. Now, what can I do for you?"

"I'm looking for work. I thought you could use a woman of my abilities," said Rachel.

"And, of course, I owe you for what happened to Tommy."

"Well, I wasn't going to mention it. Hopefully, I can do enough by myself without having to bring the past in to it."

Although Rachel was denying it, she couldn't help thinking "*too bloody true, you bastard.*" She just hoped that the thought didn't show on her face.

Fred looked her straight in the eye for a moment or two, seeming to be judging her. Finally, a smile crossed his lips.

"It's good to hear you say that, Rachel. Of course, I'm glad to have you back on board," he said. "I can always do with good men... er... people... and you were well on the way to being one of the best back then. And, I'm sure you can still be good, if not the rest, eh? It's all well and good making use of zombins, but they're only useful for the scut work, you know? I need people I can trust to make the decisions."

"Not like the bloody magicians?" Rachel said, jokingly.

"Exactly! I knew you were on my wavelength," Fred paused again. "One thing, though – are you gonna have a conscience like your cousin?"

"Well, I know he wouldn't like me to go against his wishes."

"Yeah, well. Do you have any idea how much money that little character flaw cost him?"

"I know. But, I can't do it. You understand – it's a family thing."

"Fine. Fine. No human trading. If you change your mind, just let me know. You know that Jerry Cross got enough to buy himself a holiday home on St. Lucia with the proceeds of one shipment from Eastern Europe?"

"I know. Tommy would turn in his grave, though. He always said that those girls were just trying to escape from the vampires over there..."

"And we're helping them escape. Have you seen what it's like in Romania these days? Some people might say it's worth anything to get away from Vlad and his army. But, I won't argue. I did it enough with your cousin to know how pointless it is. I've got plenty of other work for you."

#

The first few jobs that Mott gave Rachel to do were easy enough: delivering a few packages – ironically enough, quite a few of her deliveries were actually to the 'bloody magicians'; collecting money from people who paid insurance or bribes; escorting visitors around the city. It took a while before Rachel actually started to use her special abilities. She guessed that Fred just wanted to make sure she could be trusted, but eventually, she starting ghosting to help case a potential target or keep an eye on Fred's opponents – making sure their plans didn't conflict with Fred's or committing a bit of industrial spying and espionage. Fun stuff, the sort of thing that Rachel really enjoyed doing, even when she wasn't being paid for it. None of it was difficult, none of it involved any real danger and it paid pretty well, which was just how Rachel liked it. On top of that, she was able to start siphoning her money through Mott's laundry services. As she had guessed, Fred liked the idea of getting herself some extra easy money.

#

"Rachel?" Ruby called to her as was walking down Chillingham Road one Tuesday morning.

She turned to see her sitting on a wall, surrounded by her gang. It was a mix of girls and boys, the girls in short skirts and tight tops, trying desperately to look older than they were; the boys in low slung jeans and hoodies, trying desperately to look cooler than they were. Neither gender were succeeding.

Ruby hopped down from the wall and sauntered over to her, motioning her cronies to stay where they were. She was very definitely the leader of the gang, lording it over all the others, even the girls and boys who were a couple of years older.

"Shouldn't you be at school?" Rachel asked.

"Shouldn't you be at work?" she shot back.

Rachel grinned at her. In a few years' time, she was really going to be someone to contend with.

"What can I do for you, Ruby?"

"I... need a favour," she said.

"Anything."

"Can you find out who stole Uncle Phil's body?"

"What?"

"Uncle Phil. His body's been stolen. I just thought that with your powers, you could, y'know, find out who took him?" She looked up at her, hope in her eyes.

"My powers... they don't really work that way," she told her. The girl's face fell and her shoulders drooped. "But, I know some people. I'll ask a few questions, they may be able to come up with some answers. Leave it to me."

"Thanks Rachel," she said, stretching up to kiss her cheek.

"You're welcome, pet," Rachel replied.

#

Rachel did try and find out what had happened to Phil's corpse. Just not very hard. She had a pretty good idea where it would have gone, anyway. Grave-robbing was an easy way of making a bit of extra cash, if you weren't shy of some hard digging. It wasn't exactly easy to legitimately get a supply of fresh corpses to create zombins, so if you had a need for a bit of undead manpower then grave-robbing was the only course of action. You just had to be really careful that the police didn't discover what you were doing. For some reason, they weren't too happy with the idea of people using the bodies of ex-tax payers as slaves. It wasn't quite something that would get you turned into a zombin yourself, but there would be some serious renfielding in your future.

Of course, with the threat of grave-robbery higher than it had been since the time of Burke and Hare, some cemeteries had installed extra security, but to get planted in one, you had to pay for them both upfront and for as long as you didn't want to be disinterred and re-buried in a less secure establishment, which was usually for a few years until your body had degenerated enough to be beyond re-animation. Most people didn't – either couldn't or wouldn't and a lot just didn't think about it – save enough to pay the fees. When Rachel died, she was going to be cremated. This, despite the fact that she could easily have afforded to pay a mage to cast an enchantment over her coffin, but she just didn't see the point when there was such an easy alternative. One of the side-effects of being ghostkin was that she knew that she was destined to become a real ghost after her death. So, the whole cremation causing you to become a ghost controversy – which had only come about because a bunch of cemetery security firms had paid some scientist or other to conduct a study which, miraculously, came up with that result – did not really matter to her. The difficult bit, the bit at which Rachel didn't work too hard, was finding out which money-grubbing little bastard had chosen to dig up Phil's body.

#

Inspector Charlton pulled his squad car over to the side of the road in front of Rachel as she walked towards the bus stop. Seeing the police officer's beckoning finger through the window, Rachel shrugged and wandered over to her, thinking to herself that, one day soon, she really was going to have learn to drive. It was all well and good being able to send her spirit scooting around the place like a leaf in the wind, but it was sod all use when the meat had to get there as well.

Rachel climbed into the back of the squad car and smiled pleasantly at the Inspector and his colleague.

"Afternoon, Inspector," she said. "Have you managed to get anywhere with your investigation?"

"Well, seeing as I haven't arrested you yet, I still have a ways to go, wouldn't you say?"

"I couldn't say, Inspector. I think that if you're just trying to get me then that'd explain why you haven't managed to get anywhere."

"I know you did it. I just have to prove it."

"And how exactly will you do that?"

"You'll slip. Cocky little bastards like you always do," Charlton told her.

"Well, good luck with that, Inspector Charlton. If that's all, I've got an appointment to keep."

"It's not a job interview is it?"

"I've said before, I'm not unemployed. I work freelance. I'm going to the dentist's if you must know. "

"Yeah, I know what 'freelance' means…" Charlton said. "Go on then, get lost. Tell 'im to make sure your teeth are nice and clean. A nice smile will get you a long way when you finally get taken to court."

Charlton opened the rear door for Rachel.

"Thanks, Inspector. Be seeing you..."

Rachel strolled off down the street, breaking into a run as the bus drew up to the stop. She climbed on to the bus, throwing Charlton a jaunty wave as she did so.

She sat down next to an old woman who glared at her over the top of her glasses. Ignoring her, she pulled a crumpled up Elmore Leonard out of her jacket pocket and relaxed as the bus jolted off down the street.

Interlude: The Somme, August 1916.

The never-ending firing of the guns made Private Charlie Bourne wince. Aged sixteen, but claiming to be eighteen – although he was fairly certain that none of his comrades-in-arms believed it for a moment - he had joined up just a few months ago, wanting to follow in his older brother's footsteps. That Billy had died at Mons was neither here nor there to Charlie. In fact, if anything it had been an incentive for him to join up even sooner.

He was now starting to think that it may not have been such a good idea though. He had envisioned heroic action, killing hundreds of Bosch and being rewarded by King George himself. Instead, he sat around in a disgusting, muddy trench, waiting for the order to go over the top and let the Germans continue their slaughter. And being scared. The noise of the guns was bad enough, but it was nothing compared to the screams of the men who had been stuck out there in No Man's Land on the barbed wire. Every single time there was a burst of gunfire, Mick – who had only joined up a few months before Charlie, but liked to stay things that made him sound like he had survived the Boer War – said "It's the one that you don't hear that gets you, eh lad?" Charlie hadn't particularly liked Mick when he had been assigned to his battalion just a few days ago, but by now he really hated him.

But, almost worse than the noise was the smell. A vile mix of smoke and gunpowder and burning, combined with the omnipresent smell of shit and blood and humanity under pressure. It was the stink of hell.

Apart from the shooting and the screams and the stench and the terror, it was actually a beautiful day. There were no birds, no trees and little in the way of other plants that had not been ground up by the passing of troops and the constant artillery fire and everything else but it was at least warm and sunny. Back home, his dad and his little brother would be getting ready for the harvest. Even though it wouldn't be for a few weeks yet, there was still loads to do.

There was another loud whistle and, barely a few hundred yards away, a gout of flame burst into the sky as a shell from one of the German cannon landed.

"Hey, that was close, Charlie," said Mick. "But, you know what they say..."

"Yes, I know what they say, Mick. You say it every single bloody time."

Mick rose from where he was crouched, a dangerous look in his eyes. A look that turned to astonishment as he stared up into the sky behind Charlie.

"What in the name of God is that," he said, pointing above and behind Charlie.

The young private turned to look, considering for a moment that this could be a ruse to get him off his guard. But he wasn't that subtle. If Mick was going to hit Charlie, which he did on a semi-regular basis, he wouldn't bother trying to take him by surprise. He would have just slammed him in the face with his fist.

Charlie wasn't sure what he was looking at for a moment. Or rather, he knew exactly what it was he was looking at, but he didn't believe his eyes. A woman, carrying a sword and a shield and dressed in some kind of leathery armour. Flying. With wings that sprouted from her back. And looking down at them.

"Is that an angel?" Mick asked. "Like the Angel of Mons or something?"

The woman came down, her wings folding as she plummeted earthwards. Almost at the last moment, they unfurled and she twisted and skimmed over the ground, directly towards Charlie and

Mick's position in the trench. Grinning, she raised her sword.

Charlie, who was still sitting on the ground felt the sword whistle over his upturned face as she streaked past. Mick was less lucky. He fell backwards, his head bouncing to the ground next to him and coming to rest in the bucket they had been using as a toilet.

The angel... woman... whatever she was... ignored Charlie and flew on, her sword waving around. Whether she had intended Mick's death or not, Charlie had no idea, but it didn't look as if she hurt anyone else. Instead, as she flew, she scattered the soldiers around her. They climbed out of their trenches and ran for it – some of them out into No Man's Land where they were quickly picked off by the German guns.

Picking up his rifle, Charlie aimed for the woman. He paused for a moment as he wondered if shooting at an angel was a bad thing or not but all he knew for sure was that she was threatening his comrades and had already killed one of them. She had to be stopped before she did anything else. He pulled the trigger.

He was sure he hit her. He was a good shot. He always had been, even when shooting crows in the fields, so hitting her was no problem. But, she ignored it entirely, not even looking around, as if she didn't even notice it.

An enormous crash of thunder, louder than even the nearest of near misses from the German cannons, nearly knocked Charlie off his feet. Spinning, his rifle still at his shoulder he looked down the barrel into the sky. And the gun fell from fingers suddenly slack with shock.

Above him, the sky was darkening as more and more women appeared apparently from nowhere. Many, if not most, were winged like the first woman. Others, seeming to be their leaders, certainly at their head, were on horseback. And the horses were galloping through the air. The sound Charlie had heard was the thunder made as their hooves sparked lightning at each step.

And they were singing.

The women on horseback wore some kind of metal armour that glinted in the sunlight and they were charging down towards the British lines. The German guns had fallen silent, although whether this was in shock at the sight or something more tactical there was no way of knowing. But, suddenly, the only sounds that could be heard were the voices of the women. Even the dying screams of the men stuck on the barbed wire seemed to be muted.

Charlie wasn't sure what they were singing but it was certainly not in English. If anything, Charlie would have said it sounded sort of German. He fell to his knees in the mud, his hands hanging loosely by his side as the flying women and the women on the backs of flying horses got closer and closer.

A sudden volley of bullets rang out from some soldiers who were obviously not as shocked as Charlie. They were as effective as Charlie had been.

Coming low to the ground, one of the women on horseback leapt off, landing in a crouch, holding her sword before her and screaming something. Although Charlie didn't understand what she said, he thought it sounded like a challenge. And it was a challenge that was accepted. Someone from further down the trench climbed out on to the muddy ground and charged, his bayonetted rifle pointing directly at her. As he got close, he pulled the trigger. The woman shifted her shield slightly in a seemingly effortless move that deflected the bullet down into the mud beside her. Waiting until he was within striking distance, she whirled her sword and parried his bayonet attack before riposting with inhuman speed and strength, thrusting her sword into his chest, lifting him off his feet and hurling him back towards the trenches.

She stalked forwards, dispatching her assailant as she went, an almost dismissive flick of her wrist slicing her sword through his neck, and dropped into the trench.

The other women were being equally as destructive. Some others had dismounted and were cutting a swathe of death through the English trenches. Others were grabbing individual soldiers, lifting them high into the air before dropping them screaming to their deaths. Still others were charging their horses through the trenches, riding down anyone who wasn't fast enough to escape them or tried to stand up to them, knocking them down and trampling them into the mire.

Meanwhile, the German soldiers whose guns had fallen silent chose that moment to take advantage of their enemies confusion and started to fire again. Those soldiers who had escaped from the attacking women by climbing out of the trenches suddenly found that they had turned into sitting ducks for German artillery fire.

Charlie had hidden himself in a dugout at the back of the trench, pushing himself as far back as he could into the muck. Looking out as much as he could without being spotted himself, he was surprised as the legs of a deer flashed past. This was followed almost immediately by a pair of human legs landing in front of him. These legs were encased in shiny black metal armour. To the left of those legs another pair appeared, in scarlet armour. Peering up, Charlie saw that the legs were attached to bodies. They were both wearing full plate armour, one as black as pitch, the other blood red. They both held enormously long swords in their gauntleted fists. The blades were decorated with a pattern of golden leaves and flowers, twining up towards the points. The hilts were encased in elaborate wire baskets that resembled roots.

Although these two newcomers were fully armoured, the one wearing black had left his head bare. Charlie could see that it was a man, although a man unlike any he had seen before. His skin was dark blue, looking almost as if he had been painted that way, or as if someone had cut the shape of a head from the night sky and placed it atop a suit of armour. His long hair was as pure snowy white as that of Charlie's granddad. Two horns protruded from his forehead, rising up and curling back over his head. If his skin was like the night sky then his eyes were the stars shining there; glowing balls of fire that seemed to spark and flare constantly.

As the pair stood and stared around, an angry cry from above sounded. A rush of wind and a clatter of wings was followed by the loud clang of metal against metal, followed by a meaty thud as one of the winged women landed on the ground, her face turned towards Charlie and mere inches away from where he lay. Her mouth moved but no sound issued forth, just blood. And then she seemed to convulse as the black armoured being slammed the point of his sword down through her back and deep into the earth below.

Sliding it free as easily as if it was being removed from its scabbard, he looked around.

The black armoured, horned man seemed to be the leader of the pair because he turned to the other one and spoke. Charlie was amazed to discover that he could understand him. In fact, he sounded like he came from just down the road from his father's pub.

"Kalen, deal with these Valkyrie," he said.

"Yes, sire," replied the scarlet armoured being. Hefting his sword, he leapt straight up out of the trench.

"You may come out now, boy," the first man said, looking down at where Charlie thought he had been hidden.

Slowly, Charlie climbed out of the dugout. Even without the horns, this creature towered above him by a good foot or so.

"We are Oberon, Lord of Lyonesse," he said. "Where are we and why are we here?"

"What? Why? Who?" Charlie stammered. "I don't..."

"One moment, we and Kalen were hunting a hart through the woods for my lady Titania's feast this evening. The next, a rent appeared in the air in front of the beast through which it leapt. We followed and ended up here in this disgusting place. So, we demand of you once again, where are we and how did you bring us here?"

Charlie could just about remember something he had once seen. A travelling band of actors had stopped in the village and put on a play about two girls and two boys. And there was some idiots who were putting on a play inside the play. And there had been a couple of other people in it and he was sure they were called Oberon and Titania, or something like that. But they weren't people at all. They were...

"You're a fairy?" he spluttered.

"We are the King of the Faeries," Oberon replied. "And we are not used to having our questions ignored."

"You're in the Somme. In France... And I don't know what you're doing here. First there was those women and then you and... and... I don't know."

"France? You mean, this is the land of men?"

"Er... Yes?"

"It has been many years since there has been a way opened between our two worlds. And you say the Valkyrie have just appeared as well?"

"One of them came and killed Mick and then more of them and they started to kill all of us. But they left the Germans alone. What do you mean – a way?"

Oberon looked around, taking in the muddy wasteland, the barbed wire twisting across the landscape for as far as the eye could see and the corpses strewn around like a child's discarded play things.

"The land of men has changed a great deal since last we visited. What is it that has occurred here?"

"We're at war with the Bosch. That is, the Germans" Tommy said.

"Ah. We see now… and this is the final deciding battle? How many years has this battle been going? There are so many spirits up in the sky. I am surprised that you cannot see them. It seems like there can only be very few humans left alive."

"The battle?" Charlie paused, thinking back. It seemed like it had been going for most of his life. But in reality… "About a month now, I think. I mean, the war has been going for a couple of years, but this bit… yes… a month."

"And all these dead have been killed in that time?" Oberon was visibly shocked although it rapidly transformed to anger. He turned to Charlie, his fist clenched around the hilt of his sword. "Oh, what fools these mortals be… Did you not think of the dangers of so many dying so quickly and so violently? It is no wonder that you split apart the seams of your reality. You should think yourself lucky that this is all that has happened."

"It's not my fault!" Charlie said. "I didn't know. Nobody knew! And anyway, what were we supposed to do? Let the Hun get away with it? Let the Kaiser walk all over us?"

"You did not know? You think that it is reasonable for this many people to die and for there to be no repercussions? You are here and you are a human. You are part of this. Even one as dull as you must have been able to feel something of the anguish of the spirits above you. Behold."

Oberon took hold of Charlie's head in his hands and forced

him to stare up into sky. At first, all he could see was the blue sky, women – the Valkyrie? – flying around and making swift diving attacks towards the ground. But then, slowly, like a gathering storm, a dark, twisting, rolling cloud started to fade into view. And, with it, a distant wordless howl, like a whole pack of wolves mourning their leader. Suddenly, it seemed like the storm realised he was there, watching. Without changing, it somehow became a face, almost like the funny pictures that were a rabbit one moment and a duck the next. If only it had been one of them. But it wasn't. Mick was there, his face taking up the entire sky from horizon to horizon. The howl twisted and coalesced into words.

"You know what they say?" Mick said, his voice made up of the voices of every dead soldier on the battlefield. "It's the one you don't hear that gets you, eh lad?"

Oberon let go of Charlie's head and his legs gave way, sending him down to kneel in the filth in the bottom of the trench. He realised that tears were streaming from his eyes and he was repeating 'no… no… no' over and over.

"Do you see now, human?" Oberon asked.

"I promise it's not my fault. I was just doing as I was told… I don't even know if I killed anyone…"

"You were only following orders? Is that your excuse?" Oberon looked disgusted. "You will need to do better than that."

Over Oberon's shoulder, Charlie could see all of the Valkyrie swooping down to converge on Kalen. His long shining sword flashed as it span in the air. With each of his movements another of the armoured women fell to the ground either dead or dying. Nothing they could do seemed able to get through his lightning fast defence and they were equally incapable of defending themselves against his attacks. Oberon drew his sword and with a single bound was stood atop the trench. He looked back down at Charlie.

"Wait here, human. Guard the rent," Oberon said. "We shall assist Kalen. Then we shall talk more and you shall take us to your superiors."

"Right. Fine. I'll do that," Charlie replied. Climbing to his feet, he rubbed his eyes with a filthy hand and picked up his rifle.

Chapter Two

It was bloody freezing. Two o'clock in the morning, standing on the edge of the quayside, waiting for a boat to turn up that was already half an hour late. She wouldn't be able to warm up when it arrived either. She'd been given strict instructions that she was only there to oversee, not to do any of the hard work. Normally, she'd have been glad of that command, but tonight, she could really have done with getting a bit of a sweat on to banish the cold that was slowly seeping into her bones. Not even the thick duffel coat and huge sweater she'd put on was helping much anymore. And, of course, she'd forgotten gloves, so she had to keep her hands stuffed into her pockets if she didn't want her fingers turning to icicles and falling off. She didn't want to complain though, Ricky, the person standing next to her, taking occasional nips from a hipflask – and not offering her any, the bastard – didn't seemed to have noticed the weather. He was wearing a light leather jacket and a football shirt. The only way you could tell that it was cold around him was by seeing his breath turn visible. At least that meant that he was breathing.

Well, Rachel thought, *that's something to be grateful for, I suppose.*

At long last, Rachel saw a light slowly making its way down the river. It flashed off then on, off and back on again. She picked up the torch that lay at her feet and flashed back.

Going to stand at the edge of the dock, she watched the boat manoeuvre its way up to the wall of the quay. A man standing in the prow threw a rope up to her and she tied it off on a bollard.

"What kept you?" Rachel called down.

"It's not an exact science, you know?" the man said with a heavy Norwegian accent. "We have a long way to come and it's a rough sea out there. Even harder in the dark. Just be glad that we're here at all."

"You're being paid enough," Rachel replied. "Have you brought it all?"

"What? You think we'd come all this way with only half of it? Do you think we're idiots?"

"You're on that boat crossing the North Sea, not me, mate."

The sailor gave her a look that needed no translation. At that moment, a lorry drove up, braked and reversed so its tailgate was close to the boat. Ricky came over, pocketing his mobile phone and together he and Rachel pulled the lorry's back door open and lowered the ramp. Half a dozen recently deceased zombins slowly walked down and gathered in a huddle at the edge of the dock.

"Right, listen you lot," Ricky said. They all lifted their heads and focussed dead eyes on him. When he was certain he had their attention he continued. "There are a load of boxes in that boat. Bjorn there will show you which ones..."

"My name is not Bjorn," the sailor said.

"Listen to Bjorn when you are on the boat," Ricky continued, ignoring the interruption. "Do not fall in the water, because no-one will jump in and get you. When you get the boxes, stack them in the lorry."

The zombins started to climb into the boat, while 'Bjorn' huffed and muttered in Norwegian.

#

Twenty minutes later, it was done. About thirty crates, three feet long, one foot wide and one foot deep were stacked neatly against the back and sides of the lorry. Ricky had gone back to his car and pulled a briefcase out of the boot, passing it over to Bjorn. The zombins were all stood around at the back of the lorry, waiting for further orders. As Rachel watched the boat pull away from the dockside, Ricky chivvied the zombins into the back of the lorry as well.

With one last wave to Bjorn, Rachel turned away and helped close up the tailgate.

"Job's a good 'un," Ricky said. "You coming?"

"Well, I'm not waiting here for the first bus," Rachel replied. "I'll freeze me tits off."

"We've got to watch the dead guys unload the truck and then it's off to bed. The wife'll really appreciate me climbing in next to her."

"Rotting fish, corpses and sub-zero temperatures– a wonderful combination."

#

They pulled into the warehouse behind the lorry and watched the zombins unload the crates.

"Okay. I'm off," Ricky said.

"What do we do with them?" Rachel asked, jerking her thumb at the grey-skinned undead creatures standing motionless in the corner of the building.

"Mickey'll deal with them. But I'm not sticking around to speak to him. Zombins are bad enough. But he just makes my flesh crawl. If you've got any sense, you'll avoid him as well."

"Well, I've got to get a taxi, so I'm here until then."

"I'd offer you a lift home, except it's late and I really need to get back. Sorry"

"No problems," Rachel said, meaning it as much as Ricky meant the apology.

Ricky climbed into his car. Just before he started the engine, he yelled out "Hey, Mickey!"

There was a clatter as something in the back fell down.

"He'll be here in a minute. See ya." Ricky said, turning over the engine and slamming the door closed.

Rachel shuffled from one foot to the other, wondering what it was about Mickey that got to her erstwhile colleague so much. The thought of someone who could make Ricky retreat that quickly did not make Rachel comfortable.

The door at the far end of the warehouse scraped open and Mickey, the zombin wrangler, stepped through.

Almost immediately, Rachel had an idea of the problem that Ricky had with Mickey. Obviously, working that closely with zombins was not a job that attracted particularly 'normal' people. As he stepped into the room, Mickey farted loudly. He wore ragged, cut-off jogging pants and a Nike t-shirt. He didn't look as if he had ever actually done any exercise, though. Not judging by the bloated, wobbling belly that pushed out showing a pale expanse of flab protruding from above his waistband, a thin, scraggly line of pubes extending up to the deep hole of his navel. His lank, greasy hair was tied back into a loose ponytail, dirty brown locks hanging loosely around his face. Despite being in his late twenties, he had an acne ridden face that would have looked more at home on a teenager. Clumps of bristles covered his cheeks that were either an appallingly unsuccessful attempt to grow a beard or an equally appallingly unsuccessful attempt at shaving, although, considering the erupting pustules that ran across his face like volcanoes around the Pacific Ocean, too much shaving would probably have resulted in the abluting equivalent of major surgery. As soon as Mickey had locked all the zombins away, he dumped some raw meat into their bowls. Rachel watched in disgusted fascination as the zombins ripped into the meat, tearing it into shreds, blood dripping and gobbets of flesh spattering on to the floor around them.

"Not had too much contact with 'em, eh?" Mickey said. "Beautiful, ain't they?"

"Beautiful?" Rachel said incredulously, wondering what she was missing.

"Yeah. They're completely docile - follow orders, do out you want 'em to. Until they catch a hint of blood. Then, they're totally unstoppable. Keep goin' until they've got it all. So, whatever you do don't cut yersel' shavin' yer legs before you do anything with 'em." He laughed, a barking bray that was only a step or two away from complete insanity. "They're the perfect predator."

"Okay," Rachel replied. "Well, it's time for me to get out of here."

"Sure you don't wanna feed 'em? They'll eat until they're sick. It's so cool." He waved a bottle with a plain white label marked with the word 'whisky' on it. "I'm gonna crack open this bottle of whisky and watch a film or two. You can join me, if you wanna."

Rachel wondered if Mickey had ever known the touch of a woman. She then had a mental image of a 'completely docile' female zombin doing 'what you want 'em to do' and felt her stomach turn over.

"No. Thanks. Maybe another time..."

"Sure thing, whatever."

With that, Mickey seemed to forget that Rachel existed. He turned his back on her, unscrewed the bottle and took a swig, while watching the zombins eat.

"Okay. I'm going to go and wait outside. My taxi should be here anytime now."

Rachel didn't quite run out of the warehouse, but it wasn't far off.

Unfortunately, the taxi didn't turn up. After twenty minutes of waiting, she rang up the taxi company, to be told that the taxi had been there ten minutes before, but no-one had been waiting. Rachel learned an important lesson. Don't swear at the taxi booker, because they won't help you.

Fortunately, it wasn't that far into town. She just hoped that there would be some taxis still outside the nightclubs.

#

Even this late at night – or perhaps this early in the morning – people were still milling around. And, considering the temperature, they were wearing far too little. Rachel had never been one of those Bigg Market types – jeans and a t-shirt for the boys, micro skirt and boob tube for the girls. Even wrapped in her heavy coat, just looking at them as she waited in the taxi queue made her feel cold.

There was one other person who seemed to be intelligent enough to actually put some clothes on. And, seeing her, Rachel rather wished that she hadn't. Despite the bulky coat that covered her from neck to knees and the woolly hat that sat atop her head, Rachel could see that she was beautiful. Tall and slim, her calves emphasised by the heels she was wearing. Long, silky black hair hung like a curtain from under her hat. Her face was slightly oriental to look at, as if she had mixed parentage. Almond-shaped eyes and high cheek bones in a Mediterranean, olive skinned face. And those eyes were a bright and penetrating emerald green – unusually bright, maybe she was wearing coloured contacts.

The woman caught her looking. Looking? Staring. And she smiled at her. And that smile was as bright and penetrating as her eyes. It felt as if it had entered Rachel's brain through her eyes and stopped her heart. Before this moment, if she'd been asked, Rachel would have laughed at the idea of love at first sight. But, if that wasn't what this was, then she didn't want to know the real thing. It would kill her.

The woman started to walk across to her. Rachel couldn't breathe; couldn't think; couldn't move. If she didn't at least find out the woman's name, life would not be worth living in the morning.

"I noticed you looking at me," she said, her voice sending an electric thrill down Rachel's spine and into her groin.

"I'm... er... I'm... sorry. I didn't... that is... I mean... I..." Rachel stuttered and came to a halt.

"It's okay. It was a nice look. I've never been looked at that way before. It was almost like you knew me and hadn't seen me for years and couldn't believe I was here. In a way, I felt like I knew you as well," she said to her. She held her hand out. "My name is Lilly. But, maybe you already knew that."

Tentatively, as if touching her would make her disappear, Rachel closed her hand around the other girls. "Your hand is cold," Rachel said.

"I forgot my gloves," she replied, still holding on to her. Other than the coldness, her hand felt perfect. Small and delicate, Rachel could feel the slender fingers clasped around hers, her pink painted nails slightly digging into the palm of her hand.

Rachel looked back up to Lilly's face and she could see her cheeks, already flushed red by the cold, darken even more.

"I've never done this before – especially not with someone I've only met a couple of minutes before, but... would you like to come back to my place?" Lilly asked and then added hurriedly, "just for a cup of coffee. I want to get to know you better and it feels like there's no time to lose."

Once again, Rachel couldn't breathe. She had been hoping to get her 'phone number. This was more than she could possibly have imagined.

"Oh god, I'm sorry," Lilly said. "I must come across like such a slut. Really, I don't do this. I've never gone home with a woman before, but I just get a good feeling from you. I'll understand if you say no. Maybe we could meet up sometime."

"No, wait," Rachel said quickly. "I'd love to. I just wasn't expecting it. I don't think you're a slut at all. I think you're beautiful."

"Thank you. And so are you."

Lilly smiled at her. And Rachel's face cracked into a huge, goofy grin.

#

In the taxi back to Lilly's place, there wasn't much talking. Their lips didn't separate from each other for long enough to actually say anything. It was all they could do to keep their clothes on. They didn't have any coffee until quite a long time after they had arrived back at her place – a rather nicely laid out little flat in Jesmond.

Eventually, sitting in her front room, Rachel in her camisole and panties, Lilly in a black silk, knee length kimono, they had calmed down enough to sit next to each other on the sofa and actually talk.

"I don't know what came over me," Lilly said, blushing prettily.

"Neither do I," Rachel replied. "I just hope that it keeps coming over you on a regular basis."

"Oh yes," Lilly told her. "I don't want this to be a one-night stand. I really want to see you again."

"Definitely. Can I take you for dinner? Tomorrow night?"

"I'd love to."

There was a slightly awkward silence.

"I'd like it if you stayed the night," Lilly said and then glanced at the clock. "Oh god, look at the time. Stay for the next couple of hours, anyway. I have to get up and go to work and I expect you do as well?"

"Actually, no. I'm sort of an... independent contractor. I pretty much set my own hours, mostly."

"I wish I could do that. Mr Hargreaves is a bit of an ogre. He hates it when of his 'girls' arrives late."

"He's an ogre? Literally or metaphorically?"

Lilly giggled.

"Oh, metaphorically, definitely. Although he looks like he might have some goblin in his ancestry... Come on. Finish your drink. I have to get a couple of hours of sleep. I need some rest after everything you put me through..."

"I put you through? You were on top for at least half of it."

"Was that so bad?"

"Not at all."

Rachel upended her cup, downed the dregs of her coffee and then stood.

"After you," she said.

"Thank you."

Rachel was convinced that she wouldn't sleep with this goddess next to her in the bed but she surprised herself by suddenly being woken up by Lilly's iPod playing *Walking On Sunshine*. Rachel couldn't believe that she had fallen so completely head over heels in … well, certainly lust, if not love – she'd give it a few actual dates and conversations, rather than just the animalistic shagging that had gone on until about three hours before she would be prepared to even contemplate using the 'L' word – anyway, whatever it was, she'd fallen into it with a woman who not only had Katrina and the Fucking Waves on her iPod, but actually chose to play it.

Having said that. It was she had to admit, kind of apt for the way she felt that morning. Even with only the few hours' sleep she had had and the long night she'd had before with all it's ups and downs – zombins and freezing weather and (she shuddered) Mickey – she was, she had to admit, wide awake and feeling completely energised and... yes, walking on sunshine.

Fucking awful song, anyway.

She turned to look at Lilly, who was just stirring next to her, the music slowly getting through to her. She had the bedclothes partly thrown back and one leg sticking out. One long, slender, shapely, perfect leg. Even with the make-up that she hadn't managed to get around to taking off and had been fairly comprehensively smeared anyway, she still looked amazing. Rachel was glad that she herself had only worn minimal makeup the previous night because she knew there was no way that she could get away with looking like that.

"Good morning," she said.

Lilly's eyes flickered and then focused. She rubbed her eyes and then glanced at her fist,blackened with mascara and eye shadow.

"Oh fuck," she said, groggily. "Don't look at me! I need to clean this crap off my face. I need a shower. You'll never want to see me again if this is what you're going get in the mornings."

"Not at all," she told her. "I want to see you as often as possible. And, if it's in the mornings that will just mean that I've been with you for the whole night. Nothing else would matter. And, right now? You're beautiful."

"You deserve a kiss for that. But not until we've both brushed her teeth. My mouth feels like something has died in it... I've got a spare toothbrush."

"Okay, you go and get in the shower, I'll get breakfast together," Rachel told her.

"I'll get the cereal and stuff out for you."

"Don't worry. I'll find it. Go and shower."

As she climbed out of bed, Rachel patted her on the bottom.

"Be quick though. I want that kiss."

#

The next week or so passed with Rachel in a daze. She half-heartedly ran the occasional errand for Mott, waiting until she was certain that Lilly would be home from work. Then she would rush around there, usually stopping to pick up some little gift for her. The nights were spent in a haze of lust and sweat, before they both collapsed into an exhausted slumber. God, it was good.

#

The cockfighting ring was in a barn. Well, Mickey Sharp, the twenty four year-old Newcastle United defender who owned the forty acre farm upon which it was situated called it a barn. It was actually a purpose built mini-stadium, obviously ripped off from the design of St James Park, the metal tubing of the structure exposed, pre-formed concrete and glass filling in the spaces.

Rachel sat in the 'executive box', a glass of wine in her hand although she hadn't taken more than a couple of sips from it. Around her various Newcastle grandees milled around, including the Chief Inspector, a couple of senior Tory council members, Gateshead's chief rabbi, the Bishop of Hexham and most of the board members of Newcastle United itself. They were being served drinks and nibbles by girls wearing little more than silk and lace lingerie, stockings and high heels. The girls were sexy, in that really obvious way that Fred's whores tended to be, but as far as Rachel was concerned not a single one looked as good as Lilly did. Not that it mattered. They weren't there to entertain Rachel. She was just there to make sure that they got home safely after the fight and to keep count of any 'extras' that they provided, over and above their waitressing duties.

Fred had told Rachel that this was one of the best gigs in town and, considering the clientele, pretty much provided him with immunity from serious investigations. If the papers knew, for example, how much Bishop Banks loved getting blowjobs from Brittany while they were both dressed as schoolgirls, or how much blow Chief Inspector Wallace snorted from Michelle's breasts at one of these nights, or how much Councillor Fran Thomas, famed for constantly writing pieces for the Evening Chronicle espousing a return to 'family values' and stamping out the 'plague' of homosexuality threatening the sanctity of marriage, enjoyed going down on Melinda, then there could be… repercussions.

Glancing out into the barn itself, forty or fifty people, mostly men, although there were a few women as well, were milling around, drinks in hand. The biggest crowd was around the bookie, who was taking money, handing out chits and chalking odds on his board in a flurry of activity that almost made it seem like she had several arms.

"It's going to be a good one tonight," Rachel heard Wallace say. "Apparently the contender has been in fifty fights and won them all."

"That's what they always say," Fran Thomas said, one arm draped around Melinda's shoulder, gently massaging her breasts. "It usually means that they're on their last legs and barely last three rounds."

"Well, we'll see. It should be starting in a few minutes."

The party-goers in the executive box started to make their way to the seats on the balcony overlooking the arena below. Fran pulled Melinda along with her, forcing the girl to sit on her knee. Fred was going to make quite a bit from the council woman tonight, Rachel thought.

The ring itself was in the middle of the 'barn'. It was ten feet below the surface and a barrier blocked all but the most determined, or the drunkest, from falling into it. Below the executive box it was standing room only and, as a portcullis rattled up, allowing Mickey Sharp, resplendent in an immaculate tux, to step through into the centre of the ring, the spectators pushed forwards for a clear view. As Mickey stepped forwards, the bookie shut his money box and scurried away into a room that had been provided for him where one of Mickey's accountants would count up the money and take the customary twenty five per cent of the proceeds.

"Ladies and Gentlemen," Mickey said in his broad Geordie accent. "The management – that's me – are proud to present a battle extraordinary!"

On opposite sides of the ring, a couple of heavy metal gates were drawn back, allowing two heavy-set, over-muscled zombins to step forward. Metal collars had been fitted around their necks and chains, leading back into the gloom inside the gates, pulled taut as they lumbered forwards. Their dead eyes stared forwards, neither one showing any interest or even awareness of their surroundings. They were wearing very little, allowing the spectators to see how the decay had affected them, to see whether their bets were likely to pay off or not.

"On me left," Mickey continued, "is the one and only, The Byker Bludgeon."

The Byker Bludgeon had been Mickey's favourite, apparently until tonight. Formerly known as Viv Roberts, he had once been an underground, bare knuckle boxer, until the steroids he had taken to increase his body mass and strength had caused his heart to explode. Given his size, strength and underworld contacts, he was an obvious choice for being illegally zombinned. In his new post-mortal career, he had been Mickey's most successful 'signing', winning ten of the twelve bouts he had been involved in and surviving the other two well enough to only need minor stitching to keep going. But he was pretty much on the way out now, his flesh was sagging off the bone and his muscles had lost any definition they had once had. The stench that billowed out of the gate as he stepped out made those spectators who had stood above it scurry backwards, a moan of disgust rising from them. As he stood there, his once mahogany coloured skin glistened unpleasantly in the bright lights.

"On me right is tonight's star guest. Please give a big hand for the Kentish Gimp!"

This zombin was a lot smaller than Viv and was indeed wearing a leather gimp mask, mouth zipped shut. He looked lithe and healthy for a zombin, his skin glistening with oil that had been rubbed on. Already, people who had bet on Viv were shaking their heads in disgust, knowing there was a good chance that they'd blown it. The huge smile that Mickey gave to the crowd meant that he knew what a lot of them were thinking. He'd known that Viv was on his last legs and had, for once, taken the advice of the 'trainer' and put him out as dead stock. He was still big and strong enough to give a good fight and that was what most of the people were there for. The betting was just a sideshow. If there was enough blood and guts spilt by the end of the bout then, bar a few grumbles, most of Mickey's guests would go home happy.

"Now," Mickey continued. "Let the bout begin!"

As he retreated back through the portcullis, which quickly dropped into place, the chains that held the two zombins in place were released. They were pulled back and the gates closed. A buzzer sounded from their collars, signalling that they had been given a small electric shock in order to get them going.

The Kentish Gimp suddenly seem to come life, springing forwards and circling Viv, just out of reach of his long, ape-like arms, which were now swinging around trying to catch his opponent. That was probably the only advantage that Viv had over the smaller zombin. If he could catch him and get him in a bear hug, then it would very likely be over pretty quickly, even with Viv's body failing him. But the Gimp wasn't giving him the opportunity to land a single blow, skipping around the larger zombin and then, when he managed to get behind him, he would nip forwards, landing a staggering blow against Viv's back or legs before scuttling backwards again out of reach.

The bout went on like this for quite a while, Viv never quite managing to be fast enough to catch his opponent and the Gimp not being quite strong enough to fell the giant zombin. At a certain point, the fight reached its second round. Rather than stopping for a breather as would happen in a fight between live humans, it was instead ratcheted up to a new height. A valve opened above the pit and a deluge of blood and meat dropped onto the two fighters, covering them and kicking off their blood frenzy instincts.

Suddenly, instead of being a slow, lumbering monster, Viv became something entirely other. It was almost as if the blood imparted some sort of life-force to him. His movements became smoother and faster. He crouched and started to track his opponent, his boxing instincts sparking inside him. If it had only been him who had received this sort of boost then then fight would have been over in seconds. But the Gimp, already smoother and faster, went up another gear. Most zombin fighters could be beaten by a decent human fighter, as they could just move more quickly and get into a position where they could disable the zombin without endangering themselves. However, the Gimp was different. Once the blood had set off his frenzy, he seemed to turn into some kind of martial artist. He was leaping and spinning, dropping to the floor and then bounding high into the air, becoming untouchable.

The spectators gasped in amazement, seeing the amazing feats that were being performed below them. But then, a deeper, more angry undercurrent started to run through the crowd. Something was wrong, this didn't seem entirely kosher. No zombin should be able to do this unaided. It wasn't unknown for magically-enhanced zombins to fight but it was always announced before hand and would be against a similarly endowed opponent. For all this was an underground and illegal sport, it was still regulated by its organisers. For a spelled-up zombin to be put into a fight without declaring it as such was a really shitty thing to do and could mean that the owner and trainer would suffer repercussions. Knee caps being removed. A bullet in the back of the head. That sort of thing. As such, it was a very rare occurrence.

The Gimp slinked around Viv and thrust a foot into the back of his knees. He fell forwards onto his knees and, as he landed, the Gimp pirouetted into the air, an elegant but vicious kick to Viv's temple slamming him to the ground. For the final coup de grace, the Gimp leapt up once again and landed on Viv's metal collar. There was a loud crack as his neck shattered and Viv slumped to the ground. Still animated, but unable to move any more.

The crowd pressed forwards against the barriers, roaring their disapproval. Not only was Viv the favourite, but it seemed like he'd been beaten unfairly.

Another loud buzzer went off and the Gimp slumped to the ground bonelessly, lying on top of his downed opponent. The electric shock that the collars gave at the end of a fight was of a much higher voltage and was more than enough to shut down the zombins nervous system for long enough to at least get the chain attached again.

"Get it's mask off," someone shouted. "Show us it's face…"

The call was repeated over and over, building in volume as more and more people took up the cry. The bookie, usually coming back out as soon as the fight was over to hand out winnings, had chosen to stay where he was. He reckoned, probably quite rightly, that people would take back all the money they had bet, and probably more, if he went out there.

Soon enough, the whole crowd was screaming out 'Off! Off! Off!' as the trainers came out to take charge of their zombins. Once the Gimp has been chained up again, Viv's trainer started to argue with the Gimp's, emboldened by the crowd who were so obviously behind him. He reached forward to try and take the mask off but his hand was slapped away. Viv's trainer, who was almost as big as Viv himself was, looked at his counterpart, who while also pretty big, was still overshadowed, and punched him as hard as he could, first in the stomach and then, as he doubled over, jerked his knee up to meet the other's face as it came down.

With that out of the way, he turned to the Gimp and reached out for his mask. Suddenly, the Gimp seemed to spring to life, wrapping his legs around Viv's trainer's neck and twisting, flipping him over and on to the ground. Reaching inside the trainer's jacket, he pulled out the taser and quickly zapped him with it.

As he dragged his own trainer to his feet and pulled the metal collar from around his neck, a shot rang out. The Gimp fell to the ground, blood bursting from the bullet hole in his chest. As he fell, he seemed to shimmer and when he landed, his body looked different. It looked alive. No longer did it have the grey sheen of dead flesh, instead it was now pink and healthy and living.

The Gimp's trainer started to run for the gate, but another shot split the ground in front of him.

"Don't you move, you little fuck," came a shout from above.

Chief Inspector Wallace stood at the edge of the balcony, gun pointed directly at the trainer. This was probably the closest he would ever come to feeling like James Bond – wearing a tuxedo and pointing a gun at a bad guy. If only the suit fit him better, he was about four stones lighter and thirty years younger, he might have even looked the part as well.

Mickey came out into the ring and, kneeling down next to the body of the Gimp, stripped his mask off. Underneath were the fine features, pale eyes and pointed ears of a faery.

"It's a fuckin' faery," Mickey shouted. "It must've been using its glamor to make itself look like a zombin. Fuckin' 'ell."

Rachel, sitting at the back of the balcony, thought that this just showed exactly how weird the rich and powerful were.

#

The other people sitting around the table, waiting for Mott to come in, looked at each other nervously, none of them certain about why they were there or whether they were in trouble. There had been rumours over the last couple of days, a couple of jobs going wrong and some guys getting hurt. They were all trying to work out if they'd screwed up somehow or were going to be made scapegoats.

But Rachel didn't care. She leaned back in her chair, sunglasses over her closed eyes, whistling softly under her breath. Even realising she was whistling *Walking On Sunshine* didn't stop her.

Then, Fred came in. And he even stopped Rachel's happy thoughts.

Without even waiting to sit, he started to speak.

"Some fucker is talking and I want to know who. And I want him stopped. Unpleasantly."

"What do you mean, Mr Mott?" asked one of the guys. "Unpleasantly?"

"I'd have thought it was pretty self-explanatory. Unpleasantly. I want blood and screaming and entrails. Actually, on second thoughts, I probably can't trust you lot to do it properly. If I could, then I wouldn't have to worry about one of you screwing me over. I'll do it myself. Find out who's talking to Bailey and bring him to me to explain himself. Then I'll give you a demo of exactly how unpleasant I want you to be in the future."

Rachel raised an eyebrow. Someone was in deep shit. And talking to Bailey? That was really low. Mott was deeply unpleasant, hell, he'd just proved it, but at least he didn't drink your blood. Well, not that Rachel knew, anyway. And, if he did, then he didn't do it on a regular basis and it would only be to prove a point. Well, it had nothing to do with her. She didn't really spend any time with any of the other guys – they were pretty much mindless thugs. Rachel admitted that, in the past, she had been fairly thuggish herself, when she needed to be, but she had never been mindless. Now, if possible, she preferred avoiding violence and thuggery as much as she could. Frankly, spending time with Lilly made her think of other things anyway. Like getting out of this gig. Stopping all of the crime stuff and well, that was as far as she got really. The important bit was spending as much time with Lilly as she could. God, she was getting soppy. But... hell... Lilly.

#

Rachel didn't like ghosting when she was away from her bedroom. It left her body vulnerable. But she was in a hotel room, the door was double-locked and she'd pulled the wardrobe in front of it. Anyone who wanted to get to her that way was going to have to go through Narnia to get to her. And she wasn't far away from where she needed to be.

She floated across the room and out through the wall, across the street and into the bar that lay on the other side of the road. The music throbbed and she could feel the bass bouncing around the room, making the walls shake, getting inside her head and making it hard to hear herself think. This was exactly why nightclubs never got haunted. The sound made it hard to focus, beat beat beating in her brain. Already, she could feel herself starting to fray at the edges. Pausing in the middle of the room, she concentrated, reinforcing her self-image, hardening herself to the noise. It had the unfortunate side-effect of making her less invisible; she was now a slightly shimmering, woman-shaped piece of air but it was necessary.

Scooting around the room, she poked into every nook and cranny, satisfying herself that it was going to be safe. There was no-one suspicious, at least, not as far as she could tell. Nobody seemed to be waiting there, looking for anybody. Well, nobody apart from the one person she was expecting to be there. All the other people inside were desperately engaged in the practice of getting as pissed as they could as quickly as they could and copping off with one another. The Geordie young adult in all its glory.

It took a few minutes to completely satisfy herself and by the time she had, she could feel her concentration slipping. Not only did the music seem to be getting louder, but the psychic emanations from all those pissed-up girls and boys were having an intoxicating effect on her. In her ghost form, she could be vulnerable to extremes of emotion. That was how you got a poltergeist. A perfectly normal, harmless ghost that's been hanging around for years, doing no harm to anyone suddenly gets a dose of emotion, say a teenage girl with her body filled with hormones, discovering, amongst other things: boys, periods and what a complete pain in the arse her parents could be. Any one of those things could be enough to set off a 'geist. All three together and you were almost guaranteed to have lost your best china by the end of the week.

Phasing through the wall back out into the cool, fresh air of the evening, Rachel mentally breathed a sigh of relief. Having her lungs across the other side of the street made it hard for her to do it for real. Sometimes, not having your body around could be annoying. Despite how much she loved the freedom of flitting around in her ghost form, there were some advantages to having the meat to wear. Breathing, for instance. You never appreciated how good it felt to breathe until you hadn't been doing it for a while. That first breath after re-entering her body... She'd heard seriously addicted people describing the way the first cigarette felt in the morning or the initial rush when the Dust first hits your system. It sounded very similar to the oxygen hit she got when her body woke up. It's not that it stopped breathing when her animating spirit left, but it slowed right down, leaving it just a fraction away from real death. Ten or fifteen heartbeats a minute, two or three breaths. When she first started ghosting, she would occasionally just sit in her room and watch her body lying there doing almost literally nothing. She had once persuaded a girlfriend – a medical student – to hook her up to an ECG monitor. She seriously freaked when she saw what Rachel leaving her body did to it. They split up a week later, although, really, it had been over since that moment. There had certainly been no intimacy after that moment.

Yeah, there it was. That shuddering breath as her body came back up to speed. So good. She wouldn't say better than sex, especially not sex with Lilly – the things she could do with her body... – but it was right up there.

Climbing off the bed, she checked herself in the mirror. She looked like any other slightly-too-old-to-be-in-this-bar girl. A short, tight dress, sheer tights and high heels. Checking that the stuffed envelope was secure inside her handbag, she picked it up, put it down again when she realised that she would need both hands to wrestle the wardrobe away from the door, went out - picking the handbag up again as she went, crossed the road and joined the queue to get back in to the bar.

#

The sound and the atmosphere weren't much improved by being inside in her body. She went directly over to the man she was here to meet who was standing in a corner, nursing a pint of amber piss. His balding pate fringed with salt-and-pepper hair made him look somewhat clerical, although this image was broken when he turned his head and the long pony tail growing from the back of the fringe was revealed. It wasn't helped much by the heavy moustache either– the sort of growth that Rachel couldn't help think of as a 'porn-star 'tache'. His name, according to Mott, was Charlie Parsons and he was apparently the best there was at what he did, which is why Rachel had such a big wad of cash in her handbag.

"You're fucking late," Charlie growled and then had to repeat himself in a shout to make himself heard.

"Well, you know. Bars with queues and bouncers. I don't understand the popularity of the place, myself."

Charlie stared over Rachel's shoulder, his mouth twisted into a leer. She turned to look and saw a slender, blonde-haired, large breasted girl who couldn't have been any older than twenty wearing a black stretch cotton, skin tight, mid-thigh length dress, smoky black tights and heels that must have been about five inches high.

"Okay, there maybe a couple of reasons…" Rachel admitted, although she felt a bit creeped out looking at the girl in the same way as Charlie.

They looked at each other, Charlie taking another slurp of his lager.

"Have you brought it?" he asked at last.

"Of course I have," Rachel replied. "There wouldn't be much point being here otherwise, would there?"

"Yeah. Whatever. Just hand it over," Charlie told her.

Reaching inside her bag, Rachel pulled the envelope out and discretely passed it over to Charlie. Turning away from the bright flashing lights, Charlie flipped open the flap and riffled through the wad of twenties that lay inside. Then, reaching under the table, he pulled out a leather briefcase inlaid with a crocodile skin motif. Sliding it under the table to Rachel, he stuffed the envelope in the pocket of his knee length, brown leather coat, stood and made his way towards the exit without saying another word.

Rachel pulled Charlie's pint across the table, lifted it up and examined it. She didn't trust the man not to have left floaters in it. Fortunately, it seemed clear of foreign objects, so Rachel took a swig. Jesus, it was fucking awful. When she had described it as amber piss she really wasn't far off. Warm, flat and weak. She didn't blame Charlie for leaving it. No matter the amount of attractive girls there were in the place, they couldn't overcome the rankness of the lager.

Even so, she sat there, taking small sips of the drink for another few minutes, giving Charlie a chance to get well clear of the place. It did cross her mind that it left her open for a set-up, but Charlie valued his reputation too much to do that. If word ever got out that he'd screwed over Fred Mott then his business would be at an end. Not to mention his ability to walk, stand or go to the toilet unaided.

Never before had Rachel been so glad to leave a pint unfinished. But, this time, it was still at least half full – Rachel liked to think of herself as a glass half full kind of girl – when she got up, retrieved the briefcase from under her chair and followed Charlie out of the bar.

Outside, it was cool and quiet, well, quieter anyway. Music drifted out of the various bars that dotted Mosley Street and the Bigg Market seemed like a bad radio churning out a tinny tune and a bass beat. But the girls and boys milling around seemed to like it.

A man coughed behind her. She stepped to one side to allow him to pass and then almost dropped the briefcase in alarm when he felt a hand clamp tightly around her bicep.

"Miss Cantrell," a voice whispered into her ear. A gust of breath blew across her face as the man spoke. It smelt of raw meat and blood. "Did you think we wouldn't notice a business transaction going on in one of our bars?"

"What do you mean?" Rachel asked, improvising wildly. "I was meeting my friend. He's just come back from Florida and he's got something from Disneyworld for my daughter's birthday."

"And it came in such a stylish briefcase as well. Why did you think it necessary to ghost in there to begin with? Is it a particularly expensive present? Is it perhaps an original Mickey Mouse picture?"

That flummoxed Rachel. She knew that, theoretically, it was

possible to detect her in ghost form, but she'd never actually come across someone who could do it. Not even mediums were able to communicate with a ghostkin if they didn't want to make themselves known. Of course, that rule might well only apply to humans. She twisted her head to look at her captor, staring directly into a pair of pale watery blue eyes. Those eyes weren't strong eyes; they did not suggest a powerful personality, rather the opposite. They were the eyes of a weak, insipid accountant. It was instead the pale, drawn face, the ragged, pointed ears, the rat-like incisors and the tightly tied scarf around the neck that made Rachel nearly shit herself. She'd never been this close to a vampire before.

Around his head, Rachel could see a shimmering vortex of ghosts: the souls of every single person that the vampire had killed. This was one of the side-effects of vampirism that was not widely known. When you were killed by a vampire, your soul was bound to them. Most vampires that Rachel had seen had a few souls gathered around it, spitting venom and loathing at their murderer. She had, on one occasion, even seen a vampire without a single ghost – it must have fed on butcher-provided animal blood from the moment it was turned – making it the closest thing you would ever get to a vegetarian vampire. Rachel was convinced that vampires must have lacked the ability to see ghosts because surely having something like that constantly surrounding you would lead to insanity. Not that she thought vampires were entirely sane at the best of times.

"Let's go across the road into the alleyway there and we'll take a look inside the briefcase. If it is a piece of Disney merchandising tat then I'll apologise. If not, then I'm going to get very angry."

His hand still clamped around Rachel's bicep, the vampire made his way across the road, looking neither left nor right at the oncoming traffic. Despite trying to hold back, Rachel found herself being dragged along like an unruly child in a supermarket.

The alley, Drury Lane, was dark and dank. Water dribbled from overflow pipes above and down the edges of the walls. The big commercial wheelie bins stank of rotting meat and stale beer and the whole alleyway smelt of old piss. Dragging her up the alley and around the corner behind the building, they surprised a guy who was adding to the urine odour.

"Hey guys," he said. "What's going on here? You selling something good? Got any Dust?"

The vampire smiled at him and the drunkard suddenly seemed very, very sober.

"Sorry, man," he said, backing away. "I'll just… er…"

He pointed back down the alley towards the lights and people and life. The vampire nodded and let him pass.

"Now, let's see what we have here," he said to Rachel, taking hold of the briefcase and pulling it out of her hand. At the same time, he let go of Rachel's upper arm. Rachel had a brief impulse to make a dash for it, but checked it, knowing that it would be pointless. In the same way that vampires were much stronger than a normal human, they were also significantly faster.

The vampire took hold of the briefcase lock and twisted slightly, tearing it like paper. Flipping open the lid, he gave a short bark of a laugh.

"I didn't know that Disneyworld sold stuff like this," he said.

Reaching into the suitcase, he took out a bundle of twenty pounds note.

"Some of Mr Parsons' finest work, is it?" he asked.

"Well, you know. You get what you pay for."

Rachel knew that there was no more bluffing. It was time to tell the truth – well, mostly – and hope that she gets away with it.

"And Fred Mott can afford to pay for the best," the Vampire continued. "Except, perhaps, when it comes to his lieutenants. It was one of the stupidest moves I've seen in a long time, making the switch in our place."

"It's where it's always done. Fred says it gives him deniability if it's not somewhere connected with him."

"I suppose that makes a certain amount of sense. But, it's not something we can allow to continue. Not to mention that you lied to me."

He carefully closed the briefcase full of counterfeit notes and put it on the ground. Grabbing hold of Rachel's arm again, he drew her close, his meaty breath blowing straight into Rachel's face.

"How much money is in that case?"

"About twenty thousand…"

"You're lucky that I've already eaten today."

He took hold of Rachel's left hand and forced it into a fist, leaving her ring finger sticking out.

"Twenty thousand pounds in counterfeit notes? Let's see…"

Holding tightly onto the hand, the vampire took Rachel's finger and pulled it sharply backwards. The snap was almost drowned out by Rachel's scream of pain. As her hand was loosed, her balled fist fell limp. The vampire grasped her little finger.

"…one…"

And snapped it backwards. This time Rachel couldn't scream and all that came out was an agonised wheeze.

"…two…"

This time, it was her middle finger. Rachel stared at the vampire as it slowly started to press backwards.

"…three…"

Rachel felt her joint starting to strain and creak.

"No," the vampire said, releasing her hand. Rachel lifted it with her other hand and cradled it in the crook of her arm. "Ten thousand pounds a finger. That seems like adequate compensation to me. Tell Mott to keep his business out of ours."

He picked up the briefcase and headed back down the alley.

"One more thing… You're barred."

#

Pushing her way into the hotel bedroom with her good hand, Rachel flopped on to the bed. She lay there, feeling her heart slowing down and the sweat on her body dry.

Pulling open the mini-bar, she took out three miniature bottles of whisky. Cracking the screw tops with her teeth, she downed each one without pause. Taking her camisole, she tore it in half from the neck down and then ripped a strip off. Grimacing, she wrapped it tightly around the two broken fingers and the middle finger next to it and then followed it with another bottle of whisky.

Laying back again, she tried to relax, although it was difficult. Every little movement of her body sent a jolt of pain up her arm. Eventually, though, the whisky started to kick in and take the edge off the pain. Closing her eyes, she slipped out of her body.

#

"Fucking vampires," she muttered as she hovered above the slowly emptying bar. The last late-night revellers staggered down the street towards the taxi rank, holding one another up, girls and boys groping and snogging, drifting off to nightclubs or home and a bed. A little later, the bar staff came out, wishing each other a cheery good night and getting into their waiting taxis.

Looking through the window, she saw the vampire sitting, sipping a glass of something thick and red. Rachel was fairly certain that it wasn't a glass of wine. The bar manager, apparently entirely comfortable around the vampire, counted up the night's take.

Once the manager had left, locking up behind him, the vampire sat in the darkness. Then he reached for the briefcase that sat next to his chair. It was now held closed with a couple of bungee cords. Putting it down heavily on the table in front of him, he undid the cords and then opened it. Slowly, he started to take the bundles of counterfeit notes and riffle through them, counting them.

Rachel slid through the walls of the building next door to the bar. She didn't want to chance alerting the vampire to her presence. She was still stunned at the concept that she could be detected in her ghost state, which made her wonder if they could do anything else. It was bad enough that her physical body had been hurt – she could feel a distant throb in her fingers even now. For her to be able to feel it when her spirit was at such a distance from her nervous system it had to be causing a lot of pain and the three miniatures had started to wear off. Maybe this would be a good time to never return to her body – but if they could detect her, perhaps they could hurt or damage her spirit and that could be irreversible. Maybe they could even exorcise her. She didn't think they'd be able to do so, but she really didn't want to chance it. Even if it didn't work, it would probably really hurt.

In the courtyard behind the bar, Rachel found where the mains entered the building. She paused, taking a deep breath and then followed the wires inside to the central fuse box. Concentrating, she pushed both hands into the box. Sparks exploded as she 'geisted the box. Flames spat out around the edges of the door and then the box exploded, throwing it across the room. Fire leapt up the wall and licked at the ceiling, the paint immediately starting to bubble and blacken. In the centre of the ceiling the bulb exploded and Rachel heard pops outside the door as others followed suit.

Floating through the destruction, she went through the back of the bar into the main room itself. The vampire was looking around in shock as the backlights in the bar blew out, shattering the San Miguel logo mirror that adorned the wall behind the counter. Picking up the briefcase but ignoring the pile of cash that lay on the table, he ran for it, forgetting that it no longer locked properly. As he made for the door, the case flopped open, shedding notes on the floor. A brief tug on the door's handle and it flew open, as if it were unlocked.

Rachel stood in the middle of the room as flames flickered and grew around her. A smile grew as she looked at the devastation. That had been fun. Perhaps not 'adequate compensation' for two broken fingers, but even so… She paused next to the table at which the vampire had been sitting and swept the money that had been lying there inside herself.

After a couple of minutes, the fire had really taken hold. Smashes and tinkles of bottles exploding as the liquid inside them boiled started to sound in among the crackling of the flames as the tables and chairs started to catch. Through the window, she heard sirens and blue flashing lights as the police and fire brigade arrived. Ghosting back through the flames and the wall, as a window exploded, hurling shards out across the road, Rachel headed back towards her hotel room and her body.

#

"And you fell down the stairs?"

"That's right, my little boy had left a car there and I didn't see it in the dark."

"Lucky you only broke your fingers, really. It could have been a lot more serious."

The nurse was in her late forties, bobbed hair dyed black, although the roots were starting to show through a little, revealing the grey that she was trying to cover up. Her name badge identified her as Staff Nurse Sarah Addison. And Rachel didn't think she believed her.

"You're telling me. It could have been my neck."

She finished bandaging the fingers together, splints keeping them straight and immobile. Then she took a sling and helped her put it on, making sure that her hand was comfortable.

"How are you going to get home," she asked. "Do you need a taxi?"

"If you wouldn't mind, that'd be great."

#

It seemed to Rachel that the previous night's activity actually took place over several days. So, it was actually quite surprising to find that it was still quite early in the morning. As the taxi pulled up, a rubbish truck drove out of the back lane and on to the main road. Hanging on to the back of it were a couple of zombins. Rachel couldn't actually remember the last time that she'd actually seen zombins doing the job for which they'd been named – zombie bin men. She knew that they emptied the bins at least twice a week but her mother dealt with putting the rubbish out and she liked to make sure that she was in bed when they came around. It was just far too early for any right thinking human being to be up and about. Fortunately, the drugs that Nurse Addison had set her up with had left nothing but a dull throb in her hand that she was certain she'd be able to ignore once she managed to get into bed herself.

#

Despite all the money she had appropriated, Rachel didn't like to spend it on herself. She was happy, even eager to buy things for her mother, or for Lilly, but she never really felt like there was anything she wanted herself. Once she had paid for all the procedures she had needed, she had discovered that she was pretty much content. A decent home cinema system, the odd nice outfit or pair of shoes, a few DVDs a month and some books were about all she wanted. She just wasn't into 'stuff'. Even so, after a few days of having one of Mott's drivers take her wherever she wanted to go, rather than relying on buses and Metros, she realised that this was one luxury she could really start to enjoy. After all, Lilly had a job, so she couldn't expect her to take her everywhere. And she was being driven around in a top-of-the-range Alfa Romeo coupé – black leather, shiny chrome and polished wood. She was also fairly certain that she didn't want Lilly to know exactly where she went all of the time. Some of the places would have been just a little difficult to explain. Like the whorehouse on Osborne Road. She no longer had any interest in using the girls there – which caused one or two of them to pout, although Rachel suspected that it was more due to the lack of regular cash rather than any particular prowess she showed – she was just there to get Mott's share of the takings.

Stopping outside Mott's house, Rachel climbed out of the back of the car. The driver flicked on the radio as she stepped out and Rachel heard a jingle for Radio Two.

Inside, Rachel passed by the photos on her way up to the office. She was now allowed to go up without the zombin escort, a fact which really rather pleased her. Suddenly, she paused. She'd recognised one of the girls in the pictures. Sharon, the girl who whinged the most about her not coming round anymore. She claimed to be seventeen, but Rachel believed that as much as she believed her when she told her that she was the best woman she had ever slept with. It was definitely her, though, she could tell, even though her face was half turned away from the camera. She recognised the Kabbalistic tree of life tattoo on her bicep. Each of the Sephirah was actually the Venus symbol, ♀, with the topmost, Keter, made of two of these symbols interlocked. Despite – or perhaps because of – this assertion of her sexuality, she seemed to be one of the most popular girls in the brothel with the men who frequented it.

Continuing up the stairs, she got to Mott's office. The older man was typing something on a laptop, which he closed up as soon as Rachel entered the room.

"How are you feeling?" he asked.

"There's less pain now, but it still hurts when I try and move them," Rachel replied.

"Keep it moving. If you need to see a physio or a doctor or something, let me know. My doc is the best. He should be. He costs enough."

"Thanks, Fred. I think I'll be okay, though. I don't think you called me in to check up on my well-being though."

"That's what I like about you. You're not shy saying what you mean."

"It doesn't get you anywhere saying things prettily," Rachel told him.

"So true. But, I'd watch it, if I were you. Not everyone will take it as well as I do."

Rachel immediately recognised the underlying threat implicit in that statement and made a mental note to watch her mouth and say things a bit more 'prettily' around Mott from now on.

"Tomorrow night, there's another shipment coming in from Norway. I want you and Ricky to collect it again."

"Sure, no problem. I'll tell Lilly I can't make it to hers tomorrow night."

"Well, if you think you can do without a night of screwing..."

"I'll manage." Rachel couldn't help smiling. Her utter infatuation with her beautiful girlfriend was very well known amongst Mott's lieutenants and, apparently, Fred was aware of it as well.

"This is a slightly larger delivery, this time, though," Fred continued. "There are some very large boxes coming in."

"What's in them?"

Rachel knew what Bjorn normally brought and was extremely curious about what else he was bringing.

"It's a device that I've bought from a human freedom fighter group in Hungary."

Rachel had heard about these groups. A large part of Eastern Europe had been, since the mid-fifties, under the control of a new Hungarian Empire, ruled by Vlad Dracula and his consort, the Countess Bathory. They were strong enough that they were even recognised as a legitimate power by most of the human-controlled countries of the world, although very few of them tended to keep diplomatic embassies there, mainly because humans who displeased the vampiric overlords had an unfortunate tendency to... disappear. Several groups of humans worked hard to overthrow Dracula. The largest called itself 'The Soldiers of Van Helsing' and were at the forefront of vampire destruction techniques.

"Let's just say," Mott continued. "I won't be selling them on. They are going to be useful in our current situation. They may even bring you another chance for some further revenge against the... person... who broke your fingers."

Mott's distaste when he spoke of the vampires was very evident. He couldn't even bring himself to say the word 'vampire'. Not that Rachel felt much happier about them. Non-Hungarian vampires may claim to be integrated into society and deplore the activities in Eastern Europe, drinking artificial plasma and pretty much keeping themselves segregated into vampire enclaves, but to Rachel it felt like a case of the lion lying down with the lamb. The only reason to do so would be to make the lamb easier to catch. It was a cliché, but, as far as Rachel was concerned, the only good vampire was a dead one. And if she could be the one who was shoving the stake into their chests, cutting their heads off and stuffing their mouths with garlic then all the better.

"Sounds good to me. I'll look forward to seeing it."

#

The night was even colder than it had been the last time she had been down on the quayside at this time of night.

Fortunately, this time Bjorn wasn't late and Rachel had remembered her gloves. Rachel and Ricky urged the zombins down the ramp and lined them up at the edge of the quay again.

Even zombins could learn, after a fashion, and they had done this job several times before, so shepherding them into position was a relatively simple task between the two of them. Of course, Bjorn did not help. Instead he sat inside his boat's helm and watched, smoking a cigarette and drinking coffee from a flask.

And then the two live humans on the quayside froze as they heard a sound. A car's engine, the low, throaty rumble that you only got with an expensive motor vehicle echoed through the night. It was difficult to tell how far away it was because it was so quiet, but it was definitely coming towards them. Ricky pulled out his mobile and speed-dialled a number. It rang and rang as the engine noise got louder.

"Fuck," he said. "Someone's got through the guards down that way. Get the dead guys into the back and close it up."

He ran towards the lorries cab, pulled the door open and told the driver – who had Metro Radio playing and hadn't heard anything – to get going as soon as the doors were closed. The driver threw his copy of *The Sun* down on the seat next to him, dropped his half-finished cup of coffee out of the window and started the engine.

A matt black BMW came up the street and pulled to a halt in front of the lorry, preventing it from moving. The passenger door opened and a short, fat, pale man stepped out, leaning heavily on a silver-headed and tipped cane. He looked as if he would be the last kid chosen for football; as if he would have a permanently tight chest and be constantly sucking on an inhaler. He wore a smart suit with a pale pink silk shirt and a dark blue tie. On a taller, fitter, more handsome man it would have been a good look, but on this person, it looked vaguely ridiculous. Although the term 'person' was perhaps the wrong word to use. He had an inhuman, terrifying ugliness. His face was even more twisted than the vampire that Rachel had encountered in the bar. His incisors were so pointed he had to be careful when he spoke to ensure that he could be understood. His ears were ragged and pointed, looking exactly like an albino bat's wings. He didn't bother with a scarf, or even a bandage around his neck, instead allowing the bite wounds he had received when he was turned to constantly seep blood down his neck, staining the pink silk of his shirt collar a much darker shade.

Around his head, Rachel could see an uncountable number of spirits, swirling in a maelstrom of anger and hatred.

Two more vampires got out of the car, the driver and one sitting shotgun. Their own storm clouds of ghosts seemed pathetic in comparison to that of their boss.

"Fuck," repeated Ricky, but with real feeling this time. "It's Bailey."

"Mister Rogers. Miss Cantrell." George Bailey said. "How... interesting to meet you. I am given to understand that there are some objects in your lorry that may be of interest to me."

"I... er... don't know what you mean," Ricky said.

"Really."

Bailey took two steps forwards, took hold of Ricky's head with one hand, his fat, sausage fingers curling across his face, long, sharp nails digging into his cheek. Bailey's other hand snaked around his left shoulder and held it tightly. Although Ricky was much taller and more strongly built than Bailey – looking as if he could take the vampire without even breaking a sweat – he could not move an inch.

Bailey lifted Ricky entirely off the ground and pulled his head aside with such a powerful jerk that Rachel heard muscles snap. Bailey kept pulling and the skin of Ricky's neck grew tighter and tighter. His scream was tight and strangulated but there was no way Ricky could get a full-throated noise out of his mouth as his trachea was twisted and bent more and more out of shape. Thrashing his feet, he pummelled Bailey in the stomach, chest and crotch, slammed his fists into the vampire's shoulders and face but he may as well have been kicking a wall for all the effect it had.

The skin on Ricky's neck tore slightly and blood began to trickle out. Bailey paused for a moment and pushed his head forwards, a scarlet tongue slipping from between pale lips to barely touch Ricky's neck. He looked up, staring at Rachel.

"Fear makes the blood taste so much sweeter," he remarked.

A slight strain and Ricky's neck tore across. Blood pulsed out, rushing across Bailey's hands and splattering on to the floor. The screaming died away entirely but Ricky did not die, not yet. His flailing limbs continued to thrash, although they lost any real sense of direction, only landing a blow on Bailey's body by chance. Bailey was, however, ignoring him entirely, focussing on the scarlet juices gushing from his body, slurping and licking, letting it spatter across his own face and down his shirt front, the pinkness dissolving into red, the silk turning translucent and sticking to his skin.

After a couple of minutes, Ricky finally stopped shaking. Almost without thinking Bailey dropped him to the ground. One of the other vampires came over and picked him up, his head dipping down to feed on the sluggishly moving trickle that still dribbled out of Ricky's next. Taking the body back across to the car, the third vampire pressed his head in, the two of them slurping noisily.

Bailey turned to look at Rachel as she stood there, transfixed.

"So... Miss Cantrell...," he said. "Do *you* know what I mean?"

Interlude: Tynemouth, February 1996

The wind blew bitterly cold. It seemed to have come directly from the Arctic and right through every layer of Eric's clothes into the core of his body. The moon hung in the cloudless sky, casting a river of light across the sea and on to the ornate plasterwork of the Tynemouth Plaza.

He looked around warily, although he doubted there would be anyone around. It was too late at night, too cold and too crappy. Even the bloodsuckers were undercover and they didn't give a toss about weather. He jumped as a loud cracking noise came from around the corner.

"Come on, kid. No time to waste."

Eric went towards the voice and saw his cousin, Tommy, waving to him from just inside the broken fire doors. Piled next to the door were a dozen plastic, petrol-filled jerry cans, bought from several different garages earlier in the evening.

Eric tucked one under each arm and grabbed a couple more in each hand, following Tommy, who was striding confidently inside the Plaza, shining his light down onto the floor ahead of them.

"Now, you're sure there's no one around, kid?" Tommy asked.

"I didn't see anyone when I ghosted in here," Eric said. "It's as empty as your bollocks."

Laughing, Tommy cuffed him around the head.

"Get a move on," he said. "We need to get this done quickly."

Going further into the building, Eric remembered the times he'd been to the roller rink down in the basement. It had always seemed a bit seedy and on the verge of falling into dereliction – if it didn't fall into the sea first. The impression of impending ruin was made even stronger by the occasional flash of what it used to be – the odd ornamental cornice, the fancy staircase, the Roman pillars...

But none of that mattered now. Fred Mott needed it gone, apparently as a message to its owners on the errors of not keeping up the insurance payments. Tommy had told Eric that they had been pressured by George Bailey, that they had claimed that they couldn't afford to pay two lots of insurance – the place didn't bring in enough money - but that wasn't really an excuse. Examples needed to be made. And Tommy was very good at making examples.

They made their way down into the basement into the roller rink. Looking around at the DJ box and the single sad glitter ball that dimly reflected the light from the moon shining through the small windows placed high up on the walls, it felt almost like they would be doing the place a favour.

"Dump the petrol here," Tommy told him. "Then go back and get the rest."

"It's dark, I'll not be able to see where I'm going," Eric said.

"Didn't you bring a torch? Honestly, I told you to bring a bloody torch."

"Sorry. I forgot."

"You're fuckin' useless, aren't ye?"

Eric shrugged apologetically.

"Here you go," Tommy said, handing over his torch. "I've got a little 'un here that I bring in emergencies. Like if the batteries go on the big one. Or me little cousin makes a mess of things."

"Ta, Tommy," Eric said, taking the torch and dashing off.

He quickly returned, torch held between his teeth, as he tried to manhandle all the remaining jerry cans down into the rink. Seeing him, Tommy raised his eyes heavenwards and went over to help him.

"You could have made a couple of trips, y'know?" He said.

"I thought we needed to get this done quickly?" Eric replied.

"We do. But if you drop all the petrol everywhere, it's gonna make it harder, isn't it?"

"But I didn't."

"Aye. More by good luck than good judgement," Tommy retorted.

In the time that Eric had been away, Tommy had started to build a stack of chairs and tables, dragging them from the edge of the room right into the middle, building them up around a couple of still full cans and then soaking them in the rest of the petrol. Separating two of the cans and placing them back at the entry into the rink, he started to splash the rest of the petrol around the room.

"Like this," he said to Eric as he poured a liberal amount over the records in the DJ booth, spraying the fuel over the walls and equipment in there.

"Aren't there any records we can take?" Eric asked.

"No time to look. And anyway, it'll all be Britpop shite. I can't fucking stand Oasis. Fucking Beatles rip offs. Go on, get a move on."

Eric took up one of the cans and went over to the snack bar. After stuffing his pockets with Mars bars and packets of Maltesers, he doused everything.

After a few minutes, all the cans, bar one that Tommy kept back and the two that remained at the door, had been emptied. As he drained the last one, Tommy threw it on to the pile of chairs. Opening the one he had kept, he started to walk out of the roller rink, letting the petrol dribble out onto the floor, making a trail from the pyre in the centre of the room to the doorway.

"Okay. One last thing to do upstairs and then we'll set this fucker off," Tommy said, picking up the two remaining cans.

Going up the stairs into the offices and kicking a door in, Tommy took one of the jerry cans and started to splash it around, across the desk and chairs, up the walls and over the filing cabinets.

"Go next door and do the same there," Tommy told him.

"What are we doing it in here for?" Eric asked.

"Because I'm telling you to. That's why," Tommy replied.

Shrugging his shoulders, Eric picked up one of the other jerry cans and went next door.

It only took a couple of minutes to soak everything in that room and he came back out to find Tommy waiting for him.

"Sorted?" he asked.

"Sorted," Eric replied.

Tommy patted his pockets, pulling out a box of matches. He offered them to Eric.

"Would one care to do the honours?" he asked in a fake posh accent.

"Oh, one would be delighted," Eric said, laughing and taking the box.

Going to the entrance to the office he had dowsed, Eric slid the box open and took out a single match. Scratching it along the striking surface, it sparked and flared into life. Holding it for a second to ensure that it was well alight, Eric threw it into the room. The match landed on the edge of the desk and bounced onto the floor. Holding his breath, Eric saw it fall down into a puddle of petrol that had spilt off the desk. There was a soft 'whoomph' as it caught light. Eric stood there entranced, watching as the flame started to spread, climbing up the legs of the desk and across the floor.

"Come on, dickhead," Tommy said, breaking him from his reverie. "We haven't got time to admire your handiwork."

Taking the box back from his cousin, Tommy lit another match and threw it into the other office.

They ran downstairs and back to the roller rink. Lighting a third match, Tommy dropped it into the trail of petrol. Flames flashed along it towards the pyre, branching off as it met other trails that the two had laid as they had gone around the room.

They stood and watched for a minute, impressed despite themselves, but very soon the heat and smoke started to get too much for them and they beat a retreat back up to the ground level. They could hear crackling and snapping from above as the fire took hold in the offices, flickering shadows playing against the walls and they grinned at one another

"What the fuck have you done?"

They span around and came face to face with a man in a blue uniform, torch pointing at their faces. He was in his early fifties, a peaked cap covering his hair and the jacket pulled slightly too tightly across his beer belly. The fear Eric had felt subsided a little. This bloke wasn't the police, just a security guard. They would be able to get away from him pretty easily.

"Get lost," Tommy spat, putting his hand into his coat pocket.

"I'll have your guts for garters, my lad," the guard said. "The police are on their way now. You are going to be zombinned for this."

A flash of steel warned Eric what was going to happen as Tommy pulled out his flick knife and slammed it into the guard's stomach.

Gasping, the guard stumbled backwards, got his feet tangled and fell to the floor, all the while scrabbling at the wound as blood started to gush out.

"What the hell was that?" Eric asked. "We could have got away from him no problems."

"I thought you said there wasn't anyone here?" Tommy spat back.

"I didn't see him!"

"Yeah, well. This's your fault."

"We can't leave him here. He'll burn to death."

"Then he won't be able to ID us. Come on."

"We can't. We've got to get him outside."

"Eric - If you wanna do that, be my guest. I'm out of here."

Tommy span on his heels and ran towards the fire exit they had broken open.

Eric looked at Tommy's fleeing back and then towards the guard, in an agony of indecision. Making up his mind, he went over to the guard, knelt down next to him, pulled him him to a sitting position and then dragged him to his feet.

Putting his shoulder under the guard's arm, Eric staggered along. Every step made the guard gasp with pain and Eric was really unsure about whether or not they were going to make it before the fire blocked their escape. But, after what felt like hours as smoke and heat gathered around them, they pushed out into the open air.

Eric half-dragged, half-carried the nearly unconscious guard away from the building and gently laid him down on the ground. As he stood, the guard clamped a meaty hand around Eric's upper arm.

"You're not going anywhere," the guard growled through the pain.

In the distance, Eric could hear sirens. Panicking, he kicked the guard in the side, making him crumple in agony. Eyes streaming from a combination of fear and smoke, Eric ran off.

A van parked in the parking bays across the road flashed its lights at him and Eric realised that Tommy hadn't abandoned him entirely. Angling across to it, he dragged the door open and was barely in before his cousin gunned the engine and screeched away, heading into the housing estate just as a police car came around the roundabout further down the road.

Chapter Three

"What the fuck happened out there?"

The room was practically bare. There was a single metal table that had seen better years. Its surface was marked with little black scorch marks where people had stubbed out their cigarettes without bothering to find an ash tray. On one side Rachel sat in an uncomfortable orange plastic chair, the sort that church halls specialised in getting to accommodate the old fogeys when they went for their tea and biscuits. A thick, scratchy blanket that may at one time have been white or cream but had now faded into a dish water grey had been wrapped around her shoulders by someone at some point, but she couldn't remember who did it or when. The front of her blouse was liberally smeared with blood and she seemed to be missing her jacket and one shoe as well. In her shaking hands, she held a Styrofoam cup full of tea that was so weak its colour matched the general décor of the room. She took occasional sips from it, slowly and carefully bringing it to her lips to make sure that she didn't spill any of it, which was a definite possibility.

A single small window high up in one wall made a square of sunlight in the middle of the table, a cheery orange glow as the low winter sun peeked in. The clock on the wall opposite the window read '7:56'.

Opposite her sat Inspector Charlton and a female police officer – a constable. Charlton was glaring at her, his normally ruddy face almost glowing with emotion. His thinning hair was in disarray, as if he hadn't had a chance to brush it that morning. The woman, on the other hand, was not exactly immaculate, but she was certainly a lot smarter than her superior officer. She seemed to be taking almost no notice of Rachel whatsoever, showing more interest in the digital recorder that sat on the edge of the table and was, currently, playing up.

Rachel took another sip of her tea and looked at the Inspector impassively.

"Come on, Rachel," Charlton said. "I'm not due on for another..." He glanced at the clock "...one hour and four minutes. I haven't had a chance to get a decent cup of tea yet, or even brush my hair since I got out of bed. I could have let you wait for me, but I don't work like that."

"So, why are you here? Are you stalking me?"

"I got called in because the lads picked you up from the middle of a massacre and they know that I'm investigating you. This is a completely different order of things, though. One murdered human and a dozen dismembered – not to mention unregistered – zombins. I know you're a thief, even if I can't prove it yet. But if you don't say anything, you'll get stuck with the whole lot. It'll not just be renfielding this time. You'll be zombinned."

Rachel kept looking at Charlton. Then, as if coming to a decision, she heaved a deep sigh.

"I don't know anything," she said.

"Really?" Charlton replied. "You do amaze me. Just in the wrong place at the wrong time, were you?"

"Exactly."

"So, how exactly did you get covered in blood?"

"I tripped and fell over the body. I was kind of pissed."

"Would you be willing to take a breath test to confirm that?"

"No. I wouldn't. I've had a really shit night and this isn't helping. Either charge me or let me go."

"Oh, come off it, Rachel. Are you really going to try and pull that?"

"What else should I do? You seem pretty much convinced of my guilt anyway. Can't you, just for a minute – even think about the idea that I might just have been in the wrong place at the wrong time?"

"Not really, no. Do you have any kind of alibi that would suggest to me that what you say has any basis in truth?"

"I'm not even going to try. You'll ignore anything I say. Hell, the recorder's not even working, so this conversation isn't really happening anyway."

Charlton glared at the constable.

"Are we anywhere near getting that bloody thing sorted, Constable Marks?" He asked.

"Very nearly, sir. I think it's a loose connection," she said as she jiggled the power cord.

"Go and get another one. We must have a load of them. And, if we don't have any of them, get a bloody tape recorder."

"Yes sir, sorry sir," she said, getting up and hurrying to the door.

As she reached the door, it was opened from the other side. The Desk Sergeant came in, along with a slim, smartly dressed man, holding a briefcase.

"Inspector Charlton," the desk sergeant said. "This gentleman has come to see Miss Cantrell."

"Leonard Martin," Charlton said. "What the fuck are you doing here?"

"I am Miss Cantrell's solicitor."

Charlton turned to look at Rachel.

"You're working for Fred Mott now?" he said, incredulously. "I knew you were a shit but I didn't think you were scum."

"Sorry to disappoint, Inspector," Rachel replied.

"What did he have you doing last night?"

"My client is not going to answer any more questions. Unless you are prepared to make a formal charge, I have to insist that you release her."

"You are fucking kidding me," Charlton said.

"I do not appreciate that tone of voice. If you do not moderate it immediately, I will be forced to make a complaint about your conduct."

Rachel sat back in her chair, smirking.

Charlton opened his mouth to say something, paused and then closed it again. He looked from Rachel to the solicitor and back again, shook his head and, shoving his chair back violently, made to leave the room.

As he reached the door, he turned back for a moment.

"Just wait right there for a moment," he said. "I'm just getting the paperwork to formally charge Ms Cantrell with murder and possession of unlicensed zombins."

"You what?" Rachel said. She turned to Martin. "Can he do that?"

"Hmmm. Touché, Inspector," Martin said. "You're braver than I thought."

"Do you want to know the real bugger of it, Mr Martin?" Charlton said to him. "I would have probably let her go before you arrived."

"You're prepared to admit that?"

"Here? Now? While there's no recorder? Admit what, exactly?" Martin turned back to Rachel.

"My apologies, Miss Cantrell. I appear to have seriously underestimated the Inspector."

#

The cell was small and bare. The only furniture was a built-in shelf/ bed thing with a blue plastic-covered mat. It was not comfortable to either sit or lie on. Noises from outside permeated into the room: the slow, echoing footsteps of a policeman; the shouts and screams of a fellow internee; the occasional clang as another cell door was opened and closed.

Even so, Rachel was trying to relax. Her eyes were closed and her breathing was slow and measured. It wasn't the best place for her to try and do this, even worse than the hotel room. Her brain was buzzing, trying to think of a way to get out of there. She was fairly certain that she wouldn't actually be in there for too long. All the evidence against her was purely circumstantial and she could, pretty legitimately claim that she really was just in the wrong place at the wrong time. Which, considering what happened, she figured was a pretty accurate statement anyway. Being around George Bailey was pretty much the textbook definition of 'the wrong time and place'.

Slowly, she felt her body starting to sink into a trance. It was as if a duvet was being pulled up over her. Warm pressure crept up her legs and she felt her body getting heavier and heavier. When she had tried to talk about it, to explain it to others, she couldn't. It was like nothing else she'd ever felt but it was also completely natural to her. How would you tell someone who had always been blind what the colour red was like? Or someone with no sense of smell what frying bacon smelt like? The closest analogy she could come up with was as a mixture of falling asleep, being pleasantly drunk or stoned and the slow build up to an orgasm. And even that wasn't right.

Anyway, whatever it was, it was happening now. It had taken a lot longer than usual to get into the right state, but then, she was usually at home in her own bed, so that was hardly surprising. But, the feeling had slowly crept up to her head and she had felt as if she was being pushed out of the top of her skull. There was a brief moment of disorientation and then she was standing, looking at herself from the corner of the cell.

She took a moment to examine her corporeal body and was, mostly, happy with what she saw. Looking at herself like this felt more... objective... than it did looking in a mirror. Comparing the physical body that everyone could see with her spirit self that nobody could see inevitably left her feeling inadequate. She could still see some of the male features in her face, admittedly, they were covered over with the effects of the hormones and the work she had had done, but they were still there. The spirit selves of most Ghostkin tended to reflect pretty much exactly their corporeal forms, but this had never been the way for Rachel. She remembered how shocked she was when she realised that her spirit had a vagina. Shocked and overjoyed, because it meant that the feelings she had always harboured - had always hidden - were right. However, when puberty hit and her ghost started to develop into a young woman while her physical body started to develop masculine features, she fell into a deep depression. Later on, she realised that in some ways she had it better than other trans people had it. Yes, she still suffered from the dysphoria that afflicted a great many trans people, but she at least had the option of escaping her male form and spending some time looking like a girl. But, it meant that later on, she could see how she would have looked if she had been physically female from birth and she could compare it to how she actually looked now. And she always found that she fell short of where and who she should be.

Shaking herself and turning away from her body, she flew out into the corridor, along and up the stairs and through the offices. Passing Inspector Charlton, Rachel paused and looked at him. She almost felt sorry for the man. This was his chosen career, trying to catch people who had abilities he couldn't even comprehend. He may know about ghostkin and what they could do, but that was knowledge, untempered by experience. He had no real concept of what it meant, what Rachel was actually able to do. That was, she supposed, partly to do with the way the police worked. They had never been able to really integrate the whole supernatural aspect of the world into their operating practices. Partly it was a lack of understanding, almost undoubtedly a few ghostkin had gone into the force, like the few magicians who had joined up and comprised most of their occult department, but they were hamstrung by lack of finance even more than the usual run of police work. Finding a criminal when the only evidence left behind was some ectoplasm that very quickly faded into nothingness, no matter what you did to preserve it, very quickly became of secondary importance behind the robberies and rapes and murders committed by 'real', corporeal people who may have actually left behind something physical, something solid. On top of that, the laws themselves hadn't managed to catch up. Which, considering it was now nearly a century since this stuff had first happened was pretty disgusting. A week was allegedly a long time in politics, but one hundred years did not appear to be long enough to actually do anything. Although it suited Rachel fine. After all, she was one of the people against whom they would be legislating. Charlton could investigate and bluff and curse and promise all he wanted. Without the physical evidence to back up his allegation, there was no way he could pin that bank job on Rachel. Which was why being discovered unconscious amongst a pile of long dead bodies, alongside a newly dead one, must have seemed like a godsend for the long suffering Inspector. And why he was now trying so desperately to get Rachel to sweat. Which is where the whole failure to comprehend what a ghostkin could actually do came in. Okay, so Rachel's body wasn't going anywhere, but there was no way that would stop her from still having a life outside. Hell, if her dad could get her mother pregnant when he'd only just died, then Rachel was pretty damn sure she'd be able to work out how to have sex while in her spirit form. It was just another sort of 'geisting after all.

But, right now, she needed to get out of there and see Mott. He'd know by now that something had gone pretty badly wrong and he may even have an idea of what it was. But he needed to know exactly what it was that Bailey had done. And he needed to know that it wasn't Rachel's fault.

#

Well. That didn't go well. At all.

She supposed that turning up in Mott's office while he had a prostitute under his desk on her knees giving him... executive relief... probably didn't start things off well. But it was Rachel's inability to explain what had happened and why she was still alive and, indeed, completely unhurt when Ricky had been completely drained of blood and all his zombins had been dismembered. Of course, the reason for Rachel being unable to say why this should be was because she didn't have the faintest idea. She hadn't even really thought about it. She had just been glad that Ricky had said something before she had because, to be honest, she had been mere moments behind him in trying to bluff her way out of the situation. And seeing the way that Bailey had called his bluff, she was very happy that she had been slower. Actually, she would be seeing the way that Bailey had called Ricky's bluff in her dreams for a very long time to come.

And then, when Mott had started to throw things around and discovered exactly how difficult it was to hurt a ghost with an ashtray, no matter how heavy it was, it had just made him even more angry. All it had done was to utterly terrify the girl, who had scampered out of the room, tottering on her six inch tall, fuck-me stiletto heels, clutching her blouse to her chest to cover her skimpy, lacy bra. Rachel recognised her; she was Genni, one of the girls from the Jesmond whorehouse. She didn't know they did house calls, although she supposed that you did what you were told when the boss made demands. Let's face it, that's pretty much what Rachel did. Although she hadn't yet ended up on her knees under Mott's desk. Not that she ever intended to be put into that situation. Although you never knew how things were going to end up. She had the feeling that Mott really wanted to fuck her up badly at that moment.

To top it all off, discovering that his extremely expensive solicitor had utterly failed to get Rachel's situation sorted out and, in fact, may have just made things worse, really made Mott blow a gasket. Rachel got a little worried for the man. He was so red in the face and was screaming so loudly that Rachel felt sure that he was going to drop dead of a heart attack at any moment. Which would, at least, mean that he stopped yelling. The noise and the mental violence emanating from him made it quite difficult for Rachel to remain centred and focussed. She kept floating slowly backwards away from Mott, who just kept stalking forwards, getting louder and more strident.

Try as she might, Rachel couldn't get Mott to listen to her. Every time she started to try and explain exactly what happened, how she had to let Bailey take the shipment, how she had been in terrible terror for her life, Mott just overrode her and refused to listen.

After about half an hour of constant haranguing and insults, Mott finished with an explosive 'get the fuck out of here'.

#

Coming back to her body, she just lay there, her eyes closed, working through her 'conversation' with Mott. She was going to have to try again, either in person, if and when she managed to get out of her or in ghost form again. Although she thought that perhaps part of the problem was her turning up like that. Mott didn't have a problem using Rachel's ability, but she remembered, perhaps too late, that he seemed to be really squeamish when it came to actually seeing it. Back when she worked for him the first time, when she was with Tommy, she remembered how Mott had been seriously visibly shaken the first – and indeed only – time that she had asked to see a demonstration of how Rachel ghosted. It wasn't uncommon, Rachel knew one person – an old school friend – who had thrown up when he'd seen Rachel return to her body. Jake had been pretty much okay when Rachel had first ghosted, giggling as he re-arranged the empty body into various different poses and using a Ouija board to communicate with his incorporeal friend. But, when Rachel had come back there had been something about her body going from a limp ragdoll, essentially a warm corpse, into a living, breathing person again that had completely freaked Jake out. He had lost his lunch all over Rachel's bedroom floor. Which was one of the major reasons she tried to avoid ghosting around other people.

Her eyes flickered open and she found herself looking directly into Inspector Charlton's eyes.

"Have a nice little trip?" Charlton asked, apparently not as affected as Jake had been by what he had seen.

#

It turned out that the Inspector was actually there to release Rachel, although not without warning her that she should stay around, just in case anything came up.

"So, why are you letting me go? I thought you had the idea that I was involved somehow."

"Oh, I'm sure you are. But you aren't responsible for the murder. Unless you're a vampire now as well as being a ghostkin. Forensics came back and confirmed the attack as being vampiric. There wasn't enough blood in the body to be able to type it properly. And there wasn't enough on the ground to account for what he should have had inside him."

Rachel very nearly blurted out that George Bailey was responsible, before remembering that she claimed not to have been there. By covering her own back, she'd also done a pretty good job of covering up for Bailey as well.

Oh well, you can't win them all, she thought to herself.

"And what about the zombins?" she asked

"We think they were either brought by the vampires or the dead guy to help shift whatever they were down there for."

"What do you think they were there for?"

"That's all you're getting. I'm not telling your boss what we know about his business. He'll find out when we turn up on his doorstep with a battering ram and a warrant."

"I have no idea what you're talking about," Rachel told him.

"Of course you don't. You are completely innocent. It's just a coincidence that you happen to have the same lawyer as Fred Mott, one of the most expensive little rat bastards in the city. Remind me how you pay for that, seeing as you are one of the long-term unemployed?"

"Not unemployed. Freelance. And I have a rich uncle."

"Get out of my sight. You make me sick. I hope that next time I see you, you'll have a longer stay down in the cells," Charlton said, his voice dripping with loathing. He didn't usually let a case, or a criminal, get to him this way, but there was something about Rachel. Her superior attitude; how she could have so easily used her ghostkin ability to do something useful; the fact that it seemed more and more likely that the little shit was going to get away scot free. Well, this time, anyway. She'd screw up eventually. They always did. No matter how clever they thought they were. They always screwed up. Always.

"Well, I'm sure you'll understand, Inspector," Rachel told him. "If I don't share your desire. Well, mind how you go."

Charlton just looked at Rachel as she headed for the exit. She could feel the Inspector's glare burning into her back.

As the station door swung shut behind her, she breathed a heavy sigh and leant against the wall, feeling her knees suddenly turn to water. That was just too damn close. It brought back memories that she would really rather stay buried deep down in her subconscious. Memories that she had worked very hard over the last few years to lock away. Of the police raid when she and her cousin had been arrested. Tommy's execution. The hideous dullness of her time spent renfielded, being able to see everything, feel everything but from a distance, as if she was watching her life through the wrong end of a telescope. Maybe she needed to lie low for a while, maybe even go away for a bit, after the investigation moved away from her – if it ever would. She'd just gone too far above the parapets. Before, when it had just been Charlton on a lone crusade to nab his ghostly bank-robber it had been okay, a bit of fun. But now she was well and truly on the police radar. They'd be keeping an eye out for her. If they found her in the vicinity of any more crimes then they'd be all over her like the proverbial. Thank god they didn't think to ask her about the burnt down bar.

And then there was the fact that Bailey knew who she was. Which couldn't be a good thing any way you looked at it, whether he knew about the bar or not. It meant that someday – probably someday pretty soon – Bailey would try and make her into a late night snack. Which made getting out of the area even more important, really.

To top it all off, Mott was probably suspicious of her. Probably? If his rant was anything to go by, then Mott thought she was the cause of all his troubles and had been back to nursery school. Mott's, not Rachel's. That really needed sorting out.

So, on the whole, it seemed like her best plan was to get the fuck out of the city. Probably out of the country.

These thoughts were going around and around in Rachel's head as she sat on the bus taking her back home.

Climbing off the bus, passing Kerry, wishing her a good morning as the ghost girl waited next to the pelican crossing, unable to cross and unable to leave, Rachel headed up the street back to her house, her thoughts of a villa in the sun on a Caribbean beach fading away. She wasn't going anywhere without her mother. And *she* wasn't going anywhere without her husband. And *he*… Well, he wasn't going anywhere. Charlton. Bailey. Mott. She'd stand up to all of them to make sure her mom had whatever she wanted. After all, that was pretty much the reason she did this shit.

The house was very quiet. Normally, her mother called out as soon as the door opened, as if anxious to check that it was actually Rachel coming through the door. But this time, all that greeted her was the noise of Jeremy Vine on Radio 2, goading Daily Mail readers to ring in and be apoplectic.

"Mom?" she called, as she hung her coat up. "Dad?"

Her mother really didn't go out very often. Rachel could count on the fingers of one hand the number of times that she had come home during the day and her mother had been out somewhere. She always claimed that her father needed her there to look after her and no matter how often Rachel tried to point out that having been dead for thirty years he was a bit beyond 'looking after' it didn't really seem to get through to her. She'd probably just popped out to get a pint of milk or something, but, even so, each of those times when she had come in and her mother had not been there, Rachel had felt anxious. It wasn't right. Her mother being at home was one of the great constants of the universe. Coming home to find that she wasn't there was like the sun failing to come up in the morning.

She hadn't expected her dad to answer, though. The miserable old bugger never did, unless it was to berate his daughter for having done something wrong.

Going through into the sitting room, Rachel smiled as she saw her mother slumped down in the big easy chair that she called her 'listening chair', the one that Rachel has spent hours getting positioned exactly right to hit the sweet spot for the music system and the home cinema set up. She did wonder, slightly, if listening to Jeremy Vine on the brand new, high-end Bose DAB digital radio was the best use for it.

Quietly, she went through into the kitchen and put the kettle on, putting some chocolate Hob Nobs on a plate and preparing the makings of a pot of tea.

Once it had boiled, she put it all on the tray and carried it through to the sitting room. Placing it carefully on the table next to her, she looked fondly at her mother. She must be really sound asleep, she hadn't moved at all while she had been in the kitchen. She debated leaving her there to snooze, but knew she wouldn't thank her for it. She hated sleeping during the day, said it always made her feel like her head was full of cotton wool and made it hard for her to sleep at night. She poured the tea, added the milk and the two teaspoons of sugar that her mother liked and then gently shook her.

And then a little harder, calling out 'mom' as she did so.

She still wasn't moving a muscle.

Rachel shook her again, putting some strength into it and she flopped over onto her side, arms hanging limply over the edge of the chair.

"Oh, Jesus Fuck!" Rachel shouted as she leapt away from her dead mother, the tray flying into the air.

#

Rachel didn't just leap away from her mother; she leapt out of the house. She literally, jumped right out of her skin. That had never, ever happened to her, just vacating her body as if she was dropping some rubbish. But one moment, she was realising that she no longer had a mother, the next she was floating several hundred meters in the air, looking down at her house.

For a moment or two, she stared around, not sure what had happened. For an instant, she found herself wondering if this was all a dream. But really, she knew it wasn't. She couldn't get out of it that easily. Slowly, she dropped down towards the ground. Towards the house. Towards her mother. Her corpse.

The sitting room was bizarre. Surreal. Again, she felt almost certain that she was dreaming. But, again, it was just for a second. How could her mother's world still be continuing without her acting as the driving force? Surely Radio Two should be off the air, at the very least. The enormity of her death must have some impact outside the confines of this single house, this little, comfortable room. But, there she slumped, the radio playing music that Rachel didn't recognise, tea dripping down the walls, her own body lying face-down on the floor.

It was then that she noticed the figure sitting in her father's chair.

"Is this what you look like when you're a ghost?" Her mother asked.

Rachel gaped, utterly unable to make a noise. If she had been able to jump any further out of her skin, she probably would have done.

"You look quite beautiful," she continued. "Sort of like yourself and yet not quite. Like the girl you always should have been. I should be used to seeing ghosts, probably, seeing as your Dad was always around, but I suppose it's different seeing you. I'd think he'd look odd if I saw him in the flesh now."

"What happened?" Rachel asked, at last.

"I guess I must have had a heart attack or something. I was sitting down, having a little rest and I think I must have fallen asleep. And I woke up like this. It gave me quite a shock, I can tell you."

Looking back on it later, the thing that surprised Rachel most was that her mother was being so calm about the whole thing. Especially considering how freaked out Rachel was. It should have been the other way. After all, ghosts and dead bodies were very much part of Rachel's life. She had her husband around, but she never treated him any different from live people. Or maybe, she never treated live people any different from her husband. Whichever.

"Where's dad?" she asked.

"He said that now I wasn't around, he didn't want to stay. He's Gone On."

"Oh," Rachel didn't know what to say to that. On the one hand, she was quite glad to see the back of the old bugger, but on the other, it would be strange not having him around. Almost as strange as being haunted by her mother.

"So, it's just you and me now, is it?"

"Oh. Sorry, darling," she said. "But no. I'm Going On as well. I just waited to see you and say goodbye. Holding myself together is really quite difficult. I'm going to go and your join dad. And I'll see my dad and mother again. I haven't seen them in years."

Already, she was starting to dissipate. Her edges were becoming fuzzy and she was getting steadily more translucent.

She stood up out of her husband's chair and came over to her daughter, trailing smoky ectoplasm behind her.

"Can I touch you when we're like this?" she asked, sounding distant.

"Yes. Ghosts can touch each other, if they both want it," Rachel replied. She put her hand out towards her and she held it. It felt like she was being held by a cool breeze. There was no weight or substance to her. When two ghosts touched, they felt solid but this time Rachel was worried that if she pressed against her mother, she would push through her.

Her mother looked at her lovingly and then touched her cheek, a feather touch, barely there anymore. She was a faint cloud with vague suggestions of features.

"Goodbye, Rachel," she said and Rachel had to strain to hear her. "Be a good girl."

And she was gone.

Interlude: Newcastle, April 1996

"Remind me why we are here, darling," Eric's mother said to him as they walked down a corridor, guided by a young woman dressed in a smart black skirt suit. Eric found it hard to keep his eyes off her long, slender legs, encased in black nylon, her high, pointy-toed heels clicking as they walked along the concrete floor, extremely aware that he was dressed in much the same way. That his mother had insisted that he needed to do this and there had been no way he could get out of it. Not that he wanted to, but he wasn't exactly prepared for it this evening of all evenings.

"I just needed to check it out for Mister Mott. He rang before and said I needed to go and do it tonight. I'm sorry it's getting in the way of your celebration. We'll not be late for dinner, there's still loads of time."

"Didn't you tell him that you were busy?"

"Mister Mott isn't really the sort of boss who takes no for an answer. He always says something like 'if I'm prepared to take time out of my social life to work, then I expect my people to do it as well.' And he'll pay me extra for it as well."

"I still don't think it's very nice of him."

"I'm sorry, mom. It really won't take much time."

The woman took them up some stairs into a far nicer part of the building, with carpeted floors and large, framed photographs of footballers in action.

"What do I call you again?" his mother asked.

"Rachel," said Eric.

"Okay. I'll try, but you'll have to forgive me if I get it wrong."

"I will, mom. I understand. It's difficult for me as well a lot of the time."

They paused in front of a set of double doors, a sign designating the room beyond as 'The Gallowgate Suite'.

"I've always wanted to see in these places," Eric's mother told him.

"Well, I guess there is a silver lining to having to come here then?"

"I suppose so," she said half-heartedly. "My dad used to bring me to matches when I was a little girl. I always wanted to take you to see a game, but it's just too rough for me now. And you never showed any interest either. I guess you take after your dad in that one. He was never a football fan either."

"I guess that's one thing, then," Eric replied.

Eric's mother put her hand out, took her son's hand and squeezed it.

"Yes," she said. "It doesn't look like there's much of your dad in you, is there? I know you don't get on with him, but things seem to be doing better since you got the job with Mister Mott, don't they?"

"I guess so," Eric said. "He still gets at me though."

"That's just his way. He thinks you should go into the forces like he did."

"Yeah. That's not gonna happen. I mean, look at what happened to him. And they don't take people like me, either."

"I know. And I'm glad. You're my precious boy. Or, girl, I suppose I should say. I couldn't sleep at nights if you were sent to Bosnia or something."

"Well, you don't have to worry, mom. I promise that won't happen to me."

Their guide looked at them patiently as they stood debating outside the door.

"Sorry," Eric said. "This is it?"

"This is it. I hope it's what you wanted."

Eric twisted the handle and pushed the doors open.

"HAPPY BIRTHDAY!"

It was so full of balloons and crepe streamers and banners that Eric found it hard to believe that there was any room for the people. But they all managed to get in there, happy grins plastered on their faces, glasses held high and cheering.

Eric could see that just about everyone he had asked to come had made it - his entire family – everyone from his six month old niece Maggie to his granddad, all of his mom's friends from church and there, in the corner, smiling paternally, stood Fred Mott and a couple of his lieutenants.

"Whose idea was it to do this again?" Eric said, looking around the room.

"I think it was yours, dear. Oh thank you. It's lovely," his mother told him, standing there with, tears in her eyes.

"Oh, really? Oh, well, that's okay then."

"But how have you managed to afford this?"

"I saved up from my new job," Eric said. "You're only forty once and I wanted to treat you."

Eric's mother wrapped her arms around her son and hugged him tightly. He saw tears trickling down her cheeks.

"Thank you so much," she said.

"Hey, mom. No crying – this is a party. You've gotta be happy."

"Oh, silly… I am happy. So very, very happy."

Once everyone got over the surprise of seeing Eric in a dress, the party really got under way. A few people stormed out, complaining loudly about how they wouldn't stand for perversion, but Eric's mother just said 'good riddance' and hugged her new daughter tighter.

At one point, after her fourth, or possibly fifth glass of champagne, Eric's mother suddenly squawked.

"The restaurant!" She said. "We've missed our booking! They'll be so annoyed."

"Relax mom," Eric told her. "I cancelled it."

"You are such a bad boy... girl... shit," she told him. "You shouldn't have done this. You're young – you should be spending your money on yourself."

"Mom," Eric said, suddenly serious. "If I can't spend my money on you, then it's not worth earning it."

"Don't be daft," she told him. A sudden thought struck her. "Did you invite Susan?"

"I've told you before, Mom. We're not friends any more. We… fell out."

"Was it because of... this...?" she asked, gesturing at the dress that Eric was wearing.

"No. It was something else," he replied.

"You'll get over it. You just have to apologise for whatever it was that happened. She's a good girl, that one."

"It'll take more than that," Eric said, firmly.

"Okay," she replied, utterly unconvinced.

Rachel was boogying to Status Quo, doing her best guitar rock impression, and feeling really happy and relaxed now that she was finally being who she really was, when she felt a hand on her shoulder.

Laughing, she span around. And stopped laughing as she came face to face with a pair of uniformed police officers flanking a woman that Rachel assumed was a plain-clothed detective.

"Aw, what the fuck do you want?" Rachel said, suddenly aware of the silence around her. She looked around the room and saw that another pair of officers already flanking Tommy. Fred Mott was nowhere to be seen.

"Eric Cantrell?" the detective asked.

"Naw. I'm Andy Cole," Rachel replied.

"Eric Cantrell?" the detective repeated. "Please identify yourself."

Rachel gave a huge sigh.

"Aye. I'm Eric Cantrell, y'fuckin' bitch. This is my mom's fortieth birthday party. Couldn't this have waited?"

The detective ignored her.

"Eric Cantrell," she said. "I'm arresting you under suspicion of arson and assault with a deadly weapon. You do not have to say anything. But it may harm your defence if you do not mention when questioned something which you later rely on in court. Anything you do say may be given in evidence."

"Aw, fuck."

"Rachel?"

Her mother was coming across the room towards them, swaying slightly.

"What's going on love?" she asked. "What are these policemen doing here?"

The detective turned towards her.

"I'm sorry to barge in here, uninvited, Mrs Cantrell," she said. "But this is an important matter that we need to resolve as quickly as we can. We have reason to believe that your son and your nephew, Thomas McConnell, were involved in burning down the Tynemouth

Plaza."

"My son is actually my daughter and I'd appreciate it if you would remember that. And I can't believe that she would do that," Eric's mother said. "My Rachel's always been good, even when she was a boy. Tommy, aye, he's a bit of a tearaway, but he wouldn't do anything like that. I think you've made a mistake."

"I certainly hope so, Mrs Cantrell. If we haven't they'll both be renned, at the very least."

"Rachel?" his mother turned to him. "Tell her. Tell her she's wrong."

"Look, mom," Rachel said. "We'll go down to the station, me and Tommy. We'll sort it out there."

"Just tell her you didn't do it."

"Leave it mom," she said, eyes downcast.

"But... Rachel?"

"Come on," she said to the officers. "Let's get this over with."

Ignoring her mother's increasingly panicked calls, Rachel and Tommy walked side-by-side out of the suite and back down the corridor, flanked closely by the four officers and the detective.

Chapter Four

The next few hours were a blur. She must have done the right thing, because an ambulance turned up, along with Inspector Charlton, of course. Rachel vaguely remembered swearing at him, threatening to throw him out if he didn't leave by himself. Charlton must have taken her seriously, because he didn't hang around for long.

Once the ambulance had gone, Rachel found herself wandering around the house, sitting down in one place for a moment before getting up and moving somewhere else. Someone, maybe one of the paramedics, maybe Inspector Charlton, perhaps even Rachel herself, had picked up the dropped tray, cup and saucer and taken them through into the kitchen. Amazingly, they hadn't broken. *Which*, Rachel thought to herself, *was a good thing*. They were her mother's favourites and she'd be really upset if anything happened to them...

And then, she found herself on the floor of the kitchen, clutching the cup, staring at it. The pattern seemed to be swirling around, hinting at something hidden beneath the surface of the china. She wasn't sure how long she'd been there, but it had grown dark outside. Carefully putting the cup and saucer back on the draining board, she climbed to her feet and went up to her room.

Stripping naked, she lay on the bed, closed her eyes and tried to clear her mind. Getting out of her body, letting her spirit go free might help. It might...

Time had passed again when she suddenly came to. She didn't think that she'd slept. She certainly hadn't slipped free of her body. She had just blanked. When she came back to herself, she could feel every inch of her body. Every single goose bump that pocked her flesh. Every single beat of her heart. Every breath. She imagined that she could feel her hair growing. And it was awful. It was mortality. This is what had done for her mother. The breathing, beating, sweating, shitting, farting hideousness that was the lot of every human being on this planet. And she couldn't get away from it.

So, she did the only thing she could do and she forgot. She pushed herself away from all that was out there, from every reminder of the seconds of her life ticking away and she let the darkness roll over her. She still functioned, but it was automatic, almost autonomic. The things that she needed to do to still happened because they had to happen, like her heart continuing to beat and her lungs continuing to draw breath.

#

"Don't sit there," Rachel said to the Reverend Susan Donahue who had just been about to sit down. "That was mom's chair."

"Oh sorry."

This was the first time that Rachel had seen Susan since they had had their… discussion… out at Saint Mary's Lighthouse. She felt like she should be shouting and screaming at her, telling her to get out of her fucking house. But she really couldn't work up the energy to get upset about it. Okay, they'd both spoken words that they shouldn't have done. She was certain Susan probably regretted everything she had said as soon as she had said it. She knew that she did. Mostly. It didn't matter anymore. None of it did.

Then she realised the other thing that she had just thought. That she needed to tell her to get out of her house. Her house. It was how she always thought of it. After all, it was her home, it was where she had lived her entire life. It was her house. But it had never really been hers, had it? She had lived here and would always have been welcome here. It had been her home, but it had been her mother's house. And now, it wasn't. It really was her house. She wasn't sure if it was her home though. They always said that home was where the heart was. And she didn't think she had a heart anymore. Not like that, not in any way other than as a muscle to pump the blood around her body. And it's not as if she needed that either. She could quite easily live without it. She wondered if that would make things easier for her.

"I'm so sorry," Susan said, after she had settled down on to the sofa. "About this and, you know, everything."

"Thanks. So am I."

Rachel couldn't sit still. She perched down next to her for a few moments, before getting up to stand next to the fireplace, then going to sit on one of the dining chairs and round and round the room, like a long-tailed cat in a room full of rocking chairs.

"Is there anything I can do to help?"

"Er... no. Not really. I don't know. I can't remember what needs doing."

Susan looked seriously at her.

"Rachel," she said, firmly. "You need to sit down."

Rachel paused in her pacing and looked at her.

"Really," she continued. "You look terrible. Worse than you did after you were released from your renning."

"Oh. I'm so sorry that my distress is upsetting to you."

Susan looked at her, giving her a look that she has seen many times from her mother. What was it about all the women she knew? They all seemed to make her feel like she was back in primary school. Well, except for Lilly, who made her feel like an overly hormonal teenager, but that was different.

"Don't be daft," Susan said. "You know how much I loved your mother. I want to help you give her the best send-off possible. And having you like this isn't going to do it. This isn't how to show love and respect for your mom. You need to focus. She needs you to focus."

"She's dead," Rachel said, raising her voice. "She doesn't need any fucking thing now. She's dead. She's gone and she's going to be rotting in the ground."

"But her soul..."

"What about her soul? I saw her soul. We talked after she died and then she went away. Once your ghost fades away – that's it. You're finished. No afterlife. No heaven. Nothing."

"Is that really what you believe? Or is it what you're frightened of?"

"Why should I be frightened? When I die, I'm gonna be a ghost. I get to spend my death hanging around here until I eventually fade to nothing. Hell, I hope there's no afterlife. 'Cos if there is, you can fuckin' well guarantee that I'm not going to heaven. It's straight downstairs for me..."

"You can't possibly believe that. Everyone has a possibility of redemption," Susan replied earnestly.

"You see," Rachel said. "That's what I like about you. Your belief that there's some good in everyone. You forget – I'm an ex-con. And I've not exactly led an entirely blameless life since then."

"But..."

"There's no buts," Rachel interrupted. "To be completely honest, I really hope you're wrong – you and all the other religious types out there. It's my best shot."

"Look Rachel..." Susan paused and looked at her again. "No. That's not a discussion for today. We're here for your mother. Whatever you think. Whether she's gone to heaven or we're just saying goodbye to her, we want to do her proud. Don't we?"

"Yeah. You're right," Rachel acquiesced. "Thanks. Sorry."

"It's okay. I understand," Susan said. "At least we've managed to get you out of your depression."

"Yeah," Rachel said, but, even as she agreed, she could feel the dullness and greyness waiting for their chance to roll back in again.

#

And so it proved. Almost as soon as Susan had left she felt herself switching off. She tried to fight it, reminding herself of everything Susan had said. She tried to get herself annoyed again by going over the religious things she had said, but it was like trying to stop fog by turning on a hairdryer.

A few days after her meeting with Susan, she found herself standing in front of an open grave with a coffin being slowly lowered in to it. It was a beautiful coffin, extremely expensive, made of a dark wood that may have even been mahogany, with exquisite brass fittings. Lilly stood by her side, holding her arm, weeping tears that had yet to escape her own eyes.

Silently, she threw a handful of dirt on top of the coffin before walking off, passing Susan, nearly shoulder-barging her, as she intoned some sort of holy words to which Rachel wasn't really bothering to listen. The service might have been utterly wonderful, she assumed that Susan would have done her best and given her mother the best send-off there was, as she had promised. She had probably even given a stormer of a eulogy – she always had been a brilliant talker – full of emotion and passion. But Rachel hadn't taken any of it in. She vaguely remembered that she had gone up to the front of the church and said something, but she wouldn't have been able to repeat what she'd said.

She paused in front of the gravestone that she must have organised, although she had no memory of doing so. Reading the words on it, she suddenly felt a surge of anger. Words on stone. That's all they were. They weren't her mother. A name, a couple of dates and some kind of mealy-mouthed aphorism that must surely have been suggested by the undertaker, because there was no way she would have come up with it. She had a strong urge to find a sledgehammer and destroy it. Turn it into dust. That would surely be a better admission of how she felt about the whole thing than anything that could be carved into a piece of granite. Hell, an entire book – an entire library of books – couldn't encompass that. A life needed more than a few words to sum it up.

#

She'd have thought that the last thing she'd want to do would be to have sex. What was it the French called an orgasm? '*Le petit mort*' or something like that, anyway. She'd read it in a book at one time or another. And, although her French was something worse than 'rusty' – utterly shite was probably a better way of describing – she could at least translate that. '*The little death*'. And, if there was one thing she didn't want to do, it was to get any closer to death today.

So, what was it that made her nearly tear her dress off when she and Lilly got back to her house – and it truly was hers now, there was nobody else to whom it could belong anymore – and shut the door. They couldn't even get as far as the bedroom. Hell, they couldn't even get as far as the living room. They did it there in the hallway, their first intimacy since before her mother had died. Lilly's skirt pulled up high, thong around her knees, Rachel's dress and panties hastily ripped off, the lace underwear still caught on one of her shoes. What they did couldn't even be described as fucking. It was animalistic rutting. Hard and fast and vicious. When Rachel came she pushed so hard that she shoved Lilly along the hallway. When Lilly came, she bit down on Rachel's shoulder, puncturing the skin and drawing blood. Neither one of them noticed.

In a way, it was lucky that the wake was taking place somewhere else. They might well have done it in front of everyone, so urgent was her need. She'd heard that sex like this was some sort of reaction to the day, some kind of need to show life in the midst of death. And, perhaps, that was what it was. But it didn't feel like that. After she'd finished and was just lying there on top of Lilly, she didn't feel like she'd had any kind of victory against death. If anything, she felt the opposite. The fucking had been some kind of acceptance of death, mindless lust that had overtaken them both wasn't any kind of life, it was instead just another way of losing any sense of identity she had, forgetting about life and death and all that shit. Forgetting about who she was. It wasn't an acceptance of life. It wasn't a glorification of life. It was a rejection of it. It was either fucking her brains out or killing herself. To be honest, she wasn't sure if she'd made the right decision.

Finally, she rolled off her. Lilly just lay there, legs still apart, thong still around her knees and looked at her.

"Lilly," she said, at last. "I'm going away. Come with me."

"What do you mean?" she asked.

"I'm leaving Newcastle. I'm leaving the country. I want you to come with me. I love you."

"Why? Where?" Lilly seemed confused, she hadn't been expecting this. "What about your job?"

"Fuck my job," she said. "It's going nowhere and I hate it. I was only doing what I did to look after my mom. No point doing that now."

"I don't think you should be making decisions like that right now. Take some time, think it over. If you still feel like this in a few weeks or a month, then you can start thinking about it seriously, but right now…"

"No," she interrupted. "It's the right thing to do. My job... I've never told you what I do... It's not a nice job. It's the sort of job where people can get hurt. Really badly hurt. I don't want to do it anymore"

"Is... is what you do illegal?" Lilly asked quietly, sitting up, drawing her knees together and pulling them up to her chest.

Rachel looked at Lilly.

"Yes," she replied, just as quietly.

"How illegal?"

"It's probably best that I don't say anything," she said. "I just want to leave it all behind."

"I understand."

Rachel pulled herself into a sitting position as well and pressed her body against Lilly's in a loving embrace.

"And I can't leave without you."

"I understand," her girlfriend repeated.

#

After Lilly left, Rachel sat in what had been her mother's chair in the front room. It would probably always be her chair. Slowly, the light faded from the windows and the shadows in the corners of the room grew. Still she sat there. She may have been thinking, but, if she was, it wasn't of anything in particular. When she roused herself a little, her thoughts inevitably turned to Lilly. She had left without telling her what she thought of her plan. She knew that what she was asking was a huge thing. And admitting to her that she was a criminal. That was another huge thing. It didn't seem to worry Lilly too much, however, perhaps because she had said that she wanted to leave it all behind. But did she understand that the only way Rachel could do that would be by leaving Newcastle? There was no other way. She was too far into Mott's business to be left alone, either by Mott or the police. Or any of Mott's rivals.

Eventually, when full dark had fallen almost entirely and there was only a slight hint of light on the eastern horizon, Rachel found her stomach making its presence known. She pulled herself from her chair, flicked the light switch and pulled the curtains before making her way into the kitchen. She pulled open the fridge and the freezer. Nothing. Well, not nothing, there were plenty of things, but nothing she saw was in the least bit inspiring. Eventually, she pulled out a frozen pizza and slammed it into the oven. It would do.

#

Her 'phone rang, playing the opening bars of '*Lily Marlene*', just as she finished the last slice. Wiping her hands on her skirt, she pulled it out of her handbag.

"Hi Lilly," she said.

"Hey sweetheart," she replied. "I need to speak to you. Tonight. Right now."

"I'll get a taxi and come on over."

"Don't worry," she said. "I'll come and get you. See you shortly."

Realising that she was still wearing the dress she wore to the funeral and that she almost undoubtedly smelt of dry sweat after her sexual exertions with Lilly, she ran upstairs, stripping as she went and threw herself into the shower.

#

"Aren't we going to your place?" Rachel asked, sitting next to Lilly as she drove.

"No. I thought I'd take you out for a drink," she told her. "Somewhere we can talk."

"Talk? About what?" Although, actually, Rachel thought she knew what it was. At least, she hoped she knew. Was there anything else to talk about, other than her proposition? And, if she was going to say no to her, would she bother taking her out anywhere? If Rachel was going to turn someone down then she'd be more inclined to do it somewhere privately, where there wouldn't be a scene if there were any strong reactions.

"Wait. We'll be there soon."

Rachel felt a perk in her soul. Not exactly happiness, not today and she didn't think she could remember what it felt like anyway, but certainly a small rise towards a somewhat more positive state of mind.

They pulled up outside a building in the centre of the city. The ground-floor was taken up by a coffee shop. To the side was another door and it was towards this that Lilly led her. A small, brass plaque screwed to the surround stated that this door was the entrance to "*Club Egoiste*". It was the sort of place that Rachel knew well, from looking after business dealings for Mott. It was actually quite nice to come to somewhere like this for less unpleasant reasons. Lilly pressed a buzzer and after a moment, there was a gentle click as the latch opened.

She followed Lilly inside and up the stairs, her perfect arse wiggling gently from side to side in front of her face, beneath her tight, scarlet mini-skirt, her long legs encased in black nylon and sliding into ridiculously impractical but equally ridiculously sexy high heels.

Pausing at the top, Lilly handed her coat across to a woman who hung it in a small cloakroom. To the woman's side a small monitor showed the entrance. Rachel looked through an arch into a small, dark room, exotically decorated with swags of velvety material artfully draped across the ceiling and down the walls, making the place seem almost like a tent rather than a private underground drinking club. Low coffee tables and large, comfortable sofas and armchairs were scattered around the room, creating intimate, private areas where patrons could relax and enjoy themselves while waitresses, wearing a uniform that could best be described as almost but not quite French Maid, stood to attention at the sides of the room. One corner held a baby grand piano upon which an elderly black man played a gentle blues riff. A woman in a smart black dress, a lot more stylish and less overtly sexual than the waitresses, wafted from one table to another. She was tall and quite old, probably in her mid to late fifties, although her face was utterly flawless and her figure was that of a much younger woman. Her hair was immaculately coiffured in a complicated up-do, a shining natural red, although now streaked with grey, that, whilst showing her age, also managed to make her look even more attractive. She was obviously the club's hostess, her main job consisting of talking to the patrons and making them feel utterly at home.

As they came into the room, they were lit by a spot that shone directly down onto them, obviously placed to ensure that whoever came in could be seen by everyone who was already there. The hostess looked across to them and immediately her face broke into a large, apparently genuine smile.

"Lilly, my darling," she said in a deep, soft voice. "I haven't seen you for so long."

"I've been occupied," Lilly said. "It's good to see you Maria."

"And is this the young lady who has been occupying you?"

Lilly blushed at that and then followed Maria to a table in a shady little corner.

"A bottle of champagne, please," Lilly said.

The older woman nodded her assent and breezed away leaving a soft, floral scent. Rachel turned to look at Lilly.

"What did you want to tell me," she asked.

"Wait until the champagne arrives," she told her, taking her hand.

After a few minutes, the champagne arrived. After a moment, Rachel realised that it wasn't Maria who had brought it or one of the waitresses. It was actually a short, fat man. A fat, pale, horrendously ugly man in a black tuxedo, blood from a wound in his neck staining the collar of his shirt. Rachel looked up and straight into the face and fangs of George Bailey.

"Good evening, Miss Cantrell," he said. "My condolences on your loss."

Rachel sat, glued to her seat. Her first impulse was to shout at Lilly and tell her to make a run for it. But almost immediately that was over-ridden by the thought that telling her to do that would mean her death in a manner very similar to that which overtook Ricky. She'd just have to try and bluff it, for Lilly's sake as well as her own.

"Mr Bailey," she eventually managed to get out, her voice barely more than a whisper. "Thank you."

"To lose your mother so suddenly. It must be a shock."

"It was, very much so."

"It is good to see that you are refusing to let it get you down, though. You are showing your lady-friend a good time?"

"Actually, she brought me here. We have something to discuss," Rachel said. "I don't mean to be rude, but…"

"Ah, yes. I understand. I should leave you two together," Bailey said, with a thin smile. "However, I have a business proposition that I wish to discuss with you, Miss Cantrell and I am afraid that it will not keep. I am sure your friend will not mind if I steal you for a few minutes?"

He turned to look at Lilly then, for the first time. Rachel followed his gaze and looked at her as well. If she had hoped that her girlfriend would realise there was a problem, she was sorely mistaken. Lilly was looking back and forth between Bailey and Rachel, apparently unaware of the undercurrents of danger and violence that threatened the pair of them. She didn't even seem to be particularly worried by his hideous face. Either that or she was a much better actor than she gave her credit for. But then, none of the other patrons seemed concerned by his appearance either. Rachel wasn't sure which was more alarming.

"You don't mind, do you, my dear?" Bailey asked her.

"Of course not. But please, don't take her away for long, we do have something important to discuss."

"I promise. In the meantime, please have the champagne on me," he told her. "Miss Cantrell? Come with me, please."

Bailey stood and headed across the room to a door behind the piano-player. He didn't even look back to check if Rachel was following. He didn't need to; Rachel knew exactly what she had to do.

Through the door was a private room. It was richly, some would say tastelessly, decorated in gold and red with heavy, velvet drapes hanging from the ceiling and a green baize-covered oak table dominating the centre. Comfortable chairs were arrayed around it, three of them occupied by Bailey's lackeys – Rachel recognised two of them as the vampires who had accompanied Bailey on the night they had met. The third was a woman, wearing nothing but a spangly silk and sequinned burlesque-style corset, frilly, lacy knickers and fish-net stockings. Her face was heavily made-up but Rachel could still see that she was very old. Even despite her age, Rachel couldn't keep her eyes off her. There was something hypnotic about her. Just looking at her made Rachel horny.

"You have managed to inveigle yourself into Mr Mott's inner circle quite successfully recently, wouldn't you say, Miss Cantrell?" Bailey said as he sat himself down next to the old woman. He didn't offer a seat to Rachel.

"I don't know. I suppose you could say that," Rachel replied. "Although I don't know whether he still trusts me after you killed Ricky and left me alive."

"Ah. Yes. That was an unfortunate, if tasty, business," Bailey said. "I did, however, have my reasons for leaving you alone."

"Can I ask you what they were?"

"It's very simple. You are supplying me with information from the very heart of Frederick Mott's empire."

"I am not," Rachel blurted.

"You may not have realised it, Miss Cantrell, but you have been one of my best informants recently. However, it seems that your usefulness may have come to an end. I can only blame myself, I suppose." Bailey seemed almost sad at the thought.

"I haven't told you anything," Rachel said, earnestly. "I don't know what you're talking about."

"No, I don't really suppose that you do," Bailey told her before turning to the old woman. "Eve? Would you like to call your daughter through and introduce her to Mr Cantrell."

"Certainly," Eve said, in a voice that somehow sounded familiar to Rachel.

She rose and went to the door, caressing Rachel's face as she passed. Her touch made her instantly wet. It also made her shiver with terror, a woman who could do that to her, could control her and get her to do just about anything if she tried. There was a word for a creature that could do that...

(Opening the door, Eve looked through and called out.

"Lilith, darling" she called. "If you'd like to come in here for a moment?"

Through the door, wearing a scarlet mini-skirt, her long legs encased in black nylon and sliding into ridiculously impractical but equally ridiculously sexy high heels stepped Lilly.)

…Succubus.

Chapter Five

The limousine pulled up outside Fred Mott's house. Its rear door opened, Rachel stumbled out and the door closed again before the car pulled off. Her face was covered in blood and one eye was almost swollen shut.

"Yeah, you can all fuck right off!" Rachel shouted after it, slurring her words a little through her damaged lips.

Swaying slightly, she went up to Mott's front door. Holding the doorframe, she hammered the knocker.

Ignoring the zombin and the soft-core porn and everything else, she made her way up the stairs, directly to Mott's office.

"So, you've decided to come and see me in person, this time?" Mott spat, looking up at her, dropping his pen and splattering some ink on the cream vellum paper he was writing on.

"Bailey knows everything," Rachel said, closing the door behind her and locking it.

"How? How do you know?"

"Lilly," Rachel said, slumping into a chair as she spoke. "She's a succubus in Bailey's pay. She… she fucked it all out of me."

"Fuck me!" Mott bellowed. "You incompetent fucking idiot."

"It's worse, Fred," Rachel said.

Mott paused, closed his eyes and put his head in his hands, fingertips massaging his temples.

"Tell me," he said quietly.

"I've been renfielded," Rachel told him.

Mott looked up to discover a gun pointed into his face.

"Sorry Fred," Rachel said and pulled the trigger, once, twice, again.

#

The light of the moon streamed in through the window. Rachel looked out but felt nothing. Even seeing the ruined corpse of her former boss couldn't raise any emotions. There was a banging on the door as Mott's zombin butler pounded on it, trying to break it down, but it was a heavy oak door and there was no way it was getting through in a hurry.

Rachel dropped the gun on the desk, opened the window, slipped her high heels off and climbed out onto the sill. It was quite a long drop but, without even pausing, she jumped, landed and rolled on the back lawn. Quickly picking herself up, she ran around to the front of the house and down the street. The limousine sat waiting around the corner. As she drew closer, the door opened again and Lilly stepped out. She was no longer wearing the things that Rachel thought of as her usual clothes. Instead, she was dressed in a long, black, tight, silk dress, slit from ankle to thigh and from throat to navel. She was obviously not wearing any underwear although her breasts were still high and firm, nipples pressing against the material. On her feet were heels that were so high she almost stood on tiptoes. Her face, usually only lightly made-up, was now painted with thick, deep-red lipstick and heavy, smoky eye shadow.

"Rachel. Darling," she purred, a predatory smile creasing her lips. "I hope you were successful."

She stroked Rachel's face, her scarlet nails scratching gently. Even through her dulled senses, it had an effect on the renned woman.

"He's dead," Rachel replied.

"Good girl. Now, get in the car."

She did as she was told. Lilly climbed in after her and draped herself against her, unbuttoned her blouse and slid a hand inside.

"We really need to get you cleaned up. You look a complete mess," she said as she took hold of her through her bra and squeezed.

#

Standing right on the edge of the river, the Baltic was an amazing building, an old mill that had been revamped and converted into an art gallery. Of course, it was on the Gateshead side of the river, but as it was right next to the river, it was easy to forget that it was 'South'.

It was strange, but until the Baltic and the nearby Sage Music Centre had been built, most people north of the river were content to forget about Gateshead, tending to speed through it, or even better around it on the A1 bypass. But since they had opened, there was a whole corporate 'NewcastleGateshead' philosophy going on, which was essentially a way for Newcastle to co-opt the good bits of Gateshead – which to them mostly meant the Sage and the Baltic – and claim them for itself, while still being able to ignore the rest of the place. Mind you, considering that until recently, the only part of Gateshead that was famous was the '*Get Carter*' car park, which had only lasted so long because of its 'iconic' status, it was really pretty easy to ignore it.

Rachel had made sure that she was the first to arrive. It had meant hanging around for an hour before the meeting had been called, just to be absolutely certain, but it was necessary. She stood and looked out of the picture window. It was an impressive view from the meeting room on the first floor of the Baltic, looking down on to the Tyne with the bridges set out in an array before her – the pretty ones at the front, all lit up and looking glorious, the ugly modern Metro and Redheugh bridges hidden away behind them in darkness. The clear sky allowed the bright, full moon to shine down on the river, silvering the tips of the wavelets.

The door at the other end of the room banged open and the first of the others arrived. He looked as annoyed as Rachel had expected.

"Jerry," Rachel said, her false bonhomie sounding utterly fake, even to her own ears. "So glad you could make it."

"What the fuck are you doing here, you little bitch?" Jerry said. Looking at Rachel's bruised and battered face, he continued, "What happened to you? Who fucked you up?"

"I was told to come, just like you were. And this," Rachel gestured to her face, "is a private matter."

"Fucking private matter. Fuck off. Just fucking tell me, are the rumours true? Was it you who did Fred in?"

"Really, I don't want to discuss anything until everyone else arrives," Rachel said. "Why not just get yourself a drink and calm down?"

"No fucker tells me to calm down." Jerry muttered. But, he poured himself a cup of coffee and sat down at the far end of the table, nearest the door and furthest away from Rachel. Sipping his drink, he glared at the younger woman. Rachel stood in front of the windows, quite unconcerned.

Over the next twenty minutes or so, the rest of Fred's former lieutenants made their way into the room. Finally, they were all there, sitting at the long, oval table and glaring at one another.

"So," said Jerry. "We're all here. Who the fuck called the meeting?"

Rachel paused and looked at everyone. They were all different – some of them were in expensive suits; some of them in jeans and t-shirts; some looked like they were unfamiliar with the effects of soap and water; others looked like they were fresh from the shower. There were, however, two things that united them all. Firstly, they were all men. There was no place for a woman in the upper hierarchy of Fred Mott's business. As far as the late gangster was concerned, the only things that women were good for was making drinks, typing letters, shagging and giving blowjobs. The second similarity that ran through them all was their complete lack of magical ability. Apart from Rachel herself, they were all about as magically aware as the table around which they were gathered. Which suited Rachel right down to the ground.

Rachel stood up.

"I'm afraid, gentlemen," she said. "I have to admit that it was me who called you here. With Fred's death, we need to do something."

"Did you kill 'im?" Jerry shouted.

Rachel ignored him.

"And, to be perfectly honest, seeing how you lot work and how you've been running around like headless chickens for the last couple of days – throwing accusations around," Rachel paused and looked pointedly at Jerry. "I don't think a single one of you could organise a piss-up in a brewery."

This statement caused an explosion of fury, people leaping to their feet, pointing at Rachel and one another, shouting and swearing.

Only one person, other than Rachel seemed to keep his calm. Godfrey, the oldest man in the room, had been a gangster for his entire life. He had run around with the London East-End gangs when he was a kid, but had moved up to Newcastle in the 1970s. He had once explained to Rachel that he had never tried to go out on his own and start his own gang because it was 'just too fuckin' much like fuckin' 'ard work'. He preferred just sitting back and following orders. He was pretty much retired now; he certainly wasn't involved in any of the really heavy, strong arm stuff now. Instead, he just ran the brothels that Mott had owned, not necessarily making sure that they were drug-free and healthy, but that the drugs used were supplied by one of Mott's people and that the diseases were kept pretty much under control. After all this time, he'd seen everything and, as far as he was concerned, this was just another kid trying to make a play for the big time. Sometime in the next ten or fifteen minutes, Rachel would either be in charge or dead.

"Let the girl talk," he said, barely raising his voice.

"Girl. Aye, that'd be fuckin' right," Jerry said.

After a couple of minutes, the others finally shut up and sat down again. They didn't look happy though.

"That's better," Godfrey said. "Maybe the kid's got a plan. Maybe she can explain who killed Mr. Mott. We can listen to 'er and then, if we wanna, we can kill 'er. But remember, if we do 'er, we've gotta be quiet. No guns. There's too many civilians around."

"But, listen to what she's saying, Godfrey. She's saying that we're idiots," Jerry whined.

"On the whole, I'd 'ave to say that she's right. Most of you couldn't find your arses with the 'elp of a fuckin' map. So, just fuckin' listen to 'er. She 'ad the balls - ha - and the nous to organise this meetin', which none o' you lot did. And, like I say, if we want, she's 'ere and we can kill 'er without worryin' about 'avin' to find 'er."

"Thanks, Godfrey," Rachel said. "I do have a plan, as it happens."

"Let's hear it then," Jerry said.

"We need to join up with another organisation. I can't see any of us surviving anyone else coming in and trying to take our territory."

"Bollocks," Jerry retorted. "We're strong enough."

"I disagree. We're already under attack. And none of you realise it. Fred's death was just the start. Take out the head and the body will wither and die."

"'Oo is it, lass?" Godfrey asked. "Do you know 'oo killed Mr Mott?"

"The hit was ordered by George Bailey."

"You're fucking kidding me," Jerry said. "That vampire bastard? I know all you lot are scared of him, but I'll go down to his fucking office and shove a stake right through his fucking black heart, if he tries anything."

"Well, you see Jerry," Rachel said. "He's not trying. He's succeeding."

"How do you know it was Bailey? You seem to know a fuck of a lot. You still haven't told us if the rumours are true."

Jerry stood up and, reaching into his inside jacket pocket, pulled out a butterfly knife.

"I think," he said, stalking towards Rachel. "That you need to tell us everything."

Rachel backed away, keeping an eye on Jerry's hand.

"Well, the thing is we know that Bailey has already got a mole in the organisation. So, it kind of makes sense that his next move would be more overt."

"And you thought of this all by yourself did you?" Jerry growled.

"I 'ave to admit, girl," Godfrey said. "At the moment, it's soundin' like you know a lot. I'm inclined to 'ave you killed, just to make sure, you know?"

"I'm sure that Bailey would be happy to employ you all. He will need humans to run the daytime stuff," Rachel said, backing up against a set of double doors.

"And what if we don't want to work for the blood-sucking little fuck?" Jerry said. "What do you say lads. Should I cut 'er?"

"Not 'ere," Godfrey said. "It's too obvious 'ere."

"I take it that's a no to my suggestion, then?" Rachel asked.

"Take a fuckin' guess," Jerry replied.

"Does Jerry talk for all of you?" Rachel said to the others who had been sitting back, enjoying the entertainment. None of them especially liked Rachel, so they weren't going to bother lifting a finger to help her. One or two of them nodded agreement, a couple of others shrugged, but most of them just sat and watched.

"Oh well then," Rachel said. She felt around and found the handle of the door against which she was apparently cowering. Twisting it, she pulled the door open.

On the other side, a towering mass of fur and muscle had been snuffling at the crack in the door. As the door opened it raised itself to its full height. It bared its fangs and seemed to growl noiselessly. Extending its muzzle it sniffed and then stepped forward. It raised its head and howled, once again without sound. A scar across its throat showed where its vocal chords had been cut.

"You brought a fucking werewolf here?"

"Mr Bailey kind of assumed that you'd not want to work for him, so he wanted to make sure you wouldn't bother him."

"Mr Bailey? It fucking was you. You cunt..." Jerry screamed and leapt forwards, his knife pointed ready to take Rachel in the stomach.

The werewolf moved so quickly that it almost seemed to flicker from beside the door to stand between Jerry and Rachel without crossing the intervening space. It grabbed the knife in one if it's long, clawed paws and twisted. The knife skittered into the corner and Jerry screamed in pain. A swift movement of its jaws and the screamed choked away into a gurgle.

One of the men, a tall, skinny red-haired man called Ian, who had sat down closest to the doors at the far end of the room bolted. He got to the door and tried to pull it open, only to find it locked.

The werewolf bounded at him like a dog jumping for a ball. Ian didn't have time to move or make any kind of a sound before it landed on him, hurling him to the ground, its claws sinking into his chest.

Everyone else in the room froze. Godfrey turned away from the werewolf and looked at Rachel who was standing next to the door, fingering a locket on a chain around her neck.

"What 'ave you done, you little slut?" he hissed. "You've gotten into bed with that bloody vampire, 'aven't you?"

"I wouldn't quite go that far," Rachel said. "Although there was a certain amount of bedding involved... Let's just say that he had a compelling argument for me to go along with him. The rest of you are expendable."

"Now, 'old on," Godfrey said. "Let's talk about this. I'm sure that we can come to some kind of agreement."

"If you're that willing to change your mind to save your skin, how can Mr Bailey be certain that you won't change it again the next time someone threatens you?"

"What about you? What's 'e offered you to make 'you go along with it."

"Basically, he changed my mind for me. I just don't think he can be bothered with the rest of you."

"You mean 'e renned you?" Godfrey said. "You poor cow. I think I'd rather be dead than in your position."

"Lucky for you, then," Rachel said.

She slipped through the door, pulled it closed and locked it. For a moment all was silent in the other room, but that silence was soon replaced by the sound of chairs and tables being thrown around, screams of terror and agony and the heavy thudding noise of bodies being hurled against walls and floors. Someone apparently even managed to pull out a gun and loose a couple of shots. Rachel doubted they were at all useful.

Come the morning, the werewolf would have reverted to its human form, an ex-stripper called Marjorie. As Rachel left the building, she offhandedly hoped that no-one would open the doors into that meeting room before then.

#

Time passed. It had to pass. Things happened. Most of them deeply unpleasant. Even when Lilly used her, it wasn't pleasant.

Bailey also used her, although differently from Lilly. She became his messenger, his enforcer and his dogsbody. Bailey seemed to delight in degrading her.

"Here, hold this," Bailey said.

The boy was young, no more than eleven or twelve. Tears of terror ran down his cheeks.

"Please," he said to Rachel. "You're not a vampire, are you?"

"No. I'm not," she replied.

"Then please, let me go."

"No."

"Oh, god. Please… please…"

"Shut it up," Bailey said. "I hate it when lunch whinges."

Rachel pulled a handkerchief from her pocket. Not a particularly clean one, it was streaked with blood and snot. She grabbed the boy's face and tried to stuff it in his mouth. He bit down, hard, and Rachel pulled her fingers back. Stopping for a moment, she looked hard at the boy and swinging as hard as she could, slapped him full across the face. He screamed and his knees went limp. If Rachel hadn't been holding him, he would have collapsed to the floor. Once again, Rachel took hold of his face and pressed the handkerchief into his mouth. This time he didn't bite down. Now only small groans and squeaks escaped from his mouth through the material.

"Thank you, Rachel. Now, if you would," Bailey told her.

Rachel pushed the boy down on to his knees in front of Bailey. Taking a tight hold of one shoulder and his hair, she pulled his head back roughly, exposing the neck. Bailey leant forwards and, licking his lips, he gently bit down on his neck. Blood trickled down and over Rachel's hand. It was warm and slightly sticky.

Bailey took his time over feeding. The boy was awake the whole time, looking up at Rachel, pleading with his eyes. Rachel stood and looked down at him, keeping his head still, even though her muscles started to cramp.

Eventually, the boy lost consciousness and the pulse Rachel could feel in his neck got slower and slower before finally stopping. After a few more moments, Bailey looked at Rachel. His chin was covered in red.

"Do you know," he said, conversationally as he dapped at himself with a wet wipe. "There is nothing quite so tasty as a boy who is just coming in to the first full flush of puberty? All the hormones and chemicals rushing around the body, it adds a certain piquancy."

He paused for a moment, eyeing Rachel meaningfully.

"I wonder what a tranny would taste like," he continued. "Maybe I'll find out someday. Get rid of the meat, would you, Rachel?"

"Yes, Mr Bailey," Rachel replied, lifting the boy's body in her arms. With so much of his blood drained, he was almost weightless. She took it down to the cellar, pulled open a heavy door and laid it on a slab. One of Bailey's werewolves was a professional butcher and would carve the body to feed his pack-mates later.

#

Before long, Rachel's routine was basically set. She would be degraded by Bailey in the morning. Then, lunch, when she would watch and, more often than not, help Bailey degrade and murder someone else. Then, the afternoon's degradation. And then she'd be handed over to Lilly for her to do whatever she wanted. It was usually fairly unpleasant and degrading.

However, if just having someone around for Bailey to be unpleasant towards was the only reason that he kept Rachel around he would probably have grown bored and killed Rachel quite quickly. But, there were other reasons. The majority of Bailey's lieutenants were other vampires. The only non-vampires were Eve, Lilly's mother and Rachel. There were no other humans that high up in his organisation and the sort of people who would accept a job from a vampire were not the sort of people who could be trusted to do anything that needed a little bit of thought. They just about knew the right end of a knife, although they could be brutally effective with a cricket bat or a stick with a nail in it. Of course, the obvious drawback to having a team of leaders who burst into flame when they were out in the sun rather than tanning was that it made working during the daytime somewhat difficult. It was this loophole that had allowed Fred Mott to become as powerful as he was, controlling most of the daytime criminality and even being able to start taking some of the night time business away from Bailey's vampires, which Rachel realised, was the reason that he had shown up on the vampire's radar.

So, Rachel became Bailey's voice during the day when the vampire would stay hidden behind heavy velvet curtains and blackout blinds. She was therefore also expected to keep on top of the jobs she undertook when she was still working for Fred Mott. Since taking over Mott's territory, Bailey thought that having a familiar face around would make it easier for everyone to deal with the situation. Humans were, according to Bailey, easily led. He said that if they weren't reminded of the way the situation had changed most of them would be happy to let things continue on as if nothing had actually changed. And as long as it caused Bailey less hassle than the alternative, he was content.

#

Despite Bailey's expectation of 'business as usual', it had still been several weeks since she had last visited the Osborne Road whorehouse to pick up what had been Fred Mott's share of the take. She knew that there should be quite a lot of money waiting for her. It had been one of the more successful ventures that Fred had controlled, one of the few in which he had taken a personal interest, probably because Valerie, the madam, had been with him from the very start.

The building itself was fairly anonymous with no sign of it being anything other than a typical small hotel, similar to all the others along that road. The sign above the door of the building proclaimed it as being called *'L'Hôtel des Dames Jesmond'* which had always sounded so outrageously obvious to Rachel that she thought it was the perfect proof of the efficacy of 'hiding in plain sight'. The only external differences between this place and all the other real hotels being the permanently lit pink neon 'no vacancies' sign, the heavy curtains that were always pulled across the windows on the ground floor and its lack of any mention on TripAdvisor. This didn't discourage everyone from venturing through to the front desk on the off-chance of finding a spare room, where some of the younger, less experienced 'members of staff' would take turns acting as receptionist, welcoming those guests who knew exactly what the place was and why they were there and gently turning away the others. And woe betide any girl or boy who didn't take the position seriously.

Rachel strode through the doors and up to the reception desk. Sitting behind it this time was Megan, dressed in a smart, smoke grey skirt and jacket with a soft pink blouse beneath. She looked up and, seeing who it was coming through the door, smiled. And then she obviously remembered everything that she heard and her smile turned into a frown.

"What do you want?" she asked coldly.

"Now Megan," Rachel said. "Is that any way to speak to me? I'm just here to speak to your boss and to collect the usual payments. We always used to get on. I don't see why that needs to change."

"Except for the part where you work for a vampire now," she replied.

"Well, yes. That's true. But, technically, so do you now. I'm sure that if you have a problem with that, you can quit. But trust me. It's a tough world out there. You're better off here. After all, you aren't really qualified to do anything other than part your legs are you? And without your teeth you wouldn't be able to do much more than give twenty quid blow jobs to the drunks in the Bigg Market who couldn't persuade anyone else to fuck them."

Megan reeled back in her chair, almost as if Rachel had actually struck her.

"Now, be a good girl and tell Valerie that I'm here to see her. I'll be in the lounge."

Without saying another word, she went across to the doorway that led inside. Megan pressed a button on the desk and the door swung silently open.

#

The interior of *'L'Hôtel des Dames Jesmond'* was utterly unlike the stereotypical brothel that tended to be shown in the media. It was subtle and understated, decorated in soft, feminine pastel colours and flowered wallpaper with still-life pictures on the walls. If anything, Rachel thought it felt a little too corporate and sterile, as if a tough businesswoman wanted to show how feminine she was and had then focus-grouped the concept. She'd have liked a little more ostentation – a little more *'Moulin Rouge'*, a little less *'Laura Ashley'*. But she also knew that there was in fact a *Moulin Rouge* room where exactly that taste could be indulged.

Pushing through into the lounge, she looked around. This was the room where you could first be certain that you had indeed entered a place where sleeping with someone was only a euphemism. Rachel came in the middle of the day when business was at its most quiet. Not entirely dead, there were always a few customers who enjoyed a midday 'romp' and she knew that Valerie prided herself on always having a full roster of girls available. Women were sat around the room, ranging in age from those appearing to be in their late teens – although Rachel knew most of them were a few years older than that and were just very good with their make-up – to a few women in their forties and fifties. They were mostly dressed in various items of revealing lingerie, although one or two were wearing stylish cocktail dresses or ball gowns and a couple were in a slightly sexed-up approximation of everyday clothing. Rachel also saw a couple of young men in tight jeans and t-shirts – this was an equal-opportunities whorehouse and could cater for anyone of any gender and preference. She was mildly surprised to see Valerie's 'speciality' – a male faery, dressed in an immaculate white silk corset and knickers, white stockings and heels on his legs. He exuded a complex and confusing mixture of rampant masculinity and sensuous femininity. And Rachel knew that he was extremely expensive. He needed to be to be able to afford the Dust he took in massive quantities which had led him to this position. From all accounts, sex with him was utterly mind-blowing, although Rachel had never been interested. She preferred the panties with which she came into close physical contact not to have bulges in them. Although, given the way things were, if Lilly had told her to let herself be fucked by, or even to fuck, the faery, she would have done it without a moment's thought. She might even have done it before being renned, so strong had Lilly's grip been on her and her libido. But, to see him here in the lounge was unusual. His 'dance card' was usually pretty full.

Rachel went over to the bar at the far end of the room, sat on a stool and ordered a whisky. Normally, she wasn't a shorts drinker, but the first time she'd come here, she'd suddenly decided to have one. Whether it was because of the rather amazing array of bottles on the shelf, the relatively poor selection of beers and lagers or just because the place made her feel like she should be a bit more sophisticated, she had no idea. But, since then, she'd always had something strong from a bottle. And she saw no reason to change that.

One thing that definitely had changed was her solitude. Usually, the girls would have been all over her as soon she came through the door into the lounge, cooing and flirting with her and blowing into her ear – even more so after Lilly came along and they realised that she wasn't going to take advantage of any of their charms, but this time, they remained seated and watched her silently. In fact, the whole room was silent. When she had arrived there had been a single customer, sitting canoodling with Violet, but almost as soon as Rachel had entered, she had pulled him to his feet and guided him out of the room. If she had any emotions that were allowed to come to the surface, Rachel knew that she would have been quite hurt. She was well aware that any affection they showed her was utterly fake and they only showed it because she had power, but it had always been an enjoyable experience. Obviously, the power thing was negotiable because she arguably had more power now as Bailey's renned human substitute then she did when she was Mott's lieutenant. Working so closely with a vampire obviously rubbed off. Or maybe they'd heard about what went on in the Sage. Or perhaps the rumours of what she did to Mott were reaching further out. Whichever it was, she really didn't care. What she did care about was the fact that she had to wait for Valerie. She usually came down to her pretty quickly. It wasn't as if she ever let anyone screw her anymore. She said that the reason she worked so hard to get herself set up with her own place was to get away from all that. Admittedly, Valerie usually knew she was on her way, but Rachel didn't think that counted as an excuse to leave her here by herself for so long. Although it did give her a chance to sample a couple more of the really rather excellent whiskies.

Eventually, she came through from the back offices, a mix of displeasure and discomfort on her face.

"Valerie," Rachel said."

"Rachel," she replied. "What can I do for you?"

"Been busy this morning? Counting out the money you owe, I hope."

"I don't think that I owe anything," she told her.

"Really? I'm fairly certain that you do. I certainly haven't been collecting anything from you."

"Ah, well. That is because you aren't part of the organisation anymore."

Rachel paused and slowly drained her glass, placing it carefully back on the circle of condensation on the bar.

"Would you care to repeat that?" She said softly.

"It's quite simple," she replied. "Since your actions in terminating your employment with Mr Mott's organisation left the whole thing in tatters, I chose to become an independent business-woman."

"Ah, you don't get it, do you? Mr Bailey has taken over all of Fred's businesses. So the money that you owed to Fred you now owe to him."

"I disagree," Valerie told her. "Being part of a vampire's business just doesn't go along with my plans, I'm afraid. I don't think that your Mr Bailey – or any of his renfielded underlings – can understand what it takes to run a place like this. If it becomes generally known that I am partnered with a vampire, I will lose a lot of customers. I am must respectfully decline."

"I am reasonably certain that 'my' Mr Bailey does not give a flying fuck for your respect or whether you think he could run this place or not. He's not running this place, you are. And you're mistaken – you aren't his partner, you are an employee. He won't let you resign and he has absolutely no intention of letting 'independent operators' work in his city," she paused and looked at her. "Look, Valerie, I think that you will actually find that he's a better person to work for than Fred Mott."

"Please, Rachel, I'm just one small business. Bailey won't even notice that I'm here. Can't he make one exception?"

"Why should he? After all, it's not like he needs you to keep him happy with freebies… So, either get with the programme, or Mr Bailey may just change what that programme is."

"Oh, you bitch," she spat. "I bet you aren't even renned, are you? You just signed up with Bailey because he lets you be the vicious shitting psychopath that you tried to hide."

"Believe what you want to believe. It doesn't matter. All I need from you is a large bag of cash. You can either be a contributor to his bank balance or he can find another way to take your tribute from you. And if you think that customers will be put off by knowing that the place is owned by a vampire, imagine how off-putting it will be trying to fuck a girl with bite marks on her neck."

Valerie shook her head, glared at her and then slapped Rachel across the face with as much force as she could muster. She was knocked back, arms flailing, swiping her empty glass from the bar and falling from the stool. She hit the ground at the same time as her glass which shattered and sent shards of glass flying across her face.

She lay there for a moment, dazed and uncertain of what happened, before slowly climbing to her feet. A vivid red palm print stood out on her cheek and multiple tiny dribbles of blood started to make their way down her face from the glass embedded in them. Gingerly, she put her hand up to her face and pulled it away again, examining the red marks on it as if she couldn't quite understand what they were.

Valerie looked into her eyes and saw nothing. And then she got really scared. Whether the woman opposite her was renned or not, it didn't make any difference now. She was fucked. Climbing down off her stool, she stepped back.

"Cluracan," she said, looking at the lingerie-clad faerie.

He came over to them, a knife suddenly appearing in his hand.

"That's a really bad idea," Rachel said.

"I'm just making sure that you don't do anything that either one of us will regret," Valerie said.

"Oh, like maybe slapping someone?"

"I'll come on-board with Bailey," she said. "But I don't want any vampires anywhere near here. And I don't want you collecting the money."

"I'll tell Mr Bailey your terms," she said. "I doubt he'll take any notice of them, but I'll tell him. Now. The money?"

"Give me ten minutes," she said.

"Make it five," Rachel told her.

Turning away from both Valerie and her knife-wielding faerie rentboy, she reset the stool on to its feet, sat on it and gestured to the bartender to pour her another glass of whisky.

#

The warehouse appeared to be entirely deserted and thoroughly locked up. And, according to the people who had been watching it from the rooftop opposite for the last three days, no-one had gone either in or out in all that time. Rachel, however, knew that there had to be at least one person inside. Mickey wasn't going to let his zombins alone for that length of time. For a start, they'd have taken to feasting on one another. And that would even put Mickey off. Probably.

Rachel looked around at the crew she had with her, all crowded together in an alley across the road from the warehouse. If she had been able to feel anything, she'd have looked heavenwards in despair. There were a few humans who were happy to work for vampires without being renfielded. Stood there before her, awaiting her orders, were the cream of that crop. Or at least these were the ones who had floated to the surface, so calling them 'the cream' was kinder than the alternative, if somewhat further from the truth. Bailey had judged that doing this operation in the middle of the day was a better idea than doing it at night, because he said that they wouldn't be expecting a vampire to work in the daytime. Rachel reflected that, on the whole, they were correct: there weren't any vampires here. However, it was pretty much unsurprising. Considering what they expected to find inside the warehouse, it didn't really make a lot of sense for vampires to put themselves at risk. Not when they had people who could do the job for them and may as well have been wearing red shirts with the words 'cannon fodder' printed on them. And that included Rachel.

At the front of the pack was an enormous, thuggish creature of limited intellect, nicknamed Ratty. He was exactly the sort of psychotic potential zombin-in-waiting that Bailey preferred to use although he probably came closest to being the leader of the group by virtue of having learned the alphabet. Ratty was so-called due to his buck-teeth and ragged, pointy ears. Seeing those ears, you could almost wonder if he had been sired by a faery, although every other feature on his face and body belied that fact. He was either bald or he kept his head shaved, except for a single, long, slender queue at the back of his head which was plaited tightly and then waxed, which made it look an awful lot like a rat's tail. Rachel didn't think that this particular piece of visual punnery was Ratty's idea.

"Okay," Rachel said. "You don't really need me to tell you what we're here for. But don't kill anyone if you can possibly avoid it until I get a chance to have a word with them."

There was a general murmur, which Rachel took to mean assent, coupled with a little bit of upset at being denied the chance for immediate mayhem. They would just have to learn about delayed gratification.

"And don't kill the zombins at all. You know that Mr Bailey wants them for something. And I'm not planning on taking the blame if you fuck up. So don't fuck up."

Rachel thought that that should motivate them sufficiently to do their job.

The crowd of thugs hefted their crowbars and knives and, in one case, a somewhat rusty and blunted machete that Rachel thought was more likely to cause death through tetanus than any other means. She also thought that mentioning anything would be a mistake. It was probably called 'Betsy Lou' or something and 'her' wielder probably snuggled with 'her' in bed.

Remarkably silently for a bunch of people that Rachel would have bet still had difficulty tying their shoelaces, they crossed and spread out, two or three of them taking up position outside each of the few doors and windows through which escape could be possible.

The majority of them, though, gathered in front of the main doors. Rachel went over to them, wielding a large, unwieldy pair of bolt cutters. She looked at the enormous chain threaded through the handles on the doors and realised two things. Firstly, there was no way in hell she was going to be able to cut through them. And secondly, this was a very good reason for having hulking idiots whose testosterone had pickled their brains. They'd probably enjoy finding something which they could out-think for once.

"Ratty," she said, holding out the bolt cutters and feeling her arm sag a little at their weight. "Deal with the door, would you?"

Ratty came up to her, took the cutters and with a slight grunt sliced through the padlock which Rachel realised was made of metal that was a lot thinner than the chain. She hadn't even looked at the padlock. Rachel thought for a moment that maybe she had miscalculated and perhaps Ratty was cleverer than she had taken him for. However, she quickly changed her mind when Ratty started attacking the chain itself.

"Okay, Ratty," Rachel said. "That's fine. Thanks."

"What? Oh, okay," he grunted.

Pulling the chain free from the door and dropping it to the floor, Ratty pulled the door open. It squealed and jerked, resisting him, but he put his back into it and dragged it open wide enough for the others to go inside.

They went in quite slowly, letting their eyes get used to the shaded interior, after the brightness outside, spreading out cautiously.

"Mickey," Rachel called out. "It's time to come on out. We can talk about this nicely or I can shoot you in the head and feed you to your friends."

There was a titter of amusement that sounded more like it came from a party of schoolgirls than a bunch of heavyset thugs.

Well, considering their steroid intake, they probably had testicles about the same size, Rachel thought.

However this was the only reaction, the rest of the building stayed utterly silent. Looking around again, Rachel spotted a shadow moving across a glass-fronted door on the suspended walkway above. She tapped the nearest one of her men on the shoulder, one of the younger members of the party who insisted on calling himself 'Aitch', which he said was short for 'Hell-bastard', although Rachel knew that it actually stood for Harvey. Bailey had recruited him straight from borstal, where he had been sent after splitting his DT teacher's head open with a metre-long metal ruler. He held a metre rule in his hand now, one end sharpened into a point and the other bound with masking tape and a tea-towel as a make-shift grip. It looked vicious in a way that an actual sword somehow didn't. Maybe it was the knowledge that someone had actually spent time turning this from a tool into a weapon.

Aitch climbed the stairs that led up to the walkway and, without pausing, pushed the office door open. Moving faster than Rachel had ever seen one move before, a zombin leapt through the doorway and fastened its teeth on Aitch's shoulder. He screamed and stepped backwards, flailing at the creature that was trying to eat him as fast as it could, his ruler-sword completely forgotten and slipping from his hand.

He stepped back again and came into the contact with the safety rail at the edge of the walkway. It wasn't designed for holding a person who had another person wrapped around their torso however and Aitch tumbled straight over it, flipping end over end once on the way down. The two of them hit the floor and the room echoed to the sound of their bones shattering.

Although the fall may have been too much for Aitch's body to survive – which, Rachel would later realise was a good thing, otherwise someone would have had to deal with him turning – it did not stop the zombin. It hampered it severely, though. There was no way it was going to be leaping any more. In fact, the way its body lay on the ground, twisted and torn like a doll that had been played with by a particularly vicious child whose parents had never taught it how to play nice, it probably wasn't going to be moving at all. That wasn't exactly a problem for the zombin at that point, though. It had plenty of fresh meat that wasn't trying to escape.

Seeing that everyone else, that is everyone who had access to their emotions, however base and uncomplicated they may be, was stunned by what they had just witnessed, it was left to Rachel to deal with the situation.

She went over to the creature that was happily feasting. On the way, she spied Aitch's ruler and picked it up. It actually had quite a bit of heft for something that seemed to be really quite flimsy. As she approached, the zombin lifted its head, twisting it in a way that it could only do if several bones were not working in the way that they usually did, and gurgling at her. It was a pathetic sound, utterly without any sort of power. Lifting the ruler above her head, Rachel brought it down as hard as she could onto its skull, again and again, until its brain was utterly destroyed.

Dropping the ruler to the ground, she turned back to the others, who were standing around, slightly in shock at what had just happened.

"I thought you didn't want the zombins killed?" Ratty said.

"Did you want to have to deal with that one? Maybe you'd have liked to push it around in a wheelchair?"

"Well…"

"Exactly, shut the fuck up."

Rachel turned away from him and looked around the warehouse again.

"Mickey!" She shouted. "Get yourself out here now. Or I'll burn the fucking place down and I'll make certain that nothing gets out of it – alive or dead."

Nothing happened.

"Are you sure he's here?" Ratty asked.

"I'm sure. And I thought I told you to shut the fuck up," Rachel hissed back.

The silence stretched out and continued for nearly an entire minute until, at last, there was a small metallic sound as the door at the back that led into Mickey's room was unlocked.

Immediately, a couple of thugs ran across, kicked the door open and rushed inside, apparently forgetting what had just happened to their compatriot. This time, they were lucky and the only occupant of the room on the other side of the door was human. They dragged Mickey out and across to Rachel, where they held him tightly, clamping their meaty fists around his arms, as if worried that he might, somehow, be some sort of a threat.

He was if anything even more repellent than he had been the last time Rachel had seen him. It looked like he had completely given up on anything approaching personal hygiene. The stench from him had an almost physical presence, as if it were his own personal ghost. His clothes, which looked to be the same raggy pants and t-shirt as before, were now even more stained and splashed with blood, presumably, Rachel thought, from the meat he was feeding his charges, rather than anything else.

"Mickey," Rachel said in greeting. "You're looking well."

Mickey looked sullenly at Rachel through his greasy hair.

"What do you want? Wait until Mr Mott hears about this, you little shit," he said, his voice a whine as if he didn't quite believe what he was saying.

"Okay," Rachel said.

She paused a moment and then slammed her foot between Mickey's legs as hard as she could. Mickey let out an agonized howl of pain and would have collapsed to the floor if he hadn't had the assistance of his two captors.

"That is for Aitch," Rachel said. "You won't believe how much hassle that is going to cause."

Rachel then kicked him again, in the same spot and with the same force. Unable to catch his breath from the first assault on his testicles, Mickey just squeaked and tears gushed down his face.

"And that's for threatening me. You obviously haven't heard – I don't expect many people think about you. I expect most people actively avoid thinking about you… But anyway, Mr Mott has retired. All his business has been taken over by George Bailey. And that includes all of his zombins. And you."

Rachel waited patiently for Mickey to recover himself. When he did, he said "What do you mean – retired?"

"I mean that I blew his brains out," Rachel told him.

"Fuck…" Mickey said. Although he was still in pain, Rachel could see that he was trying to pull himself together. "Respect, dude. That's pretty fucking hardcore."

"So, you are now working for Mr Bailey."

"Cool. I guess you'll want all that anti-vamp stuff in the back then?"

There were several ways that Rachel had seen this encounter going. And this had not been one of the scenarios.

"Yes. Show the guys where it is."

Mickey waved vaguely into the shadows at the end of the warehouse.

"Yeah, it's in one of the store rooms back there. Oh, you'll need to be careful though, I put another one of the zombins in there at the same time as I put that other one up in the office," he said. Then another thought seemed to come to him. "Mind, it's all pretty crap, though, that weaponry. Barely damaged the zombins when I played with it. I tried to tell Mr Mott, but I couldn't get through to him. I guess you'd done for 'im by then. That's why I holed up in here and released some zombins – security, y'know?"

"Weren't you worried that they'd get to you?"

"Nah. I know how to handle 'em, man. You know that. I made sure that they couldn't get out. So it was just people who went in that'd have to worry about it."

"And if someone did go in and the zombin killed them? The door would be open then."

"Oh. Yeah. I guess I didn't think of that. Damn. I'm glad you came then. You can sort 'em out, can't you?"

#

Sitting in the beer garden of the Free Trade Inn, supping on a pint of beer and looking out over the valley down to where the river flowed, Rachel still felt nothing. She couldn't even feel annoyed that she felt nothing. She may as well have been drinking water sat in her kitchen for all the pleasure she derived. But Bailey had sent her to the pub. Having a drink was the thing to do when you were in a pub and one of Rachel's standing orders was to avoid doing anything that would draw attention to herself – unless it was something that Bailey actually wanted her to do – so, she had to have a drink.

She was actually starting to get a little bit cold, there was quite a breeze blowing and, by the looks of the clouds, rain wasn't too far away, but the person she had been sent to meet didn't like going inside buildings if he could possibly avoid it. He had always lived outside and so the concept of enclosed buildings gave him a severe bout of claustrophobia. Although, apparently, naturally formed caves didn't worry him. But, as long as he turned up, it would be okay. Although, there was no guarantee that he would arrive. Oberon wasn't the most reliable of individuals. From all accounts he'd been more than a little flaky when he was king of Lyonesse – what with all the enchanting his wife to fall in love with peasants with the heads of donkeys and the screwing around with anyone and anything he could – but, now that Titania had finally deposed and banished him from Lyonesse never to return and he was strung out on Dust all the time, as well as dealing it, he'd become even worse. But, Bailey was planning on moving in on the Dust business, which had, until then, been pretty much Mott's area and so he needed Oberon on side. Without him, the supply of Dust would be pretty much limited to a few small time Brownies and Pixies who didn't owe any allegiance to the once – and he always claimed future – King of the Sidhe. And their stuff was nowhere near as good as the Dust that Oberon could produce.

"Hey, O," Rachel said to the lanky, scruffy, horned creature as he finally clumped across the wooden boards of the beer garden to the pint of scrumpy that sat waiting for him. His skin which had once been midnight blue had now faded and turned paler, as if the sun was coming up on his body. His eyes, which had been like twin stars in that night sky were perpetually eclipsed behind a pair of dark sunglasses, although Rachel would have thought that they had faded in a similar manner.

"We have told you before. When addressing us, you call us, sire," Oberon said.

"Sorry, I keep forgetting," Rachel replied, pausing before adding, "Sire."

Oberon looked at her. If it wasn't for the drink in front of him, he may well have left at that point. Deposed monarchs do not like having the piss taken out of them.

"We understand that you have gone up the world," Oberon said, after taking a long, slow draft of the scrumpy. "We have heard that you have switched employers and handed in your resignation quite dramatically."

"You could say that," Rachel said. She was under no command not to talk about or reveal her renfielding and was fairly certain that most people who had any sort of connections had a pretty good idea about her situation anyway. Even so, she didn't say anything about it. She couldn't exactly say why though. There was no shame or embarrassment in it for her. Or, if there was, then she couldn't feel it.

Maybe, she thought, it could lead to problems. If she was known for being renned then maybe others would try to dominate her. And, if it was bad enough being controlled by Bailey – and, intellectually, if not emotionally, she knew that it was very, very bad – then having every creature with any ability in domination trying their hand on her, would be even worse. And, Oberon was certainly capable of doing exactly that. Rachel wouldn't like to place a bet on which one would come out on top. Or on what sort of state she herself would be in after the attempt had been made.

"So. What is it you want of us?" Oberon asked.

"My new employer wants to discuss a partnership with you," Rachel told him. "He wants to know what it would take for you to stop selling your product in the city."

"We do not work for vampires," Oberon said flatly. "We would not expect you to understand."

"My employer is, however, the only game in town," Rachel said.

"Thanks to you."

Rachel shrugged.

"That's neither here nor there," she said. "The truth is my employer wants…"

"Why don't you say his name?" Oberon interrupted. "We both know about whom we are referring. We will not work for George Bailey or any other vampire in this city, any other city or any other land, real or imagined."

"My employer prefers not to have his name bandied about in public. He is a private individual. However, he did anticipate your reluctance. Therefore, I have been instructed to ask you a question."

Oberon took another sip and glowered at Rachel.

"Ask us," he said.

"My employer said to ask you if your ex-wife knows where you got your product from?"

"A threat? We thought that… your employer… would be above that."

"I think it's a case of whatever works."

"We do not think that Titania, whatever her other faults may be, would listen to a vampire. She and we are of one mind on this subject," Oberon told her.

"I have to say, sire," Rachel said. "From what I know of your relationship with your ex-wife, if you were actually 'of one mind' about vampires, it would be the very first thing the two of you agreed on."

"Nevertheless."

"Are you completely certain that Titania wouldn't be willing to listen to, say, a human who was sent by a vampire? Are you prepared to give up your income, not to mention your own little habit? My employer wants to work with you because you know the business. Now that Fred is out of it, he wants to control it and he wants to make sure that it is kept out of the city. He knows exactly what he's doing and he is going to get his way. Really, it's up to you whether you help him or fight against him."

"A pretty speech, I admit. You are loquacious. Why does your employer desire a city free of Dust?"

"Let's just say that having junkies in Newcastle is not part of his plan. He wants all the humans around here clean and fresh."

"Interesting. If we choose to go along with your employer, we will require… recompense. Losing an entire city, especially one that is as lucrative as this one, would impact upon our income quite considerably. And the price would be even higher because of the nature of your employer. If we can overcome our revulsion at the very idea of working with such a creature as that."

"He is aware of that and is prepared to negotiate."

"Very well. We shall consider what you say. Come back here at this time in three days and he shall have our reply."

Oberon sank the last of his pint, stood and strode off, his cloven hooves leaving dints in the wood underfoot.

#

"He's not going to go for it."

"That is not what I wanted to hear."

"It's not what I wanted to tell you."

Bailey's office had one similarity to Fred Mott's. It only had one chair. However, other than that, it was entirely different. There was no desk, no computer, no filing cabinets and no pictures of scantily-clad girls. It was down in the cellar of Bailey's house, although this wasn't entirely obvious. Rather than an office, this was more of a library. Two of the walls were covered, wall to ceiling with bookshelves. The times she had spent in here waiting for Bailey had given Rachel plenty of time to browse and she had discovered that the vampire had an interesting taste in books. Several shelves were packed with bad romance novels, while others held lurid true crime books, the sort that were the journalistic equivalent of dog's vomit. These were hidden behind encyclopaedias and dictionaries and atlases. Rachel would be willing to bet that the latter had been bought by the foot. Certainly, the romances and the true crime looked as if they had been read and the others had quite a thick layer of dust over them. Around the room were shelves stacked with war memorabilia from all over – guns, helmets and equipment belonging to, Nazis, the allied forces, Viet Cong and more as well as the occasional piece of Valkyrie armour and Faery weaponry – which Bailey claimed he had collected himself from the fields of war after he had been vampirised. However, Rachel had found a price tag on some of the pieces and some of the Valkyrie armour was actually fibre-glass. But it wouldn't do to mention that. Rachel thought that Bailey would not be happy if it was pointed out. Not that Rachel would have cared much about the provenance of the stuff even if she had been in full possession of herself.

"So, what are you going to do about it?" Bailey asked.

"What do you want me to do?"

"I want you to get him to join, either willingly, or otherwise."

"And if I can't? I can't kill him. He's a faery. In a lot of ways, he's The Faery. Even though he's been kicked out of his palace and his veins are full of Dust, he still has a hell of a lot power. And he's immortal."

"I am sure you will work something out," Bailey said. "Use your initiative."

"I would, but, unfortunately, I don't have any at the moment. It's one of the side-effects of renfielding me," Rachel told him, completely matter-of-factly.

Bailey looked at Rachel, as if to ascertain that she wasn't being sarcastic.

"You know," he said. "It is entirely possible that your usefulness will come to an end sooner than I anticipated."

"You do need me to conduct all your daytime work for you," Rachel replied.

"Oh, go away," Bailey said, unable to hide his annoyance. It wasn't that he had been outwitted by a human that upset him, it was being bested by being told things that he already knew by someone he had himself renned. It was galling, to say the least.

Rachel turned to leave and was almost out of the door when Bailey stopped her.

"Wait," Bailey said. "I have an interesting idea. I have just finished reading a book."

#

Donella was a very pretty faery girl. She could have been seventeen if she was human, but the truth was that she was probably closer to seventeen hundred. And she had the sense that Oberon apparently lacked. Either that or she had watched 'Scarface'. She did not partake of the Dust. She was probably Oberon's only real competition when it came to selling the stuff and, if Oberon wasn't such a famous being, she would probably have been well ahead of him. In a lot of ways, having Shakespeare as his publicist was probably the best thing that could have happened to Oberon once he had been expelled from Lyonesse. The sort of human who was liable to take Faery Dust was also likely to believe that getting it from 'The King' was going to mean that they were getting a better quality of drug. Which was, of course, complete rubbish. Oberon probably cut his supply with other things more than any other Dust dealer would even consider and the only reason he could get away with doing it was because of who he was.

So, Donella managed to keep her position in the Dust hierarchy by dint of selling at high quality and high prices. It still wasn't entirely pure, no human would survive the experience, but whereas other dealers would use the standard drug dealers cutting agents –

kitchen scourer, flour, ground up paracetamol – Donella tended to mix it with cocaine or heroin. The earthly drugs would both temper the pure Dust experience and also make it feel longer lasting. It was actually the hit from the coke that made it seem like that. Dust was a very, very fast hit that wore off just as quickly, but while you were under its influence time seemed to slow right down so the few seconds it lasted felt like hours. With added coke or heroin, the hit from that drug would kick in just as you were starting to come down from the Dust and you would get a second rush from that.

Or at least, that was what Rachel understood happened.

She was gorgeous though. Whether she used a glamour or whether she looked like that normally, Rachel didn't know. Although, even if she hadn't been renfielded at that moment, Lilly still had her claws in her soul so she wouldn't be able to look at another woman with anything approaching lust. Well, woman – female creature would be closer to the mark. Lilly was after all not human and neither was Donella.

Towards the middle of the night, when the music was banging its bass beat hardest and the atmosphere in the club was composed of at least fifty per cent sweat, there was a slight lull in Donella's business. The queue of people who stood waiting to approach the little private booth where she held court had died down and she was able to sit back and sip her drink. Rachel chose that moment to go across to her. She motioned to the two vampires she had brought who put their glasses of mineral water down and came across to her. They slid in, one on either side of the faery girl, while Rachel sat opposite her, where her customers usually sat.

"Miss Donella," she said, loudly to be heard over the thumping bass. "My name is Rachel Cantrell. I have a business proposition to make to you."

"I've heard of you, Cantrell. You work for the vampires now. Fuck off. And take these two suckers with you."

She was somewhat less polite than Oberon. Or maybe she'd just acclimated to the human world better than he had.

"Can we go somewhere else to talk about this?"

"There's nothing to talk about, blood fucker."

Rachel motioned to the vampires and, faster than the eye could follow they each snapped one end of a pair of handcuffs around her wrists. The other half of each cuff was attached to the vampire, hidden under their own shirt-cuffs. Donella's scream of pain as the cold iron touched her skin was muffled by Rachel as she leaned forwards and pressed her lips against hers. Renfielded or not, enchanted or not, it was an opportunity that was not to be ignored.

"I hoped you would be reasonable," Rachel said in her ear, as she held her close. "If you want to get out of those cuffs, come with me quietly."

She stood up and the vampires followed suit, pulling her to her feet and holding her hands to disguise the cuffs connecting them. A clubber was just making her way over to them, her make up running as the sweat poured off her. Rachel thought that it wasn't just the energetic dancing that was making her sweat.

"Hey, miss D," the girl said. "Can I get some…"

"Donella is finished for the night," Rachel told her. "Come back next time."

"I need it now. I've got the cash here." And she held out a wad of five and ten pound notes.

"Fuck off, junkie," Rachel snarled, pushing the girl away and making her drop her money. The girl dropped to her knees and scrabbled for the loose cash as Rachel barged her way through the crowded dance floor towards the exit, the vampires following her, dragging Donella along with them.

Once they got outside, Donella pulled back against her captors, making them pause.

"You should have let me give her some Dust," she snarled. "Do you have any idea what happens to a DJ that doesn't get a fix?"

"That's not my problem," Rachel told her. "And don't tell me you're worried for her health and welfare? Or is it just that you'll lose a customer?"

"Take me wherever the fuck you need to take me and get me out of these fucking cuffs, blood fucker," Donella spat at her.

"Do you have any idea how little sense that makes?" Rachel said, almost conversationally, as she led her down the road to the waiting limousine. "I neither want to have sex with vampires nor do I get turned on by them feeding. I work with them. It doesn't mean I want to be one."

"I really don't care," Donella told her. "Blood fucker."

The limo took them to a warehouse on an industrial estate just outside the city. Dragging the faery girl out of the car, they went inside. It was almost entirely filled with boxes, leaving only narrow corridors between to get to the ones further back. At the front of the warehouse was a reasonably sized loading bay, large enough for a truck to park and still have room to manoeuvre a fork-lift, although at the moment, the forklifts and pallet-movers were all crammed to one side. In the middle of the empty area was a padded chair. It was made of steel tubes with both head and foot rests. The back of the chair was steeply sloped backwards so that anyone who sat in it would be lying back, not quite prone, but getting up from it would be a struggle. A man sat next to it, looking through some tools lying on a small table.

"I was wondering how I could persuade someone of your kind to do something that he didn't want to do," Rachel said, as she led Donella towards the table. "You're all really tough. Even a little weak looking thing like you could take any normal human in a fight. If I hadn't got you with these cuffs, you'd have ripped my head off by now."

"Don't think it still won't happen," Donella said, although she said it nervously, eyeing up the table and the man they were going towards.

"It was thinking about the effect that cold steel has on you lot that made me come up with this. Mr Bailey showed me an article that said that at one time tattooing ink held small particles of metal."

Donella jerked at this and stopped moving. Rachel looked at her and then towards the two vampires.

"Guys?" she said to them.

They took her by each arm and lifted her clear of the ground, carrying her over to the tattooing chair. Laying her chest down on the chair they secured her legs with more handcuffs and then placed a heavy steel chain around her neck. Finally, Rachel took a couple of keys from her pocket, unlocked one of the sets of cuffs from wrist of one of the vampires, secured that to the table.

"I thought that the best way of getting control of a faery would be to make sure that he knows that I know what hurts him. And I really can't think of anything that would hurt one of your sort more than having cold steel permanently embedded inside your body. Actually, I don't know if the stuff in the tattoo ink will hurt you, which is why I need to try it out. Consider yourself a volunteer in a great scientific experiment."

"Why me?" Donella asked, her voice weakened by the pain of the steel touching her skin.

"Because you are Oberon's main competitor," she told her. "And, once we'd persuaded him on to our side, we'd have been after you next. You can think of this as a little pre-emptive strike."

"Blood fucker. Let me go. I will kill you."

Rachel looked at the tattooist. He was an old man, scrawny and wiry. His hair, what little there was left of it, was dirty grey with a hint of tobacco yellow in it that undoubtedly came from the tightly rolled cigarettes that he smoked seemingly constantly. At least, Rachel had not seen him without one since collecting him from the half-way house that afternoon.

"Mr Fredricks," she said. "If you'd like to show us your trade?"

"You unnerstan' that I ain't done this since I came out of stir, dontcha?"

"I'm sure it will be just like riding a bicycle."

"Yeah, I never got the hang o' tha' either."

"Keep this old fucker away from me," Donella screamed.

Rachel came over to her and went down on her haunches next to her head.

"You should feel honoured, Donella," Rachel told her. "Peter Fredricks is a genius when it comes to the fine art of the tattoo. The fact that you're his first client in nearly thirty years is just an added bonus. You see, Pete, here, has a nickname. In his day he was called The Tattooist. Do you know about Jack the Ripper? The murders he committed were so famous at the time that hundreds of people wrote letters to the police pretending to be Jack himself. It was actually one of these letters that gave him the name Jack the Ripper. There were so many letters that we still don't know if any of them were actually from the man himself. The same can't be said for Peter. He only actually killed three people before he was caught, but, each of those three people had a short note tattooed to their back explaining why they had been chosen. He is even going to use the same ink and tools that he used all those years ago."

Fredricks pinched the end of his cigarette, putting it out and tucked the stub behind his ear. Then he stood up, picked up a pair of scissors and stepped towards Donella. He ran them up under her blouse along her back, cutting the silk and her bra strap in one swift movement.

Turning back to the table, he swapped the scissors for his tattoo gun. Bending over her back, he brought the machine to bear and was just about to press it against her skin when she bucked up, knocking his arm out of the way. He straightened up again and turned towards Rachel.

"I can't do this if she's gonna be like that," he said. "I always knocked 'em out when I did it."

"We'll do that if she causes any more trouble, Pete," Rachel said. "But let's try one more thing first."

She knelt down and pulled another, even heavier chain out from under the chair.

"I should probably have done this from the beginning," she said.

She dropped it over her lower back, forcing a squeal of agony from Donella and secured it tightly with another padlock. The weight of the chain and the added pain from the steel seemed to calm her down, or perhaps more likely, pushed her into semi-consciousness.

Fredricks bent over her back once again and, with a buzz from his tattoo gun, he started to work.

"Take your time, Pete," Rachel said. "We've got all night. I want a really pretty pair of fairy wings for the really pretty fairy."

"You're the boss," Fredricks replied.

#

It was raining when Rachel returned to the Free Trade. It wasn't a hard downpour, but it was insistent. The sort of rain that didn't feel like much but managed to quietly and subtly insinuate itself through every little hole in your clothing until suddenly you discovered, rather than just being a bit damp like you thought you were, you were actually completely drenched, the water was dripping off your nose and your shoes squelched when you walked. And you had no idea how you managed to get that wet.

Fortunately, she had an umbrella with her, so she could at least shelter her drink while she waited for Oberon to turn up.

Whether this time his lateness was just Oberon being Oberon or whether he was gaining some kind of pleasure or revenge out of making Rachel wait, she didn't know, nor did she care, but this time, Oberon didn't turn up until forty-five minutes after the appointed time.

"Oberon," Rachel said, once the Faery King had settled himself, shaking his head and spattering Rachel with raindrops. "Have you come to a decision?"

"Are you really expecting us to ignore what you did to Donella?" Oberon demanded.

"No. Not at all," Rachel replied. "In fact, I was hoping that you would see it and understand it for the message it was."

"We should rip out your heart."

"Very possibly. But can you be certain that, if you do that, a couple of vampires won't turn up at your door one evening? The 'only being allowed in if they are invited' thing only works for humans. Non-humans don't count for that rule," Rachel told him. "I wonder... do you think that if a faery was turned then those rules would apply to faery-kind and not humans?"

"No vampire has ever tried to turn a faery and lived to talk about it. If the faery did not kill the vampire then their blood did it instead. That threat is no threat at all."

"Oh, that wasn't a threat. Not really. I was just wondering about it. Call it a professional curiosity. No, the only real method of persuasion that I have is the horrible thing that happened to Donella. That and the possibility of talking to Titania, of course."

"You think she would speak to you after the atrocity you committed on one of her subjects?"

"I'm sorry? I didn't think that she had any interest in the faery-kind who left Lyonesse. Or is that just you? Sire."

"You little fucker," Oberon shouted, surging to his feet and grabbing hold of Rachel's shoulder. "How dare you. I'll fucking kill you."

"You've said that. Donella said something similar, although she said it better. Want to end up like her? Touch me again and you will. Really piss me off and I'll have your bollocks chopped off, so you're really like her. Now, sit down before you fall down."

"You would know about the removal of testicles, wouldn't you, once-a-man?" Oberon hissed before releasing her and, slowly, sitting.

Rachel paused and looked silently and steadily at Oberon as she counted to ten inside her head. She could see a look of worry cross his face as he realised that he may have gone too far. Then she gave him the biggest, most shit-eating grin she could, a smile that said that she was choosing to ignore what he said, but it was not forgotten and it was absolutely not forgiven.

"Now, my Lord Oberon, once and future king of Lyonesse. In the tradition of all the best reality telly… it's decision time."

She paused and looked hard at the Faery. Oberon's face was contorted into a harsh scowl and his fists were tightly clenched.

"I'm excited," Rachel said, actually sounding rather bored. "Are you?"

"I have no choice, do I?" Oberon said and, as he spoke, he seemed to deflate. He went from an imposing, menacing monarch into a shrunken junkie as he spoke, letting his glamour die.

"Not really, I'm afraid."

"I shall stop selling Dust in this city. Have your master tell us his terms. Tell him we will not speak with you again."

"Very well. I'm sure he'll be happy with that."

"There is one thing though. You spoke truly," Oberon's glamour returned suddenly, with even more force and power. He seemed to grow and, as he did so, the clouds turned darker and the rain grew harder. Looming over Rachel he pointed at her and spoke with a booming voice. "You described us as the once and future king of Lyonesse. Bear that in mind. We have lost our throne before and we have always returned to that position. And always stronger. When we are restored to our rightful position, then you should beware. Our retribution will be swift and ruthless. I pity your position, once-a-man. To have your will overcome is a terrible thing. But this does not mean that we shall not forget your insults. Nor shall we forgive them. Ever."

Interlude: The Lake District, July 1966

"Not far now, George!"

The shout came from a tall, blonde woman about one hundred yards ahead of him. She'd said that exact same thing about half an hour ago. Why he had ever agreed to go on a hiking tour of the Lake District with her, he would never, ever be able to work out. Not only was he completely unsuited to walking long distances – being short and fat was all very well when all you did was stand behind a bar serving pints all day, less so when you were walking miles up and down great big bloody hills – and he really doubted that she was actually going to get into her knickers. And he was going to miss the World Cup Final! And listening to it on his tranny wasn't going to be anything like watching on the telly. And, to top it all off, it was raining. Again. It hadn't stopped for one moment in the three days they had been here. It wasn't really pissing down, it was just a constant drizzle that seemed to get everywhere. The water dripped from his hair his into eyes and off the end of his nose and even managed to get inside his raincoat. And yet, she was striding ahead, looking for all the world as if she couldn't ask for anything more. And she was wearing shorts!

So, all in all, it had been a completely terrible holiday so far and the prospects weren't looking good for it improving at all over the next couple of days. He was really looking forward to getting back to work. Except he'd still have to work with Sheila having to put up with her constantly laughing at him behind his back for all this. Strange how walking for hours behind somebody – even somebody with a backside and legs like hers – could make you really hate them.

Reaching the summit of a rise, Sheila stopped and waited for him, sitting down on a rock at the edge of a road and gazing out at the countryside around her. When she glanced down the road to see George huffing and puffing his way up towards her, he was convinced that he could see the laughter in her eyes which was not quite making it out from between those two perfect, utterly kissable lips. Not that he had. Kissed them, that is. The closest he came to it was when she gave him a quick peck on the cheek last thing at night before settling down to sleep in her sleeping bag. And leaving him to lie there, struggling to find a spot on the ground that wasn't cold and lumpy.

"Look, George," she said as he finally reached her, a wide sweep of her arms encompassing everything around them. "Isn't it magnificent?"

Even in the mood he was in, even with the rain and the mist and everything else, George had to admit that it did look utterly amazing. They were standing about three quarters of the way up a hill – well, *they* called it a hill, George would have called it a mountain – and looking out over a valley towards some beautifully barren hills on the far side. The green grass was marred by the occasional scree slope and a few deep scars that looked as if the ground had been torn open. Ullswater lay at the bottom of the valley, calm and serene, stretching out into the distance, long and thin. There was the occasional farm house or barn on the slopes of the hills and a network of dry-stone walls that looked almost as if they had grown there rather than being built. The distant whistle of a shepherd calling to his dog was the only human sound he could hear. Other than that it was just the sound of birds singing and the occasional bleat of a sheep.

"Aye, I suppose so," he said. "Still, I'd rather be looking at it through a window with a pint in my hand."

"Oh, you," Sheila replied. "That's no way to experience the countryside. You have to get out into the open air. You've got to soak it all up."

"Well, I'm soaking something up," he muttered. "Where is this place we're going to?"

"Not far. Let's go."

He was about to complain that she had been able to have a rest while he caught up with her, but he was too late. She was already off again, settling her rucksack on her back as she went.

'Not far' was apparently only another hour's walking. When they finally reached the farm where they would be camping down for the night, George wasn't sure if he was soaked from the rain – which had slowly grown heavier as they continued on – or from the sweat that seemed to be cascading from every inch of his body. As the farmer's wife – an old harridan called Mrs MacReady who had obviously seen a way of making a few bob by letting idiots who wanted to go walking sleep in one of her barns – showed them to where they would be staying for the night, which included a long list of rules nailed to the wall, George felt like he wanted to just lie down and die. Once Mrs MacReady had left, he did the first part of that, shucking his rucksack and collapsing on some bales of hay that had been provided for bedding.

After about half an hour of lying on the hay, groaning softly to himself, George realised that he really wasn't going to get any sympathy. In fact, lifting his head and looking around, he realised that Sheila had actually disappeared. Her rucksack was open and some of her things were lying on her sleeping bag.

Some... of... her... things...

Lying on top of the pile of clothes was something quite small and white. He looked around guiltily to make sure that there was no-one around and then pulled himself up from the bale and went over to her sleeping bag. Reaching out a hand, he picked up the item that lay there. It looked almost like a pair of bikini bottoms, kind of like the ones that Ursula Andress wore in Dr. No. But these were cotton and so light. He could barely feel them sitting there on his hand. His hot, sweaty hand. These things had, at some point, been wrapped around Sheila. Touching her bottom and... and her...

Hands shaking, he lifted the panties to his face. They smelt clean, feminine and fresh.

"What the hell are you doing, you pervert?"

The shout pulled him completely from his reverie. Dropping his hands, he saw Sheila standing just inside the door to the barn, her hair wrapped in a towel, wearing a long, heavy dress that seemed to cling to her body.

George looked at her and felt his face turning hot.

"I wasn't... I mean..."

"I thought you were different," Sheila said. "I thought you were a nice guy."

"I am... I'm sorry..."

"I can't look at you... Please... just go away..."

Shaking with embarrassment, George stumbled out of the barn, hands tangled in his hair, as if he was trying to pull it out by the roots. As if, by hurting himself, he'd somehow atone for the crime he had committed and show Sheila that he was a nice guy. That she would like him again.

Wandering around with your hands covering your face is very rarely a good idea. Even less so when you are wandering around somewhere with which you are unfamiliar. And even less than that when the unfamiliar place is a farm that, until very recently, has had several days' worth of rain falling on it. It didn't take long for George to step in a puddle and discover that it was actually a pothole. His ankle twisted and he went down heavily, splashing into the water and sending wet, liquid mud splashing up and over his entire body.

George just lay there, the pain from his foot washing over him. Slowly, as he stayed still, the pain ebbed away, almost like a tide going out, slipping down his body and back into his leg and foot, becoming bearable, but always threatening to roll across him once more if he moved a single muscle. He knew that he was going to have to do something about it. He couldn't just lie in that puddle for the rest of the night and he was fairly certain that if nobody came when he screamed as he fell, they weren't going to come and stumble over him now. He was also reasonably certain that he needed to go to a hospital. Although where the nearest one was from this godforsaken hill he had no idea. Carlisle probably. Still, for the moment, he was going to just lie there. He felt in no hurry to move. It was going to take a fair bit of courage to do it and that was one thing that George was lacking, just then.

So, he lay back, lying his head back in the mud, feeling it squelch up around his ears and looked up into the darkening sky.

He could, without moving his head much, see pretty much all around him. The farm actually lay on the brow of a hill and he had fallen so he looked across the valley. It lay pointing east-west, so in one direction, the sky was already black, while in the other the clouds were lit by an almost artificial looking rose pink glow. In some funny way it looked like one of the painted backdrops that he saw when he went to see a Western at the cinema. Although the wet, green hills of Cumbria were about as far from the arid stone and desert that John Wayne and Audie Murphy rode across as you could get. Lights were on in the MacReady's farmhouse and, across the valley he could see more yellow pinpoints as other farms prepared for the oncoming night.

The whole thing: lying there, exhausted from the day's walking, the mud slowly drying on him and the warm summer breeze blowing against him, just a hint of rain in there, even the dull throb that emanated from his ankle, all came together to send him into a lull. He wasn't falling asleep, it wasn't that comfortable, but he was certainly not entirely awake. Slowly, above him, the stars started to light up, first one or two and then more and more, almost as if they were more farmsteads off in the distance, flicking on their own lights. And, you never knew, maybe there were farms out there. After all, if ghosts and faerie and what-have-you existed, there's no reason at all why the Martians, Venusians and Gort shouldn't.

His reverie was interrupted by a rough, Cumbrian voice coming out of the dark.

"What are you doin' down there lad?"

George jerked, waking up the pain that had been slumbering in his ankle and sending it climbing up his body, coming out of his mouth as a heartfelt yelp.

"You hurt yerself?" the voice asked.

"Yeah," George replied, his own voice roughened by the pain. "It's my ankle. I think I've twisted it. "

"Come on. Let's get you up and into the house. I'll get the wife to clean you up and we'll take a look."

The owner of the voice stepped forwards and he matched the voice: rough and Cumbrian. His clothes were a patchwork quilt of repairs. His face, where an enormous snow white bushy beard didn't cover it, was deeply lined, almost as if he'd taken the plough to his own forehead and cheeks. His hands, as he reached forwards to help the younger man stand, were gnarled, the knuckles like walnuts. The obvious arthritis did not seem to slow him down though, as he helped George get up, seemingly without effort. George certainly didn't need to put his damaged foot on the ground.

"You'll be the young man who came in earlier on then?"

"Yes, that's me. Bailey, George Bailey," George replied.

"You can call me Wilf. Enid told me there was a couple here and I was coming out to say hello."

"Enid? You mean Mrs MacReady?"

"That's her. The wife. Come on let's get you in the house, then we'll let your young lady know where you are. She'll be getting worried."

"No. I don't think she will..."

"Oh. Had an argument have you?"

"Sort of..." George said, blushing.

"Ah well, I'm sure seeing you in dire straits like this'll get to her. Accident's always help young love."

George nearly laughed at that.

"No. We're not together like that. We're just friends. Well, we were..."

"It can't 'ave been that bad, can it, lad?"

George muttered something which Wilf seemed to accept as a reply. They hobbled on to the farmhouse and the old man pushed the door open, calling out to his wife.

The scowl remained on her face as she came into the kitchen.

"The young'uns hurt himself," Wilf said. "Get 'im cleaned up and we'll take a look at him."

"I think I might need the hospital," George said as he sat down.

"I'm sure you'll be fine," Wilf told him. "Enid is a wonder with bandages and the like."

#

For all that she seemed like an evil old harridan, Enid MacReady did indeed know her way around a bandage. Before long, George was cleaned up, cup of tea in hand and wearing an old dressing gown that belonged to Wilf. Enid had his foot up on her lap and was gently prodding and probing it.

"It's twisted pretty bad," she said. "But it's not broken."

Wilf was sitting opposite watching his wife tend to their visitor a look of concern on his face.

"The lad's good and healthy then, is he?" he asked.

"Oh aye," she said. "He'll be limpin' for a couple of days, but he'll be right as rain. And I'd be willin' to bet that a lad like that hasn't never taken any of them drugs that everyone seems to be on about these days."

"Oh no..." George said, earnestly. "I've never touched it. I guess I just like staying in control. Well, apart from a couple of pints on a Friday night, y'know?"

"A couple of pints? That's nearly an armful!" Wilf said.

Taken by surprise – he wouldn't have thought that the old man was a fan of Hancock, even if he had misquoted – he nearly sprayed his tea all over Enid as he spluttered a laugh.

"Steady on, lad," Wilf said, getting up and coming over to him. "We can't have you choking to death. That'd be a right waste."

Standing behind him, Wilf clapped a hand on George's shoulder.

"Y'know, lad," he said. "I think you'll work out right nice."

"Thanks," George said. "You've been really good to me. I guess I'd better be getting back to the barn. Sheila'll be wondering where I've got to."

"Oh, there's no hurry lad," Wilf said, his voice loud in George's ear as he bent down next to him, placing his other hand on George's shoulder. "There's plenty of time yet."

Suddenly, George felt intimidated by these two old people. Perhaps it was just old fashioned country courtesy but it just felt a bit creepy. He tried to get up but Wilf's hands on his shoulders kept him firmly in place. The old man was a lot stronger than he first appeared.

"All that country living has really given you some muscles, eh, Wilf?" George said, half-laughing.

"I'm not sure you could call it that, lad," Wilf replied and Enid let out a sudden bark of laughter that made George jump. "It's certainly not living that has given me this strength."

For one moment, George felt an agonising sharp stab as Wilf suddenly sank his teeth into his neck. He was about to yell out in pain and anger when the pain changed and a deep, comforting, somnolent warmth started to emanate from the puncture wounds, rippling in waves through his body. He knew he should probably be struggling, that the old man was doing something that he really shouldn't be doing, but it just felt too good. Too nice.

After a time that felt like all the time in the world and yet nowhere near long enough, Wilf lifted his head from George's neck. George could feel blood dribbling down on to his shoulder and down his chest, a liquid warmth that kind of felt like that time he'd gone swimming in the sea at Whitley Bay and hadn't bothered getting out when he needed a piss. Wilf came round in front of him, incisors now jutting out over his bottom lip, chin covered in gore, a smile on his face.

"Oh yes. You are a good, clean lad, aren't you?" He said. "So few people your age have blood that isn't filthy with drugs these days. But you're not like them. As you said, just a few pints of beer. And that just gives your blood a nice tang to it. You really will work out right proper."

Dazed and confused, George looked up at the old man's – the old vampire's – face, not sure what he was saying, watching as Wilf lifted his own wrist up to his mouth and bit down. The way the teeth slid through the skin like a hot knife through butter was really quite fascinating to watch. His blood, thicker and darker than George's own, looking half congealed already, slid over his wrist and splatted in heavy gobbets on the floor.

"Drink this lad," Wilf said, placing his wrist gently against George's lips. "You'll not believe how good it is."

The thought that he shouldn't do this – that he should try

and escape briefly surfaced in George's befuddled mind, but it disappeared as soon as the first drop of the vampire's blood touched his tongue. George suddenly realised how thirsty he was and how thirst-quenching this sweet, delicious, smooth liquid was that was slipping into his mouth and down his throat, better than the best first pint on the hottest day, better than anything. He knew that after tasting this, nothing else would be enough.

When Wilf pulled away this time, there was no confusion about whether George had had long enough. He knew that there would never be enough time to get all he wanted.

His hands reached out but Wilf evaded his grasp.

"I know, lad. I was the same when I got me first taste. But believe you me – good, clean human blood makes the stuff in my veins taste like stale piss. And, the sooner you get some inside you, the better and stronger you'll be and the easier the transition will be."

George lifted his head and stared at Wilf, realising the truth in his words. He could the hear the steady beat of a heart, even as he heard his own slowing and stopping. Swinging his head, he focussed on the source of that constant rhythm and came to look at Enid. He tried to rise but Wilf held him back in the chair.

"No. Not Enid, lad," he said. "She's mine. You'll have to find your own."

That was okay. George knew where to get blood that was younger and fresher than the old woman's. After all, he'd really wanted to get his teeth into Sheila, even before that evening.

Chapter Six

If there was one thing to be said for being renfielded it was the fact that life was suddenly not very hard at all. Rachel had no important decisions to make, because her entire life was decided by Bailey. Anything she had to decide was as a consequence of, and predicated upon, Bailey's wishes. She was utterly unable to do anything that would contradict his instructions. She could give a convincing impression of being self-aware and able to form opinions of her own, at least to those who were unaware of her position. But it was all merely a façade. Bailey would point her in a direction and, like a little tin toy, she would be let go to do her stuff.

As well as not having to make any decisions, she did not have to worry about any of those annoying emotions. The day that she was renned she had also buried her mother and discovered her girlfriend was actually a succubus who was using her as an unwitting mole. She may not have got on with her father but, nevertheless, she had also lost him at the same time as she had lost her mother, without even the chance to have one final farewell argument with the old ghost.

In the dark of the middle night, when Bailey had sent her to rest, Rachel would find herself contemplating these things – in a purely abstract manner – and wondering about them. She could feel that they were still there, shoved deep down inside and locked away, just waiting to be set free when she was eventually freed. In a way, she was not looking forward to that day. Although, she was also able to see that it was probably not a day that would come for an awfully long time, if at all. Bailey was not the sort of person – creature – being – whatever – to take pity on anyone or anything. He would use Rachel for as long as he saw fit, until she was no longer useful. When that day eventually came, Rachel thought that she would be released from her bondage only to immediately become lunch. And there was really nothing she could think of to get herself out of the situation. Fortunately, like all the rest of her problems, this did not worry her in the slightest.

#

The debate was very, very dull. Why exactly anyone would want to watch a debate about the pros and cons of leaving street lighting on through the night was beyond her. In a world where the night held vampires, werewolves and other horrors, not to mention the more human terrors, surely it was worth spending a few extra pounds to keep things illuminated. But, apparently not. Or perhaps it was. Neither side of the debate was exactly sparkling in their attempts to persuade.

So, in a way it was fortunate that Bailey had plans for that evening. And that was why she and several vampires were watching it. There were also some human thugs that Bailey had brought along that Rachel was fairly certain hadn't been renned.

It was just getting to the 'high point' of the debate when Bailey stood up.

"Ladies. Gentlemen," he called from the public gallery. "If I may have a word."

Leaping over the rail, he jumped, surprisingly lightly for a short, fat man with a limp, down to the chamber floor.

"I have been thinking recently," he said, as he walked towards the chairperson, "that we vampires have not had enough recognition. I think there may be a certain amount of inequality in the way that humans treat vampires."

"What do you want us to do about it?" a brave councillor called out.

"Well, it occurred to me that just as humans don't bother giving their food any say in matters concerning them, so we vampires should feel the same way. So, if you want to continue in your nice, harmless, mindless way without being harassed too much, then I suggest that you do as I ask."

"Are you threatening us?" the brave councillor called out again.

"Well, a threat is often seen as something that is not acted upon," Bailey told him.

Bailey leapt from where he stood in front of the chairperson on to the table in front of the councillor. He took hold of the man by his hair and pulled him to his feet.

"I do not make threats. I merely tell you all how things are going to be from now on."

Sinking his teeth into the councillor's neck, he pulled hard. Blood spurted onto the floor, splashing over his stunned colleagues.

"If more of you do not want to end up like this, then I suggest that you acquiesce. I want a tithe. Ten per cent of the taxes you take from the good citizens of Newcastle. Or I shall take ten per cent of the citizens."

He looked around at the assembled councillors. Blood dripped from his jaws and down his chin.

"I will not take your answer now. Instead, I will expect a front page headline in tomorrow evening's local newspaper. If there is no such headline then I will assume the answer is no and shall take the appropriate action."

He went to the double doors at the far end of the chamber and pulled them open.

Turning back to the assembled councillors, he bowed.

"Ladies, gentlemen," he said. "I trust that we shall be able to work together and I will see you soon. One way or another."

He walked out and the other vampires, leaping down from the gallery followed him. His human thugs trooped out of the doors in the gallery. Rachel and a handful of others, who had been there to view the ordinary proceedings and were somewhat shocked and surprised by what they had seen, remained where they were.

#

Unsurprisingly, the following days newspaper headlines – not just the local paper but the national ones as well, were full of the replies from the council. Although she had not been there the evening before, the mayor had chosen to set herself up as the figurehead for the consequences. Whatever they turned out to be.

The answer was, of course, 'no', although it was phrased a lot more belligerently and with more bravado. A bravado which was somewhat undermined by the fact that the mayor, most of the councillors and their families had left the city for an 'undisclosed location'.

As well as the local politicians, the national ones got in on the act. The Prime Minister applauded the councillor's position and said that whatever happened, he would ensure that Newcastle would not become a 'vassal state of Dracula'. It actually created cross party agreement for once. The leader of the Opposition claimed that he would support anything that the PM proposed to prevent this 'flagrant attack on the civil rights of our law-abiding citizens by this evil creature of the night'.

Of course, Bailey didn't actually expect to get any sort of capitulation. Sowing unrest among the human authorities was just the first step. If they had agreed to his demands then it would have made the rest of his plan a lot easier, but either way, it wasn't a problem for him. Having them refuse just made it all that much more enjoyable for him.

However, until he actually chose to reveal his plan to the rest of the world, Bailey had to keep the façade up. So, he had to play the part of the 'super-villain'. Which entailed making a reply. He had spent the day waiting for the evening's local newspaper to be published and moving his base of operations from the centre of town to a significantly larger abode in Darras Hall. It was one hell of a safe house.

The one obvious problem for a vampire when he was trying to send a message to a lot of people was his inability to appear on film. The medium of radio had been all well and good forty years ago but now people didn't believe it unless it was on the telly and they could watch it again and again on YouTube. So, for Bailey to get his word out, he had to resort to a little bit more subterfuge.

Rachel was almost surprised that Bailey didn't dress her up like Nosferatu or a Universal movies vampire. Despite their actual existence, those two images were, for many, if not most people, still the images that the word 'vampire' conjured up. Instead, she wore one of Bailey's usual 'natty' suits. This one was puce. Rachel didn't know where he got them from and wouldn't have wanted to know, no matter what state of mind and body she was in. Well, she may possibly have found out, but only to avoid shopping there.

It didn't particularly matter what she was wearing though. Rachel was sitting in front of a series of high wattage lamps that shone with searing intensity, turning her into a sharp-edged silhouette that showed off her rubbery bat-wing ears and her bald cap to brilliant effect while hiding every other feature. Another light, this one with a red filter and of much lower power, was pointed at her face. It didn't really illuminate anything as it was pretty much completely washed out by the light projected upon her from behind. What it did was highlight some of the wrinkles and creases in her face, make her eyes shine a little with what could be mistaken for an unearthly glow and show her lips moving, in case anyone watching thought that what they saw was not real.

"Are you ready?" Bailey asked Rachel.

"As ready as I'll ever be," she replied.

"Your public awaits, Miss Cantrell."

Bailey nodded towards the vampire who was manning the camera and he held his hand up, all his fingers splayed out. He counted back the seconds with his fingers and, when he reached one, he pointed at Rachel.

"Good evening, ladies and gentlemen," Rachel said, trying hard to put on a masculine voice, a voice that she had spent hundreds of pounds and hours learning to lose. "You will be aware of the request I made to your civic councillors, regarding the payment of a tithe. As I explained at the time, I think that it is only fair that we vampires should be recompensed for allowing you to live. After all, if we took it into our heads, we could devastate the city and turn it into a ghost town almost overnight. You may think that you would be safe during the day and you could hunt us down. But, believe me when I say that we are better hidden during the day than you could imagine and we are nearly invulnerable during the night. How many of you can truly say that you would have the courage to attempt to drive a stake through the heart of a vampire? Do you truly believe that, in these irreligious days, a cross is going to make any difference to most of you? It is not our belief in a higher being that powers it, it is your own. And there are so few true believers out there now."

She paused and took a drink of something heavy, viscous and red. The overpowering sweetness of the watered-down strawberry jam almost made her gag, but she managed to hold it in.

"Your politicians speak of refusing to bow down to terrorists. Trust me when I say that your terror is the last thing on my mind. I merely want a society where vampires are shown the respect they deserve. After all, what respect do you show your cattle? Oh, you may kill them humanely and feed them well and let them roam through the fields but that is only because doing so makes them taste better. The only way I can get your attention is by taking that which you hold dear. And humans hold nothing in higher regard than they do money. I do not want to have to kill you all. That would, in the long run, lead to a war between humans and vampires. And you can judge how well you would come out of that by looking at the way humans live under Count Dracula and his consort. I want vampires to live peacefully with humans. But I want to do so in the correct way. With vampires at the top of the pile. Therefore, I shall bypass your politicians and appeal directly to the people of Newcastle. I do not ask for much. I have not demanded human sacrifices. I have not asked for first-born children or virgins or any such thing. Not yet anyway. All I want is some money. Tell your politicians to give me what I ask or I may have to rethink my stance. Thank you for listening."

She took another long, slow pull on her drink and then the vampire cameraman indicated that they were done.

"Excellently done, Rachel, "Bailey said. "That will keep them on their toes. Just as I wanted. And, when they refuse, the consequences will be their own fault."

\#

Jenny and Andrew Ferguson were sitting down to watch the evening news. The twins had just settled down – they were only six months old and had just started to sleep for longer than three or four hours at a time, so their parents were finally able to start feeling vaguely human again as opposed to sleep-walking zombins, which had been their default state since the girls had been born. There had even been some vague discussion about perhaps, maybe, finally having sex again.

Suddenly, someone started to bang on the door. Not just the usual rattle of the door-knocker. This was a real, heavy fist-hammering-on-the-door banging.

"I'll get it," Andrew said. "Whoever that is had better not wake the kids."

With a sigh, he pulled himself out of his chair and went to answer. Standing on the step was a woman, wild-eyed and breathless. At the end of the garden path stood a group of three or four others, looking, apparently anxiously, back down the street. As Andrew pulled the door open, the woman pushed her way inside and fell to her knees, coughing and wheezing.

"Please," she panted, after a few moments when she had caught her breath. "Vampires. They're after us. They already got someone back there. Help."

"Of course," Andrew said. "Come in, come in."

The woman turned back to her companions.

"He said we can go in."

"Vampires can't get in to someone's house unless they're invited in," Andrew said as the group followed him in. "And I damn sure won't be doing that."

As they went into the front room again, Jenny looked up at Andrew questioningly.

"Vampires," Andrew told her. "They were chasing these guys. We need to call the police."

"I am truly sorry," the woman said.

"No – no worries. We've got to look after each other," Jenny said.

"That's not what I meant," the woman said.

One of her companions slowly opened his mouth, showing his teeth. His fangs.

"I'm afraid you should have left us outside. Your invitation was all that was needed."

Andrew realised that not all of them had come into the front room at the same moment as the last vampire did so. He was holding two small bundles in his arms. The girls were soundly asleep, snuggled up in their little pink, flowered, oh-so-cute baby sleeping bags that Jenny had bought over Andrew's opposition. Andrew lunged forwards but was effortlessly held back by another vampire. Jenny stared, soundlessly, her face drained of all blood, her eyes wide with terror and tears slowly starting to slide down her cheeks.

"Please," she said. "Don't hurt them."

"They won't feel a thing," one of the vampires said, as he took a step towards her. "And you won't see anything happen to them."

Rachel stepped outside the room. She hadn't been specifically instructed to stay and watch, so she didn't.

There were little grunts and moans and even a couple of murmured pleadings from inside the room. All the sounds quickly died away and there was only an ominous silence.

#

This tactic was repeated extremely successfully for the next three nights. Four or five times each night, Rachel along with different groups of vampires would inveigle themselves into someone's house and then everyone would be slaughtered. Sometimes, by the end of the night when the vampires had taken their fill, they wouldn't even drink from them. Instead, they would just kill them, leaving the rooms spattered with blood and body parts. Eventually, though, people learned and they stopped answering the door. After sundown, Newcastle became silent. There were always a few people around, quickly making their way from one place to another – district nurses, doctors and paramedics hurrying to attend to the ill and infirm, police cars patrolling, the occasional fire engine making its way to an emergency. There were even a few foolhardy souls who refused to let the fear get to them and went out to the pub. And, these people seemed to be okay. Not a single one of these people were reported as going missing. It was almost as if they were too easy.

Despite what Rachel had said in the broadcast, the sales of religious icons went through the roof. It was truly 'panic buying'. Crosses, Stars of David, crescents, even such things as the word 'Om' in Sanskrit and yin yang symbols started to show up on doors and around peoples necks. Churches, synagogues, temples of all kinds reported a sudden surge of worshippers.

And then, a couple of weeks after the last reported attempt to gain access, a brick was thrown through the front window of Martin Lightfoot's house. The double-glazed glass shattered and Martin himself nearly had a heart attack as the brick landed about a foot away from where he was sitting. The brick was quickly followed by a liquid-filled bottle, a burning rag stuffed into its neck. It flew past Martin's head and shattered against the back wall of the room, the petrol inside the bottle splashing all around and igniting with a 'whoomph'.

Martin's boyfriend, Pete, who had just been putting his dressing gown on, after having had a shower, came running downstairs at Martin's shout of terror. Seeing the living room blazing, Pete pulled at Martin's arm, dragging him away and out of the room, out of the house. As he went, he grabbed his coat from where it hung over the end of the bannister. It still had his mobile phone in the pocket and, as soon as they were outside and a safe distance from the house, he pulled it out and dialled for the fire brigade.

Just as he was put through, he felt Martin go limp next to him. Turning, he caught a glimpse of someone with his mouth latched firmly on to Martin's neck, just before he was grabbed from behind and pulled backwards off his feet. He felt sharp teeth at his neck and cried out. The phone fell from his hand, while the operator called out "hello? Which service do you require?"

This next stage of Bailey's plan seemed to last for weeks. Slowly, the city started to empty. First, the students started to leave. It was probably easiest for them, as everything bar the most vital services seemed to have shut down or were only working on a skeleton basis and that meant that the majority of lectures were cancelled – except for those given by the fanatical educators, which were the ones which were usually the most sparsely populated anyway. The buses and the Metro had all but stopped, which meant that people ended up congregating at bus stops and in stations. For a while, they grumbled about it in that very English way people have of complaining without actually doing anything.

"Bloody hell," one man said. "It used to take twenty five minutes to get from here to Whitley Bay. Now it takes me an hour and a half to get home. And there's never any bloody seats on the train when it does turn up."

"Aye. Ah hear ya," replied a second man.

Further up the platform towards the entrance, a ripple ran through the crowd, as if someone had fallen over. The ripple turned into a wave front as people pushed against one another, seemingly trying to get away from someone.

"What the fuck…?" the first man said, standing on his tiptoes, trying to see.

"Ah, y'knaa what it is. It's prob'ly some pissed bloke flailing around or throwing up everywhere."

"Or the vamps have come for us," a teenager said, laughing. A few people laughed at this comment, while others stared at him with mild disgust for even daring to try to make a joke, no matter how weak, about such a serious situation.

There was another shove, this time from behind and then a woman on the other side of the track started calling and pointing, shouting at them to get away.

"Come on, man. Whose shoving back? I mean, what's the point?"

And then he heard the first scream. It was a cry of pure, unadulterated terror and it seemed to freeze everyone in their tracks for a moment.

Then, a woman jumped down onto the tracks and ran straight across. She was followed by another and another and then the floodgates opened as people leapt, lemming-like, from the platform and scrambled over the lines to get to the far side.

The first man saw what had caused the stampede and, without even thinking, he pushed aside those people in front of him, leapt down off the platform edge and followed. The vampires *had* come for them.

Unfortunately, at that moment, almost as if the vampires had planned it that way, the Metro train from the coast towards the town centre arrived around the bend. It had slowed down and was coming to a halt, but it still had the full length of the platform to go.

The last thing the man saw was the terrified, screaming face of the train driver as he frantically pulled on the emergency brake.

After that, people stopped travelling on public transport. If they had nowhere else to go, they tended to stay at home, not quite huddled together, but not straying too far from one another, hoping and praying that their home wouldn't be the next to have the window smashed by a Molotov cocktail.

#

It was the third time that Rachel had stood on the quayside waiting for a boat to arrive. The major difference this time was that it was the middle of the day. The sun was shining brightly and the gulls were screaming in their constant search for food. But, apart from Rachel, the coach driver and a man who was sitting on the edge of the quay smoking, his legs dangling over the edge and a semi-automatic rifle at his side, there was nobody around. All the fishmongers and cafes that lined the street were closed up, their shutters firmly locked.

The boat that tied up at the edge of the quay was larger than Bjorn's boat. Even before it had tied up properly a gangplank had been extended from the deck to the quayside. Rachel's guard stood at the head of the gangplank, rifle at the ready, cigarette discarded.

A large, ugly man, one ear missing and a scar running from the hole where it should have been down his neck and inside his shirt, came ashore and held his hand out towards Rachel.

"Are you Miss Cantrell?" he asked in a heavy Eastern European accent.

"That's me," Rachel said.

"The Count sends his regards to Mr Bailey and says that he hopes that his plan succeeds. He said for you to tell Mr Bailey that if there is anything he can do, Mr Bailey just has to ask."

As they talked, two more men climbed off the boat, one with a machine pistol in his hand, the other holding a rope that led back on-board. It was quite loose in his hands and he looked bored as a young woman followed him, the rope looped around her neck and then trailed from her to loop around that of a young man following her and then another girl and another boy and on and on. It was obvious that their spirits had been thoroughly broken and they were now little more than sheep willingly being led to the slaughter.

"I'll pass the message on, I am sure he'll be really pleased to hear that."

The sailor reached inside his coat and pulled out a small package.

"This is the special item that the Count promised Mr Bailey."

"Thanks. He's been looking forward to getting this."

After a couple of minutes, all of the roped-together people had disembarked from the boat and were standing in a huddle.

"There you go," said the sailor. "Twenty girls and boys. All virgins and all clean of drugs and disease. I hope that Mr Bailey enjoys them."

The sailor who had guided the captives off the boat came over to them and offered the rope to Rachel. For a moment, Rachel didn't quite know what to do, but then she took it.

"Thanks again," she said.

Turning away from Dracula's minions, she headed towards the coach, forcing the others to follow her.

The sailors didn't look back as they returned to their boat and cast off. Rachel, on the other hand, watched as they sailed away until the coach started to drive off, its passengers sitting as far away from Rachel as they could.

On the seat next to Rachel was the small package that had been the actual reason for the sailor's journey.

#

It was probably the first time that the mayor had stood in front of the famous black door of number ten Downing Street. She had met the Prime Minister a couple of times before, but it had always been on the times when he had come to Newcastle, either canvassing or just seeking publicity. Admittedly, the PM had no particular reason to come to the city. His constituency was somewhere in the South East and he was an avowed Southerner. His party tended to target the areas that seemed to be most in need – the North, or in Scotland or Wales – rather than in the South, as hotbeds of laziness, asylum seekers and benefit fraud but, considering that sometimes his party seemed to be lucky if they made it into second place in those areas, it was hardly surprising.

But, there stood the mayor of Newcastle City Council, on the television, in front of the doors, looking slightly uncomfortable to be standing next to the person she had once memorably described as 'an upper-class idiot who was a shining example of everything that was wrong with the private education system and had no concept of the needs and desires of the ordinary British citizen'. So, when she smiled at him it looked a little forced.

"It is absolutely the last thing I wanted to do," she said. "But the on-going situation in Newcastle has forced this upon me. I have been in conference with the Prime Minister and we have agreed that we have no other alternative than to declare martial law in Newcastle and the surrounding areas."

She paused and stepped back, persuading herself to grant the Prime Minister another tight little smile as he stepped up to the microphone.

"Thank you, madam mayor," he said. "This has been a most trying time for you and you have conducted yourself admirably. Please, let me be the first to say that I have absolutely no desire to see British troops posted on the streets of a British city, let alone one that should be as bright and vibrant as Newcastle." He pronounced it 'Newcarstle'. "However, as Mrs Goodwin said, we feel there is no other alternative. As of midday, all police have been issued with regular firearms. By this evening, troops from Catterick Garrison will have arrived to reinforce the police and, as well as being armed with regular firearms they will be carrying anti-vampire equipment that has been developed by the freedom fighters in the so-called Hungarian Empire. I can assure the citizens of Newcastle that we are anticipating a swift conclusion to this situation and they will be able to go back home and start to get things back to normal."

The cameras of the press photographers started to flash and reporters started to call out questions. Bailey wasn't interested in that, however and he pressed a button on the remote control. The television flicked off and the vampire sat back in his chair.

"What are you going to do now," Rachel asked.

"I don't need to do anything," Bailey replied. "Everything is going exactly as I hoped. We'll keep going and soon it'll all have paid off."

"Aren't you worried about the soldiers with their anti-vamp tech?"

"To be able to use it, they need to be in the same place as a vampire. If they aren't then it's just another useless lump of metal. And, if all they've got is something made by those Hungarian hicks then, even if they do get anywhere near me, I don't think I need to be worried. It takes a little bit more than a lump of wood to get through to me these days, thanks to the Count."

As he said this, he played with the ring on his left finger. It had not been there for long and he was obviously still unused to it. It was a brass ring, faded and tarnished and utterly unlike Bailey's usual taste in jewellery.

#

Bailey was not lying. For all the use that the soldiers and police made of their much-vaunted anti-vampire weaponry over the next few weeks, they would have been better off carrying around a lump of metal. At least then they could have used it to frighten off the few foolhardy souls who had taken the opportunity of an evening curfew to try their hand at a bit of looting. Wherever the military were, the vampires weren't.

Despite that, the vampire attacks started to taper off. Before too long, there were no more than one or two a week; more than the usual number of attacks, but still a lot fewer than there had been at the beginning of Bailey's reign of terror. Some people were even asking if the vampires had finished whatever it was they were doing or even if the army had just frightened them off. Some people even came back into town, although it was hard to tell exactly how many, because they remained inside as much as those who had stayed.

#

It was a cold October day when Rachel found herself back in Heaton again. She had been through there a few times since she had been renfielded but never stopped.

But now, she sat on the bench in front of the bank where she had committed her last criminal act as an independent operator. She looked across to the crossing, expecting to see Kerry but failed. That almost made her feel something then. She had abandoned her. It hadn't been her decision or, at least, not lately. Before Bailey had got his claws into her she had been so distracted by her work for Mott and, when she hadn't been working, she had been screwing Lilly. And she had, of course, been completely screwing her. But not in a good way.

She walked over to where Kerry usually stood. She assumed she'd still be there, she hoped she would still be there. It was entirely possible that she had faded or moved on. Rachel would have been glad, if she could have been, if Kerry had finally allowed her death to take her to… wherever people went when they died… but she would, at the same time, have been sad that she hadn't been able to say goodbye to her. If she had been able to feel anything.

At last, a line of lorries rumbled down the street and pulled into a side street. As they pulled up, Rachel hurried over to the first one and climbed up into the cab.

"You took your time," she said to the driver.

"Sorry boss. The traffic was a bitch." Which was, very obviously, a lie. The only way that this job could ever happen was because of the absolute lack of any traffic whatsoever. Rachel had never seen Chillingham Road this empty, not even at two in the morning. But, she had been sitting and waiting for about half an hour and not a single vehicle had passed. It was kind of eerie, as if she was the last person left alive.

"Well, you're here now," Rachel said, choosing not to follow up on the untruth. "Let's get them out."

They both climbed out of the cab and went round to the back of the lorry. The driver pulled the ramp down, unlocked the rear doors and opened them. It was lucky that zombins were even less aware of things than the average sheep. They had been squashed into the back of the van so that there was absolutely no room to move until the doors were opened, at which point, the front rank fell out and landed with a thump on the ramp, rolling down to the ground before dragging themselves up no worse for wear.

As the other zombins made their way down the ramp, Rachel found herself staring with what would have been described, in normal circumstances, as utter surprise. She'd found Ruby's Uncle Phil. He wasn't looking especially healthy. His flab was flopping around in a way that it never did when he was alive, his jowls were really drooping, the skin threatening to tear. Rachel stared at him, unsure of what to do. She'd promised Ruby, but that was ages ago. Surely she'd have forgotten by now. And she was fairly certain that Bailey wouldn't let him go. Creating a zombin was expensive, certainly a lot more expensive than creating a renfield. Bailey was not renowned for letting his investments go easily. There was no way she could feel guilty for not doing anything about it now, so it must have been just the sudden unexpectedness of coming across something from her previous life, back when she had a life, cropping up now. Anyway, she had a job to do at the moment and that was something that could very easily wait until later. Or perhaps another time entirely.

It may have been a coincidence, or it may have been Bailey's sense of humour, that the first road Rachel had been told to hit was the one in which she ostensibly lived. But, there she was, standing in front of her own house once again. She was just about able to see through the net curtains and she could vaguely make out the living room. Everything looked to be under a thick layer of dust. At least everything still looked to be there. Being so obviously un-occupied could have been an invitation to petty criminals and burglars. In a way, it was down to Bailey's reign of terror that it had remained secure for so long.

Feeling inside her pocket she pulled out her keys and went up to her front door. Unlocking it, she pushed at it, pressing hard against a mountain of mail. Then, stepping back, she ushered the first four zombins inside.

Very soon after they entered, they came out again, carrying the music system that she had spent months building – obsessively reading magazines and articles online, making lists and talking to music geeks in shops. They took it into the back of one of the lorries and placed it carefully. Zombins may have been unfeeling, brain-eating monsters from beyond, but they were excellent furniture removal men.

It didn't take them long to remove every single item of worth from inside her house, leaving it almost entirely bare. They even took cutlery and crockery, ripping out the entire set of kitchen cupboards and just carrying them out with their insides intact. By the time they had reached that point, however, Rachel was no longer watching them. She had gone on to the next house, belonging to Mr and Mrs Marks, a very pleasant old couple. He was an old ex-miner and she had spent her entire life running the household. Fortunately, they had a very wealthy son who worked as a plastic surgeon in Southern California. He was always on at them to move over there permanently but they always resisted. They were as stubborn as Rachel's father had been. But at least they had both been alive. Rachel assumed that they had escaped to America. They certainly weren't in their house anyway.

#

And so it went. From house to house up the street and everyone single one was empty. This was quite an affluent part of Heaton, though – she'd heard these streets being referred to as 'Heaton Village'. Admittedly, it had only been referred to as such by estate agents who wanted to make the area seem more exclusive and so bump up the house prices, but it was certainly true that the area did have a different feel compared with the streets on the other side of Chillingham Road. Whether that was because they were all houses on this side and terraces of flats on the other, Rachel couldn't say and, even when fully in control of herself, she couldn't really bring herself to care, but there you had it. These more affluent (she wouldn't say rich, but they were certainly richer) people had all managed to get away from the terror in the city. It could be argued that coming back home again to houses that had been stripped would be a small price to pay for still having their lives. No doubt their insurance would cover it anyway.

Rachel soon saw that the zombins had managed to get the hang of the job and they didn't need her to point out where they needed to go. So, she went and sat on the wall in front of her own house, looking through the window and into the front room. The net curtains hadn't been taken, but they were in disarray, half pulled open to show the bare room behind them. With the exception of the bad wallpaper and a single over-turned chair that looked like it had had one of its legs snapped in the burglary, there was no sign that she or anyone else had ever lived there. After a couple of minutes of sitting, staring through the glass, Rachel turned to face away from the house. It wasn't upsetting, but, as she looked through the window, she found herself thinking that she should be saddened by it. There was no longer any sign or memory of either the family she had known or those that they had kept alive in memory. It was a bare shell with no emotion left in it.

As each lorry filled up, it was driven away somewhere. Rachel didn't know exactly where it was going, but she could certainly guess. There were only two or three places in the city that Bailey would be able to store this much stuff until she could dispose of it. Bailey's plan was such that he was going to need a lot of money to make sure that it was going to work. And, as far as he was concerned, if the humans weren't going to stick around, then he may as well use their belongings instead of just using them. Ultimately, it would all lead to the same thing.

Rachel got up to inspect the goings on and see if there was anything she needed to do. She didn't think there would be, but she thought she would do it anyway. She glanced down the street towards Chillingham Road and saw that there was indeed something she needed to do. Standing, looking back at her, his mouth gaping in shock, was Inspector Charlton.

"Cantrell!" he shouted. "Stay right there, you bitch."

He stormed up the street towards Rachel, a smile starting to show on his face.

"I knew you'd come back and I knew I'd catch you one of these days, but I have to admit, I didn't think it'd be when you were doing anything like this," he said as reached Rachel.

"I don't like to be too predictable," Rachel replied.

"Just you stay there and don't use any of those freaky powers you've got, either."

"Don't worry, I haven't used them for quite some time now. I think I might have forgotten how, to be honest," Rachel told him.

Charlton flicked the switch on his walkie-talkie.

Quickly, Rachel looked around. Spotting a brick that was coming loose on the wall next to her, she grabbed it and pulled. It came free more easily than she'd anticipated.

Charlton paused and loosed the switch.

"Put that down Rachel," he said. "That's really stupid."

"You need to walk away from here, Inspector," Rachel told him, calmly. "You need to forget about this."

Charlton placed his hand over the butt of his pistol.

"If you threaten me with that, I will have to shoot you," he said, just as calmly. "I am going to take you in and there is nothing you can do about it. Just accept it. You had to know this was coming."

"Please, just go away. I don't have any choice over this," Rachel told him.

"What do you mean? You've always had a choice. Just think what you could have done as a copper. Now. Drop the brick, tell all the zombins to stop what they're doing and come with me."

Rachel waited for a moment, looking at Charlton. Then, hefting it quickly, she hurled it as hard as she could at the police Inspector. Her aim was spot-on and the brick smashed into his face, crushing his nose across his face. He fell backwards, his cap flying off over a garden wall.

Without waiting, Rachel leapt onto him, bringing her brick down again and again. Quickly, Charlton stopped struggling and just lay there on the ground, blood pouring from a face that held no identifiable features. It was a mask of blood and ground meat, with nothing but a ragged slash for a mouth.

Rolling off, Rachel stood and looked down at the body, then looking at her hand, still clutching the brick but now dripping with blood. One of the zombins, carrying a Tiffany Lamp, paused as it went past and looked at the bleeding mess on the ground. It dropped the lamp, which shattered turning an exquisitely designed, extremely expensive piece of furniture into hundreds of shards of exquisitely designed, extremely expensive pieces of broken glass. It took a step towards Charlton and then another, its fingers twitching as the scent of blood activated something in its dead brain.

Wielding the brick again, Rachel clubbed the zombin in the back of the head, making its knees give way. It tumbled to the floor, next to Charlton. One of its hands started to finger-crawl its way over to the body, before Rachel stamped on it, twisting her heel, the zombin's bones snapping audibly.

One of the things that scared most people about zombins, in fact zombies in general, was their silence. They made no noise. There was no groaning or moaning, no grunting or snarling. Nothing. They probably didn't feel pain, but if they did, there was no way of knowing, because they didn't react to it. They would walk through fire and keep going on, completely uncomplaining, even though they were ablaze, until the flames finally roasted their brains or burnt through their spine. So, just snapping the bones in one hand wasn't really going to do anything other than make it use the other hand to get to the meat.

Which is exactly what it tried to do. First, using its other hand it started to pushed itself up, managing to get part of the way, but then unbalancing itself and tipping over on to its back. Trying to use its broken hand to help it, it failed miserably, the hand just giving way and slipping uselessly to one side.

Looking around, Rachel noticed that the garden, in front of which she was standing, contained a rock garden. A nicely designed, healthy looking herb garden with thyme, sage, parsley, mint, coriander and many others growing in profusion. All over a bunch of really big rocks. She leapt over the wall and took hold of the largest one she could see. The soil and the plants had really bound it in tightly, as well as it being very heavy, which meant that Rachel really had to strain to free it from where it lay. It came suddenly, sending her tottering backwards, almost tripping over a rose bush and dropping the stone, narrowly avoiding her foot.

Not daring to pause for a moment, Rachel hefted the rock once again and half-ran out of the gate. The zombin had dragged itself to its knees and was squatting to push itself to its feet. Rachel breathed a silent thanks that the damn things were so slow when they weren't under orders, lifted the rock above her head and brought it down with all her might upon the head of the zombin. One followed the other down to the ground and barely paused as it cracked skull and smashed brain into the tarmac. The zombin shuddered once and then lay still. As still as Charlton.

Looking down at the police Inspector, Rachel said to him, "I tried to warn you."

A gentle rattle came from the ruined remains of Charlton's face. It took a moment for Rachel to realise that he was still breathing. Very shallowly, but still. He was alive.

Rachel turned and called to the drivers of the remaining lorries. Who, she noticed, had all disappeared very swiftly when Charlton had made his appearance.

"Bloody hell," one said. "You've done a right number on him, haven't yer?"

"We're finished here. Get the zombins packed away and get out of here before any more police show up," Rachel told him.

As the zombins were herded into the back of their lorry, Rachel watched. Perhaps the adrenaline rush from having to deal with first Charlton and then the zombin had loosened her renning, just for a moment. Because as Ruby's Uncle Phil started up the ramp, Rachel managed to startle herself by making a decision. Stepping forwards, she pulled Phil by the shoulder. Phil stepped out of line and turned to stare at her.

"Come with me," Rachel told the zombin.

Obediently, it fell into step behind Rachel as she turned and made her way back down the street, away from the crime scene and towards Chillingham Road.

\#

Walking down the street, spattered with blood, a zombin trailing along behind her, Rachel thought it was quite a good thing that there wasn't anyone around. It must have been a very odd sight. While seeing zombins around wasn't that unusual, they were almost always criminals that had been executed for their crimes. As such, they always wore the Community Service issue orange overalls, which had the dual effect of warning everyone that there were dead people at work and, because they were waterproof, holding any fluids that may ooze as they started to break down.

Fortunately, she didn't have far to go. Walking up to Ruby's flat, Rachel wondered what the reaction would be. She didn't think her mother would be too happy. She'd probably got another 'uncle' for her daughter by now who, if Phil's temperament when he was alive was anything to go by, wouldn't be overjoyed to see his woman's previous lover. Especially in his current state. Still, Rachel had made a promise and she didn't want to have to break that promise, considering all the other things that she'd done. Compared to all those other actions, it was a small thing, a practically non-existent thing, but Rachel thought it was important. Having been able to make the decision and not having specific instructions to the contrary, it was actually something she could do.

She paused in front of the door and looked behind her to check that Phil had kept up. She didn't have to worry. It would have been harder to get rid of him.

She pressed on the doorbell and waited. A clatter of shoes on wood indicated that someone was coming down the stairs and then the door swung open. It didn't open very far, stopping as it reached the end of the chain. Ruby peered out at her.

"Rachel?" she said. "I haven't seen you in months. What are you doing here."

"Hi Ruby," she said. "I've been kind of busy. I can't talk about it. I... your uncle Phil... he's..."

"You've found out what happened to him? Hold on a moment," she told her, before closing, unchaining and re-opening the door. "What happened to him? Where is... oh."

She had noticed the corpse standing at the end of the path.

"Uncle Phil?" she whispered, as tears started to trickle down her cheeks. "What happened to him?"

"George Bailey had someone dig his body up and turn him into an illegal zombin," Rachel explained. "I've not seen him before now."

She pushed Rachel out of the way and stumbled towards Phil.

"Uncle Phil?" she said, putting her hand out to touch his hand.

As she reached for him, a spark leapt between them. Rachel smelt the sudden, strong tang of ozone and, for the second time that day, the second time in a long time, felt surprised when Phil suddenly lifted his head and looked directly at the girl standing in front of him. His eyes were clear and his skin had lost a little of its grey sheen.

"Ruby?" he croaked. "I thought I was…"

"I'm sorry, Uncle Phil," Ruby said to him. "You are. You died months ago. But, I couldn't let you go without saying goodbye."

"How am I here?"

"Rachel Cantrell brought you to see me. She found you. Someone's turned you into a zombin. She's saved you and brought you here."

"I… I remember."

He swung his head around to look at Rachel. Although he had some semblance of his life and humanity back, there was still something fragile about his body, as there was around all zombins. It didn't usually matter, as they were normally a lot stronger than they seemed. But Phil looked to be using his remaining life-force up very quickly.

"Rachel… Cantrell? You saved me? I remember you, Rachel. Did you save me? I don't think… I don't know…"

"What does he mean, Rachel? What's he saying?"

Rachel just shrugged.

Ruby turned from Phil and went over to Rachel. Rubbing her hand across her eyes to wipe the tears clear, she looked at him, taking her hand.

"What did you do?" she asked.

There was another spark, a bigger, louder one, accompanied both by the ozone and a stench of burnt hair and flesh. Rachel was hurled backwards, through the doorway, cracking her head and back on the stairs.

"What the fuck…?" she said, her voice drenched with astonishment. "That fucking hurt."

And then she slumped down, head lolling to one side as unconsciousness rolled over her.

Interlude: The Land of Faerie. November 1924

Stepping through the doorway, Francis Emmerson stumbled and fell to his knees, landing in a puddle of muddy water.

"You," he said, pointing to a younger man who had come through the doorway before him and had been patiently waiting for his superior. "Go and get me a clean pair of trousers before the guy shows up."

"That will not be necessary. I am already here."

The voice, a slow, lazy drawl, came from behind him, hidden by the void of the doorway. Emmerson span around, his hand half-reaching for the pistol he had concealed inside his jacket. Sitting there, an amused smirk on his face was the largest faerie that Emmerson had ever seen. All the others to whom Emmerson had talked while setting up this meeting had been uniformly slender and beautiful, so similar in physique that they could all have been related, if he ignored the outlandish colours of their skin. Not that that would have mattered to Emmerson, he was used to dealing with families. This one – he had never worked out if it was correct to call a male Faerie a man – was anything but slender and beautiful. The chair he was sitting on would probably be better described as a throne – gaudy and golden and encrusted with gems. Actually, he didn't so much sit on the throne as engulf it. His violet-skinned fleshy body overflowed it, his belly hanging over the arms, his own arms resting on the enormous bulge that surged out from his huge, pendulous breasts and lay on his massive thighs, covering them almost down to his knees. His fingers had rings on them that could never conceivably be removed, the bands engulfed by the meat so it looked as if the jewels were attached directly to his finger. Even his bald head was fat, rolls of flesh gathering at the nape of his neck and making his cheeks and nose bulge. He had so many chins that they seemed to merge into his cleavage. His eyes were still completely clear however, and the stars that seemed to shine in them burned brighter than those of any other faerie he had ever met.

Emmerson glanced at his subordinate, a brief look that contained several paragraphs of information, mostly related to the discussion that would be forthcoming about the exact meaning of preparation and being the advance party. The recipient of his look, the young man who also happened to be Emmerson's sister's daughter's husband so would probably get away with just the discussion, winced.

Looking back to the vast form sitting in front of him, Emmerson smiled and smoothly moved his hand from his holster to proffer it in greeting.

"Mr Varagon," he said. "A pleasure to finally meet you."

"Count Varagon," Count Varagon replied, ignoring the hand. "And I hope we can conclude this business swiftly."

Varagon gestured around him.

"I loathe all of this," he said. "I want to be back in my halls by nightfall."

Emmerson looked around and utterly failed to find anything hateful. It looked to be a total paradise. He had always thought of retiring to a place that looked like this, although probably closer to home. It reminded him a lot of photographs he had seen of California, where the Redwoods grew.

The door from Earth had opened into a wide parkland surrounded by trees and hills. As his gaze followed Varagon's gesture, it was captured by the sight of deer peeking out of the undergrowth at the edge of the forest. It seemed to stare back at him for a few moments before turning tail and dashing away. A bee buzzed past the end of his nose, intent on whatever it was that bees did. A big bird – maybe a hawk? – he wasn't a birdwatcher, unless it was the pigeons that crapped on his window ledge – floated effortlessly in the clear blue sky.

A sharp cough brought him back to the business at hand. He focused on the corpulent faerie with whom he was planning on doing business.

"Of course, Count," Emmerson said. "This shouldn't be much more than a formality."

"Come and sit, so we may discover the final details", Varagon said, pointing to a chair that had been placed at a table under the eaves of the forest.

As Emmerson walked scross to it, Varagon clicked his finger. His throne creaked somewhat alarmingly and gave a little shudder. Emmerson had time to consider how difficult it would be to lift Varagon on to his feet if the throne were to actually break before it started to move. The legs of the throne moved and Emmerson realised that they were folded away underneath the seat. They stretched and the whole throne stood up, walked across to the table and then re-settled itself.

"Jesus H. Christ," Emmerson said. "Y'know, Count, I know people who would love a chair that did that."

"I do not think there would be enough magic in your world to sustain it for very long," Varagon replied. "But I am willing to discuss it after we have concluded our negotiations on the current matter."

Emmerson sat down and his nieces' husband brought over the briefcase he had been carrying. Inside was a single file with only a few sheets of paper inside it. Emmerson spread them out on the table and then looked up at Varagon, his face hardening. No matter the place or the person sitting opposite, this was, in the end, just another negotiation and it was his job to get the best deal.

"How much of the product can you supply?" He asked.

"As has been told to you on several occasions by my subordinates, I can supply you with as much Dust as you need, for as long as you need."

"I have found over the years that subordinates have a tendency to exaggerate. Before I finally make a deal, I like to hear it from the organ grinder and not from the monkeys."

"And now you have heard it," Varagon replied.

"But y'know," said Emmerson. "The thing that confuses me? What exactly are you getting out of all of this? You say that you can supply all of the Dust that I can sell but not a single of one you have ever said what it's gonna cost me? Now, much as I believe in the goodness of my fellow man, I've got two problems with this scenario. Firstly, I reckon that if you have all of a fella's goodwill and a dime, you'll have enough for a cuppa coffee. Secondly you ain't a man."

Emerson drew his gun from his holster and, without actually aiming it, gave the very strong impression that it could very quickly be pointed at Varagon's forehead and the trigger pulled.

"So," Emerson continued. How's about you tell me exactly what I'm letting myself get into before I get into it."

Varagon smiled and then very deliberately blinked. And something about the way he blinked made Emmerson's eyes start to water. And, in the time it took his eyelids to flick closed and then re-open, Varagon had moved.

No longer was he slumped, seemingly boneless in his mobile throne. Instead, he stood at Emmerson's side, a knife in his hand held ticklingly close to the gangster's Adam's apple. The faeries other hand cupped Emmerson's head softly, almost lovingly, while holding it as steady as a rock at the same time.

"May I suggest, Mister Emmerson," Varagon said, his voice unchanged, still utterly complacent and uncaring. "That enquiring too much into the business of your elders and betters is an excellent method of shortening your already mayfly-like existence."

Emmerson's niece's husband shouted, a wordless cry of annoyance and confusion and started to move towards the pair, his hand reaching for his own pistol. For the briefest of moments Emmerson felt the knife move away from his neck.

Afterwards, when he was trying to explain the sequence of events, how everything had turned to shit so very quickly, to his grieving niece and his livid sister he would be unable to say if the knife that became embedded in the boy's right eye was the one that had been at his own throat and a new one replaced it or vice versa.

"There is nothing physical that we need from your world," Varagon continued, seemingly oblivious to having just killed someone. "We have no need of your weapons. We do not want your money. We do not desire your bodies, although I might have swived your boy there if I had not had to kill him. Trust me when I say that you have no way of comprehending the compensation which we shall receive for this transaction. In our world there was a bird – a goose, I believe it was – which was reputed to lay eggs of solid gold."

"'S a fairy tale," Emmerson gurgles.

"You know the story? Good. Consider this another version of that story. Another tale, told by a different faery. The one difference being, if you continue to ask impertinent questions, it will not be the goose that ends up slit from beak to gizzard. My metaphor may not be entirely apropos but I am certain that you understand. Say 'yes Count Varagon'"

"Yes, Count Varagon," Emmerson repeated.

"Good. It would have been such an annoyance having to find another human intermediary."

The throne lifted itself up the ground once more and made its way round to where Varagon stood. With a sigh, the rotund faery collapsed back into it, the knife returning to the folds of his clothing as he did so.

"I must apologise for the death of your servant," Varagon said. "Good help is so hard to find."

"I'm gonna catch hell from my sister for it," Emmerson said, gingerly dabbing at his throat.

"Family. Such a delight and yet such a burden."

"Tell me about it. And look, Count, I really don't wanna be disrespectful. I really do understand what you were telling me, but I gotta know, even vaguely, what are you getting out of this deal? I mean, is this stuff gonna kill my customers?"

"Are you telling me that you actually care for these people who will be partaking of the Dust? These - what do you call them – junkies?"

"Hell no," Emmerson would have laughed if he wasn't still trying to calm down. "It's just economics. But, if they die too quick, then we can't get as much money as we can out of them and they can't spread the word and grow the market. I mean, your guys showed me what this stuff does and the junkie who tried it loved it and is desperate for more of it. But, if he dies the second or third time of using it then it's not gonna benefit anyone. Knowing what you are getting out of it just means that I'll be able to plan better to make sure we both profit."

"You make a very powerful point. One that I must admit I had not contemplated." Varagon replied thoughtfully. "It is difficult when dealing with – and please forgive me for saying this – with lesser species. For we faerie folk, taking Dust is merely an amusing diversion to distract us from the ennui of our eternal existence. I have no doubt that your customer's time on your earth will be curtailed by using the Dust, but I do not think that they will perish too swiftly. However, it may also be sensible to adulterate the substance a little, to make it a little less potent."

"Yeah, yeah," Emmerson replied. "We always water our stuff down, even with more down-to-earth stuff. It makes it go farther and increases the profit margin, y'know?"

"Very good. Now, for the final time, are you satisfied with our arrangement?"

"Well, I guess so. I just hope it don't come back and bite me on the ass, somewhere down the line."

"My dear Mister Emmerson, in my experience, very few things ever lie dormant. If your behind remains unmarred by this event then I am certain that another will take a goodly chunk from it at some point. I, however, will not be the cause of any rear-end damage."

"Okay. I guess that's gonna have to be good enough," Emmerson said reluctantly.

"I am SO glad," Varagon replied, before slowly hauling himself out of his chair and holding his hand out towards Emmerson.

Emmerson put his hand out to take hold of the faerie's, but instead Varagon clasped his wrist and pulled him close, pressing his lips to Emmerson's.

Pulling away, Emmerson slipped and fall backwards to the ground. Dizziness washed over him for a moment as if he had just been spinning around.

"Hey! What do you think you're doing? I ain't no fuckin' fruit. Fucking, goddamn…"

"No, you misunderstand, Mister Emmerson. This is how we seal a contract. That is all. There was nothing sexual intended I assure you. The first delivery of Dust should now be awaiting you upon your return to your home."

"Well… okay, I guess. Just warn a guy next time…" Emmerson replied, scrubbing his mouth with his sleeve. "I guess that's it then."

"Indeed. I believe you are correct."

Emmerson picked himself up from the ground and tried once again to brush his pants clean, although he quickly realised the futility of his actions and gave up, consoling himself with the thought that with this new deal, he'd be able to buy himself dozens of pairs of pants. Going across to his nephew-in-law's corpse, he picked him up, grunting with the effort.

"Please, do apologise to your sister for me and tell her reparations shall be forthcoming," Varagon told him.

"Yeah, sure thing." Emmerson replied.

"Until next time, Mister Emmerson," Varagon said. "Please do take care and let me know if there is anything else we can do for one another."

"Of course."

Emmerson staggered back to the doorway and, without looking back, stepped through and disappeared. Varagon looked at the place where he had gone for a moment or two and then, with a wave of his hand, dismissed the portal.

As soon as it had disappeared a faerie that until that moment had been standing in the shadows beneath the trees utterly motionless and totally unseen by Emmerson stepped out into the open and walked across to Varagon. This one was much more the stereotypical faerie that the human had been used to dealing with – tall and slender and almost feminine in appearance, with chestnut brown hair, pale green skin and eyes that twinkled like distant stars. He came up to stand in front of Varagon, paused a moment and then sank to one knee.

"My lord," he said. "Is everything as you desire?"

"It is perfect, Aodhán. Emmerson has agreed to be our Earthly distributor. Once again, dreamstuff will flow into our coffers. We just hope that our wife will be happy. For once."

"I am sure she will, sire. The lady Titania knows that everything you do, you do for her."

"We just wish that she would show it now and again," Varagon grumbled.

Varagon stood up smoothly and, as he did so, he changed. His skin darkened, turning a deep midnight blue. Snow white hair sprouted from his scalp and tumbled down his back, long and straight. His knees twisted and turned as white hair sprouted from his calves and his toes and feet seemed to melt and deform, turning into cloven hooves. The clothes that had previously clung to his obese form slipped off and fell in a puddle around his feet. The only features that the faerie now standing before Aodhán shared with the form of Varagon were the still flaring, nova-like eyes.

Out of the distance, galloping at a speed unheard of on Earth came a horse that was so black it seemed like a horse-shaped piece of the night sky had fallen to the ground. It slowed and stopped in front of its master who leapt onto its back. Without urging it took off again, carrying a naked Oberon, king of the Faeries back to his palace and his beloved queen.

Chapter Seven

Returning to wakefulness was not a happy experience. Although, having said that, the fact that she could experience the sadness and grief that hit her as she remembered everything she had done over the last few months sent a thrill through her. She finally came back to herself completely with tears of self-hatred fighting with tears of joy. The two conflicting emotions, after so long without anything, were threatening to tear her apart.

Eventually, rubbing her sleeve across her eyes to clear them of tears, she opened them and looked around. She was lying on an old, dirty brown, velour sofa. Springs pricked up into her back and legs, although her head was resting comfortably on a cushion. Sitting across from her, on a pine dining chair, Ruby watched her carefully. Her face was creased into a frown of deep concern. Behind her, slouching bonelessly, stood Phil, ignoring Rachel entirely, all his attention focussed on Ruby, his face shifting between zombified detachment and a look of deep love, almost worship, for his 'niece'.

Unsurprisingly, Ruby's mother didn't seem to be around.

"What the fuck happened?" Rachel said. Her voice was little more than a whisper. It felt as if she had been screaming her throat raw.

"I didn't know you were under an enchantment," Ruby told her. "I think I must have broke it."

"Thank you," Rachel said as she pushed herself up to a sitting position. Her elbows shivered under the strain and threatened to give way and send her sprawling back onto the sofa. "It was Bailey, he'd renfielded me. I didn't know you could do that."

"Neither did I," Ruby told her, then her face broke into a huge grin that lit her face and made her look much more like the little girl she would have been if the magic hadn't worked it's stuff on her. "Dead good, isn't it?"

"Definitely," Rachel gave her a weak, shaky smile in reply. "You're really powerful. When you get a bit older, you're going to be a serious force to be reckoned with."

"And fucking gorgeous," she said.

"Don't swear," Phil said, quietly, his words little more than breaths of air. He was looking less and less lively by the moment as Ruby's untrained magic-casting started to wear off and the spell performed by whichever one of Bailey's tame enchanters it was that made corpses rise started to re-assert itself more and more.

"Sorry, Uncle Phil," Ruby said.

"I've got to get out of here," Rachel said. "Bailey will be expecting me back to report on how the operation went. And, when I don't turn up... Shit, one of the drivers'll tell him that I went off with Phil."

"Don't swear," Phil repeated.

"And he'll work out where I went."

Rachel stood up, tottered on her feet and fell back onto the sofa again.

"I don't think you're going anywhere," Ruby said. "Hang on."

She went over to a sideboard, climbed on a chair and pulled a bottle of whisky down from the top. It wasn't a very good whisky. The label was grey and it was called 'Value Scotch Whisky'. Grabbing a tumbler, she poured out a healthy slug of it and offered it to Rachel.

"Mom always says this is what she needs to get her going. Especially after she's been out on the town the night before."

Rachel eyed the glass of amber liquid. It didn't look too much like whisky, instead there was a distinct look of something she flushed away first thing in the morning. While she could appreciate something that was a bit rough and somewhat less than 10 year old Single Malt, she thought that this one was not going to quite live up to that standard. Still, beggars can't be choosers, she told herself. She accepted the glass with a nod of thanks, paused for a moment in anticipation and knocked it back, hoping that it would shoot straight down her throat and bypass her taste buds as much as possible.

It still made her utter a strangled 'Jesus Fuck', though, as it went down.

"Don't swear," Phil said again. This seemed to be his last coherent thought as his face and posture both collapsed into the limp listlessness that characterised a zombin with no orders.

Despite the awfulness of the drink – Rachel was loathe to name it whisky – it did the job and she felt a warmth flow through her veins as the alcohol burned away in her stomach. She was at last able to stand and make her way, still a little unsteadily, towards the front door.

"I'll take Phil with me," she said. "Your mom really won't want him around the place. And, to be honest, I don't think he's going to last much longer. I think your spell really took it out of him. I'll make sure he gets put back where he should be."

"Thanks Rachel," Ruby said. "What are you going to do about Bailey? He'll know you're not renned anymore, won't he?"

"Well, if he doesn't yet, he will as soon as he sees me," Rachel said. "I dunno. I'll think of something."

Suddenly, Ruby threw her arms around Rachel and squeezed her tightly.

"Thanks Rachel. I'll not forget this, really I won't," she said.

"I should be thanking you," Rachel told her. "You freed me from Bailey's control. There's nothing I can do to repay that."

"Good luck," she said. "Be careful."

"Ah, I'll be fine. I can sort Bailey," Rachel said, giving her another smile, this one a lot stronger and more confident than before.

As she shut the door, leaving Rachel and Phil standing there, she added, "Somehow."

#

Standing on the street, looking up and down, failing to see a single person, made Rachel feel even more bereft than she had inside Ruby's flat. Only having a zombin for company, even one with its personality restored, was not a particularly positive thing. Especially when that zombin's personality was Phil Marshall. And his personality, along with his entire body was rapidly disintegrating.

Despite what she had said to Ruby, she didn't have the first idea about how she was going to go about 'sorting' George Bailey. If the police and the military hadn't succeeded, then how the hell was she going to? She supposed she had a couple of advantages. Firstly, she knew where Bailey was. Having seen the way they were scouring Newcastle, without going into the surrounding towns and villages, Rachel reckoned that it would take them to just this side of Ragnarok before they found his house out in Darras Hall. Although, considering the reports that regularly came out of Norway, that could be anytime from next Sunday onwards. Secondly, she was a ghostkin, which meant that she had powers and abilities, 'beyond mortal ken'. Or even mortal Barbie. Which should help a bit when she was trying to knock off a bunch of vampires.

Even with those two wonderful advantages, though, she reckoned that she would still last about thirty seconds. She thought, briefly, about just getting the hell out of there and finding somewhere warm and sunny to hide out. *Preferably where the sun shone twenty four hours a day, seven days a week.* But, she couldn't think of anywhere quite like that just at the moment and, without it, she reckoned that Bailey would be able to find her. And, find her he would. Bailey would not take kindly to losing his little human puppet, nor would he like the idea that there was someone who could actually break his control over someone he had renfielded. Which led to another thought. She owed Ruby something and leaving her behind meant leaving her in danger. *Fucking hell, was she actually getting a conscience?* She guessed that, if she tried hard, she could put it down to self-preservation, but, really, she knew – and not all that deep down, either – that it wasn't just that. She needed to try to stop Bailey. Partly because she wanted revenge for the months she'd spent being humiliated and degraded – which reminded her, she needed to do something with Lilly as well – but also because she really hated seeing Newcastle like this and she didn't see anyone else actually doing anything about it. She had a horrible feeling that if there wasn't some kind of breakthrough soon, the government would just leave the place and allow it to be run by Bailey. *Which was, of course, exactly what the miserable bastard wanted.* Hell, they'd probably end up negotiating something with him anyway. After all, it's not like these people actually voted for this government. Losing the North East would probably help cement the government's power. *Christ, she needed to talk to someone.*

Reverend Susan Donahue looked out from her pulpit and felt a mixture of gladness and sorrow. She was glad that so many people had managed to find their way to church after so long a drought of believers. She was, however, sad that it took a crisis of this magnitude to drive them here. And she was fairly certain that most of them would disappear when it was all over. Still, if she did her job well, maybe she could get some of them to stay. She almost wished that some angels had appeared at the same time as the faeries and the Valkyrie and the dragons and everything else. But, at the same time, she berated herself for wishing that. She didn't need physical proof to bolster her faith. And there were some extremely convincing arguments that the lack of anything Christian appearing actually helped to prove their existence. All these other things that had appeared had generally been accepted as being mythological or legendary. Fictions, in other words. So, it stood to reason that if God, Jesus and the angelic choir did exist then they wouldn't appear along with all these other storybook characters. The lack of any appearances by Allah, Jehovah, Vishnu or Buddha was slightly annoying, but it wasn't an insurmountable problem.

Finally, the silent introspection and prayer was done. Susan gave the benediction and the service ended.

Slowly, everyone filed past. She had a kind word for most, asking after the health of relatives and welcoming newcomers with the sincere hope that they had enjoyed the service and would return soon.

Eventually the last worshipper had shaken her hand and departed. She took a tube of disinfectant gel out of her pocket and rubbed it onto her hands and went back into the church, to discover that the last worshipper had not actually left. She was, instead, sitting in a pew, reading through the bible.

"Can I help you?" she said.

The woman turned around.

"Rachel Cantrell," she said. "I haven't seen you since your mother's funeral. Where have you been? I mean, I know that you only came along because of her, but I did rather hope that you wouldn't give up quite so quickly."

"Yeah, sorry, Reverend," Rachel said. "I've been kind of busy."

"So, what brings you back after all this time?"

"I need your advice and your help, Reverend."

Susan was taken aback by this. In all the many, many years in which she had known Rachel, even back in their time at school, she had never, ever known her to ask for advice and, if anyone had ever tried to offer any, it had been flung back in their face with a contemptuous sneer.

"Please, call me Susan. I think we've known one another long enough and said more than enough to each other to be able to dispense with any kind of formality," she said, "And, of course, if there is anything I can do to help you, you just have to ask."

"You might regret saying that," Rachel told her. "But thank you."

She paused and took a deep breath.

"I need some holy water," she told her. Now that it was out, it didn't seem like such a large request. Indeed, it probably wasn't. When she wanted to know what it was for, though, that could be when the problems started. And she'd want to know...

"Of course. That's no problem. What is it for?"

...Immediately.

She looked at her a moment, considering whether or not she should tell her the truth. A simple lie would be easier and save Susan a lot of heartache. After all, she reckoned that the Archbishop of Canterbury probably wouldn't countenance the use of religious paraphernalia to do what she intended to do. And, there was always the question of plausible deniability. But then... Ah, fuck it.

"I want to kill vampires with it," she said.

She looked at her silently and steadily for a minute.

"You're not kidding, are you?" she said at last.

"I wish I was," she replied. "I wish I could just leave and forget about the whole thing, but I can't."

"What happened to you?"

"George Bailey renfielded me," she said. Actually finally being able to come out with those words and tell someone else felt like a dam had broken in her heart. Everything that had happened to her, everything she had done suddenly washed over her. She slid off the pew, down onto the cold, stone floor of the church, curling up almost into a foetal position.

"Oh god," she said, as the tears fell from her eyes. "What have I done?"

At that moment, in that place, she couldn't tell if she was praying or blaspheming. At that moment, in that place, she didn't think there was much difference.

Susan quickly knelt next to her, put her arms around her shoulders and started to rock her gently, almost as if she were a baby.

"Whatever happened to you," she whispered to her. "Whatever you did. It wasn't you."

She had dealt with people who had been freed from renning before, when they had finished their stint at Her Majesty's Pleasure. She had even been there for Rachel when she had been released after her first, lawful, period of being renned and had decided to continue her transitioning to living as a woman which had been so cruelly interrupted by her arrest. She had been one of her first cases when she was still in university studying religion and starting her training to become a lay minister. Not that Rachel had wanted any help that time. She was determined to do it all - transition, recovery from her time renning, all of it - by herself.

Susan had never, ever come across anyone who had had it done to them by a vampire and who had not been cared for by someone responsible. She had, of course, heard stories of renned convicts being used and abused by unscrupulous individuals who were meant to be looking after them, but few of the stories seemed to have any actual basis in fact. She had always been led to believe that someone who had been renfielded was able to act in self-defence, but that was lawful renning, done by a legally appointed Mage of the Court. She thought that it must differ, quite significantly, from being renned by a vampire. She couldn't imagine what she had gone through. And, to be honest, she didn't want to. She looked at Rachel's neck, exposed as she tried to curl deeper and further into herself, and was both happy and slightly surprised not to see any obvious bite marks there. Whatever else had happened to her, she didn't appear to have been a vampire's meal.

She sat back on her haunches for a moment, looking thoughtful. She had suddenly remembered a drunken conversation she had had with her husband, shortly after all of this had started. It had been a silly remark, she couldn't even remember which of one of them had said it, but it came back to her now.

"You know, Rachel" she said. "I might be able to do better than holy water. Have you heard of chrism?"

#

"I do not like him being here."

Rachel guessed that she wasn't actually supposed to hear that. Unfortunately, when someone was as annoyed as Susan's husband was, voices tended to carry, even when supposedly whispering.

"I don't like him and I don't like that zombin he's got with him. The damned thing talks. And didn't you tell me he was some kind of gangster?"

Rachel couldn't hear Susan's reply. At least, not what she was saying. He could hear a feminine-sounding, calm and reasonable murmur that came in the moments when Susan's husband was quiet and he assumed that was her. She was very good at remaining calm. She always had been, even when she was a little girl she had been remarkably imperturbable. Apart, obviously, from that one time. That, combined with her unshakeable faith in God, made her ultimate career in the church a foregone conclusion. It had also meant that, even when Rachel had been an insufferable shit, which had been pretty much constantly from the age of about eight until they had stopped being friends around the age of thirteen – some would undoubtedly say that it was still the case – Susan had always been there for her. She really didn't deserve her, not then and not now.

"I don't think you should claim him - sorry, 'her' - as a friend, either. I mean, what are you doing helping 'her'? Can you even trust 'her'?"

Rachel sipped her tea, while the argument continued in the

kitchen down the passageway.

"And that's meant to make me feel okay with it, is it? 'She's' an old boyfriend, therefore everything's okay. God, just saying that makes me want to throw up. It's perverted. And, I mean, you told me what he did to you. Isn't that enough to tell him to just get lost?"

Susan's reply, while the words were still unheard, the tone was becoming a little more strident.

"It's bad enough having to deal with all the crap that's going on out there," her husband said. "I wanted us to go away, to go to London and stay with my mother until all this stuff was sorted out. But no, you needed to stay here. You had a 'flock' to deal with. Do you think any of those arseholes out there give a toss about whether you're here or not?"

This time, Rachel couldn't hear anything of her reply. She knew that when Susan got angry she never raised her voice. Instead, she went in completely the opposite direction and got very, very quiet.

"So you had a full house today? Well, whoop-de-fucking-do." Her husband did not get quieter. "Do you seriously think that any of them believe that you can help them against a vampire trying to rip their heads off? The church is a last resort for most of them."

Rachel had had enough. She put her tea on the coffee table and stormed down the passageway into the kitchen.

"Oh, Rachel. No," Susan said as she came in.

"Do you have any idea what a complete fucking twat you sound," she said, ignoring Susan, ironically because she was too angry for her. "The whole point of the church is to act as a last resort. It's there to bring hope to the hopeless. Whether there is a god or not is fucking immaterial. A shitload of people have fucked off and left everyone else in the fucking lurch. Your wife could have done that, god knows, enough other priests, vicars, fucking... I dunno... imams and rabbis did just that. But your wife, she knew that she had a job to do. She's pretty fucking amazing. She didn't need to help me, but she didn't even have to think. She saw an opportunity to do some good and maybe, just maybe, help everyone and she took it. If you can't see that then you are a bigger fuckwit than you seem to be. And you seem to be a pretty fucking big one at the moment. And, one other thing –

you asked her if any of them believe that she can stop a vampire? I can name one person, at least, who has every faith in her ability to do just that. Me. I came to her because I believed that she could help me and I couldn't think of anyone else who could."

"This is my house," Susan's husband said. "You do not speak to me like that in my house. Get out of here. Get out of my fucking house."

"It is not your *fucking* house," Susan said, her voice low and bitter. "It is my house. It is God's house. You live here with me not the other way around. I had to stay and I was glad that you stayed with me. I thought it meant that you supported me. Now I see I was wrong. If you can't see that I am needed here – and that helping Rachel is part of that job – then you don't know me as well as I thought you did. And I certainly don't know you. If you still want to run away to London, then you'd best do it. If you are going to stay here then I need your support and your strength. Complete, one hundred per cent and absolutely unstinting."

"You just want me out of the way so you can see if there's still a cock in those knickers," he said to her, his voice slippery with spite. As he said the words, though, his face changed, as if he hadn't known what he was going to say until it was out of his mouth. "Oh shit, I'm sorry, Susie. I didn't mean that... it... it just slipped out."

"Leave," Susan said. "Now."

She turned away from him and towards Rachel.

"Come on, Rachel. I'll show you what we need to do."

She led her out of the kitchen and down the passageway to her office.

"Grab your tea from the front room," she told her, as they passed the doorway. "We may be a while."

#

When Susan had told her that it would take three days to prepare the chrism properly, she had nearly sighed in deep despair. Just in time, she had managed to hold it in, reminding herself that this was probably the biggest favour anyone had ever done her. It would probably count as one of the biggest favours in the history of the world, up there with the guy who had carried Jesus' cross for a little while. So, she resolved to remain quiet and do what she could to help her speed things up. Which, to be honest, would probably not be much more than making cups of tea for her. And eating. It wasn't until she had stopped that she had realised how hungry she actually was. Thinking back over the last months, she realised that, she had only really eaten enough to keep herself alive and no more. Looking at herself in the mirror, she realised how incredibly skinny she was. Her elbows were knobby outcrops on arms that were almost skeletal. Her ribs showed starkly under her skin and her face was little more than a skull with deep-set eyes and sharp cheek bones. What was odd was that, despite the ravages of neglect that her body showed, she was clean. That was one thing of which Bailey had always made sure. That and allowing her to keep taking her hormones. Although it may be more true to say that he didn't think about it. Whether he would have been bothered about it if he had, she didn't know, nor did she care to speculate.

Really, this enforced rest would be a welcome thing. She would need to gather what little strength she had in order to see it through to the end. She had few illusions about what that end would entail and who would ultimately come out the victor, but she did have to try. And, if she was dead, then she wouldn't have to deal with all the guilt that her recent actions caused. Unless Susan was right and the only thing she had to look forward to after this suicidal assault on a vampire's stronghold was a delightful afterlife in the pits of hell. But then, if she was at all honest with herself, which she was discovering appeared to be a side-effect of her new-found conscience, she would – she almost said probably, but that honesty made her mentally edit that word out and replace it with 'definitely' – be going there anyway. Saint Peter would take one look at her, laugh and kick her arse straight downstairs.

She did have one job to do while Susan slaved over the preparation of the chrism. Twice a day, morning and evening, she had to take a bucket full of raw meat, the cheapest, stringiest stewing steak that Susan could get from the butcher's and go out into the back garden to the shed.

The second morning she was there, immediately after she and Susan had eaten breakfast together and she had assured her that it was all going well, Rachel filled the bucket and went outside. Unlocking the shed door, she pulled it open.

"Oh, shit," she said.

Lying on the ground, eyes open, mouth agape, Phil had quite obviously breathed his last. There was absolutely no animating force behind those eyes and, as she watched, a single bluebottle climbed out of his mouth and buzzed away. Rachel had known that Ruby's spell had put a fatal strain on Phil's zombin frame, but she had hoped that he would have lasted until after it was all over. This was both annoying and frustrating. She couldn't really find it in herself to see it as sad, though. Phil had, after all, actually been dead for a long time and all that had really happened was his body had finally stopped moving. After dealing a potentially fatal blow to Susan's marriage and involving her in something that could end up with her own death, there was no way she could leave a zombin corpse in her garden shed. Once the spell that animated them had gone, putrefaction was surprisingly fast as if nature wanted to catch up. There was only thing for it. She was going to have dig a grave. Looking at her arms, she knew this was not going to be an easy task.

Interlude: Heaton. March 1997

Eric couldn't sleep. It was hot, he was really uncomfortable and the thing between his legs was making itself known. Fortunately, he had an excellent remedy for it. Inasmuch as he wouldn't feel how his body felt - how much it made him feel like the boy he didn't want to be - it would be great. Abstractly, he knew that he'd still have to deal with it later, but he was fourteen. He didn't really let the future impinge much on his consciousness. He was all about the here and now. Focussing on the future meant focussing on what was happening to his body and what was going to continue to happen with it. And that really hurt.

Lying back on his bed, he started breathing deeply and slowly relaxed. Over the last few months he had discovered relaxation techniques normally reserved for advanced yoga practitioners and Buddhists. If he had been told this though, he would have scoffed and told you what you could do with your yoga shit. All he knew was that if he wanted to do what he wanted to do, he needed to be as calm as he could be.

Calm, relaxed and consciously not focussing on what he was doing this for, Eric vacated his body. He'd only been able to control this for a year or so, although he'd been doing it since he was an infant, which his mother had said had really scared her the first time he'd done it. Discovering his little body limp and barely breathing at eighteen months or so was the worst moment in her life. If it hadn't been for her ghostly husband, finding Eric's spirit crawling down the wall towards the kitchen focused on getting his bottle, bringing him back to his body and settling him in, she would have lost her mind then and there.

Obviously, having a ghostkin baby was a very strong possibility, it just wasn't the first thing that sprang to her mind when she saw her baby's body lying there. Through those early years, it seemed like Eric would go exploring nearly every other night, roaming farther and farther afield as his strength grew. When he was four, Eric's father discovered him wandering through the cemetery up in High Heaton, running around and annoying all the restless spirits that inhabited it. Although he was unable to physically punish his son, Eric's father was more than able to blister his mind with words and threats that he learned while he was alive and onboard ship. It worked for a little while and Eric kept himself close to home for a good few months after that, although he slowly started to tug at his restraints again, testing the patience of both his living and dead parents.

His unconscious spirit walking became more and more infrequent as he got older until he was about eight when it seemed to stop completely. Suddenly discovering what normality was like was a huge comedown for the young boy, being unable to go anywhere and do anything without any boundaries was terrible and he compensated by trying to do it corporeally. Which didn't work. He spent many, many hours in detention and exclusion over those next few years. And every night, when he lay in his bed, he would try to force himself out of his body, growing more and more frustrated and angry at his lack of success. It was made even worse by his father's insistence that he couldn't help – claiming that his ghostly existence had not been a choice seemed like a cop out to Eric.

So, that night, a few weeks before his twelfth birthday when he had suddenly slipped free of his body and floated there a couple of feet above it, had been huge. Even more so though was the discovery that his ghost self was female. He had spent the entire night practising and getting stronger and better. He hadn't spent an entire night inside his body since then. One of the things that he often wondered about was whether his father had ever noticed the differences between his son's corporeal body and his ghost self. Whether it was one of the reasons for the apparent dislike of his son.

Tonight was going to be special. He'd had the idea a few weeks ago, when Mark Farmer had talked about seeing Maggie Ryan with her top off. Maggie was one of the few girls who had grown anything approaching something that could be called breasts and Farmer, who had until then been a bit of a joke – crap at PE and a swot and a teacher's pet – suddenly became a celebrity. Nobody quite believed him until Maggie had come up to him and slapped him as hard as she could across the face. She had been excluded for that, mainly because she was too embarrassed to say why she had done it, but all the kids had known and in the boys' minds it answered the question of whether or not Farmer had been making it up. After all, surely no-one would react like that if hadn't been true.

So, if Mark Farmer, who was a bit of an arsehole, could become popular for just seeing a girl's tits, surely Eric, who was much more popular, would become an absolute superstar by seeing a totally naked girl. He reckoned that he could handle a slap to the face and it would be totally worth it. And he knew exactly who it was he wanted to see. Susan Edwards was even more developed than Maggie Ryan. And he had wanted to get back at her ever since she decided that she didn't want to be his girlfriend any more. It was one of the things that confused Eric though. If he was really a girl on the inside, why did he still like girls? But he definitely did. He had no interest in boys -

not *that* way. He wanted to be a girl and he wanted to kiss girls - and more, if he could work out how girls would do that together.

He rose up through the ceiling and out of the roof of his house and up into the sky before angling himself over towards Armstrong Park. Susan lived in the houses on the far side of the park, down next to the Ouse Burn. It would have taken about twenty minutes for Eric to walk there, but, flying in his spirit form, it took no more than five, which was something else he loved about his ability. Being able to shoot around the city like Superman was just amazing and was the thing he had missed most of all in the years he had been unable to spirit walk. He would almost be willing to give up all the rest if he could just keep this one.

Gliding down towards the Edwards' house, Eric saw three or four pretty water sprites playing in the water of the Ouse Burn. Their skin shimmered as the moonlight caught their naked, wet skin and they slid over and around each other, like rapidly running water. One of them glanced up and saw Eric. Being supernatural creatures they were able to perceive other similar beings, including a spirit walking human. They quickly stopped playing with each other and rose up out of the water, their long silver-blue hair, plaited with river weed, falling down over their breasts and called out to him to come and play, that they knew lots of fun games that they would love to teach him. Eric paused for a moment, looking down at them, as they draped over one another, water dripping, playful smiles on their lips as they called to him. He was tempted. If they could see him, they could perhaps touch him. And who knew what they would be able to do? But, he had a mission. And anyway, he had read enough Grimm and Perrault to know what happened to mortals who fooled around with otherworldly beings. He waved at them and rose higher into the air once again.

Hanging in the air in front of the house, Eric suddenly felt a touch of apprehension. *Was this the right thing to do?* Well, he actually knew the answer to that one. Obviously, he knew he was invading a friend's privacy, for the sake of his own popularity. Although on second thoughts, that was perhaps pushing things a bit far, to say that she was a friend. After all, she hadn't spoken to him in months after she had decided that he wasn't 'Christian enough' for her. Which was fair enough, he'd pretty much come to the conclusion that there wasn't any God. There was too much other magical and otherworldly stuff that did exist – faeries and vampires and wyrms and werewolves and, well, him – for him to concern himself with something magical and otherworldly that didn't seem to have an effect on the world. He thought he'd explained this quite well to Susan at the time, but she hadn't taken kindly to it.

Anyway, that was all in the past now. If she didn't want to be his friend then he was quite content to let her be an enemy. And all was fair in love and war or something.

He had never been in her bedroom, never been in any rooms other than the kitchen and the living room, so Eric wasn't sure of where she would be. He paused in front of her house and tried to work out what he should do. There were a couple of lights on upstairs and he thought that one of them would probably be her room. He chose one of the lights and floated towards it. If he had been in his body, he would have been holding his breath in anticipation as he passed through the wall.

He had gone to bed especially early this evening and so he was hopeful of catching her before she did the same. He had visions of her wearing something lacy and see-through, the sort of thing he'd seen when flicking through his mother's catalogues, imagining himself wearing and filling them the way the women in the pictures did. But even as he thought this, he knew the truth was likely to a be a lot more mundane – she'd be naked, if he was lucky, but knew that flannel pyjamas or a long nightie were more likely.

As soon as he entered the room, he knew it wasn't hers. Rather, it was that of her little brother, Liam, an annoying brat six years younger than Susan that Eric had never liked and had tortured whenever he had been able, insisting that he had been a mistake and his parent's hadn't actually wanted him. Smiling to himself, Eric went over to Liam's bookshelf and, willing himself to turn a little more substantial, ran his hand long the shelf, knocking all the books to the floor with an enormous crash.

Liam was lying in bed, reading a comic book and nearly wet

himself when the books appeared to leap off the shelf. He screamed and, within moments, Susan was there, dressing gown wrapped tightly around herself, followed soon after by both of their parents.

"What happened?" Susan asked.

"The books," Ryan said. "They just fell down."

"They can't have just fallen down," their father said. "You must have been doing something."

"I wasn't. I was just looking at my comic and they fell down."

"Books don't just fall down, Ryan."

"These ones did," the boy insisted.

"Maybe they weren't stacked properly," their mother said. "And they just decided that now was the time to fall over. It happens sometimes. Let's all just calm down and we'll sort them out in the morning."

"P'raps," their father said. "Whatever. You should have been asleep half an hour ago, Ryan. We'll discuss it in the morning. Back to bed, Susan. Have you said your prayers?"

"I was just finishing my homework, then I was going to, daddy," Susan said.

"Good girl. Off you go."

Eric followed her as she turned and went out of the room. She went down the corridor and into the other room that had a light on.

It looked like Susan had been telling the truth, books lay open on her desk and she went straight back to them and sat down.

If there was anything worse than doing homework, it was watching someone else do it. And, for the next fifteen minutes, that is what Eric did. Susan slowly and methodically completed her maths homework, going back and double checking her answers and doing everything she needed to do to ensure that she had done her best. It was excruciatingly dull. And to make it worse for Eric, she kept her dressing gown tightly wrapped around her body, not giving a single hint of what lay underneath.

However, eventually, she closed her books, gathered her belongings and slid them into her school bag. Standing up from her desk, she stretched and yawned before going to her wardrobe and taking out a clean skirt and blouse, ready for the next day. She went into the bathroom and Eric paused outside. He wanted to see her naked, but he not while she was in there.

After a few minutes she re-emerged, and went back into her room. Eric followed eagerly. At last, this was going to be it. What he'd been waiting for the whole evening.

She went over to her bed and kicked her slippers off. Then she knelt down next to it, pressed her hands together, closed her eyes and started to murmur softly to herself.

Eric was aghast. *Really? Kneeling next to the bed and talking to the big beardy man in the sky? I mean, come on... who did she think she was? Christopher bloody Robin? Surely nobody really did this stuff anymore?*

"Jesus Christ", he muttered.

Suddenly, Susan stopped and looked up. Slowly standing up, her hands dropping to her sides, she turned around. Her lips were still moving in silent prayer, but her fear-filled eyes were scanning the room.

Eric suddenly realised that she had some sort of an aura around her, a softly glowing pink light that seemed to flow from her pores and to puff from her mouth with each silently spoken sacred word.

Looking from one side to the other, she tried to see something that she wasn't sure was really there.

"Hello?" she said softly. "Is there someone there? I can feel you... it's okay... I want to help."

Eric knew that it was time for him to leave. He knew that it was a really bad idea to stick around. But somehow, he couldn't move from where he floated, up in one corner of the room. Whether it was something she was doing – the light that was emanating from her holding him there somehow, or if it was just his own curiosity preventing him from slipping away back through the walls, he couldn't say.

Continuing to scan the room, Susan's gaze passed over him and for a moment, Eric felt her eyes lock with his. The pink light had turned them blank, obscuring everything, but she could apparently still see out of them. Eric wondered if she was even aware of it.

Her gaze continued on but then paused and came back, fixing

back onto his face. She stared, scrunching her face up in a desperate attempt to make out what she was seeing.

"I... I can see you," she said. "What's your name? Do you understand me?"

She paused for a moment and then suddenly took a step backwards. Her calves struck the bed and she fell backwards, nearly falling off the other side. Eric got a very quick glimpse of her knees as her dressing gown flew up.

After a moment, she climbed up off the bed, her face contorted with rage, her pink aura flushed a darker red.

"Eric Cantrell?" she whispered through gritted teeth.

If he could have done, Eric would have blushed. He hadn't counted on her being aware of him at all.

"Eric. Cantrell?" She repeated, more slowly and with a lot more menace. "What are you doing? Was that you in Ryan's room? What am I even asking for? Of course it was. Why are you here?"

"I just…" he started to say.

Eric had no idea whether or not she could hear him or if she just didn't really care, but she interrupted him, a look of understanding washing across her face. Tears sprang to her eyes and started to roll down her cheeks and her face turned as red as her aura with embarrassment.

"You wanted to see me naked, didn't you? You… you…" Words seemed to fail her. Eric could tell that she wanted to swear at him, to call him all the bad names that she had heard but never used. "Just wait until I tell your mother…"

That shook him. His mother would kill him. Suddenly, he found that he could move again. Without another thought, he fled back through the wall and up into the sky. As he shot back across the park and towards his home, he wracked his brains, trying to work out how to recover from this. It was going to be difficult. Really difficult.

Chapter Eight

On the whole, Rachel would have preferred it if Susan hadn't insisted on driving her out to Darras Hall. But, Susan had insisted and Rachel did actually need her. Catching a bus with a rucksack full of clinking bottles was not an ideal part of the plan.

What she did do though, was insist that she drop her off about quarter of a mile away from Bailey's house.

Climbing out of the car, she retrieved her rucksack from the boot and shouldered it carefully. Walking through the streets of Darras Hall, she felt like there were hundreds of pairs of eyes on her. To be fair, it was probably less than ten pairs, although as she went out of sight of one house another set would be clapped on her. The residents of the area would not be happy with someone who looked as skinny and unkempt as her wandering around their well-kept gardens. After all, not even three days of eating well could stop her looking like a total junkie. And the denizens of the area would want only the best, highest quality drug addicts around them. Still, at least she could guarantee that at the moment, it was only going to be humans who were watching. There was at least one more hour before dusk so she was pretty much safe from the attentions of vampires. Of course, they would have zombins and humans, renned and otherwise, keeping an eye out for them, but she reckoned that she'd be able to avoid them. Zombins especially weren't renowned for their stealth.

Coming around the bend in the road which hid Bailey's house, Rachel paused. Carefully, she removed her rucksack and put it on the ground beside her. Hunkering down next to it, she undid the top flap and lifted out several bottles. They were filled with a pale, golden liquid, their caps screwed down tightly. From a side pocket she pulled some rags. At least, they were rags now. Earlier today they had been some of Susan's husband's best linen shirts. Unscrewing the caps, she slipped the rags into the neck of the bottles and, pulling out a roll of masking tape, secured them firmly in place. Rachel figured that by the time she was in a position to throw the bottles, the rags should have soaked up enough of the liquid to make it easy to light.

She left a couple of the bottles there, underneath a bush, then putting the others back in the rucksack, she continued to make her way towards Bailey's house. She crept slowly forward scanning all around her, checking over her shoulder to make sure that there weren't any suddenly silent and subtle zombins creeping up behind. All was quiet. She didn't want to say that it was 'too quiet' because she just didn't want to sound that clichéd. And anyway, if she did seriously think that, something would have to happen. She gave a slight grin. A cat would probably leap out and scare the shit out of her before running away and leading her right into the arms of something evil that would rip her face off.

The way that thought ended wiped the smile off her face. She was actually, knowingly, purposefully making her way towards something – several somethings, in fact – that would very probably be very happy to rip her face off. And then drink her blood. And then, if she was really unlucky, she would survive, only for them to do it to her again. That thought made her pause again and seriously consider just what the fuck she was doing. Did she really think that a bunch of Molotov cocktails, chanted over by a woman she had gone out with when they were both seven years old and apparently granted some kind of mystical powers by a greater being that Rachel in which didn't even believe was going to be of any use against a bunch of hard bastard gangster vampires?

She didn't have anything else to hand though and, if a consecrated Molotov cocktail wasn't going to do the trick because she had problems believing in the all-powerful, omniscient being that handed down the blessing then a cross wasn't really going to be much better. However, maybe she didn't actually have to believe in God for it to work. She didn't have to believe in Ruby's magic for her to break Bailey's hold over her. She certainly didn't have to show any faith in Bailey's ability to take control in the first place. The question of belief had never even come up. So, she considered, maybe Susan just had 'bog-standard' magical abilities that came from the same place as all the other sorts of magic, from Ruby's natural abilities to Oberon's

Faery Glamour to Rachel's own ghosting powers. But, just because Susan chose to believe in a deity that hadn't manifested itself like Odin, Horus or Quetzalcoatl, didn't mean that her magical abilities weren't any less true. After all, what were prayers and blessings if not the religious equivalent of spells?

That conclusion was one that Rachel could really get behind and, whether or not it was true, it certainly helped her feel better about what she was doing. She still thought she was very probably going to die horribly but at least now she had a chance of taking a few of them with her. Maybe she'd even get an actual shot at Bailey and do some damage to him. Wipe his smug grin from his ugly bat-face.

As she got closer to the house, she unshouldered her bag again and pulled out one of the bottles. Reaching into her pocket, she failed to find the lighter she had bought from the garage on the way here. An electric shock of fear and annoyance shot through her, sending a cold sheen of sweat down her spine. Swapping the loose bottle over, she felt in her other skirt pocket and then her coat pocket. It wasn't until she felt it banging against her phone in her inside jacket pocket that she relaxed and actually remembered putting it in there 'for safe keeping so it wouldn't fall out anywhere'. Arsehole that she was.

#

The house was at the end of a long driveway which swept around the side of the house and up to the front which faced away from the road. It looked like a Georgian mansion, or it would have done if it had been half again as big and built a century or so earlier. Still, it was a big place and very pretty. The only downer on the whole property prices thing was that the basement was essentially a charnel house. Being so far away from all its neighbours was a definite plus. No-one could hear the screams of Bailey's victims. And Bailey couldn't hear the terrible music that was drifting over from one of the houses nearby.

Bailey kept an office on the ground floor as well as down in the basement. It wasn't one he went into very often, using it for when he had to meet people who probably wouldn't be happy having to deal with the stench of blood while talking to him and had the clout to make him concern himself with their feelings. Rachel crept up to the window and sneaked a peak through it. The office was empty.

Pulling a wooden stake from the side pocket of her rucksack, she reversed it and used the shaft to break one of the panes in the window as carefully as she could. The glass cracked with a sharp snapping sound and Rachel froze, waiting to see if the sound alerted anyone. It didn't seem to, so after half a minute or so she tapped at the crack again. Slowly, ever so slowly, she manoeuvred one of the broken parts of the pane out of the frame and let it fall inside. It landed on the windowsill, not falling far enough to smash or make any more noise. Taking care not to cut herself, she pulled the remaining pieces of glass from the window, placed them on the ground next to her and, slipping her hand inside, unlatched the window and pushed it up.

Putting the rucksack through, she followed it into the office. Standing once again inside Bailey's house, knowing how close the vampire leader was made Rachel shiver. Up until this point she hadn't been truly frightened but now she could barely bring herself to walk towards the door that led into the rest of the house.

Slowly, unable to remember if the door creaked or not, she pulled it open. It was soundless. Carefully, she poked her head out and looked around. The hallway was as empty as the office. So far, so good, she thought. Creeping out of the room and into the hall she headed back towards the kitchen and the way down to the cellars. Checking her watch, she saw that she had about another half an hour before she could expect any of the vampires to be up and around. That should give her plenty of time to do what she needed to do.

The kitchen was fully equipped with the highest quality kitchenware. Despite Bailey's utter lack of interest in any form of sustenance that wasn't warm, liquid and spurting from a human jugular, he kept an excellent range of foodstuffs for his unrenned human servants. This was considered one of the perks.

Rachel looked through the doorway of the kitchen to discover Ratty, rooting through the fridge, carelessly pushing aside jars and bottles, making the occasional one fall out and rattle at his feet, causing him to jump around and swear as vinegar from a jar of pickled gherkins or a two-thirds empty bottle of wine that had probably been there for about three weeks, splashed out as they hit the floor. Despite his self-inflicted gymnastics, however, Ratty did not consider being a little more careful. Eventually, he stood up, with a satisfied 'hah'. In his hand was a whole, untouched, u-shaped smoked sausage, still in its wrapper. Putting the plastic between his teeth, he tore it open and extracted his succulent treat. Dropping the wrapper on the floor, next to the remains of the food that had fallen out while he searched, he took a large bite, pushing the fridge door shut and turning around. As he turned, Rachel smashed him in the face with a meat mallet that she had picked up from the counter-top. Bones crunched, blood spattered and teeth, mixed with bits of pink sausage meat, flew everywhere. Ratty stepped back on an errant gherkin and his foot slid out from under him, sending him crashing to the ground. As he fell, the back of his head met the marble counter with a solid thud. Rachel leapt forwards onto him, knowing that she had to make her surprise attack count. If Ratty was still conscious then Rachel had no chance of getting down into the cellar. Her mission, most probably along with her life, would be over. She had once seen Ratty get in a fight with one of Bailey's other non-renned thugs. Ratty's ears had gotten a little more torn up and his nose had been re-broken for him, but the other guy was unlikely to walk again. And he had been a lot bigger than Rachel.

Rachel brought the mallet down as heavily as she could on top of Ratty's head. The prongs on the mallet's face broke through his skull with an unpleasant cracking noise, eerily reminiscent of a hard-boiled egg being smashed with a spoon. Raising the mallet, she hammered it down again, causing Ratty's skull to split open, exactly like an egg that had been hit by… well, a meat mallet.

Sitting back and breathing hard, she looked at Ratty's now still form. One thing was for sure, he wasn't coming back from that. He was still breathing, although it was very shallow, but he was completely unconscious. Rachel didn't feel much remorse. This was after all a man who would happily hold a young girl steady while a vampire fed from her while remaining in full control of his own –

admittedly limited – faculties. Frankly, he deserved everything he got.

#

The cellar door stood before her, slightly ajar. Creeping down the stairs, again taking care to make sure that they didn't make a noise, she kept watch for Ratty's friends, renned guards or zombin servants. Rachel kept a firm grip on the meat mallet, still dripping gore, as she stepped from the bottom step onto the concrete floor of the cellar. This side of the vampire's offices looked a bit makeshift. The steps led down to a narrow corridor, walled on one side by the original brickwork of the house and on the other by a breeze block wall. Facing the stairs was a metal door, padlocked and barred. Behind that, Rachel knew, was Bailey's larder, currently holding the final remnants of Dracula's gift. She fished in her pocket and pulled out her key ring, quickly sorting through them and selecting one. Fitting it into the lock on the bars, she opened them and then did the same with the padlock. Pulling the door open, she looked inside. It was completely pitch black.

"Hello?" she said, quietly.

She heard a gentle whimpering in one corner.

"Cover your eyes," she said. "I'm going to turn the light on."

"Please… no…" There was a girl who was still alive and conscious anyway. "Let me go. Please. I won't tell anyone."

"It's okay," Rachel told her. "I'm going to help you. Here comes the light."

Flicking the switch in the corridor, the room lit up. It was as dismal as she remembered it. There were two people – a girl and a boy - still there, huddled together on a single mattress in one corner of the room, they were filthy and stinking and naked, with dirty, blood-stained bandages wrapped around their necks. Even the dull glow from the forty watt bulb made them moan with pain and lift their hands up to their eyes.

"You aren't one of them, are you?" said the girl who had spoken before, her Eastern European accent made even stronger by her fear.

"You're human like us. Why are you doing this?"

Rachel remembered many of Bailey's victims saying some variation of that to him at some point in their incarceration. The guilt sent an almost physical stab of pain through her chest.

"I'm truly sorry. I couldn't help myself, but I'm going to help you now. Wait here for a few more minutes and I'll get you out of here."

She put her rucksack on the floor and shucked off her jacket and shirt, leaving her in her camisole.

"Put these on," she told them. "Wake up the boy and get ready. I'll be back in a few minutes. I'm going to close the door again, but I won't lock it and I'll leave the light on."

"Where are you going?" she asked.

Rachel squatted down, pulled the rucksack open and pulled out a couple of bottles.

"I'm going to burn the fuckers," she said to her.

She turned for the door again but paused as she reached it and looked back.

"What's your name?" she asked.

"Eva," she told her.

"I'll be back soon, Eva," she said. "Be strong."

Back out in the corridor, she looked back and forth, listening carefully for any signs of life. She had been remarkably lucky so far and was desperately hoping that it wouldn't run out just yet. At one end of the corridor, a heavy door blocked off Bailey's private apartment, where he had his main office and his… Rachel didn't want to call it his bedroom, but the only other word she could come up with was 'crypt'. The other end had a somewhat plainer door, behind which the other vampires in Bailey's group had their rooms. It had also been where she slept, when Lilly hadn't been using her, both of which were memories she tried to avoid thinking about too much. Well, this would help to exorcise one of them at any rate. Slowly, with a heavy tread, she walked towards it.

Behind the door was… well, it was a perfectly ordinary room. Large and messy with several comfortable, over-stuffed sofas, it held a television, Blu-ray player, a music system and a couple of games consoles. Most of the vampires in Bailey's pack were turned relatively recently and had been quite young when he had created them. As such, they were still very much in the thrall of their mortal, human creature comforts. They enjoyed nothing more than spending a few hours on some online shoot 'em up using their insanely fast reflexes to destroy the opposition. Apart, that is, from drinking the blood of innocents. Or even the not-so-innocent.

The room had another couple of doors in it. One, she knew led to a cupboard that was full of junk. The other led to the vampires' sleeping chamber – that was a much better phrase than either bedroom or crypt. They only had one for all of them to rest in, but really it was all they needed. During the day they were entirely quiescent, almost comatose. It took an awful lot to wake a vampire from its daytime slumbers. Well, Rachel certainly had some serious plans to give them an extremely rude, not to mention warm, awakening.

Carefully, she pushed the door open and sneaked a peek. There were half a dozen vampires all comatose on their beds. Pulling her lighter out of her pocket she flicked it on and set the flame to the now damp cotton rag.

The chrism wasn't exactly the real thing. Usually, it was olive oil that was consecrated. The liquid in these bottles was somewhat different, however. This was high grade, unleaded petrol. Susan insisted that it would still work. It wasn't the liquid that was important, it was the ritual. In theory, she could consecrate anything from 7-Up to Hydrofluoric acid. The former wouldn't have been as effective against the vampires and the latter would have been really difficult to transport. And neither one was especially flammable. So, petrol it was…

The rag flared up quickly, almost making Rachel drop it with surprise. Quickly, she hurled the bottle as hard as she could into the middle of the room. It shattered and the petrol splashed everywhere, exploding with a huge '*whoomph*' of air. The sheets on the beds caught light and the vampires stirred, starting to return to consciousness.

Rachel pulled another bottle from her rucksack and threw it towards one side of the room. It hit the wall above the beds on that side and shattered. Petrol showered down on the prone vampires. Immediately it touched them and even before the flames lit the liquid, their skin started to blister and smoke. That finally woke them up. Almost as one, they started to scream and thrash. And then the petrol caught. The beds burst into flames, the vampires that lay on them following suit.

Remembering what she was doing and pulling himself away from the mesmerising view before her, Rachel pulled another bottle from the bag and turned towards the vampires on the other side of the room. They had managed to wake up and climb from their beds.

"Cantrell," one of them shouted in recognition. His voice was strained with pain and fear as the touch of the holy oil burned into his skin. "You will die slowly for this."

Rachel threw the bottle in her hand directly at the vampires. The one who had called out to her ducked and leapt forwards through the flames. The others weren't as fast and were liberally sprayed with petrol that almost immediately set them alight.

The first vampire had managed to get through the flames and was making his way towards her. His hair was burning fiercely, making it look as if he was wearing some kind of novelty hat. Rivulets of burning petrol dripped down his face, into his eyes, over his ears and onto his shoulders. There was no way that he could see anything, but still he kept coming, arms outstretched and fingers grasping. Pulling another bottle – a hasty glance showed that she still had a couple left, enough for Bailey – she quickly unscrewed the cap and shook it out, spraying it over the oncoming horror.

Rachel bent down and picked up the meat mallet that was lying where she had dropped it. Waiting until nearly the last moment, she lashed out, both hands around the mallet's handle, smashing the vampire backwards and knocking him off his feet into the flames. Writhing and screaming, hands and feet drumming the ground in an agonising dance, the vampire was utterly engulfed in flames.

Leaving the door open, to allow the flames to spread, she turned and ran back through the living room and out into the bare corridor.

The door into the cell was open.

"Fuck," Rachel swore. "I told them to stay put."

Running up to the door, she looked in and saw that they had actually done as they had been told. Standing over their corpses, not even bothering to drink from them, hands red and dripping, Bailey was looking straight at Rachel when she looked through the door. As Rachel looked at the scene before her, two more spirits slowly coalesced and took their place in the maelstrom of ghosts that surrounded the vampire.

"Good evening, Rachel," he said. "Is there a problem you wanted to discuss with me?"

Even as she looked at Bailey, Rachel could feel the vampire exerting his will. Her head started to feel fuzzy and her hands started to shake.

Slowly, she reached into her rucksack and pulled out a bottle of petrol. She took hold of the top and started to twist it.

"Really, Rachel," Bailey said, his voice barely more than a whisper, insinuating itself into Rachel's head, making it hard for her to focus, to remember what she was doing. "There's no need for that. You've had your fun. You've actually done me a favour and shown that those others were not as strong as I thought they were. So, just relax and let go. Trust me."

Rachel's fingers slipped from the bottle top and her arm fell to her side. For a moment, she felt herself doing exactly as she was told – relaxing and trusting. But then, her glance fell on the two bodies, lying on the dirty mattress that had been used by countless others just like them and who had died in the same way: exhausted, terrified and, in the end, utterly alone. Not a single person who cared knew where they had gone or when they had died. For all intents and purposes, those two and all the ones who had come before them, had just disappeared. And Rachel had been part of that.

The shock of disgust mixed with guilt acted like being dowsed with ice cold water. With an almost physical jolt, Rachel found herself in full control of her faculties. She looked at Bailey and saw him for what he was – an overweight, ugly, runt of a creature in a bad suit who controlled through bullying and fear. Without his vampiric powers he would be nothing. He would be less than nothing. Surely by now, without those abilities, he would have died, almost undoubtedly alone, unloved and most probably unnoticed.

Sharply, she smashed the neck of the bottle against the metal doorframe. It snapped neatly across and fell to the ground, barely a drop of the chrism spilling out. Then she threw it with all her strength across the room at Bailey.

It was unlit but the fire was only part of the strength of the liquid. Hitting Bailey square in the chest, it splashed across him, soaking him. Wherever it touched exposed skin it sizzled.

Bailey squealed and stumbled backwards, tripping over one of the corpses that lay behind him and landing heavily on the floor.

Pulling out the final bottle and her lighter, Rachel strode forwards to stand over Bailey.

"Please," Bailey whined, his voice shaking and weak with pain. "I had to do it. I tried to fight it, but the thirst was too strong."

"Bullshit," Rachel replied.

Unscrewing the final bottle top, she held it over Bailey's head.

Suddenly, viciously, Bailey lashed out, smashing his foot into Rachel's ankle. Arms flailing wildly, sending the final bottle flying Rachel stumbled backwards, falling and cracking her head hard on the floor. For a moment, she felt dizzy as if Bailey was taking control again, but quickly realised that it was only the shock of hitting her head.

And then Bailey was standing over her in much the same way as she had done with Bailey mere moments previously. The vampire was still smoking and blistered but he barely seemed to notice it.

"As I was saying, Rachel. There really is no need for any of this."

Rachel kicked out, hoping to surprise Bailey in the same way she had been. It was like kicking a concrete block.

A sudden boom and a burst of flames from down the corridor distracted Bailey. He looked up, away from Rachel and saw the orange glow of the rapidly growing fire that was taking control and starting to threaten the rest of the cellar. Realising his vulnerability, covered in petrol in a burning building, Bailey stepped back.

"We shall have to continue this conversation another time," he said.

Rachel stared at the vampire as he seemed to... fade. He grew translucent and somehow smoky. And then, his body fell into nothingness. His clothes fell into a bundle and from every hole, smoke poured out. The smoke, a thick, roiling, oily gas that didn't look in any way good or even safe to breathe, moved towards the door and out into the corridor. Rachel leapt backwards as it threatened to touch her. She wasn't prepared to chance Bailey being able to do something to her while he was like this.

However, Bailey didn't seem interested in doing anything to her, just in getting away from the flames. *Which, come to think of it, was actually a sensible decision.* Allowing Bailey enough time to flow up the stairs, Rachel followed behind.

The main house was in uproar. For a building that had seemed almost entirely deserted when she came in, there were an awful lot of people trying to get out. Fortunately, their desperation to evacuate over-rode any curiosity as to what Rachel was doing back there. After having disappeared for several days, she would have expected to be questioned in any normal circumstances. If they weren't intent on escaping from the building that was rapidly catching alight. All Rachel had to do was to follow them.

Standing in front of the house, watching the smoke start to boil from the open doors and windows, everyone seemed confused. The garden was heavily shaded and the sun was now low enough in the sky that the vampires should have been able to get out into the open without any problems, but they weren't coming out. Without them around, the renned people were incapable of making any decisions. And those who were in control of their own minds didn't have much mind to do anything with in any case. And, of course, the zombins just stood around waiting for either orders or meat.

Rachel started to slowly inch her way towards the bushes at the edge of the garden. She desperately hoped that her luck would hold. She just needed a few more moments, another yard or two and then she'd be away.

"Rachel?" someone said.

Shit.

"What are you doing? Where've you been? Do you know what's happening?"

It took a moment for Rachel's brain to come up with anything. But that moment was all it took for everything to start to fall apart.

In the deep shadows at the edge of the garden, where the trees grew tallest and thickest, a movement caught her eye. Smoke was starting to rise and thicken there. Thick, heavy, oily smoke, forming into a humanoid shape and then turning opaque.

To be frank, one of the last things that Rachel wanted to see was George Bailey's genitalia. However, as he had left his clothes behind when he had turned to gas down in the cellar, Bailey had no option other than to appear naked when he re-solidified.

"There's Bailey now," Rachel shouted, pointing towards the nude vampire.

As the crowd of thugs and renned people turned to look, Rachel bolted. Leaping over the gate, barely touching it as she cleared it, she hared off down the road.

"Kill her! Kill Cantrell!" she heard Bailey shout, but she didn't slow down to check how quickly his order was being followed. Instead, she sped up, making for the corner at the end of the road.

As she turned that corner, she skidded to a halt, almost tumbling over as she stopped.

She reached under the bush and pulled out the two bottles that she had placed there earlier on. Patting her pockets she felt for her lighter.

Then she patted them again.

The third time she patted herself down, she was getting a bit desperate. Even so, the lighter refused to be in any of them. She briefly closed her eyes and swore heartily. But there was nothing she could do. Having a pair of Molotov cocktails without anything to light them with was as useful as having a couple of bottles of cheap lager. Perhaps less so. At least, with the lager she could offer it to her pursuers to drink.

She could hear heavy footsteps pounding along the road towards her. Hefting one of the bottles, she stepped back around the corner and threw it directly at the head of the guy in the lead.

In a way, she was quite glad that she wasn't able to light it. It had been bad enough seeing the vampires burning. For all their faults, these people weren't vampires. It could, perhaps, be argued that in a way they were even worse. After all, the vampires were inhuman.

There was an implication in the description that said that to try and apply human values and morals to them was to fundamentally fail to understand them. It would be like expecting a lion to turn vegetarian through the use of persuasive language when there was a dead antelope lying around. However, these people had chosen, of their own free will, to work for the vampires. So, really, anything that happened to them was their own fault. But, even saying all that, Rachel would have found it really difficult to allow a human to burn to death.

Still, it didn't stop her from trying to brain one of them. The petrol filled bottle was heavy and connected heavily with the front-runner's forehead. His legs collapsed and he tumbled to the ground, directly in front of those following him. The next pursuer was too close to do anything other than trip and send himself flying face first into the ground, landing in a spray of blood and teeth. The third was luckier, but still unable to clear the barricade of his prone companions, although the fourth succeeded in avoiding them, only to be met by Rachel's final bottle. This one was not so well aimed and hit him in the chest, which slowed him down and caused him to lose his balance. But only for a moment as, arms cartwheeling, he managed to keep coming.

Rachel span around and took off again. This time she had nothing else but her own strength, speed and stamina. And she didn't have much of any of them. She quickly felt her breath coming hot in her throat and her chest start to heave. She had never been particularly fit, preferring to rely on her ghosting ability rather than any physical abilities she may have had. But, after all the months of neglect she had suffered under Bailey's control, she was even worse off.

She felt the breeze as her nearest pursuer's hand grazed her shoulder and put on a desperate, final burst of speed, knowing it was pointless, that at any moment she was going to be caught and held and handed over to Bailey. And then, being renfielded again would be the best she could hope for.

It came as something of a surprise when a sleek, black Saab sped out of a side street and only just missed her. It was probably even more of a surprise to the thug who was close behind her because it entirely failed to miss him in any way whatsoever. He bounced off the car's bonnet and into the bushes at the side of the street, destroying the meticulously pruned shrubs and gouging a furrow in the lawn on the far side.

Chapter Nine

Rachel didn't stop. And neither did the car. It quickly caught up to her and pulled up in front of her. She was scrambling over the crumpled bonnet when she finally caught sight of the driver.

Susan was sitting there, her face white, her eyes wide and staring and her hands wrapped tightly around the steering wheel.

"Get in, you idiot!" she shouted.

She jumped from the bonnet, ran round to the back door, wrenched it open and hurled herself in, so hard she cracked her head on the door on the far side. With the door still hanging open, Susan stamped on the accelerator and dragged the wheel around to the left. With a squeal of tyres that left Rachel's pursuers coughing and spluttering in a cloud of smoke and Rachel falling off the back seat and threatening to throw her back out on to the road, she sent the car careening down the street and away.

Once she had managed to get her breath back and made sure that the door was secured, Rachel leant over to the front seat.

"I thought I told you to leave," she bellowed at her.

"And where would you be now if I had?" she shouted back.

"That's my problem, not yours."

"That's bullshit. When you arrived on my doorstep it became my problem," she told her.

That made Rachel shut up as she realised the truth in her words. She swore loudly and kicked at the roof of the car.

"Careful! This car is nearly new!" Susan said, pointedly ignoring the large, thug-shaped dent in the bonnet. "And I'd appreciate it if you wouldn't blaspheme like that."

"Sorry," Rachel said. "But I fucked up. Bailey's still alive. And if he's seen you, he'll be coming for you now."

"My faith will protect me – that's true isn't it? A vampire only reacts to a cross if you have faith in it."

"As far as I know," Rachel told her. "I've never met anyone who had that much faith." She paused and looked over at Susan. "Well, you know, present company excepted, that is."

She gave her a sheepish grin in the rear-view mirror.

"I always said that atheism was bad for the health."

"Yeah…" Rachel replied.

#

Pulling up to Susan's house and climbing out of the car they were both shocked when a dozen policemen suddenly appeared as if from nowhere. They were all in full riot gear and had been carefully hidden behind hedges and cars, obviously waiting for their arrival. As they came out of hiding, some pointing pistols and others hefting rifles, Rachel noticed that every single weapon was directed right at her, ignoring Susan.

"Get down on the ground," the sergeant – one that Rachel didn't recognise – shouted from where she crouched behind a car, his torch shining right in Rachel's face, forcing her to squint to see anything.

"You are fucking kidding me." Rachel said, looking around her in bewilderment. This was one too many things to happen today.

"Get down on the ground, you bitch," the sergeant shouted again.

"I haven't done anything," Rachel protested.

One of the policemen came up close to Rachel and kicked her in the back of the knees, forcing her down to the ground.

"Tell that to Inspector Charlton, shit head," she said.

"That wasn't my fault," Rachel said.

"That's okay. It won't be my fault when my gun blows your brains out, either."

Swinging his rifle around sharply, the constable cracked Rachel across the base of the skull with his rifle butt.

"You are under arrest for the attempted murder of Inspector Mark Charlton, the murder of Jennifer and Andrew Ferguson and others to be named at a later date and arson," the constable told her as she knelt down across Rachel's back, knee jammed into the base of her spine, wrapping a pair of handcuffs around her wrists. "Listen: You do not have to say anything, but it may harm your defence if you do not mention when questioned something which you later rely on in court. Anything you say may be given in evidence."

With her face jammed into the tarmac, Rachel couldn't say anything without getting a mouth full of gravel. She was able to hear perfectly, though. And she heard another police officer coming up and slapping the cuffs on Susan, arresting her for aiding and abetting a known fugitive.

A few moments later, the constable stood up and, yanking on Rachel's handcuffs, dragged her to her feet. She briefly contemplated protesting her innocence but a swift look at the faces of the officers around her as they holstered their weapons told her that this was neither the time nor the place. Anything she said would be used as an excuse to beat her. She looked over to Susan, who was being escorted by a female officer to the black maria that had come around the corner. She was being treated better than Rachel was, although not that much better. She wasn't in danger of being seriously hurt, but she wasn't being treated with kid gloves either. Even before Rachel had properly regained her balance, she was being pushed to follow her. She half-stumbled her way to the back of the van and crashed against the steps, feeling the skin being peeled from her shins as she slid down them to lie in a heap on the ground.

"Get up you little fucker," the constable said jabbing her in the side with his boot. Grabbing the handcuffs once again, the police officer hauled Rachel up the steps, into the caged interior. Almost immediately, the heavy back door slammed shut sending a loud boom reverberating back and forth throughout the interior of the van. A dirty grey light filtered in through a few tiny grime-coated windows high up on the side and back, highlighting the dust that floated in the air, making it glow. As the engine revved, the black maria moved off with a sudden jerk, causing Rachel to lose her balance again and fall heavily against the side of the cage.

Opposite, in a separate enclosure, Susan slumped down onto the floor, head down between her knees. Rachel started to kneel down, but quickly rose again as her damaged shins touched the floor. Hunkering down, she rested her forehead against the wire of the cage.

"I'm sorry," she said.

Susan looked at her, stared at her with tears in her eyes, grunted once and then dropped her head again.

#

The atmosphere in the police station was icily vicious. The officers on duty watched her as she went past, like a pack of wolves eyeing up an injured deer. It was almost a relief for the cell door to clang shut behind her.

It wasn't the same cell as the last time she had been in here, but the differences were minimal. The smell was the same – equal parts urine, vomit and desperation but the graffiti was different. Which was something.

Rachel sat down on the thin mattress and gently rocked herself backwards and forwards. Sitting. Waiting.

She didn't have to wait long. There was a metallic 'chunk' of the lock and the door opened. For a moment, the way was open and she wondered if this was some sort of escape opportunity. But then, from behind the door, stepped the police sergeant who had been in charge of Rachel's arrest. He held his hands behind his back. His smile was not one that promised happiness and laughter. At least, not for Rachel.

"Look, George Bailey is planning on taking over the city. Everything he's done so far has been to terrify everyone here into going along with his plan. He wants to turn Newcastle into his own little vampire city-state thing," Rachel said.

The officer didn't say anything. Instead, he brought his hands out in front of him. His left hand was fine. Gloved in black leather, there was very little worrying about it at all. However, his right hand was different. As well as the matching glove, it also held a long, heavy baton. His smile grew wider and nastier.

"I've got a message for you from the master," he said.

"The master?" Rachel asked, dread settled over her heart like an eagle landing on a baby rabbit.

"Mister Bailey. He told me to tell you something."

"Fuck," said Rachel. "What?"

"He wants you to know that you have really disappointed him," the officer said. "And he wants to make sure you don't go flapping your mouth about his plans until he's good and ready for people to know about them."

The sergeant stepped into the cell, lifted his baton and smashed it down towards Rachel.

Forewarned, she rolled off the mattress, onto the floor and towards the corner of the room. The sergeant stood, blocking the doorway, swinging his baton with great skill. It was vicious and violent and Rachel, rolling this way and that was lucky that it took so long before it connected with her shoulder, forcing out a grunt of pain.

That first blow was quickly followed by another, this time to her hip, and then another to her elbow – on the same side as her already damaged shoulder, rendering that arm entirely useless. Quickly, Rachel was backed up into the corner of the cell, trying unsuccessfully to protect her head. She lashed out with her feet, but it was like kicking a tree. Each blow would make her attacker take a step back but, almost immediately, he would be back in position, lifting his arm and dropping it mechanically and methodically, aiming it exactly where it could cause the most pain and be the most debilitating. Making it worse, it was all done in complete silence; the only sounds came from the crack and crunch of the baton landing somewhere on Rachel's body and the grunting of the air being repeatedly forced out of her body.

"Sarge?" someone – a woman – said. "What're you doing?"

There was a pause in the violence but it only lasted a few moments and, when it resumed, it seemed to be with greater force.

"Stop it, Sergeant Braithwaite. You'll kill 'er."

The officer stepped in to the cell and put her hand on the sergeant's shoulder. He span around and hit her full force in the face with his baton. She nearly flew backwards out of the cell, crashing into the cell door on the other side of the corridor and slumping down. Sergeant Braithwaite turned back and continued beating Rachel.

Rachel felt as if she was looking at the world through the wrong end of a telescope. All she could see was the rising and falling of the long, black baton. All she could feel was pain, although even that was fuzzy and distant, which was, in a way, quite nice. All she could hear was a distant ringing in her head. That wasn't really very pleasant at all. It was, in fact, kind of annoying. It seemed to be the only thing that was preventing her slipping into a coma.

The dark tunnel, through which she saw the world, grew longer. Rachel could feel finally herself slipping away. The rhythm of the baton hitting her body seemed to mirror that of her heart. They mingled until she could no longer tell the difference between one and the other.

And then, she was looking down at the cell, at the sergeant and at herself. At least, she assumed it was herself. It was difficult to tell. All her senses rushed back, but there was no pain and no fear. She had left that behind when she had slipped free of her body. Whether or not she was ever going to return to it was not something she could tell at that moment.

Although the pain was gone, she still had the ringing in her ears. It took a moment for her to realise that it wasn't her. Someone had set off the alarm. It could only have been ringing for a matter of seconds, but it felt to her like it had been going on for hours.

First one police officer ran into the cell, then another and another. They piled onto the sergeant and forced him to the ground. Even as he went down, his arm was still rising and falling, beating Rachel and his workmates with equal vigour. Eventually, one of them managed to grab hold of the baton and drag it out of his hand, throwing it across the cell and out into the corridor, where it fell next to the still prostrate form of the officer who had come in earlier.

Even with the mound of burly coppers pinning him down, Sergeant Braithwaite still writhed and flailed, swearing and screaming, demanding that they help him mete out his master's vengeance. Although it should have been a very uneven struggle and soon over, the battle just went on and on. As Rachel watched from her vantage point at the ceiling, it seemed as though the larger force was slowly but surely being defeated. Perhaps it was because they were reluctant to use their full force on him while he had no such worries, perhaps he just wasn't feeling them but the Sergeant managed to shake first one loose and then another. Rising again, he seemingly forgot about them. Instead, Braithwaite turned his back on them and started in on Rachel's body once again, this time scuffing and bloodying his once shiny steel toe-capped boots. The sickening thud and crunch of armoured leather on flesh and bone made Rachel want to get out of there. The other officers slowly picked themselves up off the ground, shaking their heads in stunned astonishment.

One of them, the first to have been knocked out of the melee was closest to the door of the cell. He turned, bent down and straightened again, the baton, still dripping with Rachel's blood, now clenched in his fist. He took one step forwards and then another. He was bigger and obviously much stronger than either the Sergeant or Rachel. For a split second, Rachel was convinced that he was going to join his superior officer in beating the life out of her body.

"Sorry Sarge," the constable said, as he swung the baton down with all his might where it connected heavily with the back of the sergeant's neck, just at the top of his spine, sending him spinning across the room, face coming heavily into contact with the tiled wall. He bounced back and landed, spread-eagled and unconscious on the floor next to Rachel's body.

Suddenly, all was silent, apart from the heavy breaths of the officers as they fought to regain their composure and the ringing of the alarm bell.

"Well? What the fuck are you waiting for?" the officer holding the baton asked of his workmates. "Get the Sarge cuffed, check out the prisoner, check on Gillen" – he motioned to the still unconscious female officer lying outside – "and get an ambulance. Fucking move it!"

#

The atmosphere in the meeting room was somewhat subdued. Chief Inspector Wallace was not used to having to sit in the audience but, since the army had come in and started sharing the station, they seemed to have taken over. And so these 'strategic planning sessions' had become more like the General standing behind the podium that Wallace had always thought of as his and telling Wallace and the other police officer's what they were going to do. And now, he had had to explain what had happened down in the cells. When that Sergeant woke up, Wallace was going to string the bastard up by his guts. Wallace was a firm believer in the short, sharp shock approach to justice, which sometimes meant a certain amount of give and take in the whole 'innocent until proven guilty' thing. Not that he'd ever admit it to a civilian – or even one of these bloody soldiers – and Cantrell was a shit and probably deserved a bit of retribution. But this was far too much. No one had yet been able to tell him if the woman was going to live or not. If she died then, frankly, Wallace was out of a job. Hell, even if she lived then his career prospects weren't looking too hot.

"So, explain to me once again what happened to this woman who could have given us vital intelligence as to George Bailey's whereabouts?" General Hamilton said.

"Why don't you explain to me," Wallace retorted. "Why none of your men chose to come and see what the problem was and give my men a hand?"

"They, naturally, assumed that it was a problem with some criminal that you had arrested," Hamilton replied. "Considering you had chosen not to bother to tell us you were mounting this operation to arrest Cantrell, we had no reason to think that you might need assistance. After all, it was one of your men in your own cells…"

"This was an operation that was undertaken by Sergeant Braithwaite without authority…"

"Well, if you can't control your own men…"

Wallace surged to his feet, pointing at the General and was about to scream something at him that would have undoubtedly put even more of a strain on the cooperation between the military and police forces, when he noticed something occurring behind the General that struck him as utterly dumb.

It was quite a small thing, really. But it was something that he had never seen before, outside of one of those magician acts they occasionally get to entertain the men at the Christmas Party while they try and get as drunk as they possibly can as quickly as they possibly can. But, it was nowhere near Christmas and Wallace was utterly stone cold sober.

Behind General Hamilton, a single whiteboard pen had lifted itself from the pot they were held in and floated across to the board on the wall. The top of the pen popped off and fell to the ground and then slowly, with apparently infinite care, the pen carefully placed itself against the board and started to write.

IT WAS BAILEY

the pen wrote.

RENNED COP

it continued.

Something that he had read as he skimmed through Rachel's file came to the forefront of Wallace's mind.

"Cantrell?" he said, disbelief plain in his voice.

YES

"Oh. Great. A bloody ghost," said Hamilton.

Rachel considered writing 'fuck off' on the board, but it really wasn't worth it. She had more important things to say.

I TELL U WHERE B IS

she wrote.

Hamilton and Wallace looked at each other.

"Where?" Wallace asked.

MAP

"You want to show us on a map?" Wallace asked again.

"Of course she does," Hamilton said. He turned to a soldier.

"Get one," he ordered.

The soldier almost ran from the room. Quickly, he was back again, carrying a dog-eared A-Z map book and held it out towards Hamilton.

"Will this do, sir?" he asked.

"I assume so," he said. "Offer it to Cantrell."

The soldier turned around, unsure of where to look. Glancing back at his superior, he received a peremptory flap of the hand.

"Errr… Miss Cantrell?" he said, holding the book out.

Rachel put all her psychic weight into a single thrust that snatched the book from the soldier's hand and hurled it, pages fluttering free, into the far corner of the room. Picking up the pen again, she scrawled a line under the word 'map'.

"What's wrong with that thing?" Hamilton asked.

"Maybe she needs a flat map," Wallace said, utterly failing to keep his pleasure at seeing the army's failure out of his voice.

Rachel hit the tip of the pen against the board several times for emphasis and made a tick mark.

"I'll get one," Wallace said and, feeling so superior now, went out. Coming back quickly, he held a brand new folded map of Newcastle. Directing a few of his own officers, he pushed a couple of tables together and opened the map out full, placing a pencil and a pad of paper next to it.

"That may be easier to use than the whiteboard," he said.

Rachel lifted the pencil and, slowly, she drifted over the map. She brought the pencil down on to the map somewhere close to the centre of town. It dipped, touched down on the map as she lost control of it for a moment and then lifted again. It wobbled on a couple of inches and then came down again, more firmly this time. She scrawled a circle around a street and then wrote next to the circle

CLUB EGOISTE

before allowing the pencil to drop.

"He's there? Are you sure?"

Rachel didn't pick the pencil up this time, instead, she pushed it, rolling it towards the pad of paper. A detective, realising what was happening, picked it up and placed it on the pad. Rachel realised that was the first time she had actually felt grateful towards a policeman.

NOT SURE BUT PROBABLY

"How do you know?" Wallace said.

IT'S HIS OTHER HQ.

"Cantrell would know, sir. She's apparently been working with Bailey for months now," the detective who had helped with the pencil said.

"So why is she helping us now? What if it's a ruse?" Hamilton demanded.

WAS RENNED. NOT NOW.

"How do we know she's telling the truth?"

"With all due respect sir," the detective said. "Miss Cantrell has just been beaten nearly to death by a police officer who appeared to be under Bailey's control. I'd say the fact that she's helping us rather than haunting us is pretty bloody miraculous. We should listen to her."

"Well said, detective," Wallace said.

Hamilton huffed out a breath, but he remained silent.

"We'll send out some men to check it out," said Hamilton.

DANGEROUS. LET ME GO

"No. Absolutely not. I'm not happy about this anyway. So, I want you well out of the way, in case this does turn out to be a trap. I mean, we only have your word for it that you aren't renfielded anymore," Hamilton said.

Unseen by anyone else, Rachel shrugged her shoulders and let the pencil fall.

Interlude: On board the HMS Sheffield, near The Falkland Islands, May 1982

Sub-Lieutenant Mark Cantrell looked over the side of the ship at the churning South Atlantic waters below. It was a calm, quiet day and it seemed hard to believe that his ship was involved in a war. Still, it had only been a couple of days since the Belgrano had been sunk. Some of the lads had been saying that they reckoned the Argies would do something back sometime soon.

To his left, Able Seaman Owen Bahari, a tall, slender faery stood with his head held high, his shoulder-length black hair blown by the cold winds that seemed to come from the very heart of Antarctica. He seemed to be smelling the air.

"There is something coming," Owen said. "You should warn your captain."

"What?" Mark asked, feeling somewhat irked, as ever, by the lack of respect the faery-folk showed for humans. Captain Salt wasn't just his captain, he was the captain of the whole ship – and that included the bloody faeries. But, as he knew from experience, saying something about it would just get him that supercilious look-down-the-nose at him as if he had only just come to the faery's attention and was no better than a lump of dog shit.

"I don't know," the faery said, looking uncomfortable at having to admit such a thing. "The wind brings me omens, but they aren't being specific."

"Maybe you're just smelling penguin crap," Mark said.

Owen looked at him.

"No," he said and Mark could hear the many different things that were contained in that single syllable. None of them were complimentary. "Something is coming. It is something bad. You should warn your captain."

"The captain is probably on duty at the moment. We can let him know if and when your penguin farts get any clearer."

Owen looked at him again. This time, he didn't even need to open his mouth to articulate his feelings for the sub-lieutenant standing in front of him. After holding his gaze for a moment or two, Mark felt compelled to look away. Dropping his eyes, he felt his cheeks burning with embarrassment and anger. If a human able seaman had looked at him that way, Mark would have had him disciplined. But the rules were different for faeries. The fact that they were allowed to get away with bloody girlish hair like this one had was enough proof of that. So, bringing Bahari's attitude to the attention of the senior faery officer on board wouldn't get him anywhere. If anything, it was likely to get him in trouble. There was a reason why, when they had to ship together – which in the current circumstances was pretty much unavoidable – human and faery slept in different parts of the ship.

Apparently satisfied, Owen turned and walked off, clattering down the steps to the deck below.

Mark watched as Owen walked away down the length of the ship, humans of all ranks parting before him as he barely paused to show the minimum amount of respect to those who were of sufficiently high rank. *Which*, Mark thought bitterly, *obviously did not include a sub-lieutenant*. He was always amazed at how faeries could do it.

They talked of their 'glamour' as if it were something entirely natural. For them, it probably was, but for humans it was just scary. He could almost understand why all of the girls – including Mary, loathe though he was to admit it – and some of the guys he knew, both in the Navy (not that you admitted that you knew anyone like that) and back home were utterly infatuated with them. He had to admit to feeling the same way about the faery girls he had seen. If one of them were to crook a finger at him, he'd forget about Mary in a moment and leap into bed with her. Hell, it wouldn't even need to be a bed. A convenient back alley would do. He'd probably feel terrible about it afterwards, but he didn't think he'd have much say in the matter at the time. In a way, it was just as bad as the stuff that the vampires did.

He turned and looked back at the ocean. Almost cursing himself, he lifted his binoculars to his eyes, just in case the faery's omens had something to them. He scanned back and forth, pausing, tense, when he saw something moving, but relaxing again when he realised that it was just a cormorant.

Looking at his watch, he realised that he should have been following Bahari. He was due on duty down in the engine room. Ever since he had been a kid, he had loved getting filthy and getting his hands inside an engine. It had reached the point now where he was pretty much happy turning his hand to just about anything. His dad had been a miner and had imparted a love of just getting stuff done to his son. He always hoped that when he and Mary finally had a kid that he'd be able to do the same. The one good thing that could come out of all of this bloody war, as far as Mark was concerned, would be a promotion so he could be Chief Engineer on a ship. He'd like to stay on board the 'Shiny Sheff', after spending so long working his way up the ranks, working on her engine, it felt almost as if she was his, in the same way that the old Morris Minor he'd fixed up by himself had been his. But in the same way that he had sold it and bought a shiny new Escort – one of the first Mark II's at that - when he could, he'd be happy to move to a new ship if it meant moving on up.

As he ducked his head to step through into the engine room, he spotted Bahari, heavy gloves protecting his sensitive flesh from all the exposed ironwork, already hard at work, wrestling with a bolt that seemed to have seized. At least down here, Mark mused to himself, the bloody Faeries had to do what he told them.

Ducking into the Chief Engineer's little cubby hole office, he saluted smartly and received his work orders for that shift. Glancing through them, he saw that there was nothing too onerous – mainly general maintenance and a few minor repairs. He was about to ask if there was anything a little more demanding that needed doing when the whole ship shuddered. A huge '*boom*' knocked him off his feet, papers flying everywhere. Tiny shards of shrapnel peppered his face and he threw his hands up to protect himself.

"What the fuck...?" the Chief Engineer shouted, as the red alert sirens started to blare out a somewhat belated warning. "We've been hit!"

Mark pulled himself to his knees and then stood up a little shakily. Staggering back down to the entrance to the engine room, he looked through the door into a corridor that was starting to fill with smoke but was being vented through a gash in the hull and a ragged hole in the floor that had certainly not been there a minute or so ago when he had been walking along it.

"I don't think it exploded, though," he called. "We've been holed amidships – it's above the waterline, down on deck two, I think – but whatever it was didn't blow up."

"Thank fuck for small mercies," the Chief Engineer said.

"There is a fire though," Mark continued, as he span and hit the emergency switch on the fire control panel beside him.

For a moment, a moment that seemed to stretch out and out, nothing happened.

Water spurted from the sprinklers above, but quickly died away to a trickle before giving up completely.

Turning to the panel once again, Mark pressed the emergency switch once again, more carefully this time, in case he'd somehow managed to switch it off last time. This time there wasn't even that sad little dribble.

"Chief," he called. "We've got a problem. The water pressure's gone on the fire main."

Looking back into the corridor, he saw flames starting to lick up the walls of the corridor from the rent in the side of the ship.

Pulling a fire extinguisher from the wall, Mark ran down the corridor to the hole. He knew it probably wouldn't do much, but he reckoned that every little helped, at least until the fire crew could get the hose going. Aiming it into the flames, he depressed the lever to send a burst of fire-retardant foam into the flames. They flickered momentarily, before coming back as strongly as ever, almost as if they had fed on the foam.

It seemed like it had taken forever but was probably only moments later that another sailor joined him, dragging the hose along with him. Glancing at his comrade-in-arms, he saw Bahari, a look of intense concentration on his face.

"I guess it was a bit more than a penguin," Mark commented by way of apology. He dropped the depleted extinguisher and helped the faery get the hose into position.

Bahari looked at him for a moment, his face still unmoving, not betraying his thoughts, before he turned back to look at the flames and twisting the nozzle on the hose. Water sprayed out but it was consumed by the steadily intensifying flames as readily as Mark's foam had been.

The flames suddenly burst upwards as something on the lower level reached ignition point. The fire forced them both backwards, threatening to consume them if they didn't move quickly enough.

"I don't think there's anything we can do here," Mark called back into the engine room. "We need to start evacuating the place."

"Aye, well, it's lucky I don't wait for your recommendations, isn't it?" the Chief Engineer called back. "Now, get your arse in gear and get in here."

"Come on," Mark said to Bahari, dropping the hose and starting to move back to the relative safety of the engine room. Bahari, however, shook his head, continuing to aim the spray into the inferno.

"You go," he said. "I shall continue to fight the fire."

"Don't be an idiot. It's not going to work. The ship is fucked. We need to get out of here."

"Now it is you who can foretell the future?" Bahari asked, completely deadpan.

"In this case, yes, I bloody well can. Now move it. That's an order!"

"I must humbly refuse, Sub-Lieutenant."

Mark put his hand on the faery's shoulder, intending to pull him back out of the way but, suddenly, he found himself cheek pressed up against the wall, his own arm twisted uncomfortably up behind his back. Mark was able to see that somehow, the flow of water had not deviated in the slightest and still sprayed directly at the base of the flames, Bahari controlling the hose with one hand and Mark with the other.

"You only endanger yourself by doing this," Bahari hissed into his ear. "This is my duty. Whether or not I am successful is immaterial. So, once again – I must humbly refuse. Mark."

When Bahari let him loose, as quickly as he had first twisted him around, Mark stumbled and dropped to his knees. As he pulled himself to his feet, another explosion rocked the ship and knocked him down once again. A sheet of flame gouted up and along the ceiling towards the engine room door.

Mark watched as the fire slipped down the wall and in through the still open door, frozen into immobility with the shock of apparently being engulfed by fire and yet not having it touch him. It wasn't until the moment passed when flaming debris from pipes and wiring that ran along the ceiling started to drop on to his head that he gained control of his senses enough to start to stand for a second time.

As he started to make his way towards the engine room, he realised that the hose was loose and spraying around. He looked backwards and saw Bahari. The flames that had miraculously left Mark unscathed had not been so kind to the faery. In one moment that seemed to last forever, Mark saw every wound that the fire had inflicted on the once handsome creature that now lay before him, gasping for air like a landed fish. His face had been seared red, as if it had been pressed onto a hot plate. His eyes seemed to stare blindly and Mark realised that he wasn't actually staring, there was nothing in the sockets with which to look. The liquid inside his eyes must have boiled and burst, dripping its humours down his cheeks. His hands looked like two over-boiled hams, his fingers reduced to nubs of flesh, tipped with white bones sticking out from them.

Where it had not burnt away, his uniform had been welded to his flesh, the metal buttons and insignia that had bedecked his front now seemingly part of his body.

What amazed Mark was that he was still alive.

He went back to the body, and gingerly reached out. Taking hold of one of Bahari's arms, he pulled and stumbled as the flash-broiled flesh slipped and fell away from the bone. Seeing the faery's tissues still in his hands followed immediately by what, in nearly any other circumstance would have been the appetising smell of perfectly cooked meat, Mark couldn't help but spray the contents of his stomach across the deck in an explosive rush of vomit.

Parting his hands, the meat fell from them and landed with a thud that, although quiet, Mark was still able to hear above the roaring of the flames. He took a single step back towards the faery, unsure of himself, if he could do anything to help him, if, in fact, it wouldn't be more of a kindness to let him die. Possibly even to speed his death somehow. Then, he glanced back towards the engine room and knew that he had no more choices. The flames were taking hold in there, getting dangerously close to the tanks that held diesel oil. Once that went, he knew that it would really be all over.

He looked at Bahari one last time, a look of sorrow and apology on his face and then turned his back on him. Running towards the access hatch, he dived through the flames that surrounded it, a trained dog through a burning hoop. He didn't pause after landing, but headed straight for the hatch at the far end of the room. Out of the corner of his eye, he could see flames licking at the tanks, looking almost as if it were sentient and searching for a way inside, looking for entry into a honeypot full of goodness.

Reaching the access hatch, he pulled on the handle. The handle turned smoothly, but the hatch remained closed. Locked.

He didn't even bother banging on the door. There would be nobody on the other side of it. They were evacuating. The Chief Engineer must have assumed that the last explosion had done for them both rather than just one of them. Now, in a funny way, it had.

Now that it was inevitable, Mark suddenly felt a lot calmer. He looked around him and saw how beautiful the flames were. Their roiling, tumbling shapes reminded him of the waters of the ocean. Waters that were just outside the thin metal skin of the ship.

He slid down the wall and sat on the ground. It was really hot in there. He could really do with a drink after all that exertion. He remembered that there was a water cooler in the Chief Engineer's office and pulled himself up again, walking across to it and, pulling a cup from the holder, poured himself a drink.

He turned and looked out into the engine room. As the last drop of water slid down his throat, he saw a pipe that was attached to one of the tanks that held the diesel oil finally give way. A spray of jet black liquid shot out, momentarily pushing back the flames before catching alight itself. The fire climbed up the spray and entered the tank. There was a brief moment when everything seemed to go completely silent, although that may have just been an illusion caused by intense concentration.

The last thing that Mark saw as a living, corporeal human being was the bizarre sight of a large metal tank bursting and letting out a huge gush of fire that seemed to head directly towards him.

Chapter Ten

The picture was really pretty shaky. It certainly wasn't in anything approaching high definition. But then, considering it came from a webcam secured to a soldier's helmet that was hardly a surprise. What was surprising, at least to Rachel, was that it actually looked less realistic than Call of Duty on her PS4.

The other surprising thing was that Rachel had actually done as she had been told. When Hamilton had told her that she was not allowed to go with the soldiers to take down Bailey, she had never, even for a moment, considered disobeying him. She didn't think it was anything to do with the military mind-set – her father had been a navy man through and through and had spent all of Rachel's life (not to mention most of his own death) trying to instil a sense of obligation and discipline into her. And it had just made Rachel rebel even more. It got to the point where the only way that anyone was able to get Rachel to do anything was to specifically order her not to do it. Which had led to some really quite bizarre psychological mind-games. When her mother had caught her smoking a cigarette at the age of eight, she had just shrugged her shoulders, said 'fair enough, if that's what you want' and offered her a can of Special Brew. Of course, she had refused the drink and immediately stubbed out the cigarette. It had only occurred to her several years later that this was actually exactly what she wanted. But it was, of course, too late by then.

Maybe she wanted to be trusted. Which was in itself something of a first. There were people she had wanted to trust her, including people who held a position of power – although that mainly meant Fred Mott. And she had needed Mott's trust because those in his organisation who lost that trust tended to 'leave' the organisation quite quickly. And quite terminally. Mainly, though, the only form of trust Rachel had really wanted had been when she was after a girl and Rachel told her "No, I'm really interested in you as a person."

So, really, from previous experience, Rachel should have been actually looking over the shoulder of the soldier with the webcam rather than virtually doing so. All she could think was '*I hope he appreciates this.*'

Hamilton, however, seemed to have forgotten her. So, for that matter, had Wallace. They were both staring intently at the screen as it showed the soldiers making their way up to the innocent, anonymous doorway while passers-by gawped and diners in the coffee shop below the club looked out, forgetting their lattes and moccachinos. The door had been re-painted since Rachel had last been there. Now it was deep red with shining brass door ornaments. The lead soldier didn't bother ringing the bell or using the knocker though. After trying the handle to make certain that it was indeed locked, he lifted one of his heavy boots and slammed it against the door. With a loud crash, it flew open, banged against the wall and rebounded again. The soldier who had booted it open caught it and pushed it fully open again before running down the stairs.

The soldier with the camera was the last to enter. The picture jerked around as he went up, the echoing of everyone's boots on the stairs made it really difficult to hear what was happening. At the top of the stairs he passed the lead soldier who had stopped, aimed his rifle into the cloakroom and was shouting something at the woman in there. There was a lot of shouting in the club itself, mainly of the 'get down on the ground' and 'don't move' variety, with some screams and shouts of fear and surprise mixed in – presumably from the staff and patrons. At least, Rachel hoped it was from them rather than from the soldiers. She didn't want to think what could have happened to make a soldier scream in terror like that. As the soldier went through the arch, he looked around him, checking on everything that was happening. The picture on the screen swung backwards and forwards wildly, making it almost impossible to follow anything. It was just about possible to see his comrades arrayed around the room, guns pointing in several directions, trying to keep everyone covered.

Hamilton, wearing a small headpiece and microphone, spoke.

"Okay, Corporal," he said. "Deploy the A-V weaponry."

Rachel didn't think he meant 'audio-visual'.

The corporal, who appeared to be the be-cameraed soldier, confirmed his order and relayed it to the rest of the soldiers. Roughly half of them placed their rifles over their shoulder and unholstered large pistols. Ignoring the people in the room, they spread out around the edges, trying the various doors that led into other parts of the building.

Then, someone came up to the corporal. A beautiful woman, with a beguiling smile on her lips. Rachel recognised her as Eve, Lilly's mother. She span around, screaming "that's a succubus!" forgetting in her sudden panic that the people in this room were as about as psychically attuned as the table and they couldn't hear her.

Apparently, she wasn't quite right. While neither Hamilton nor Wallace showed any sign of having heard anything and, indeed, appeared to be utterly fascinated by the face on the screen, a private, who had been standing on guard at the back of the room suddenly rushed forwards. He snatched Hamilton's microphone from his head and almost screamed into it.

"It's a fucking succubus!" he shouted. "Kill it! Kill the fucker!"

The picture shook, as the corporal jerked backwards. He lashed out, an almost automatic reaction to the violence of the order, hitting her and knocking her backwards across a table on the floor. As she fell her face contorted, transforming from an image of calm, serene and absolute beauty to one of hatred and fear. Not a single feature of her face had changed and yet it was suddenly deeply ugly. Both Hamilton and Wallace jerked back in their chairs, an almost identical expression of disgust crossing their faces.

The corporal's reaction was just as visceral. With a grunt of revulsion, he aimed his assault rifle at the woman writhing on the floor and pulled the trigger, not letting go until he had loosed all thirty rounds into her body. The viciously loud rattling chatter of the rifle spitting its bullets made the picture break up into static and the speakers squeal as they were overwhelmed by the noise.

When the picture came back the woman lying on the floor was barely recognisable as anything human. She was, instead, a lump of torn meat, bloody and twisted. Blood pooled on the floor and had spattered the people surrounding her. Everyone in the room was completely still and silent. Back at the police headquarters, it was equally quiet, apart from a constable who was being noisily sick into a waste bin.

Rachel watched as Eve's spirit rose from her body. It was a hideous, vile thing, ragged black bat wings sprouting from its back, its hide covered in greasy black hair. Its lizard-like face had goat eyes, a vivid yellow with seemingly bottomless black rectangular pits for pupils. Twisted goat horns sprouted from its forehead and curved backwards until they almost touched its shoulders. Reaching forwards, its fingers ending in raggedly jagged nails, it snarled soundlessly and hurled itself at the corporal. Its incorporeal form passed harmlessly through him, the only effect being a cold shiver that ran through him.

The private who had been able to hear Rachel was not so lucky. This guy was obviously a lot more psychic than he had any right to be. His face grew pale, he dropped the microphone and pointed a finger at the screen, backing away, his mouth working as he desperately tried to say something.

"Calm down, private," Rachel said. "It can't hurt anyone anymore."

That wasn't entirely true. If there was anyone there was as psychically inclined as the private then it could have a pretty good chance of possessing them. Rachel glanced at the screen again, where the paralysis was rapidly wearing off and terror was taking over. It was going to be a lot harder for the soldiers to maintain order now.

The private looked around him and then saw Rachel, translucent and a couple of feet off the floor.

"What's happening?" he asked. "How can I see that? How can I see you?"

"You've never seen anything like this before?" Rachel asked.

"No ma'am. Not while I was awake," he said.

Rachel found it hard to believe. She'd seen a few psychic awakenings before but they usually happened when the person in question was quite young. Although, looking at this soldier, that might still count.

"How old are you, private?" Rachel asked.

"Eighteen, sir."

Well, that was on the older side for it to happen, but it wasn't unheard of. Maybe he'd just never been this close to something this psychically potent. Which was understandable. Ghostkin weren't that common and Rachel was feeling under a certain amount of tension at the moment which was well known as a psychic intensifier. If it got any worse she might find herself starting to 'geist.

"Okay," she said. "Don't worry about it. You've just been woken up psychically."

"What do you mean?"

"A part of your brain that was asleep has woken up and it lets you see and hear ghosts and spirits," Rachel explained.

"I don't understand," the private said.

"Look – what's your name, private?"

"Johnson, ma'am. Nigel Johnson," he said.

"Okay. Nigel. You can now see ghosts. If there is a dead person around then you'll see them. If someone dies then you'll see their spirit leave their body."

"That's insane. That's impossible," Nigel said.

"That's the way it is," Rachel said.

"Can I ask what the hell you are doing, private?" Hamilton said, his voice soft and gentle and as poisonous as a snake.

Nigel snapped to attention. This was what he needed. Some discipline, something he was used to and that was in his proper frame of reference. None of this ghosts and ghoulies and monsters stuff.

"Sorry sir," he said sharply and smartly. "It seems that I am able to see spirits, sir."

"Spirits? You mean ghosts? Is that meant to excuse your breaking ranks and... snatching my comms away from me and having the Corporal shoot that woman?"

"Yes, sir," Nigel pointed towards Rachel. "She said that the woman was a succubus. I don't know what that is but she seemed to think it was important and no-one else seemed to be able to hear him."

"A what? A succubus? What the hell is that?"

"I don't know sir. But, when the Corporal shot her, I saw something horrible, sir. Coming out of her body, sir. It was... it was..."

"Well? What was it you saw?"

"A demon, sir."

"A demon?"

Nigel looked down to the floor.

"Yes, sir," he mumbled.

"You're relieved of duty, private," Hamilton told him. "Until I can investigate this further. You'd just better hope that..."

Hamilton was interrupted by Wallace calling out to him.

"Something's happening," Wallace said. "Come and look."

Hamilton dismissed Nigel and turned on his heel, returning to the screens. Picking up his comms unit, he settled it back into place.

"Stay here," Rachel said to Nigel. "I need you to talk to these two for me."

"Sorry, ma'am," Nigel whispered. "I've got my orders."

Rachel looked helplessly at the private as he left the room, nearly marching as he tried to maintain the discipline that he had allowed to slip so grievously.

Back at the club, the soldiers were still desperately trying to maintain order, among the panicking clientele who, as far as they were concerned, had just seen a soldier shoot an unarmed, defenceless woman. It was apparent that some of the other soldiers, who had seen the same thing, were on the verge of loosing rounds as well. They were trying to herd all the civilians into one corner of the room and they were being resisted. One man, who must have been in his late forties, hair starting to turn to grey, belly showing a definite preference for plenty of good food and drink, was standing, refusing to move, shouting and thrusting his finger in the face of the soldier who was trying to move him.

"What do you think you're doing?" he yelled. "This isn't China! We have rights here!"

"Look, sir," the soldier said, trying to remain calm and only partly succeeding.

"Don't 'sir' me, you little thug," the man interrupted.

"What is going on?" a bellow from the other side of the room interrupted everyone.

Everyone spun, the picture on the screen from the corporal's camera blurring as he turned and then coming back to something sensible again as it focussed on a doorway as the door seemed to slam itself closed.

"What's he looking at?" Hamilton said. "What's happening?"

"It must be Bailey," Wallace replied. "They say that vampires don't show up on a screen."

In the Club itself, it was obvious what had come through the door. Only a vampire would have those long, dangerous incisors, those bat-winged ears and skin so pale it couldn't have been touched by sunlight for years. Even so, he was almost entirely unthreatening. He was short and fat. His hair was plastered greasily across his head. He wore an immaculate dark purple suit, obviously of very high quality. It fit him perfectly and managed to de-emphasise his size and shape. It didn't make him look any more impressive, it just made him look a little less squat. The scarlet tie and pale blue shirt that he had chosen to complement the suit entirely failed to do so.

"Who the fuck are you?" the corporal asked.

"I believe I may be the person you are looking for. My name is George Bailey and I'd like an explanation for why you chose to kill my hostess and terrorise my guests?"

"You're coming with us," the corporal said, lowering his gun and moving towards him.

The corporal reached Bailey and took his arm.

Back at the headquarters, Rachel was standing directly behind the two commanding officers screaming at everyone around him, knowing that it was pointless, but needing to try anyway.

"Tell him to shoot! Shoot now."

Unfortunately, since Nigel's departure there was no-one around who could hear her. Hamilton and Wallace were glued to the screen.

What happened next was almost too fast to follow on screen. Suddenly, the corporal was lying on the floor, his helmet half underneath him, the camera pointing off into the corner of the room. The only thing it could see was a sudden flood of deep red liquid that flowed across the floor, rippling as it ran and pooling against the wall.

The microphone was muffled now, underneath the unmoving corporal but it was still possible to hear some of what was happening.

The sharp chatter of automatic weapons fire was interspersed with a heavy '*chuffing*' noise as if someone was pumping a very large bicycle tire. This was followed by a clattering sound as something landed on the floor. At one point, a heavy wooden stake bounced into the camera's view and rolled to a stop in the pool of blood.

In amongst the noise of gunfire, shouts and orders could be heard from the soldiers.

The suddenness that everything had turned from being mostly in control to an absolute disaster had frozen everyone in the control centre. Eventually, Hamilton shook himself out of his utter paralysis and stabbed at a button on the console in front of him.

"Get your men in there," he shouted. "They need backup, they're getting killed in there."

After a moment, another screen came to life. There was a fuzz of visual static which cleared to show another camera image of the outside of the club. Another group of soldiers were running across the road to the door. The first one to reach didn't pause. He hurled himself at the door, intending to barge it down. Instead, he bounced backwards and fell in a heap at the feet of the soldier following close behind, who almost tripped over him, saving himself only with an ungainly leap. The rest of the backup team came to a swift halt.

Back downstairs in the club, the gunfire and the noise of the anti-vampire guns were quickly starting to fade away as first one and then another was silenced. Each time one gun stopped, it was replaced by a brief, cut-off scream or a shout of terror.

"What's happening? Why isn't the A-V hardware stopping him?" Hamilton said.

At last, there was no more gunfire. Everything was silent. Through the muffled microphone, it was just about possible to hear someone talking, although no words could be made out. And then the screaming started again.

It didn't last for long, though. After a few minutes, the club was entirely silent, apart from the noise of the soldiers outside the club hammering at the door, trying to break it down. Then the corporal's body was rolled over.

Standing there, in full view of the camera, was Bailey. Although he couldn't be seen himself, the blood that covered him from head to foot showed his form clearly. His suit was a tattered mess, ripped away from his body, leaving nothing but shreds hanging from his shoulders and around his waist. He was covered in blood, from head to foot, although none of it seemed to be his own. He held the corpse of a pretty young woman, wearing the uniform of a waitress, her throat ripped open, the blood running from it already slowing as her heart stopped pushing it around her body.

Almost nonchalantly, Bailey lifted the girl and drank from her for a moment, before letting her drop to the floor like a discarded doll. Rachel could see her spirit rise from her body and entwine itself around Bailey's body, joining the forms of all the others that congregated around him.

"I don't know who is watching this. Although I assume that Miss Cantrell is with you, in one form or another," he said. "But, as you have seen, you can do nothing to hurt me. Your soldiers outside will be unable to get in – the door is held with a wizard lock. And, if they do succeed in getting in, do you really think they will be any more successful than these other grunts you sent in? Once darkness falls, I shall be away from here. And then there will be reprisals. You have brought this upon yourselves."

Bailey turned on his heel and walked out of the camera's view. All that could now be seen was the wall of the club. A wall that was covered in sprays of blood that dripped down, making it look like a piece of modern art.

"Jesus fuck," breathed Hamilton. He pressed the button on the console that connected him with the soldiers outside the club.

"Pull back," he said.

"Sir?" came the reply.

"Pull back," Hamilton repeated. "Create a perimeter and hold there."

"Yes sir," the soldier at the other end said.

Releasing the button, Hamilton slumped back in his chair. He took off his cap and threw it on the console, ran his hands through his hair and sighed deeply.

"What the fuck do we do now?" he said.

Rachel wasn't sure if it was a rhetorical question or not, but she knew she had the answer or at least a large part of it. It wasn't especially an answer she liked, but it was the only one she had and it was probably the only solution that was going to be of any help, short of a very big bomb. And she was fairly certain that it would prove to be really difficult to get authorisation to blow up one of your own cities.

Carefully lifting up a pencil, again, she started to write on the pad in front of Wallace.

I HAVE AN IDEA, She wrote. *GET NIGEL HERE.*

Chapter Eleven

Rachel thought that by now she'd have grown used to seeing herself from the outside. Most of the time she was fine with it and thought no more of it than she would looking in a mirror. This was different though. She barely recognised herself. It wasn't just the bandages and the splints and the bruising; the machines all around her, all connected in some way, either strapped to or penetrating her skin. Her body looked... vacant. Obviously, that's exactly what it was. When she was ghosting there was nothing in there. It was just a sack of meat kept going by the autonomic processes of her body. And that was fine. She knew that, she expected that. This was different though. In the same way that a house that had been left vacant for a weekend had an entirely different atmosphere to one that was completely unoccupied, so did her body. It felt cold and unwelcoming. She was scared to go near it. Just to be in the same room as her own body made her feel like she was on the verge of 'geisting. She really didn't want to get any closer to it. But, at the same time, she couldn't move away. Almost as soon as she entered the hospital she could feel the drag of it like a toy boat in a bath with the plug pulled out. And as she got closer the feeling got stronger. Despite her extremely powerful disinclination to go anywhere near it she didn't think she was going to be able to resist. And leaving the room was definitely not an option. But, she knew that the very moment she relaxed and allowed herself to go with the flow, she would be lost. The toy boat analogy was particularly apt – if she returned to her body, she would flow away down the drain and into the dark. And then she'd be right in the shit.

The question though was whether or not her body could survive without her spirit there to prop it up. There was remarkably little scientific study into what happened to the body of a ghostkin that had been beaten to within an inch of its life and then abandoned by its owner. Rachel guessed that it was probably something similar to being in a persistent vegetative state and, as far as she knew, if they didn't die then they healed okay. They just didn't wake up. So, in theory, if it didn't die, it should be fine. And, while her body looked like complete shit at the moment, she didn't think there was anything life threatening happening to it. For a start, she was in a – very nice – private room in a hospital, rather than an operating theatre. Admittedly, it was an Intensive Care Unit, but that at least meant there was something there to care for and somebody to do that caring. What worried her though was whether or not she'd actually be able to get back in when the time came. She had this horrible feeling that if her body healed without her inside it, it might... somehow... get used to not having a spirit occupying it and reject her when she did decide that it was time to 'go home' again. She didn't think it would get up and walk around by itself, but maybe there just wouldn't be any way in. She had accepted the fact that she was going to walk the earth as a disembodied spirit when her physical self finally died. Hell, in a lot of ways she much preferred the freedom of ghosting than of being inside her body. But the point was, up until her actual death, she liked having a choice. Much as she did love the whole 'leap tall buildings in a single bound' thing she could do as a ghost, not to mention the excellent burglary abilities it gave her, she also loved a lot of the physical, corporeal stuff as well. Having a really good cup of tea. Bacon and eggs. Spending the cash she'd stolen. None of that would be possible when she died. And, although she'd still be able to have sex – just look at how she had been conceived for confirmation of that one – she didn't think it'd be all that enjoyable. Connecting with the physical world was incredibly difficult. It always felt as if it was all being done through a foot of cotton wool. It was fine for doing some stuff – like picking up bundles of cash – but the smaller stuff – writing, for example – was really bloody hard and needed a lot of concentration. So, keeping yourself going and not, for example, falling through the floor, while in the throes of orgasm sounded like it would be nigh on impossible.

None of this, of course, actually helped in any way whatsoever with her current problem. No matter what she couldn't actually return to her body at the moment. She had a job to do. She had a 'mission' for fuck's sake. Maybe if she didn't get back into her own body, she could possess a Barbie and really live out the fantasies of her eight year old self.

But, she had also needed to do this: to come and see her body. Unwillingly, she added the thought '*one last time*'. Because there was a fairly strong chance that this job could destroy her spirit. There was a really pretty major possibility that Bailey would be able to renfield her while she was ghosting. Normally, she'd guess that it wasn't possible, but now that the bastard had had his – psychic, if not actual – teeth in her once before there was a powerful connection between them. And, if Bailey did manage to bend Rachel to his will then that would be it. Even if Bailey let her live, in whatever form of life she could have as a renfielded ghost, she was pretty sure that it would be even less pleasant than it had been before. And, frankly Rachel expected that if she did fall under Bailey's power then the vampire would find some way to end her life, both spiritually and physically.

Still, if there was some small chance that she could do something, Rachel had to do it. If only because having a city that was under the control of a vampire was really cramping her ability to do some nice, high grade criminal activities herself. Not to mention the fact that the bastard really deserved a good beating for everything he'd done to Rachel – and everything he'd made Rachel do. That in itself meant that she really, really wanted to drive a stake deep into bastard's chest and laugh as he turned to dust. And then piss on the dust. *Although, admittedly, that last bit could be a bit difficult at the moment.*

Of course, being able to do anything to anyone meant first getting away from her body. And that was proving somewhat easier said than done. Even while she was just standing there, looking at herself, she discovered that she had slid, almost without realising it, closer to her body. And she was accelerating. The closer she got, the stronger the pull. She could hear her own heart beating. It tugged at her concentration like the bass beat in a nightclub, getting into her head. She was losing focus. She looked around and made a foolish grab for the end of the bed, her hands passing right through them. But she touched her own foot. It was like an electric current passed through her. For a moment, the world turned grey and shadowy and she forgot where she was. Then, when she came back to herself, she found herself standing in her own body, the waist of her spirit-self sticking grotesquely up from her own belly while she looked down at her own comatose face, like some kind of freakish conjoined twin. Her spirit, usually fixed in a refined, perfected replica of her own physical form had started to lose that fixedness, had started to turn to mist at the edges. And that mist was swirling down in a spiral, touching her body and seemingly drilling into her chest. She could feel the empty darkness that lay inside her own body and it was bigger than her spirit would be able to fill. Once she was in there, she would be stuck for who knew how long.

"Ah. Here you are... what the fuck..." said a voice from behind her.

Struggling to turn her head, Rachel twisted and saw Nigel standing there, his mouth so far open it looked as if he had dislocated his own jaw.

"Help... me..." Rachel managed to whisper.

Nigel jumped at that and came forwards, looking somewhat unsure of himself, but still mostly willing.

"What do you want me to do?" he asked.

"Take... hand..." Rachel told him. "Pull..."

Nigel grabbed hold of the hand that lay limply on the bed, dislodging a cannula and some kind of sensor attached to a finger, setting an alarm off.

"No..." Rachel said. "Ghost hand..."

"Oh. Shit. Sorry," Nigel said and dropped the body's hand. He looked confused for a moment, before reaching out and putting his hand on top of Rachel's incorporeal, nearly dissolved one.

"That feels really weird," he said.

"Pull," Rachel moaned, her voice now sounding for all the world like a ghost in a fifties B-movie.

Closing his own hand around Rachel's, Nigel pulled. And was amazed to feel resistance. Slowly, the hand came up from the body, but it felt like he was trying to straight arm lift a really heavy weight. The arm followed and then Rachel could feel the rest of her being dragged backwards. It felt like she was being torn in half. It wasn't painful as such. Not yet, anyway. Instead, it was like she had pins and needles throughout her entire body. But, as Nigel pulled, the intensity increased and the pins and needles started to feel as though they were heating up.

It seemed to take an eternity for Rachel to get so far that she was free from the knees upwards, but then she stopped. Nigel kept pulling, but his feet slipped on the shiny floor of the hospital.

"What's going in here?" asked another voice, this one belonging to a woman.

Susan came into the room and stared at the scene before her, her eyes going wide as she realised the identity of the person in the bed. Since being released from custody she had grown increasingly worried about Rachel. Seeing her like this confirmed her fears. It was made more bizarre by seeing a soldier apparently miming 'windy day' in front of the sleeping woman.

"Help me," Nigel said through gritted teeth. "Grab hold of my waist and pull."

"What are you doing? Who are you?" Susan demanded. "Is this some kind of joke? I got a message that Rachel Cantrell wanted to meet me here. What is happening? What's wrong with her?

"Get hold of my fucking waist and fucking pull," Nigel said.

Shocked, Susan did as she asked. She took hold of his webbing belt and, with all the strength that she had, strength backed up by the deep and abiding faith that held her up when her body weakened, she yanked.

They didn't move far, just a few inches, but Rachel felt one of her legs slip free from her body, leaving her attached just from one ankle down. She took the psychic equivalent of a deep breath and pulled. She was free, still stretched out like a balloon in a strong wind, but no longer in contact with her body.

"Keep going, Nigel," she said. "Out of the room."

Slowly, step-by-step, Susan dragged Nigel backwards to the door and Nigel dragged Rachel. At last, just as Nigel felt as if his arms were going to be wrenched from his sockets, Susan stumbled backwards, tripping over the sill of the door. They both fell backwards, Nigel's backside landing heavily on her midriff. But that was the impetus that was needed to succeed in getting Rachel out of the room.

Once out of there and away from her body, the drag seemed to fade. Rachel could still feel it, but it was now at a manageable level. With only a little help from Nigel, she would be able to move away from it.

"Thanks, Nigel. You're a lifesaver," she said. "And thank Susan for me as well."

"The General sent me to find out what you were doing," Nigel said as he slid his weight off the woman.

"And thank god he did."

A nurse stormed along the corridor, her face black with fury. She stood over the two who still sprawled on the floor.

"What the hell is going on?" She demanded.

"It was Miss Cantrell," Nigel said. "She was being... I don't know... she couldn't get away from her body..."

He trailed off, realising how ridiculous he sounded.

"You know what? I don't care. You're causing a disturbance and upsetting the patients. Get out of my hospital," the nurse said. "I don't know what was going on in there and I don't want to know, just... just go."

"Yes, of course," Nigel said, suddenly embarrassed. "I'm really sorry. You don't know..."

He trailed off. Even winded and exhausted, the nurse had a glare that could peel paint. Not a single Sergeant had been as scary as she was at the moment. Nigel picked himself up off the ground, saluted smartly to her and, Rachel holding on to his shoulder, nearly ran out of the hospital. Susan followed closely behind.

#

The street was quiet. This was mainly because the army and the police had set up a pretty much impenetrable cordon around the area. Behind that everything was in turmoil. Despite, or perhaps because of, the fear that had settled on the city, hundreds of people had turned up to watch what was going on and, hopefully, see the creature that had been terrorising them for so long, brought to justice. Or maybe just see a large wooden stake shoved through his chest. The media was out in force as well, training their cameras on the set up in the street around the club, which must have made for fascinating viewing on the twenty-four hour rolling news channels, as all that could be seen was a couple of soldiers on guard outside a formerly empty shop opposite the club where the army and police had set up their headquarters. There had been some talk of setting up in the café below but they quickly vetoed that idea when someone suggested that perhaps Bailey might be able to penetrate the ceiling and wreak havoc in there. Even so, they had sent one single soldier in to the shop with a high-powered, directional microphone in an attempt to work out what was going on in the floor above.

Rachel was able to see all of this from her vantage point flying along above the drab green army Land Rover that slowly pushed its way through the crowd. Reporters and camera operators pushed microphones and lenses through the open windows, calling out questions and demanding information.

Once through the cordon, the Land Rover made its way to the front of the shop and Hamilton, Wallace, Nigel and Susan all climbed out.

"I'll go and talk to the press, shall I?" Wallace said. "Tell them we've got a plan and all that."

"You could just tell 'em all to bugger off," Hamilton replied. "I'd have thought that they'd want to get away from here, what with the sun going down and everything."

Wallace looked at Hamilton but didn't say anything before turning smartly on his heel and walking towards the nearest edge of the crowd.

"Now, Cantrell... Dammit, Private. Is she here?" Hamilton asked.

"Yes sir," said Nigel. He pointed at where Rachel floated above the shop awning, but neglected to mention that she was miming exactly how much of a wanker she thought Hamilton was.

"Good. Cantrell. You know what you have to do, don't you? Just go and recce the area. Come straight back and tell us what the situation is and what the bastard is doing. Not that you'll be able to do very much like that, eh?"

"Got it, boss," Rachel said and Nigel repeated, blushing as he said 'boss'. "Go and have a look for Bailey and come back and tell you what's going on."

"Be careful," Susan admonished.

Rachel looked at her and smiled. If Susan was still supporting her, even after everything that had happened, then she must still be doing something right. She turned away and flew across the street, heading for the café window. Just before she went through it, she turned and called back.

"You know," she said. "If you'd just let me do this in the first place, when I said I wanted to go, a lot of people might still be alive."

Nigel decided that discretion was definitely the better part of valour and chose not to relay that particular comment.

Shaking her head, Rachel pushed on through the window and into the café.

It was even quieter in there. The constant background drone of the crowds was muted almost to nothing. The whole place showed signs of being rapidly vacated, presumably when the soldiers had first stormed the club. Cups of tea and coffee, now cold with a skin formed over the surface, half-eaten cakes and sandwiches, even a baby's bottle that had been dropped and then left, were all over the place. For a moment, Rachel was convinced that everyone was hiding and they would jump out and say '*boo*' to give her a fright. Which, considering she was the ghost, traditionally the bringer of fear and the purveyor of '*boo*' was kind of funny. She didn't smile though. The thought of what she was here to do stopped anything approaching jollity.

Rachel kind of wished that she did have her body. If there was one thing a body was good for, it was taking a deep breath and heaving a heavy sigh just before doing something really stupid. Not having lungs and not breathing meant that you couldn't really do that as a ghost. Not properly.

Having delayed as long as she felt she reasonably could under the guise of working up courage Rachel gently floated up through the ceiling and into the club above.

#

The inside of the club seemed even quieter than the café below. It was certainly helped by the drapery and the plush furnishings that helped to damp down the sounds, but a large part of it was almost undoubtedly caused by the number of corpses that lay strewn all across the floor. Whether or not they were actually acting to damp the sound was perhaps open to debate but Rachel couldn't help thinking of the phrase '*quiet as the grave*'.

A flash of bright colour caught her eye as the sun came out from behind a cloud and sent a shaft of evening light through one of the small windows near the ceiling to fall on a woman's body. She had long, dyed, bright-red hair complemented by a beautiful, emerald green satin dress. A dozen red roses were strewn across her body, looking almost as if they had been placed there. When she was alive she had obviously been beautiful, but her death had disfigured her face, turning it into an ugly mask of terror. The red of her hair mingled with the deeper scarlet that had flowed from the gash in her chest, looking almost as if her hair had in some way been coloured by the blood. It didn't look as if Bailey had drunk from her; he had just slaughtered her, along with everyone else in the room.

Deliberately turning away from the woman, Rachel looked around the room again before facing the door through which she had been taken on the night that Bailey had renfielded her. It felt like such a long time ago now. Years rather than the months it actually had been. It had been bad enough the first time she had been renned. When it had been ordered by the courts as punishment for her crimes. But that had been different. She could still remember what she had done back then, but it was more distant, as if she was remembering looking at something through fog. It had been her doing it but it had been at one remove, almost as if she were ghosting and watching her body do it independently. This time though, it was much more like it had been her. Although intellectually she knew that she had had to do what she had been told, at the time it had felt like she had been completely free to say 'no' at any time, to back out of the deal and walk away. But she hadn't. She had held those boys and those girls while Bailey fed from them. She had killed Mott. She had shoved that brick into Sergeant Charlton's face and had not given a damn. She had done everything that Lilly had demanded of her – no matter how degraded and debasing. And each and every one of those actions remained crystal clear in her mind.

Slowly, she made her way forwards towards the door. Pausing before it, she closed her eyes. She had the option of going back. Of reporting what she had seen. But that was really only delaying the inevitable. She had volunteered for this course of action. Without knowing exactly where Bailey was and what she was doing, there would be no way of planning anything. Rachel had to watch him, to be able to tell the soldiers and the police who were waiting outside as patiently as people like that could wait, when the vampire made a move. It would only be a matter of seconds, maybe a minute or so at most, that Rachel could give them to prepare, but even that tiny advantage might be enough. It would have to be. And, if Rachel was to waste time going back and telling them that there were a load of bodies in the room but she hadn't seen Bailey… Well, it would be pointless, really. And it would prove exactly how scared she was. And, no matter how much she told herself that she didn't care what General Hamilton and Inspector Wallace thought of her, she didn't want them to think her a coward.

So, she opened her eyes again and pressed forwards, through the wooden door into the room beyond.

#

The inside of that room was entirely different to the rest of the club. There were no corpses in here for a start, although Rachel didn't think that would remain true for much longer. Three people sat around a table looking almost as if they were waiting for her: Bailey, a girl and a woman. Almost as if he was a connoisseur tasting wine, Bailey was slowly sipping at the blood that oozed from the girl's wrist. Rachel knew that before long, certainly by the time Bailey was ready to make his escape from the club, the girl's spirit would have joined the cloud of ghosts that swirled around Bailey's head.

She was probably aged somewhere in her late teens or her early twenties and was dressed in the uniform of one of the club waitresses. It was quite difficult to tell much about her because her face and actually much of her body was obscured by that of the woman who was nearly on top of her, kissing the girl with undisguised passion, caressing and groping her all over. One hand had pushed up the girls skirt and was rubbing her between the legs. It was certainly sexual but it wasn't in the least bit sensual. It looked almost violent in the way the woman was using the girl, as if she were feeding on the girl as much as Bailey. The woman was dressed in a skin-tight black PVC mini dress that was short enough to show the lacy tops of her fishnet stockings as she sat astride the girl.

Rachel watched the scene for a moment until Bailey paused in his drinking and looked up.

"We have a visitor," he said, licking his lips clean. "You should say hello, my dear. After all, you haven't seen her in such a long time. A pity that in this form she can't bring you as much pleasure as she used to do. And, of course, vice versa."

At that moment, Rachel realised that Bailey could see her. And, if that was the case, then it was more than likely that he could see all the spirits that were swirling around him, angry and vengeful. The revelation stunned her for a moment. Surely anyone who had to live with that much hatred aimed at them all day every day would be insane by now. To be able to ignore it was an utterly hideous idea. It was inhumane. Which is when it clicked for her. It was indeed inhumane. But then, vampires weren't human. Maybe the number of spirits you had swimming around you was a sign of your own strength, a method of counting coup.

The woman lifted her head from the girl who gave a soft moan of disappointment. She tried to pull the woman back to her, at the same time as she pushed her wrist forwards, attempting to get Bailey interested in drinking again. Both ignored the renned girl. Instead, the woman dismounted her and sat back against the sofa, flipping her long, blond hair back out of her face before looking over to where Rachel's spirit floated and smiling.

"It's so good to see you again, Rachel," said Lilly. "I heard about what happened to your body. It's such a shame. I enjoyed it so much."

That almost made Rachel change her mind about not appearing a coward.

"Have you come to discuss something, Rachel?" Bailey asked. "Or have you just come to view your handiwork? After all, this is all your fault. If you hadn't burnt my house down and then squealed to the police about where I was, all these people would still be alive. Including Jessica here."

"Jessica..." Lilly said softly in the same way she had once said Rachel's name. "She is such a delightful creature. So much energy. It will be such a shame when she dies. But don't feel guilty, Rachel, darling. I'm sure you were just doing what you thought was the right thing to do."

"Now, Rachel," Bailey said, with an oily charm. "Why don't you come over here and let's see whether we can't talk about this. You were so helpful to me before. I don't see why you can't join me again. I can forgive everything you have done. It wasn't your own fault. Whoever it was that made you see things differently must have really screwed you up. I have only ever been your friend. After all, didn't I make sure that my beautiful Lilith here introduced herself to you?"

Even in her ghost form, Rachel could feel Bailey's words start to wrap themselves around her brain. For a moment she even found herself wondering if it had actually been that bad. *After all, Bailey had given her a lot of responsibility. And he would only have done that if he liked and trusted someone, wouldn't he? And Lilly...*

"You should tell me who it was that did that to you – who it was that broke your spirit so thoroughly? I will have to have... words with that person when we are finished with today's business."

Rachel was about to open her mouth to speak when she glanced at Jessica. She had slipped to the floor and was rubbing herself against Lilly's stockinged leg, moaning softly and licking at her own wrist as the blood dripped down to where it was already starting to pool on the floor. Rachel had a sudden flash of inspiration. She didn't see Jessica down there on the floor. Instead, she saw Ruby. Far too young to be doing what she had already done, she wouldn't last two minutes with these two. And, if Bailey did manage to get anywhere near her, none of her magical abilities would help her.

"No." she said, wrenching the word from deep inside herself. "You can't have her."

Rachel started to sink down, pushing herself to fall as fast as she could. She needed to get out of there. She couldn't stay there, no matter what. Bailey nearly had her there. If he hadn't made the mistake of making her think about Ruby, Rachel would have been gone again.

"Stop right there, Rachel," Bailey said. Rachel froze, waist deep in the floor. "Come back. We haven't finished speaking."

Slowly, reluctantly, Rachel slid back up to floor level.

"Do not move," Bailey told her. "Stay exactly where you are."

"I need you Rachel. I want you. You were mine before and you shall be mine again." Bailey's voice was low and slow and sonorous now, venomous and yet seductive. Rachel realised that this was it. She had lost the bet. "You will give me everything and everyone you hold dear. No one will be more important to you than I am. Your only thought will be to please me. You would fuck your mother and then hold her while I drank her if I wanted it. I am your Lord. I am your Master. I am your God."

It was as if Rachel could see the words. Each one hit her with the force of a bullet, penetrating to her core and ripping it apart. She could feel her sense of self dissolving under the force of Bailey's voice. She was being dismantled and rebuilt to conform to Bailey's wants. Rachel tried to hold on to thoughts of Ruby... of Susan... but they were not enough. As each word and each phrase struck home, she grew more and more lost. Oddly, though, she didn't feel herself fraying at the edges, as she had when she was losing herself to her own unconscious body. Instead, she seemed to grow stronger, as if she was growing a protective shell around her spirit; as if Bailey's words, at the same time as they were ripping her apart, were reinforcing her self-image. Although, it wasn't really a self-image. It was an image of her that conformed to Bailey's intentions. It wasn't a shell so much as a cell.

Finally, Bailey took Jessica's hand and helped her up from the floor.

"Now Rachel," Bailey said. "If you would just wait a few minutes until Lilith and I finish what we were doing, we can discuss what we need to do to deal with the people outside."

Lilly lay back on the couch and pulled her skirt up to her waist, revealing the fact the she wasn't wearing any underwear. With a little cry of lust, Jessica knelt between her legs. Bailey took the girls wrist once again and, rather than delicately lapping at her blood, started to tear at the flesh with his teeth, sucking the blood down as it started to gush. Rachel floated and watched, impassively.

It only took a few minutes. Slowly, Jessica stopped moving. Lilly pushed her head away with a sigh and sat up, not bothering to re-adjust her clothing. The girl slumped backwards, head lolling, eyes closed, her breath so faint that it barely caused her chest to move.

"Damn, I was so close," Lilly complained.

Bailey continued feeding for a little while longer before finally dropping Jessica's wrist. It fell down and lay across her waist, without even a trickle of blood oozing from the wound.

Rachel watched as Jessica took a breath. There was a long pause before she took another one. And then there were no more. Her skin took on a milky sheen as ectoplasm oozed from her pores and lay across her body like a second skin. Slowly, it started to rise up, making directly for the whirling maelstrom of silently screaming spirits that constantly followed Bailey.

Almost without realising it, Rachel reached out a hand to Jessica's spirit as she rose. As she came into contact with her, a spark of recognition and empathy passed between them. She was angry and confused and in pain. She wanted to know what had happened to her.

Although Rachel had been told to wait, it had only been until Bailey and Lilly had finished. Which they quite obviously had. So she no longer had anything to wait for. Somewhere, deep inside herself there was a spot where she was screaming in anger and confusion and pain. The difference between herself and Jessica was that she knew what had happened. To both of them. And she let that knowledge flow out of her and into the newly dead girl's spirit.

The results were startling.

The milky translucence of her ectoplasmic form grew darker and more solid, like a cloud turning thunderous. Instead of just floating steadily upwards towards the other spirits that were gathered around Bailey, she seemed to take control of her movement. She darted back and forth like an angry wasp and then sprang forward, her arms outstretched and her fingers curved into talons, reaching for Bailey's face.

Rachel was not sure who was more shocked, Jessica or Bailey, when she hit him, snapping his head backwards on his neck and then continuing on through his body. If he hadn't been seated, he would undoubtedly have lost his footing. As it was, his head bounced off the wooden back of the seat with a resounding thud. Swearing and leaping to his face, Bailey put a hand to his face, where she had hit him to discover three tiny trickles of blood starting to run down his cheek.

Jessica pulled herself backwards from the vampire, obviously nervous and unsure of herself, expecting and fearing a riposte. As she did so, her spirit form brushed the spirits that had been trapped by Bailey. They seemed to fall on her and suck her in to the centre of their mass.

Bailey, seeing that, smiled cruelly before turning back to Rachel.

"Still some fight left in you then, Rachel?" he said.

Above him, the swirling spirits had slowed. They started to darken and billow, blooming outwards and downwards. As if from a great distance, Rachel heard a scream of rage, first coming from one voice and then a second picking it up and then another and another, until a choir of anger could be heard, never seeming to get any louder or any closer.

A spirit burst free from the cloud, its mouth gaping wide as it seemed to give voice to all its hatred, even though it didn't sound any louder than a whisper. In the moment before it hit Bailey, Rachel saw that it was Jessica once again venting her rage on her murderer. This attack hit him square in the chest, sending him stumbling backwards, forcing him to hold on to the table to stop himself falling. Another spirit followed Jessica and then a third and a fourth and more and more, all of them as black as a thundercloud, flashes of bright ectoplasmic lightning coruscating through and around them.

The attacks came faster and faster until each spirit started to blur into the next until it seemed like Bailey had a column of black smoke rising from his body.

As each angry spirit – each one truly 'geisting now – slammed into Bailey he shuddered and fell backwards, slumping to his knees, head bowed under the onslaught. Feebly, he waved a hand, trying to fight off the onslaught but it was no good. Rachel could hear the crack of bone, clear in the nearly silent attack, followed by an agonisingly loud intense scream of pain as Bailey's arm splintered.

There seemed to be a moment's pause in the attack as all the poltergeists raised themselves to the ceiling. Then, in a flash they dived down, smashing into Bailey's back. This time, though, it didn't seem to hurt him. As each one touched him, it seemed to be absorbed into his body, disappearing as if it was really nothing more than a cloud.

And then, it seemed to end. Apart from the steady drip, drip, dripping of blood that came from seemingly every inch of Bailey's body, everything was still and silent.

Bailey looked up at Rachel, his eyes a startling white in a face that was a mixture of darkly flowering bruises and jagged gashes, making him look even more inhuman and vile than he normally did. He smiled, showing a mouth full of jagged, broken teeth and when he spoke it was barely comprehensible.

"Lilith, come here," he said, blood spraying as he spoke. "I need to feed from you."

"What the fuck just happened?" Lilly asked in a quiet voice.

As Bailey tried to answer, he started to gag. He seemed to be trying to speak, to breathe, to do anything, but something was stopping up his throat. His one good leg collapsed under him, sending him tumbling to the ground and then he was writhing in agony, flailing about, feet beating against the floor. There was a single, loud, internal crack, his back arched and Bailey's sternum split wide from crotch to gullet as every single spirit of every single person he had ever killed by feeding on their blood flew from him, sending his own blood and offal across the room to decorate the walls in a hideous new colour scheme.

The spirits whirled around the room, faster and faster, picking up first smaller objects and then progressively larger and heavier. Lilly ran for the door, tugged on it and managed to get out just as she was threatened with joining the maelstrom.

Rachel remained in the middle of it all, watching, impressed.

The lights ripped free from the ceiling, sending a shower of sparks across the room. The bare wires flailed around and, as the psychic tornado increased in power, electricity started to arc out and earth itself against the few things that still remained fixed to the ground. A burst of energy flared out connecting to a power socket causing a huge gout of flame to burst from it, engulfing Bailey's body and setting alight to everything around it.

With a speed that almost matched their final explosive act of revenge against Bailey, the spirits slowed and stopped, their rage apparently spent. Everything that had been rushing around the room fell to the floor. The spirits returned to the pale luminescent beings they had been before being roused and then, one by one, blinking out of existence.

At last there were only two spirits left. One was Jessica, the other was beautiful, tall and slim, her long hair haloing her face. They both looked at Rachel, smiling. Then the woman took Jessica's hand as they too faded away to nothing.

The fire in the room was really starting to take hold now. With one last look at George Bailey's charred remains, Rachel left and followed Lilly.

She found her in the entrance to the club, trying to push her way forwards against the wizard lock that Bailey had constructed. Spinning around, she stared wildly at Rachel. Seeing her standing there, covered in the remains of her former boss, Rachel had absolutely no feelings towards her whatsoever.

"Please, Rachel. Darling," she pleaded. "I can't get out."

"There's nothing I can do, Lilly," Rachel told her. "You'll just have to hope that the spell ends before... well, just before..."

"There must be something," she continued. "What about everything we meant towards each other. I thought you loved me..."

"Strange. So did I," Rachel said and then turned her back on her and slid down into the floor.

Interlude: Heaton, Newcastle upon Tyne, June 1982

Dragging herself up the stairs seemed like the hardest thing she had ever done. *Actually, no.* She changed her mind as she paused half way up the stairs. The hardest thing had been to stand straight and tall this afternoon, the way he would have wanted. He never appreciated tears and things like that. He had always said that he had married a woman, not a girl. 'Girlish' emotions annoyed him.

But. When the rifles had been pointed into the air to fire a single volley. When the Rear-Admiral had handed over the neatly folded Union Flag - the flag that would have been draped over his coffin, if there had been anything to put in one – and the Distinguished Service Medal – the medal that should have been pinned to his chest. She had very nearly broken down then. Without the coffin, without some kind of sign that he was never coming back the whole ceremony had seemed strangely unreal until that point. The navy had taken her man away and had swapped him for a tri-coloured piece of cloth and a piece of metal. That really didn't seem like a fair exchange.

Finally, reaching the top of the stairs and their... her... bedroom, she started to prepare for bed. Mechanically, she undressed. She slipped off her shoes – black, patent leather heels - and placed them back in the wardrobe. Her smart black dress went on a hanger. She'd only worn it for a few hours, it didn't need washing. Her bra, panties and stockings came off and went into the wash basket. Naked, she padded into the bathroom, took her toothbrush, squeezed toothpaste onto it and cleaned her teeth.

As she leant over the washbasin to rinse and spit, she caught a movement out of the corner of her eye. She started and tried to catch her breath, a bad move when your mouth is full of toothpaste suds and water. She spluttered, spraying the mirror with water and spattering herself.

Swearing, she picked up the flannel and wiped off her breasts and belly, turning as she did so. There was nothing there. Of course there wasn't. They didn't have any pets, nor did they have children and the house wasn't haunted. She herself was the only thing in the entire house that moved. *Well*, she thought, *it was pretty understandable really*. The day hadn't been exactly stress-free. Seeing things that weren't really there was probably the least of her worries at that moment.

#

The bed was very wide and very cold. She had grown used to it, but now, now that she knew he wasn't going to come back to fill and warm up that space... Well, it felt like an abyss. She lay there on her side, perched right on the edge of her side of the bed, feeling that if she moved any nearer the middle of the bed or even just lay on her back, she would slip into that abyss and fall, following him into the darkness of the oceans that had swallowed him up.

Sleep was elusive. She had been laying there, eyes closed, unmoving and uncomfortable, for at least an hour. Suddenly, she had an undeniable sense that there was somebody else there in the room with her. Her eyes flicked open, but she remained unmoving and scanned the darkness of the corners of the room that she could see. A figure by the door made her jerk in shock. Being so close to the edge of the bed, she didn't have much room for sudden movements like that and suddenly found herself half on the floor, feet wrapped in the sheets and nightdress up around her waist.

Maybe she had been asleep. When she looked again, she saw that the 'figure' was just her own dressing gown hanging on the hook on the back of the door. Untangling herself from the bed clothes, she climbed to her feet, cursing her own stupidity.

"Mary," a soft voice said from behind her.

A screech of fear escaped from between her lips as she span around. There, in the shadows by the wardrobe was another figure. This time, she knew that there wasn't anything there to confuse her. She knew that she was wide awake. Someone else was in her room with her.

Slowly, she backed away, her eyes fixed on the unmoving form on the other side of the room. She reached behind her, feeling for the door knob. If he only stayed still for another few seconds she'd be able to get out.

"Mary."

The voice was definitely coming from whoever it was standing there, but it was quiet and gentle, almost as if someone were calling for her from a long way away and the sound was being carried to her on the wind.

It repeated her name for a third time and then added "please. Wait."

Her hand closed on the handle and she pulled it downwards, but something made her pause. There was something in that voice. Something familiar. It sounded like... But that was ridiculous. That would mean someone, somewhere, had been lying to her. And there was no reason for anyone to do that. Was there?

"Who... who are you?" she asked shakily.

"It's me," the voice said. "I came back for you."

Her hand slipped off the handle and it flicked noisily back into place, making her jump again.

"What do you mean?"

"I couldn't leave you here alone. I had to come back."

"Mark?"

She moved her hand upwards, feeling now for the light switch.

"No. I don't want you to see me yet."

"Is it really you?"

The figure seemed to slip from one shadow to the next, coming towards her, without crossing over the lines of light where the street-lamps shone between the curtains. He'd always hated the fact that she never bothered about having the curtains completely closed. He had claimed that the light disturbed his sleep. Although she was the one who had to poke him to make him turn over and stop snoring.

And then the figure was beside her. Behind her.

"It's really me."

Gently, almost like she was being caressed by a feather, she felt something caress the side of her neck in the exact spot that he always kissed. The spot that sent shivers down her spine and made her weak at the knees.

She could smell him. That distinct mix of aftershave and sweat that meant she knew he had been working hard and needed looking after. But there was something else mixed in. It brought back memories of last bonfire night when they'd gone down to Cullercoats Bay with the guys who manned the lifeboat. Mark had kept in touch with them after he'd joined the navy and would go out with them occasionally when he'd been home on leave. But that night had had a distinctive smell – the salt of the sea, mixed with smoke from the bonfire and the gunpowder from the fireworks. And when the two of them had snuggled down together to share a bottle of Grolsch, she'd got all that mixed with the smell of him. And that was the combination she could smell now. She remembered reading somewhere that you didn't smell anything in dreams. She didn't know if it was true or not, but the way that something smelled had never stuck in her head when she'd remembered her dreams.

She felt the touch against her neck again, stronger this time and, involuntarily, she felt herself react to it. Goosebumps grew down her arms and the shudder went down her back and up from her knees, meeting at her middle. She knew he knew what it did to her. And she knew what happened after this.

The third time she felt the touch – no, not a touch. This time it was definitely a kiss – the third time he kissed her neck, she closed her eyes and sighed softly. She couldn't explain it. And she didn't want to have to. He had come back to her. Their wedding vows had said 'until death do you part' but they had been wrong.

She felt him guiding her towards the bed, felt him pushing her down and the spaghetti straps of her nightdress slipping off her shoulders. She kept her eyes closed as his lips, cool and damp now against her skin, slowly made their way down, from her jaw line, down her neck and across her clavicle.

She sucked in her breath as she felt them reaching her breasts. A gentle graze of his teeth made her arch her back and press the now fully-erect nipple into his mouth, making contact with his tongue.

He kissed and licked and sucked back up to her lips again and she felt his weight upon her. She pulled the skirt of her night dress up to her waist, parted her legs and bent her knees. She knew without a doubt that she was ready for him. She'd been ready for this for a long time. So, when he pushed gently into her, she shuddered and moaned with pleasure, almost coming at that first touch of his cock inside her.

As he slid back and forth, the sensations seemed to come and go. One moment, she could feel him deep inside her, the next there was only an insubstantial whisper of sensation rubbing against her. When it came back again it felt like a thrust but without the pressure. He was just suddenly… there… inside her. And god, it felt good. Just being suddenly filled up with his cock was an astounding sensation.

Her first orgasm, when it came, was fast and hard and left her breathless. She wouldn't have described herself as multi-orgasmic. Not least because she had only really come across the concept recently when reading a copy of Cosmopolitan that Janice had left behind. It had really made her giggle when she read the article. Although it had really turned her on as well. But, this time, she knew that as soon as that first one had washed over her another one was building up. She found herself desperately hoping, in the moments when the pulsing of blood in her head and in her crotch quieted enough for her to think anything that Mark wouldn't finish before she climaxed again.

All this time, even during her orgasm, she had followed Mark's instruction and kept her eyes closed. But, as she felt his cock start to pulse and his thrusting grow erratic, she knew he was on the verge and the sensation pushed her over the edge for the second time.

She looked up into the eyes of her beloved. The man she had loved. Had married. Had lost her virginity to. And who she thought she was never going to see ever again.

As her orgasm took her again, she screamed out his name, a scream of desire, of thankfulness and of a release of pain.

This climax was deeper, more intense and longer lasting than the first one. It sent shudders of ecstasy through, starting in her – another word she got from Cosmopolitan and thought she would never use – her pussy and rippling out to all her extremities. She'd never had an orgasm in her fingers before. Her eyelids fluttered, trying to close, to bottle up the pleasure inside and focus it all on herself, but she forced them to stay open. She wanted to see her husband. This might be the only time he would come to her. If she was never going to see him again, she wanted her last memory to be of him climaxing along with her.

As she looked at Mark, she saw the moment he came. His eyes squeezed shut and she felt him press hard against her, thrusting deep inside, his whole body shuddering. A low moan escaped from between his lips. And he burst into flames. The skin was flayed from his head by an unseen, unfelt wind, leaving a blood-covered skull that quickly charred black. And he still he came, she could feel him inside her, pulsing and burning at the same time. The heat growing more intense the more he came. His denuded eyes stared at her, the grin of his skull moaning in pleasure. Or was it pain? Maybe it was both. His arms, pressing into the bed on either side of her head spurted molten fat across her face. His eyes burst and dribbled from their sockets.

And then he was gone.

She scrambled from the bed and flung herself into the corner of the room, tears coursing down her face, her mouth stretched wide in a scream that echoed in her head but somehow didn't seem to escape from between her lips.

#

Minutes passed. And she didn't die. And she continued not to do so. Slowly, her mouth closed and the noise inside her skull calmed down. She lifted a hand up to her face, tingling where she had been burnt by… where she'd been burnt. She didn't know what she expected to feel. Blistering at the least. Maybe it had burnt a hole in her face. She didn't know. Touching seemingly unblemished skin was perhaps an even bigger shock for her. She slowly climbed to her feet and made her way across to the dressing table pulling her nightdress up over her shoulders, from where it lay scrunched around her hips. As she approached the mirror, she closed her eyes, nervous and unsure. No, not nervous. Terrified.

She stood, facing the mirror, hands grasping the back of the chair tightly. Finally, summoning up her willpower, she forced herself to open her eyes. It seemed to take a similar effort of will to focus on the image in the mirror and when she finally did so, her knees gave way and she almost fell to the floor. There was nothing there. Her face remained untouched by anything except time and mourning. She breathed a word of thanks and pushed herself back to her feet, using the chair to steady herself again.

Had it all been a dream? If so, she didn't remember either falling asleep or waking up, although the latter could probably be explained away by the terror she had felt. If it had been a dream, it was perfectly understandable. After all, the day had been a traumatic one, so dreaming of her husband was understandable. She knew that she'd done so in the past. Although it had never been so… erotic… or so utterly terrifying as tonight's dream was. But it was the only real explanation that made sense. Although there were all these creatures out there - which she knew included such things as ghosts - she'd never actually seen one, apart from the zombins and they just looked like grey-skinned people with a nasty skin condition, really. So, for her first encounter with a creature from the other side to be an… encounter like that… with her dead husband was too far-fetched to believe. It really was.

She realised her crotch still tingled, from both extremes of the dream. The pleasant sensation she remembered from a really good time but mixed up somehow with the memory of the feel of something burning to nothing inside her.

Suddenly embarrassed, despite being alone in the house, she pulled her night dress up and gently pressed her fingers against her labia. Everything seemed fine down there. But, as she felt around, she slipped her fingers through something that seemed to be leaking out a little. It wasn't her own juices. It was thicker and stickier.

Mark had always insisted that she go on the pill when he came home, although she always stopped taking them when he was away. He refused to use a condom, because he didn't like how they felt. So, she recognised exactly what it was that slipping out from inside her. It was proof that she hadn't been dreaming.

Epilogue

Rachel stood and looked at her body on the other side of the window. She could still feel it pulling on her with an inexorable force, but now she knew what to expect and she managed to hold herself back.

In the six weeks since the *Club Egoiste* had burnt to the ground, her body had started to heal. Physically, at least. However, it remained in a comatose state and there was no guarantee that it would ever wake up.

She had eventually managed to persuade her doctors that she wasn't a figment of Private Johnson's imagination and that she should be consulted over all procedures to do with her physical form.

The doctors had never dealt with a ghostkin before, at least, not as far as they were aware. Certainly, they had never dealt with one in ghost form. They were a little confused to say the least. Not to mention their difficulty getting their heads around her status as a trans woman.

Several of them had tried to persuade her that the best chance of recovery was for her to return to her body. The theory they put forward was that doing so would somehow jump start her body and wake it up. However, when Rachel pushed them they had to admit that it was just an idea and they didn't actually have any idea whether it would actually work or not.

Having experienced the black hole that lurked where her spirit should sit comfortably inside her body, Rachel didn't think that she was prepared to try it without some significantly stronger assurances.

And so there she stood, looking helplessly and hopelessly at herself.

"What now?" she said.

Acknowledgements

This book has been a long time coming – I think it's been around five years since I started to write it. And in the intervening time a lot has changed. I started my transition and became a lot happier. In the course of things, Rachel also transitioned and, despite appearances, she's also a lot happier.

I have a fair few people to thank for helping me get Ghostkin into print – either directly through criticism and suggestions, or indirectly through helping me get through and get on with life.

So… huge thanks and lots of love go out to – Jean Rogers, Chaz Brenchley , Eleanor and Cal Burns, Dylan Falconer, Amy and Rachel Tysoe, Katrina Stonoff, all the Readers of the Lost Art, all the Sloths (especially the Trans Sloths), Carol Bird, Shaun Mellor, Sean Mellor and Jane Slater, Kirsten Murray-Borbjerg and all at Focus Shift, Kerry Gowland, Amanda Glenister and Ash Carey. I'm sure that I've forgotten some people but when I sat down to write this my mind went completely blank. Which is annoying. If you feel that you should be here but aren't, I'm really, really sorry and I do love you as well.

Lastly, of course, I owe everything to Candy and Max, my wonderful, beautiful, amazing wife and my brilliant son. They have helped me so much both pre-transition and during. It has not been the easiest time for them (Candy especially has had to deal with a teenage son and a wife who is having her second puberty – let's face it, the woman deserves a medal) but they have been strong and there for me whenever I've needed them. This book would not exist without their unfailing support. I love them so much.

THE END